RUMORS *of* PEACE

Books by
Gary E. Parker

FROM BETHANY HOUSE PUBLISHERS

The Ephesus Fragment

Rumors of Peace

A WORLD AT PEACE IS WHAT
EVERYONE LONGS FOR—OR IS IT?

RUMORS *of* PEACE

GARY E. PARKER

CPL

BETHANY HOUSE PUBLISHERS
MINNEAPOLIS, MINNESOTA 55438

Published by Bethany House Publishers
A Ministry of Bethany Fellowship International
11400 Hampshire Avenue South
Minneapolis, Minnesota 55438
www.bethanyhouse.com

Printed in the United States of America by
Bethany Press International, Minneapolis, Minnesota 55438

Library of Congress Cataloging-in-Publication Data

Parker, Gary E.
    Rumors of peace / by Gary E. Parker.
        p. cm.
    ISBN 0–7642–2257–0
    1. Peace—Religious aspects—Christianity—Fiction. 2. Peace
movements—Northern Ireland—Fiction. 3. Peace movements—
fiction. I. Title.
    PS3566.A6784 R86 2000
    813'.54—dc21   99–051011

GARY PARKER is the author of numerous works of fiction, including *The Ephesus Fragment, A Capitol Offense,* and *Beyond a Reasonable Doubt,* in addition to his work as a national consultant on theological education. Gary, his wife, and two daughters make their home near Atlanta, Georgia.

PART ONE

A hard beginning maketh a good ending.

John Heywood, 1546

*Therefore, if anyone is in Christ, he is a new creation.
The old has gone, the new has come!*

Paul, 2 Corinthians 5:17

ONE

Though trying to appear unhurried, Ian O'Fallon felt certain that anyone looking at him would immediately see his nervousness. His stride felt jittery and his heart thrummed in his chest like a heavy engine—*boom, boom, boom.* He licked his lips but his tongue felt as dry as sandpaper. If someone had asked him to speak, he didn't think he could, not even one syllable. Keeping his neck stiff, he nonetheless swiveled his gaze out and back, out and back. He saw no one.

O'Fallon glanced at the sky. Dark clouds covered the moon and sloped down to the ground, a filmy drape over the white stone walkway under his feet, producing a mist that bordered right on the edge of a full-scale rain. The fog comforted him somewhat, made him feel less visible. Maybe, if the fog held and no one saw him, he could stop this, stop it before—

He glanced at his watch—10:41. He had nineteen minutes.

His arms held like sticks at his sides, O'Fallon stared straight ahead as he scurried up the walk toward the Belfast City Hall. A multidomed stone edifice that served as the centerpiece of Donegal Square, the building had stood as a symbol of stability for far longer than O'Fallon's thirty-four years could even conceive.

O'Fallon wanted to go to the far left wing of the building, the wing where he worked every day as a tax clerk, the wing where a bomb waited to explode at 11:00 P.M. Encased in a tan leather briefcase, the bomb lay in a desk drawer in an unused office on the second floor near the middle of the wing, a location that guaranteed the maximum damage but the minimum possibility of bodily injury.

He checked his watch again. 10:43. He walked faster, his shoes clicking quickly over the sidewalk. The building loomed larger and larger in his vision, a white colossus that dominated the capital city of Northern Ireland like a Mount Everest. In less than sixteen minutes, the explosives in the briefcase would destroy approximately one-third of that building.

O'Fallon tried again to lick his lips, but his tongue stuck in his mouth. Inside his head, a voice accused him of treachery but he pushed the voice aside. Fifteen minutes to go. He reached the far side entrance to the building and jerked to a stop. A uniformed policeman with a gray handlebar mustache nodded at him. Past the policeman, O'Fallon spotted a number of other men, several of them in suits and ties. But that didn't fool him. These men were also security officers, only of a more sophisticated lot. They served a variety of nations—his own, plus the governments of the English, the Irish Republic, and the Americans.

Inside City Hall, a roomful of negotiators sat around a conference table on the first floor, each of them busy trying to find a solution to Ireland's age-old hostilities. The security officers outside the building protected the negotiators in the conference room.

"Identification, please," said the policeman.

O'Fallon nodded, his photo tag already in his hand.

"You're out a bit late, aren't you, laddie?" asked the officer, taking the ID.

"To be sure," O'Fallon said, forcing a smile. The word "sure" came out "shurr," with the "r" slurred, the lyrical tone of the Irish riding it. "But I work on the second floor. Stupid me, left me wallet in the office. I'm sitting at the pub and I've just quaffed meself a pint. But then, would you believe it, I went to pay for me pint, but me wallet was nowhere to be found. That barmaid's not a-smilin' now, I'll tell you that. A bit of a fix, to be sure."

He paused and swallowed, trying not to glance at his watch. If the copper smelled any hint of desperation, he'd get suspicious. With three terrorist attacks in Belfast in the last month, the level of vigilance in Northern Ireland had escalated to unprecedented heights. The police searched citizens without cause, bomb-sniffing dogs patrolled the streets at all hours, and city officials had called in scores of retired officers to beef up security at all public buildings. That's why the diplomats had met in emergency session tonight—to try to find a way to stop the resurgence of violence.

The policeman fingered his mustache. He glanced at O'Fallon, then back to the photo. Curly brown hair, thin goatee, eye color indistinguishable in the dark, narrow face, five nine, and one hundred fifty-seven pounds.

"Wait here a second, laddie," the officer grunted.

O'Fallon pocketed his hands and stared at his feet. His heart thumped loudly. He wondered why no one heard it but him. The accusing voice intruded again, and this time he couldn't push it back.

People will die, said the voice.

But I'm here to stop it, thought O'Fallon. *At the risk of me own life*.

The policeman sauntered back over, one hand busy with his mustache, the other holding the photo. A squatty man in a gray suit and open black raincoat hung behind the officer, his eyes on O'Fallon. Hanging his head to obscure his face, O'Fallon felt like screaming for the officer to hurry. But he couldn't. So he waited, his skull about to explode with tension. The policeman handed back the photo. O'Fallon took it but didn't put it away. It stuck to his sweaty hand—a laminated reminder of his identity, a mocking picture of a man who had become nothing more than a murderous terrorist. Though he had come to disable the bomb, that didn't matter now. Unless he managed to breach the security ring that guarded the City Hall building, a number of men and women would end up dead and maimed beneath tons and tons of Irish stone.

"Sorry, old man," the policeman said, rolling the end of his mustache. "But no one enters the building tonight, not even those who work here."

"But me wallet," O'Fallon said, desperately trying to stay calm. "I need me wallet to settle up with that barmaid." His voice sounded whiny. He had less than ten minutes.

Apparently losing interest, the short man in the ankle-length raincoat turned away and walked back toward the building. O'Fallon kept his head twisted anyway.

"It'll have to wait till Monday," the officer said. "No entrance, that's the order of the day. Too many high and mighties here for such as you to come and go. Peace discussions, big emergency, you know about that." He smoothed down his mustache.

"I know," O'Fallon said, trying to stay light. "But I'm a bit desperate here. That barmaid is a big woman, and she won't serve me again until I pay her up, and I've a whole day tomorrow

ahead of me without a pint if I don't." He leaned closer to the
policeman and his voice dropped to a whisper. "That's a wee bit
tough on an Orangeman."

The policeman froze and focused hard on O'Fallon. A hint of
recognition flickered in his eyes. "An Orangeman, you say?"

O'Fallon chewed his lip nervously. He didn't like mentioning
the Orange. If the policeman wasn't a member of the one-hun-
dred-thousand-strong men's fraternity, he would no doubt push
him away with a snarl and a curse. People held strong views
about the Orange, a Protestant group with a sworn dislike for all
things Catholic. Swearing to maintain a free Northern Ireland,
the Orange rejected any peace process that called for unification
with the Irish Republic or any break in Northern Ireland's union
with the British. They hated the Irish Republican Army.

*An Orangeman should love, uphold, and defend the Protestant
religion and sincerely desire and endeavor to propagate its doctrines and precepts; he should strenuously oppose the fatal errors
and doctrines of the Church of Rome and scrupulously avoid
countenancing (by his presence or otherwise) any act or ceremony
of Popish worship; he should, by all lawful means, resist the as-
cendancy of that church, its encroachments, and the extension of
its power.* The Orange code had been pounded into O'Fallon's
head for years.

"Yes, I'm of the orange," he said, holding his breath. The policeman rubbed his mustache. Less than five minutes remained.
The peace discussions going on inside City Hall had indeed
sprung up without warning. A "security measure," said the news-
casters when the news had leaked out late that afternoon. The
negotiators planned to meet, then disperse before any of the terrorist groups active in Northern Ireland had a chance to disrupt
them.

Ian shrugged casually. "A day without a pint is a sorry day. I
truly need me wallet."

The policeman grunted. "Hold one more second, laddie. Let
me see what I can do." He turned back toward the building and
spoke to the man in the raincoat.

O'Fallon glanced at his watch—four minutes and forty seconds. His tongue felt swollen. His heart pounded. His palms
dripped sweat as the policeman spoke softly to the stumpy man.
Eyes down, O'Fallon tried to listen but heard nothing save the
voice in his own head.

You're a murderer!

Ten seconds later the policeman stepped to a second officer, talked to him for a couple of moments, then headed back to O'Fallon, his head shaking. O'Fallon's heart fell.

"Can't let you inside," the officer said. "But I've sent one of me boys to fetch the wallet for you. Wouldn't want a fellow Orangeman to expire without his pint."

For several seconds, Ian stood immobilized. In less than three minutes he—the son of a gentle shoe cobbler and his schoolteacher wife, politically neutral until three years ago, a man of slight build and easy temper—would become a murderer.

He stared at his shoes. He and his companions hadn't planned it this way. Yes, they had detonated three bombs in the past month—one in an out-of-business pub on Trafalgar Street, one in a deserted schoolhouse just north of the city, and one in a dry cleaner's five blocks from the mayor's residence. But each had exploded late in the night, exactly as they planned. No one suffered, no injuries occurred. To no one's surprise, the Irish Republican Army had claimed credit. Messages to the daily newspapers and television commentators made it plain that these attacks came from the IRA in an effort to destroy the peace talks.

But Ian O'Fallon knew better. The IRA hadn't set those bombs. He and a cell group of seven other members of the Orange had. But the IRA received the blame. A brilliant strategy, really. Destroy shabby buildings in Belfast, make sure no one gets hurt, and blame the IRA. The most recent peace effort remained on hold, and the militant group that insisted on a reunited Ireland and a retreat of all British presence took the brunt of the international community's displeasure.

In less than two minutes, the plan would fail. People would die and he could do nothing to stop it. O'Fallon glanced up at the officer, noticed the lines around his eyes. The man had to be sixty, maybe older, probably a grandfather.

"How long in the Orange?" Ian asked.

"Fifteen years."

Ian glanced at his watch. Barely two minutes. He rubbed his forehead, then started to back away. He stared past the officer but didn't see the man in the raincoat. The bomb would explode in seconds. Ian moved back another two steps.

"A bit of advice?" he asked, his eyebrows raised at the policeman.

"Sure, always open to advice."

"Come with me," Ian whispered.

"Wha—?"

"Come with me!" He turned and began to move away.

"But your wallet!" shouted the policeman.

Ian grabbed his back pocket and pulled out his wallet. Running now, he held it up for the man to see. "I have me wallet!" he shouted. "As a brother of the Orange, I'm telling you to run!"

"Wha—?"

Ian sprinted away, his small feet flying across the thick grass that fronted City Hall. Thirty yards away, he twisted back, his feet still moving. He saw the mustachioed policeman moving after him, but not nearly fast enough. The ground trembled beneath his feet. A rumble followed the tremble. A split second later the whole world seemed to end. The left wing of City Hall imploded in a huge whump of noise and crash and dust and crumble.

The explosion knocked Ian off his feet, and his face plowed chin first into the wet lawn beside the walk. He tasted dirt, spat out a stream of saliva, and pushed up from the ground. The smell of smoke swept out from the explosion, and the sky seemed to have turned red with fire. A piece of stone the size of a pillow landed to his right. A second piece, this one no bigger than a small biscuit, hit him in the shoulder, and he winced in pain but didn't stop moving. From somewhere in the distance, a siren began to scream and voices shouted from all directions.

On his feet again, Ian took one last look toward City Hall. To his horror, he spotted the mustachioed policeman lying on the ground, a huge piece of stone on his left leg, pinning him down. Though knowing it was foolish, Ian immediately sprinted back to the policeman and knelt down to his side. Blood covered the man's mustache, but his chest moved up and down, up and down.

Grabbing the heavy stone, Ian pushed upward. Fueled by fear, his adrenaline surged and the rock moved. The policeman opened his eyes.

"Can you move?" Ian shouted, his voice thin against the noise coming from the bombed building.

The policeman nodded weakly. A second siren wailed in the distance.

"Okay, when I lift, you pull out!"

The man nodded again. Ian gripped the rock and squared his legs under his back. Grunting, he lifted upward. His back creaked. The rock moved. The policeman jerked, then jerked again. His legs shifted, then slid from beneath the rock. He rolled to the left, and Ian dropped the stone. Squatting, he took the policeman's head in his hands.

"I . . . I have to go . . . have to . . ."

"I know," said the officer.

"I didn't mean to hurt you. Didn't mean to hurt anyone . . ."

The man nodded. "Go, brother," he mumbled. "Go before . . . before it's too late."

Ian gently lowered the man's head, stood up, and looked back at the destruction he had caused. He saw the squatty man in the black raincoat hobbling in his direction, a weapon in hand. His heart heavy, Ian pivoted and ran into the wet night.

TWO

A chorus of sirens wailed like hungry children. Smoke the color of pewter rolled across the ground. A scattering of people, all of them appearing dazed and disoriented, ran haphazardly, first in this direction, then in another. Black soot covered one man's face. A woman's right forearm was covered with blood and twisted at an odd angle back toward her elbow. A stiff wet breeze blew the smell of smoke and charred skin in a south-westerly direction across Donegal Square.

His thick blond hair blowing in the wind, Casey Sterling tucked his chin and stared straight ahead into the glare of the camera light that illuminated his face. Over his left shoulder, an ambulance sped away into the soggy night, its siren blaring. The ghostly smoke, a blanket across the top of the ground, parted and bowed at the ambulance as it passed. Behind Sterling, four men in dark uniforms scurried by, their shoulders hunched against the wind.

Sterling wrinkled his nose as if to dispel the smoke. Another siren wailed as a second ambulance darted away. Three more jammed into the space it had just vacated.

His hands steady, Sterling lifted a note pad close to his face and stared at the jottings on it. A mixture of discordant sounds—the spray of water from fire hoses, the groans of the injured, and the shouts of would-be rescuers—pulsed and blared at him from every side, but he never lost his concentration on the pad. The smoke blanket snaked around his ankles as if to envelop him, and the smell of something charred roiled up from his feet and across his nostrils. His stomach lurched but Sterling didn't miss a beat. He tightened his abdominal muscles, cleared his throat, and faced the camera again.

Behind the camera, the operator held up three fingers, then two, then one, then winked. Sterling dropped his notes to his side, held up a microphone, and began to speak, his voice a smooth baritone, the only calm in the midst of the chaos.

"Another tragedy in Belfast, Northern Ireland, this evening," he began. "The third in the last month. In this attack, a bomb blasted through the northern section of the City Hall building no more than half an hour ago. As you can see behind me"—he pivoted and pointed his note pad at the carnage to his back—"a section of wall the width of a basketball court and almost as long is destroyed—blown up by parties as yet unknown. The blast occurred at just past 11 P.M., Belfast time, ripping through this historic old building. Now almost a third of the building is gone, blown up by those who continue to believe that violence is the only way to settle the centuries-old dispute between the Catholic and Protestant segments of the Irish population."

Stepping four steps to his right, Sterling edged closer to one of the ambulances. His cameraman immediately followed him, their movements seamless on the screen. A policeman rushed at them, his gloved hand faced palm out. "Halt there, sirs!" shouted the officer. "This area is off limits!"

Sterling and the cameraman paused, a symbiotic couple working their steps in harmony. A gurney wheeled past and jerked to a stop at the back of an ambulance. Two men and a woman flipped open the back door of the vehicle. Sterling's cameraman never missed a beat, the camera light spotlighting the bloody figure on the stretcher as if the person were a rock star. Though nodding to the policeman, Sterling didn't back up. Instead, he turned from the officer and faced the camera again. The smoke blanket crawled past Sterling's waist and became a belt just under his armpits. He wrinkled his nose and spoke again, his voice solid as a piece of granite.

"As you can see," he said, his head tilted toward the gurney, "the perpetrators of this crime have accomplished their purpose. At least three people are known dead, fourteen are wounded, and more are still missing. What the final death toll will be, no one knows." Sterling eased away from the ambulance, his cameraman following as if dancing with him. He led, the camera followed. He turned, the camera followed. He dipped, the camera followed.

Feeling the rhythm, Sterling almost smiled. He loved moments like this, when everything fell so perfectly, so purely into place. Situations didn't always unfold so well. Sometimes he had to scrounge around like a stray dog in a pack of stray dogs, digging and snarling after any scrap he could find. But tonight, except for a couple of local, almost amateurish broadcasters, he had the feed bowl to himself. A friend in the U.S. State Department had tipped him off late yesterday about a secret meeting in Belfast. Dropping everything, Sterling had caught a red-eye flight from Atlanta, set up shop outside City Hall, and hogged the spotlight all day—the only American journalist on the scene.

He almost smiled again. The bombing hadn't come as part of the original package. But, since it had happened, someone had to report it, and that someone just happened to be him. A few more breaks like this one and he'd have that anchor desk quicker than he ever imagined.

Focusing again, Sterling took one more step. Now the domed figure of City Hall sat directly behind him again. Sterling stopped. The smoke blanket reached his neck, and he wondered if his audience could see it, wondered if they could smell the sour air, an aroma that Sterling had smelled more than once, but one that always shocked him with its putrid reminder of death. Inhaling as little as possible, Sterling pressed to finish the broadcast as the smoke blanket clawed at his throat.

"The almost four-year-old peace in Northern Ireland is now definitely broken. Whether anyone can reestablish it after this latest abomination remains to be seen. This is Casey Sterling with CBC news, live from Belfast. . . ."

As the camera lights blinked off, Sterling felt himself about to choke. Jerking his notebook to his face, he waved it out and back, out and back, out and back. Behind him, a team of emergency workers pushed another hospital gurney toward an ambulance. Sterling stood on tiptoe to escape the smoke but it didn't help. The smell of death swallowed the top of his head and he dropped his gaze. A second later a strange sensation overcame him, a sensation he hadn't felt in over ten years. His left arm went numb and almost as quickly his hand, then his forearm and shoulder began to shake. Within another second the shaking had spread like the smoke up and over his body, and, try as he might, he couldn't do a thing to stop it.

THREE

ATLANTA, GEORGIA

Locking his fingers behind his shaggy mane of silver hair, the Reverend Russell Chadwick leaned back in his chair and surveyed the group gathered around the oblong table that centered the conference room of his office suite. All but one of the four had worked with him for over twenty years, their friendship enduring more bone-wearying revivals and Saturday meetings like this one than he could remember.

Chadwick's gaze—his eyes were still clear blue in spite of his seventy years—landed on the man directly to his right. Rodney Kent, whose hair always stuck out at odd angles and whose nose resembled a robin's beak, had been the baritone soloist for every Chadwick crusade in the last two decades. Chadwick smiled. Rodney was so short his head seemed to perch atop the podiums from which Chadwick preached. But when the little man opened his mouth and bellowed out an old hymn, no one noticed his diminutive size. Chadwick had no doubt that if a surgeon ever sliced Rodney Kent open, he would find lungs larger than saddlebags.

His back stiff, Chadwick stood and tilted to the left, then the right, stretching the muscles that ached more and more these days.

"You okay, Russ?" asked Lester Boggett, a rotund, freckled redhead, the chief financial officer for the Russell Chadwick Evangelistic Association.

"My back again, Lester," Chadwick said. "Nothing new."

"You need to listen to your doctor, go on and get that surgery," said the redhead, his Southern accent evident in every syllable.

"We fork over big bucks to that guy to keep you fit, but you don't pay him a lick of attention. It's money flushed right down the toilet. I've a good mind—"

Chadwick lifted a hand, cutting Lester off. "A man my age doesn't need surgery," he said. "It's like putting new tires on a twenty-year-old pickup truck."

Lester stared down in a pout. Knowing his friend's tendency to take things personally, Chadwick placed a hand on his hamlike shoulder.

"I know you're thinking of me," he said. "But we've got the London crusade in a month, then Chicago. Maybe when those are finished . . ."

His voice trailed off and he moved from Lester to the window a few feet away. Studying the Atlanta skyline, he stretched his back again. Atlanta was gorgeous in mid-October, one of the few big cities that had kept enough of its hardwood trees to actually enjoy some color.

If he had it figured right, he'd never get the disk surgery his doctor said would alleviate the pain that constantly gripped him these days. An operation meant four to six weeks completely off his feet, then another three months at less than full speed. And, truth be told, no one could guarantee him that he'd ever regain his full health. So why waste the time on a body that Parkinson's disease had already started to attack? After Chicago, he had Vancouver, and after Vancouver, Rio de Janeiro, and after that—well, after that another city beckoned, just like always. One city after another, one crusade after the next.

Chadwick closed his eyes, and his entourage started to chatter among themselves, taking a break in rhythm with his own. A sense of gratitude hit him as he thought of their loyalty. These three men—Rodney Kent, Lester Boggett, and Ted Shuster, the backup preacher, crusade organizer, and overall smartest man he'd ever met—were his core group, and no matter what the issue, they followed his lead. That didn't mean they never argued with him. Quite the contrary—at times their debates made a cat-fight sound like a tea party. But eventually, if discussion didn't bring consensus to their disagreements, his verdict became the final decision.

Eyes open again, Chadwick gazed out at the late afternoon sun. None of the three ever spoke of the deference they gave him. It was just there, as natural as breathing, as much a part of their group as the spades games they liked to play when they traveled

long distances. Chadwick sighed. Sometimes leadership was a
heavy burden. Though he didn't like to admit it, Lester and Ted
spent more time with him than they did with their families, and
that made him feel guilty. At least Rodney, a lifelong bachelor,
didn't cause him that heartache.

Leaving the window, Chadwick stretched out his arms and
fingers in a vain effort to reach his toes.

"You're only 'bout four feet away from actually bein' able to do
that," Boggett said, grinning.

"At least he can still see his toes," Kent countered. "Unlike at
least one of us in this room."

"Not that his toes are anything to look at," Ted added.

Chadwick laughed and raised back up. His men liked to tease,
and he caught his share of it, in spite of their respect for him.
Personally, he liked the banter. It made him feel normal, or at
least as normal as the "Best-Known Evangelist since the Apostle
Paul," as one writer had tagged him, could ever feel.

Rubbing his back, Chadwick walked to the refrigerator in the
corner and took out a bottle of water. The bottle in hand, he faced
his crew again. Boggett had turned on the television suspended
from the ceiling over the table and was flipping through the channels. Kent, his tiny feet swinging off his chair, thumbed through
a magazine. Probably a business journal, Chadwick guessed.
With the money he'd made from the sale of millions of CDs, Kent
liked to dabble in the stock market. A bit of a day trader, he kept
a laptop computer around to execute trades when he had slow
minutes.

Next to him, Ted Shuster looked ready to jump into the middle of the table and start preaching. Immaculately dressed in a
charcoal gray suit, ice-blue shirt, stylish maroon tie, and black
wing-tipped shoes, Ted sat straight, his posture clean, his profile
handsome. Always eager, the man had more energy than a five-
year-old.

Sipping his water, Chadwick sat down on a sofa by the refrigerator and looked at the fifth person in the room and the latest
to join his group. Her name was Valerie Miller and she was his
niece.

Now thirty, Valerie had come to him from Rome about five
months ago, fresh off a discouraging stint as a State Department
media relations officer with the U.S. Embassy to the Vatican. His
sister Sarah's only child, Valerie looked like a model—high, clas-
sic cheekbones, eyes green enough to compete for attention with

a pair of emeralds, and thick auburn hair cut just below her ears. Her only flaw, if you could call it that, was a scar the size of a little finger's nail near the bottom of her right cheek where it merged with her neck.

Smiling to himself, Chadwick remembered the day Valerie received the scar. He and his family of five—wife and one son and two daughters—had taken a couple of days off to visit Sarah, her husband, Tyrone, and their only child, Valerie, in Charlotte, North Carolina.

Valerie had wandered off to play with his boy, Todd. The two of them climbed a magnolia tree by the house. Hoisting up to a limb too high for her nine-year-old skills, Valerie fell out. Hitting a branch just before she hit the ground, she broke her right wrist and cut her cheek—a laceration that required six stitches and eventually left a scar that makeup could never quite cover completely.

But falling out of that magnolia hadn't scared Valerie too much. She continued to tackle life head on. She had attended private religious schools until college, winning numerous awards as she went—prizes in academics, piano performance, and student government. She entered Duke at the age of sixteen and majored in language studies with an emphasis in Italian. Also capable in Spanish and Turkish, she earned a Ph.D. at Georgetown in International Studies at twenty-five, then signed on with the State Department. State sent her for short assignments in London and Israel. Then came the Vatican. But that had turned out badly. For the first time in her life, Valerie had learned the meaning of fear. As a result, she had come to him with a sad heart and a shaken faith—a young woman trying to find the courage to climb trees again. Chadwick looked up from Valerie as Boggett flipped through the television channels again.

"Hold it there, Boggs," he said, his eyes suddenly alert to the images on screen.

Boggett notched up the volume.

"What in the world is—?"

The sound of a siren wailed through the room.

The face of Casey Sterling, a prominent international journalist stared back at Chadwick. A chaotic scene flashed in and out of focus behind the newsman. Sterling's familiar voice cut into the office, and Chadwick's entourage immediately fell quiet.

"What we do know is this," Sterling said, his face grave. "It's been only a week since the last terrorist attack in North Ireland,

and matters are escalating daily. The almost four-year-old peace in Northern Ireland is now definitely broken. Whether or not anyone can reestablish it after this latest abomination remains to be seen. This is Casey Sterling with CBC News, live from Belfast, Northern Ireland."

The screen flipped back to a studio setting. An anchor said, "We'll be right back with more on the developing situation in Northern Ireland."

His heart heavy, Chadwick trudged back to the table. "We did a crusade there two years ago," he mumbled. "I thought we made progress, thought the Lord had . . ." His voice trailed away as he placed his forehead in his hands.

"You did make progress," Kent said. "But that place is a quagmire, has been for centuries. No one has been able to do anything there."

"It seems so useless," Chadwick moaned. "Everything we've done, all these years . . . all those sermons . . ."

"But that's all wrong," Boggett insisted. "You've touched millions of people, changed more lives with your preaching than any man in history."

"You've done everything you can," Ted added. "The Lord didn't call you to fix political problems. The Lord called you to preach, and you've done that faithfully, more faithfully than anyone. Your whole life has—"

"But the world is still such a mess!" Chadwick groaned, his frustration overcoming his naturally sunny disposition. "Here it is the new millennium and anywhere you look—Kosovo, Rwanda, North Korea, Iraq—you see violence, terrorism, bombs, and biological warfare. . . ." He rubbed his forehead and the room was quiet.

The television screen went black, then switched from commercials to the news studio again. Everyone but Chadwick stared at the monitor. More tragic images from Northern Ireland flashed on screen. The image changed again, this time landing at the United States State Department where a spokesman called for the competing factions in Ireland to remain calm and not let the terrorism disrupt the fragile peace negotiations.

Chadwick lifted his eyes. "I've got to do something," he said softly.

"Let's declare a national season of prayer," suggested Kent. "We'll call all our prayer associates, thousands of them, get them involved, get—"

"Let's not wait that long," chimed in Boggett. "Let's pray right now, all of us."

Chadwick nodded and the crew instantly bowed their heads. Leaving his chair, Chadwick dropped to one knee, his hands holding the conference table for support. His men looked at one another. Chadwick lifted an eyebrow at Ted. Ted clasped his hands and closed his eyes.

"Almighty God," he began, his voice a bit too loud for the room. "We're not worthy to come into your presence. But you have given us permission. So we dare to enter your throne room of grace. . . ."

Chadwick's right knee began to quiver. He shifted slightly and refocused as Ted continued.

"We're powerless in a matter like this," Ted said. "But we know that you, O God, are not. You have the power to act, to stop this madness, to call men and women to repentance and reconciliation . . ."

Chadwick's arms began to tingle. Ted wasn't known for his short prayers, but unless he broke his pattern and finished quickly, he'd have to stand up or risk collapsing on the floor. If that happened, his men would know just how frail he had become in the last few months—not a prospect he liked to consider.

"So we beseech you to act, Lord Jesus," Ted said. "We call upon you to perform a Holy Spirit miracle, to—"

Chadwick grunted against the pain in his knee. Ted continued to pray, his tone deepening. A flash of heat zipped through Chadwick's ankle, up his knee, and into his thigh. He grabbed the table with both hands and tried to pull up, but his right leg wouldn't support him and he sagged back down. His hands left a trail of sweat as they slipped away from the table.

On all fours now, Chadwick's nose faced the tan carpet. His head throbbed and he thought he was about to faint. A sense of detachment hit him—a sense that he had left his body and wavered in the air above it.

"Show us what to do, Lord Jesus," Ted pleaded. "Show us how we can fulfill your call upon us to become peacemakers in this world. . . ."

Ted prayed on but Chadwick no longer heard him. As if hit by a bolt of lightning, he suddenly realized he had to do more than pray. With his physical condition becoming more fragile each day, he knew that if he wanted to make any real difference in Northern Ireland, he had to try something unprecedented. As Ted's prayer droned on, Russell Chadwick lay prostrate on the floor and tried his best to imagine what that could be.

FOUR

Ian O'Fallon kept one eye glued on Casey Sterling and one eye focused on his five-year-old daughter as she played on the floor of his small, but immaculately kept, three-room apartment four miles outside of Belfast. His daughter—Heather by name—was the best product of his lifelong romance with Rebecca Lawrence O'Fallon, a romance that began in childhood when Rebecca moved to Belfast at the age of six. Their baby Heather had curls the color of carrots and skin as white as fine snow. The curls framed her face in such a way that she looked angelic to Ian—an example of exquisite beauty in a world that held little of that most precious commodity.

Heather's mother—a pure redheaded Irishwoman with more energy than a volcano and twice as much heat—had died only three years ago at the age of twenty-six. Now she was cold, cold and dead and . . .

"Over here, me sweetheart," O'Fallon said, shaking off the memory of his deceased wife, his right hand held out to Heather. "Here in your daddy's lap for a minute before I put ya to bed."

Shaking her head, Heather squealed, tapped her feet once, twice, then scooted away from her daddy's hand.

"I'll get ya," O'Fallon called, rising from the two-seater sofa where he sat. "I'll get ya and tickle your tummy until ya cannot breathe."

Heather darted across the room. O'Fallon gave chase, his slender frame jumping a coffee table that separated him from his daughter. Heather stopped by a chair in the adjacent room and stared back. Her brown eyes gleamed. O'Fallon reached for her, his hand delicate, much like the rest of his body. His eyes were just as brown as Heather's and equally as soft at the edges. But those who knew O'Fallon knew better than to let his fine features and gentle eyes fool them. An expert with all types of explosives, O'Fallon carried more hatred inside him than his one-hundred-fifty-seven-pound frame seemed capable of supporting. And why not? A bomb had killed his good wife Rebecca, a bomb placed under the counter in the restaurant where he had taken her to celebrate the recent announcement of a new baby to be born to them, a boy this time, he was sure, a future soccer player, for certain.

The Irish Republican Army, a paramilitary band of terrorists that sought the unification of all Ireland in a nation completely free of British rule, had taken credit for the explosion that killed Rebecca and six others, seven if you counted the unborn child in Rebecca's womb—which Ian did, of course.

Until that night, Ian had lived a quiet, common life, growing up in a small flat above his father's shoe shop. His father made new shoes, repaired old shoes, sold polish and shoe-shining materials, and basically tried to stay out of the fiery politics that had plagued their country for as long as anyone could remember. When Ian married Rebecca, he took a job with the city of Belfast as a tax clerk, and she inherited his old job keeping the books for the family business.

In the second year of their marriage Heather was born. He and Rebecca planned on having at least three more babies. But the bomb that exploded within feet of his dear wife's face as she paid the bill for the dinner ended all their hopes for more children. For that matter, the bomb ended all their hopes.

Rushing from the men's room, Ian had found Rebecca crumpled against a shattered wall, her wavy hair streaked with blood, her big brown eyes already dimming. Sirens blared somewhere above his head, but Ian knew the ambulance wouldn't make it in time. Taking Rebecca's head in his lap, he kissed her forehead and told her to hold on, help was coming. She smiled weakly at him and touched his cheek.

"Heather," she whispered. "Tell her I . . ."

Her breathing stopped in midsentence and her head rolled back, and Ian placed his fingers on her eyelids and pulled them shut. Then, still squatting in the floor of the destroyed restaurant, he gritted his teeth and swore revenge on those who had murdered his wife. And so a terrorist was born.

When he was with Heather, though, as he was now, he was a
father instead of a terrorist. He was a daddy, a man who loved a
daughter more than anything, even his own life.

Heather stuck out her tongue. O'Fallon returned the gesture.
Behind him, he heard the voice of Casey Sterling on the television.

"The perpetrators of this crime have accomplished their purpose," the newsman said. "At least three are known dead, fourteen are wounded, and more are still missing. What the final
death toll will be, no one knows."

"It's way past your bedtime," he said, grabbing for Heather,
regretting all the while that he had left her for so long at his
mum's house while he did his awful business. "So come here to
me, ya little pipper."

Pulling her close, he tickled her tummy. Shrieking loudly,
Heather squirmed and twisted in her daddy's delicate hands. His
shrieks as loud as hers, he hauled her back to the sitting area
and tossed her gently onto the sofa.

"I love ya, sweetheart," he said, burrowing his chin into her
belly as he continued the tickling. "I love ya and your mummy
loves ya. Don't ever forget that, okay?"

Heather nodded, her curls bouncing as if someone had coated
them with rubber. She grabbed her daddy by the cheek and
pinched him hard, and he stopped tickling her and just rested in
the feel of her chubby fingers on his face.

The phone rang. O'Fallon hesitated. It was almost midnight.
He had picked Heather up from his mum's after his desperate
escape from the City Hall explosion, and he didn't want to talk to
anyone. The phone rang a second time. Reluctantly, he pulled
away from Heather.

"Hold here, sweetheart," he mumbled, grabbing for the phone.
Heather rolled back on the sofa and stayed still.

"O'Fallon," he said, keeping his voice low so Heather wouldn't
hear.

"Murphy here. You see the news?"

"Watching it now." O'Fallon turned his back to Heather.
"Heavy damage, it seems."

"You okay?"

"Sure, why not?" He said nothing about returning to the
building.

"Well, I don't know. Second thoughts, maybe, life's regrets,
that sort of thing."

"Life's dangerous," O'Fallon said, rubbing the back of his neck. "One never knows what the day will bring."

"What's next, you think?"

"More of the same, I suppose. Retaliation, then revenge for the retaliation, then revenge for the revenge. Fairly predictable."

"Until the last four years or so. Things pretty quiet through that time. All this Good Friday Peace Accord stuff."

"But now that peace is shattered again."

"Aye, and a good thing too."

"So now the struggle begins anew. An eye for an eye, a tooth for a tooth . . ."

"A man can set his watch by it. See you at the pub in the morning for a spot of coffee?"

Thinking of the man in the raincoat, Ian shrunk his shoulders. "I think I'll spend tomorrow with me family," he said. "I'm not feelin' so well."

"Monday mornin', then?"

"If I'm feelin' better. I'm sure they'll need several days to open City Hall again."

"I'll call ya Monday, then."

O'Fallon hung up and turned back to Heather. Almost asleep, her eyes drooped. Cupping his hands under her back, O'Fallon carried her to a bed in the room just off the eating area. Pulling a blanket up to her chin, he kissed her on the forehead, then flipped off the light and left the room. Ten seconds later, he stood in front of the mirror in the bathroom and stared at his face. For the most part he liked what he saw. Brown hair, very curly. A narrow chin, but not overly so. Dark brown eyes like his daughter's. Skin as white as milk.

Sucking in his breath, O'Fallon grabbed a pair of scissors from a drawer under the sink and began to snip away at his goatee. Though he didn't know how well the man in the raincoat had seen him, he didn't want to take any chances. Even though the authorities had no reason to connect him to the bombing, the man might want to question him anyway, see what he knew. Worse yet, he didn't know if his fellow Orangeman had reported his warning, his urging him to run. Though not likely, if the man had relayed his words, the authorities would surely want to chat with him. Either way, he needed to take a few precautions.

Finished with the scissors, he laid them down and picked up an electric shaver. Five minutes later the job was done and

O'Fallon rubbed his chin. Without the goatee he looked much younger, less sinister.

He picked up the scissors again and started working on his hair, bangs first, then sides. Unable to see the back, he grabbed the electric razor again and worked away, the buzz of the shaver the only sound in the room. Another five minutes passed. He finished with the sides and back and ran the blade over the top once more.

Laying down the shaver, he stared at himself for several seconds. If the man in the raincoat could recognize him now, it'd be a miracle.

Satisfied, O'Fallon switched on the water and washed his face, the cold water like a shot of electricity into his skin. Rubbing soap into his hands, he lathered up, soap on his forehead, then his cheeks and under his eyes, then his chin and neck. Taking a towel from the rack by the sink, he rubbed the soap into his face, at first gently but then harder and harder. Becoming more and more desperate, he scrubbed his skin, the towel rough against his cheeks. His skin turned red, then redder as he worked to clean away the residue of his evening's work.

Dropping the towel, he sloshed handful after handful of water into his eyes, then down his face and throat. For an instant, he felt panicky and he threw more and more water onto his face, his fingers rubbing it as if trying to remove ink from a white shirt. But then, suddenly, like a dog coming out of a lake, he shook himself, his thin shoulders quivering, his face jerking side to side. The water slid down his throat into the collar of his black shirt. He picked a clean towel from the rack and dabbed at his face. Finished with the towel, he tossed it to the floor and stared back into the mirror. But it was no use. In spite of the shaved head and chin, it was still there, the stain, the . . . well, he didn't know what to call it, but it was angry and hateful and he couldn't wash it away, not now and not ever, not after tonight.

O'Fallon squinted. No doubt about it, his eyes had changed. Anyone who knew him would see it. They were harder at the edges and more haunted from the inside out. Whereas before they were brown like sweet chocolate, they looked now like pools of sludge, thick and oily, dark and dangerous.

He, of course, knew why they had changed—no mystery to that. Though he had been a soldier with the Orangemen since the third month after Rebecca's death, he had never done anything really harmful until tonight. But now he had murdered, and his eyes reflected his new status.

Stepping from the bathroom, O'Fallon walked to a green trunk sitting at the bottom of Heather's bed. Squatting, he unlocked the trunk and lifted off the top. The hinges squeaked in the quiet room, but Heather didn't budge. Reaching into the trunk, O'Fallon ran his hands over the contents. Over twenty sticks of Tovex, a sophisticated form of dynamite, a box full of blasting caps and electric timers, enough firepower to do far more damage than he had ever dreamed of doing. He rubbed his chin as he stared at the tools of his trade. A clerk and a daddy by day, but a terrorist by night. Within a matter of weeks, he knew the chances were good he'd become a murderer again. Would it feel different the next time? Easier maybe?

Heather jumped in her sleep, and O'Fallon dropped the trunk lid and locked it back. Standing, he moved to Heather's side and leaned over to kiss her.

"Sleep tight, my angel," he cooed. "Daddy's here, daddy's here."

Heather didn't move. But if she had, if she had opened her eyes, she would have seen her daddy the murderer wiping tears away from his big brown eyes.

FIVE

His jaw determined, Russell Chadwick reared back as much as his aching back would allow and tossed a horseshoe at the steel rod that poked out of the dusty ground of his backyard just a few feet behind his garage. The horseshoe clanked against the rod, then settled in on it. Turning to his wife, Mildred, he stuck out his tongue.

"That's twenty-one!" he playfully taunted. "Game over!"

"I don't think so," Mildred said, waving a finger. "You threw first, so I have to throw last. Now step back and let me at it. If I get two ringers, you wash the dishes."

Chadwick and Mildred had been tossing horseshoes together for over forty-five years, and he almost never beat her. The daughter of a man who had spent at least a couple of summers playing for the old Brooklyn Dodgers, Mildred was a natural athlete. When she threw a horseshoe, she looked like poetry in motion—arm flowing backward, foot stepping forward, back arched perfectly, hand extended completely, horseshoe gliding through the air. *Clang.* The first horseshoe dropped over the steel rod as if honed in by radar.

"That's eighteen," she said calmly. "Another one and—"

"Careful now," he interrupted her. "Don't let the pressure make you choke. And it's about dark out here too—almost seven o'clock. You miss it and you have to fry me catfish Friday night. Get that smell all over the house. And grease popping everywhere, a real mess to clean up. You know you don't want that."

Mildred glanced at him dismissively. Chadwick grinned and took a deep breath. Mildred toed the line they had drawn in the dirt to mark the throwing point. Chadwick studied his wife's profile. The sun, almost gone now, threw its last rays into her hazel gray eyes. Her hair, though gray like his, remained lustrous and thick. Her body, always slender and strong, had remained so to this day. She wore her khaki slacks, tennis shoes, and a light green jacket with the style of a woman half her age. Even at sixty-seven, she still looked beautiful to him. Better still, she still made him go out and play horseshoes with her, even after a terrible day like today. With Mildred, he always knew he'd find what he needed—play, encouragement, advice, sometimes even rebuke.

Her eyes focused, Mildred shifted into action. The horseshoe flew up and out into the air just as Chadwick heard a car pull into the driveway. *Clang.* The horseshoe bounced once, twice, then settled. Two car doors slammed but he kept his eyes on the horseshoe.

"You missed!" Chadwick shouted, moving quickly toward the opposite stob. "It's not a ringer!"

"Is too!" Mildred argued, right behind him. "The prongs are on the edge, but they're there, right there. Look."

Chadwick knelt slowly, his right knee weak. "It's close," he said. "Too close to call."

"It's on there!" Mildred raised her voice, her fingers marking the spot in the dirt. "Right on there."

"Too close!" Chadwick countered.

"Hey, what's going on?"

Chadwick looked up as his son, Todd, a stockbroker, approached them across the grass, his sixth-grade son, Taylor, right beside him.

"It's your mom again," Chadwick said, standing. "Trying to cheat me out of another game."

"I'll be the judge," Taylor said, obviously having witnessed such an exchange in the past. "Whose shoe is this?" He pointed to the last one Mildred had thrown.

"Can't say," Mildred cut in. "You just tell us if it's a ringer or not."

Taylor bent over, his concentration intense. After several seconds, he stood and shook his head. "A close one," he said, "but I think it's a ringer."

Chadwick raised his hands into the air, feigning disgust. Mildred danced a jig at his side, then stopped and hugged Taylor as though he'd just given her a million dollars.

"You're my boy!" she shouted. "Come on in and let me cut you a slice of coconut cake."

"Before supper?" Taylor asked.

"You called it a ringer," Mildred said. "If you want cake before supper, you've got it."

Muttering, Chadwick followed her and Taylor inside, Todd trailing behind. Thirty minutes later, they sat down to eat. Taylor said the prayer. They ate simply but well—corn bread, barbecued chicken that Mildred had baked earlier in the day, green beans, a mixed vegetable salad.

"You see that Northern Ireland stuff on the television?" Todd asked, his mouth full of corn bread.

"Yeah," Chadwick said. "Makes me sick to think about it."

"You'd think someone could do something," Mildred said. "I mean it's been eight hundred years. One war after another."

"They say three are dead," Todd said. "More wounded. But nobody's got any answers."

"I—" Chadwick started to say something about the feeling he'd experienced at the office yesterday, but then he decided against it. Why utter something so vague? He swallowed and stayed quiet. The meal passed quickly, and after finishing off a piece of coconut cake with milk, Todd and Taylor stood to leave.

"Betty flying in tonight?" Mildred asked, standing with them.

"Yeah," Todd said. "At ten. She's finished with that Austin conference."

Chadwick stood too and walked them to the door. On the steps leading to the garage he gave his son a quick hug. "I'm glad Betty doesn't travel but a couple of times a year," he said.

"You and me both," Todd said. "And I'm glad Mom is here to feed us when she does."

"Yeah, no maid to cook for Grandma," Taylor said, obviously pleased.

Chadwick and Mildred both squeezed Taylor, then watched son and grandson walk to Todd's car. Closing the door against the autumn chill, Chadwick glanced at his watch. Almost eight-thirty—not long until his nine o'clock bedtime. But he had dishes to do first.

"Come on," Mildred said, kissing him on the chin. "I'll help with those dishes."

"And I'll take you to dinner this weekend," he said. "Skip the catfish."

Yawning, he put his arm around Mildred and walked her to

the kitchen. Thirty minutes later he led her up the stairs of their two-story brick home. An hour after that, he closed his Bible, turned off the light, kissed Mildred on the cheek, and lay down to sleep.

Within minutes, his light snoring filled the room. Outside, the moon climbed into the black sky, and stars twinkled like street-lights on a main street a billion miles away. The clock passed eleven, then twelve, then one.

Perspiring in spite of the cool night air, Chadwick stirred in his sleep and rolled over. Mildred lay beside him, her breathing regular and deep, her hands folded neatly over her stomach. Chadwick's eyelids flickered but didn't open. He tossed again and his pillow dropped to the floor. He moaned slightly. Inside his head, a flitting image floated through his sleep, a lion crossing a desert. Flowing mane, heavy paws, blood dripping from his mouth. The lion roared, tossed his head, and reared up on his hind legs.

Chadwick jerked slightly as he dreamed, a jolt of fear running through his subconscious. Materializing from the sand of the desert another creature rose up and roared.

He struggled to see. What was it? Fuzzy . . . brown . . . A bear, that's what it was. A bear bigger than any bear in the history of the world. A giant grizzly with claws like meat hooks. The claws were bloody like the mouth of the lion.

Chadwick groaned again and the sound stirred Mildred, but not enough to wake her.

The lion saw the bear and his mouth opened, and his teeth flashed in the glare of the sun. He emitted a roar that shook the ground. The dust of the desert rose up under the lion's paws.

Chadwick felt himself sweating but he didn't wake up.

The bear and the lion moved toward each other, each of them growling. A wind whipped through the lion's mane, and the desert sand became thick in the air. The smell of rotting flesh flowed from the gaping mouths of the lion and the bear, and flies buzzed in and out around their teeth.

The lion and bear stepped closer and closer. The bear swiped the desert with a massive paw and the lion crouched, his head huge, teeth exposed, flecks of saliva dripping from his jaws.

Chadwick opened his mouth to scream, to keep the lion and the bear apart, to keep them from killing each other and spewing blood across the desert sand. He tried to shout, to command them to stop. But his tongue refused to work. He gritted his teeth as he dreamed, and beads of sweat now dotted his face.

The bear rushed the lion, and the desert sand swirled around them. The lion opened his mouth and the two were almost at each other's throats. They were going to kill each other. Neither would survive . . . neither . . .

A lamb darted toward the lion and the bear. A spotless white lamb. It appeared from out of nowhere, a speck of a creature, its legs spindly and shaking. The lamb bleated once, twice, three times.

The lion and the bear halted in midair, their charge broken by the bleating of the lamb. They tumbled to the ground and crouched in the sand, their eyes watching the lamb, their stomachs touching the earth, their teeth still bared, low growls rumbling in their throats.

The wind whipped higher and higher in the desert. The sand grew thicker as the lamb stepped between the two creatures, then lay down and rolled over on its back, exposing its neck to the lion and the bear. It bleated once more.

The desert sand blew even heavier now, and the swirl from it covered the lion and the bear and the lamb, obliterating them all in a dull yellow cloud—

Chadwick woke with a jerk, his body covered with moisture. For several seconds he lay still, trying to get his bearings. He glanced over at Mildred. She continued to sleep, on her back as always, as neatly as a store mannequin. Chadwick rolled over, picked his pillow off the floor, and tucked it to his stomach. Not given to much dreaming, he wondered what this one meant. It was so vivid.

It had made him feel helpless. Helpless and scared. A lion and a bear fighting to kill each other. But what did that mean?

Still confused, Chadwick tried to go back to sleep. The clock beside the bed glowed 1:37 in red numerals. He closed his eyes. More minutes passed, then another hour. But sleep refused to come.

Giving up, Chadwick climbed out of bed, slipped on a robe, and made coffee in the kitchen. Sitting in the breakfast nook, he sipped at the coffee and stewed over the dream. But he couldn't quite figure it out.

Leaving the table, he told himself to forget the dream. Just a bad night. Maybe he could read awhile. Grabbing a Bible from his study, he read for almost an hour from the Psalms and then tried to pray. But the dream kept intruding, and he finally gave up his praying and walked back to the bedroom.

Crawling back in beside Mildred, Chadwick sighed. The Ireland mess had consumed him all day—intruding on his thoughts through church, lunch, and his afternoon nap. Such a tragedy!

A jolt of energy hit him and he sat up in bed. He knew what the dream meant! It symbolized conflict, conflict between two strong and determined foes, foes like those in Northern Ireland! The lamb represented Jesus, the lion and the bear the opposing sides in the hostilities!

Certain he had figured it out, he checked the clock, saw it was still only four-thirty, then closed his eyes to sleep again. But his mind remained restless. The dream kept bothering him, prodding him, as if he had missed something crucial beneath the surface of what he had figured out. Another hour passed.

Finally, frustrated by the insomnia, he climbed out of bed again, showered, shaved, and dressed. Thirty minutes later, he called Ted, apologized for waking him so early, and asked him to have everyone meet in the office at 8 A.M. Might as well get the week off to a quick start.

Leaving Mildred in bed, he alerted one of the two bodyguards who stayed with him twenty-four hours a day, spent another thirty minutes in prayer, then climbed into the backseat of a black town car and told his driver to head to the office. Until he settled the meaning of this dream, he suspected he'd not get much of anything else accomplished, no matter how urgent.

SIX

BELFAST, IRELAND

At just before 1 P.M., Ireland time, Casey Sterling lifted his eyes from the computer screen he'd been studying and grabbed a telephone off the desk in his bedroom suite in the Irish International Hotel. Punching in a number, he did what he did just about every other day of his life, no matter his location. He called his mother, Lacy Drew Sterling.

Exactly four rings later she answered.

"Hey, Mom," he said, "I'm in Ireland."

"Of course you are," she said, her Southern accent drawn out like a fishline in the sun. "You're on television, remember? I know where you are almost all the time."

Carrying the phone to the window, Sterling smiled at his mother's down-home Southern tones. Having long since cleaned up his own accent—the result of expensive speech lessons—he now had the capacity to adore rather than resent his mother's small-town ways. He stared out the window into the small park area that bordered his hotel. Mom always sounded so pleased when he called, as if it had been months since they had last talked.

"I was the only American here for several hours," he said. "Had the stage all to myself. 'Course all the networks are here now, a whole herd of cameras, you can hardly walk through 'em all."

"But you were the first," said his mom, her pride evident in her voice.

"That's the idea," Casey said.

"You were great as usual. Better lookin' than Brad Pitt, and taller too."

"You're my mom," Sterling said. "You have to say that."

"If I'm lyin', I'm dyin'."

Sterling knew he had one of the most recognized faces in the world, but his mom's bragging still embarrassed him.

"You comin' back to the States soon?" Mom asked.

Casey saw an elderly couple standing in the park under a tree, a flock of doves at their feet. The couple sat down on the bench and tossed the doves some kind of bird feed.

"Probably another day or so," he said. "But yeah, if nothing else breaks over here, I'll come home by Friday at the latest."

"You gon' drop into Swansboro and give me the pleasure of seein' you this time?"

Sterling left the window and stepped back to his desk. Though he loved his mom more than anything, he didn't like going back to Swansboro, South Carolina, any more often than absolutely necessary. Too many memories were buried in that two-red-light coastal town, and most of them were bad. Swansboro conjured up too many bad smells—the aroma of fishing boats that had served too long and been washed too seldom—and too many bad sights— sun-bleached warehouses with the windows broken out and the wood crumbling. An image of his dad flashed through Sterling's head, but he quickly squashed it. Talk about bad memories.

"I don't know, Mom," he said. "Let me get back to Atlanta, then I'll see. Maybe you can come down to my place instead. Lots more room, better dining, I'll take you to a play. You always like that. We'll go to the Fox Theater."

"You know better than that," she said. "That Atlanta scares the livin' daylights outa me. Too many cars and not enough space. I get all tight in the chest just thinkin' 'bout comin' down there."

Sterling nodded. His mom almost never left Swansboro, her home since the day she was born just over fifty-five years ago. Only eighteen the year he came into the world, Lacy Drew Sterling carried her small-town ways like a badge of honor, al- most daring someone to make fun of her upbringing. Though she assured him that she liked the tailored clothes and quality jew- elry he bought her, she almost never wore any of it, except for the rare occasion she did give in and come to Atlanta.

"I can't wear all that fancy stuff here in Swansboro," she'd say when he questioned her about it. "Like puttin' cashmere on a cow."

Sterling didn't argue. In spite of the fact that his mom had the looks of a much younger woman, she had never really accepted how exceptional she was.

"I'll see if I can make it up there, Mom," he said, his tone apologetic. "But I can't promise."

"You don't need to worry about him, son," Lucy Drew said softly. "His liver's done give out on him. He won't bother you none this time."

Ignoring his mom's last statement, Sterling picked up a piece of paper, crushed it, and studied his computer again.

"I may skip over to Kosovo for a couple of days before I come back to Atlanta," he said.

"That place gettin' dicey again?" The sound of fear edged into his mother's words.

Sterling tossed the paper into a wastebasket in the corner and concentrated on the computer screen. Always trying to anticipate the next news, he read daily Internet reports from around the world, each of the updates bringing him the most recent news from every imaginable spot across the globe. The face of Milo Prikova, the Albanian leader of the KLA—the Kosovo Liberation Army—stared back at him. The man had a beard as thick as bear's fur, and the scowl that lurked in his black eyes and at the corners of his down-turned lips seemed to crawl off the computer screen into the room with Sterling. He knew from past reports that Prikova had lost his entire family in the Serbian cleansing of the ethnic Albanians that had pushed the Allied NATO forces into the bombing campaign of 1999.

After the bombing forced the Serbs out of Kosovo, the authorities had found the bodies of Prikova's wife and two daughters in an unmarked grave no more than a thousand yards from the burned-out home where they had once lived. A third child, an eleven-year-old boy, had disappeared, and everyone presumed him dead.

His hatred of the Serbs fueling his actions, Prikova had made the KLA his private army, using it to exact revenge against those who had murdered his family. In spite of the best efforts of the thirty-five thousand NATO peace-keeping forces still active in the area, Prikova kept stirring the pot. Though his forces had not mounted a major offensive in over a year, a couple of Sterling's sources had recently told him to keep his eyes peeled. Something might happen soon after the New Year.

Staring at Prikova, Sterling wondered what the man had felt

when he found the graves of his wife and daughters. What anger had that created in him? What despair? And what about his son? What would happen if and when Prikova finally discovered his body?

An idea came to Sterling and he keystroked the print command on his computer, then focused on his mom again. "Kosovo is a definite possible," he said. "A bit of digging and a man might still find a story there."

"You take too many chances. The hostilities ended 'bout two years ago. No reason to run way over there. Come on home and see your mama."

Sterling pulled the printout from the computer and stretched back up. "They don't give anchor desks to people who sit around in their office drinking espresso," he said. "When I'm in the field, I'm in the living room, simple as that."

"They'll have to give you one of them anchor jobs soon," his mom said. "You're the best-lookin' boy out there . . . and the smartest, too. You just wait. It can't be long now, you'll see."

"I'll call you when I leave here," he said. "If I do go to Kosovo, I'll let you know."

"Don't forget to come see your mama."

"I'll see what I can do, but I can't promise that I'll come to Swansboro."

"Love you, Casey boy," said his mom.

"You too," he said.

Hanging up the phone, Casey stared at Prikova's picture one more time. His enemies called him "The Mad One" and accused him of atrocities that equaled or surpassed any that the Serbs had visited upon his people. According to those who now hunted him, Prikova had the temper of a wounded jackal and even less scruples. If he had ever known the meaning of mercy, he had surely forgotten it, and he had a commitment to his cause that most saw as fanatical.

Sterling sat on the windowsill and tried to see past the printed report. An engineer before the breakup of his country, Prikova had built roads and bridges and dams. Highly respected in his field, he had worked with the government on a number of contracts, and the people who knew him then spoke of him as a man of intelligence and charm.

Carrying the paper to his bed, Sterling plopped down and read further. Prikova had studied for over a year in England at the Polytechnic Institute of London and knew people in all walks of life. Until the war in Kosovo, westerners acquainted with him said he had always been an intense but reasonable man. But then came the destruction of his native land and the death of his family. War made good men do bad things.

Making a firm decision to go to Kosovo, Sterling closed his eyes and took a deep breath. War wasn't the only thing that could have such an effect on good men. He wanted revenge too, and no one he loved had ever died in a war.

———

His bodyguards on either side, Russell Chadwick took the elevator to the tenth and top floor of the RCEA Building—a modern steel and glass complex on the northeast perimeter of Atlanta. Entering the main suite, a complex with sixteen offices, a conference room with seating for forty, and a theater-style auditorium he often used for staff meetings, he saw that his crew had already arrived. Still disturbed by the dream from the preceding evening, he immediately called everyone into the boardroom.

His hands shaky, he steadied himself at the edge of the conference table and studied his people as they situated themselves. As always, Ted wore a starched shirt, this one white, a dark suit, and an expensive gold-tone tie. Boggett, on the other hand, looked like an unmade bed. His tie hung crooked around his neck, and the top button of his wrinkled shirt didn't quite connect to the buttonhole on the other side of his chunky neck.

Chadwick grinned and faced Kent, the only one without a tie. Kent held a cup of hot tea, his slender body covered by a long-sleeved black shirt and charcoal gray slacks. He looked neat, as always, but not stuffy. A laptop computer sat on the table beside him, its monitor closed against the keyboard.

Valerie Miller sat beside Kent, her elbows on her chair arms, her ice-blue blouse a sharp contrast to her tan skirt, her auburn hair shining in the light from the window behind her back. She looked happy this morning. Maybe she had begun to sleep better. For a second, Chadwick wondered why she wasn't married yet, but then reminded himself that people married later these days. Besides, God used a lot of single people—like Jesus, for instance, or Paul. No sin in being single.

Taking a deep breath, Chadwick mentally rehearsed his opening words. Though still not sure exactly what God wanted, he had no question that the Lord had tried to speak to him in his dream. He'd seen no lightning flash and heard no thunder. Not exactly Moses and the burning bush but . . . .

"Sorry to call you here this early," he said. "I know we weren't scheduled to meet until ten."

"No problem," Ted said.

Everyone nodded their agreement.

Chadwick rubbed his hands together. "Okay, here's the deal. I didn't sleep much last night. This Ireland situation is weighing heavy on me."

"We're all prayin' about that," Boggett said, a jelly doughnut in hand.

"I wonder if prayer's enough in this case," Chadwick said, his index finger tapping his chin. "Maybe we can do something else, something more direct."

"We'll call the President," Kent offered. "Tell him to turn up the heat, get the factions back to the bargaining table."

"That's not enough, either," Chadwick said.

"But what else can we do?" Ted asked. "That's about as far—"

Chadwick threw up a hand. "I don't *know* what else to do," he said. "But last night I had this dream."

"But you don't ever dream," Boggett said.

"Well, I did last night. I saw a lion and a bear. . . ." Chadwick described the combatants. "And then a lamb came between them. The lamb knelt between them and they stopped fighting."

"Jesus is the lamb," Ted offered. "Jesus is the only one who can stop such terrible things. The power of the Lord."

"That's my thought too," Chadwick said, his brow furrowed. "But somehow I don't think that's all there is to it. I feel like I'm supposed to *do* something here, but . . . I don't know what." He slumped into a seat and propped his head on his hands.

For almost a minute, no one spoke. Chadwick studied the top of the table. Boggett nibbled at his doughnut.

"Jesus," Ted repeated. "The lamb is Jesus."

"We all know that," snorted Boggett. "Tell us something we don't know."

Silence came again. Chadwick ran his fingers through his hair and left his seat for the window. Boggett took another bite of doughnut.

"We're not much help," Ted said.

"Dreams ain't my thang," Lester said, his accent dripping. "I'm a nuts and bolts guy, a pragmatist."

Chadwick faced them again, his brow furrowed. Then his eyes sparkled and he turned to Valerie.

"You haven't said anything," he said.

She straightened as if caught taking a cookie from a jar.

"Do you have any ideas on this?" he tried again.

"Well, I don't know," she said. "I'm so new and—"

"Never mind that," he said. "Tell me what you think."

Valerie put her hands on the table, palms together. "Okay," she began, her voice unsure in spite of Chadwick's encouragement. "I agree . . . with Ted, Jesus is the Lamb. But . . ." She hesitated, then averted her eyes.

"But what?" Chadwick asked, pulling it from her. "Go on."

Valerie stared at her hands. "Well . . . maybe we're forgetting something here, something important. Jesus wants us to do His work, right?" She looked at her uncle for affirmation.

Chadwick nodded.

"Jesus said, 'Blessed are the peacemakers for theirs is the kingdom of heaven.' "

"Right."

"Well, maybe that's us. We become the peacemakers for Jesus, the lambs in His stead."

She stopped as if afraid to say more.

"Go on," Chadwick encouraged.

"I'm not sure I should."

Chadwick walked to the seat beside hers, sat down, and took her hands in his.

"Look," he coaxed. "This is Uncle Russ here. You're with friends. And I trust your judgment."

She nodded.

"So go on, tell me what's on your heart," Chadwick said.

Valerie hesitated once more and he squeezed her hands. She finally spoke, her words pouring out quickly. "Well, what if you . . . you personally are the lamb?"

Boggett laid the last scrap of his doughnut on the table. Kent stopped drinking tea in midgulp. Ted caught his breath, and all three men stared at her as if she had just taken the Lord's name in vain.

"What do you mean?" Chadwick asked.

Valerie shrugged. "I'm not sure exactly. But as you were describing your dream, I . . . had a thought. What if—?" She stopped and shook her head as if to shut off the notion.

"What if what?" Boggett challenged.

"No, it's nothing," Valerie said. "Just a crazy idea."

"The Bible is full of crazy ideas," Chadwick said, his interest

piqued. "Moses told the king of Egypt that God wanted His children to go free. God commanded Gideon to take three hundred
soldiers and go to battle against thousands of Midianites. A virgin woman gave birth to a baby who became the Savior of the
world. Pretty crazy stuff, if you ask me."

Valerie smiled briefly. "Well, you said you felt like God wanted
you to do something more direct." She seemed to gain confidence
as she spoke. "So, what if you're the lamb? God's peacemaker on
earth? What if you went to Northern Ireland?"

"To do what?" Kent challenged.

"Think about it this way," Valerie said, her voice steadier.
"Reverend Chadwick is a pastor to the whole world. Known for
his love for others."

"But he's a Protestant!" Kent countered. "The Catholics in Ireland won't give him the time of day!"

"And it's too dangerous," Boggett added. "Plenty of nut cases
in a place like that who'd like nothin' better than to put a big hole
in the most famous preacher in the world. Imagine the security
problems we'd face."

"I said it was a crazy idea," Valerie said.

For several seconds, the room settled into silence again. Boggett grabbed for his doughnut but saw it was almost gone and
left it on the plate. Chadwick studied his men, trying to determine how to handle the matter. As the first woman to take part
in such discussions, Valerie's presence added tension. His men
weren't exactly male chauvinists, but they weren't accustomed to
a feminine perspective either. But once she started working for
him, Chadwick had decided to involve her precisely for that reason—to give his crew a fresh look at things, a new way to view
the world. After all the years of male-only influences, he believed
he and his men needed to hear her voice. Plus, she needed his
encouragement. If he ever expected her to gain her confidence
back after the recent trauma she'd suffered, he couldn't shut her
down just because Lester and Rodney disagreed with her idea.

Chadwick faced Valerie again.

"Talk to me," he coaxed. "Spill it, everything on your mind."

Boggett flinched. Kent inspected his belt buckle. Ted never
moved, but his eyes stayed glued to Chadwick.

Valerie straightened her shoulders. "I may be way off base
here," she started, her tone still reluctant. "But here's what I
think the dream means. . . ."

Kent, Boggett, and Shuster listened suspiciously as Valerie

continued. Watching them from the corner of his eyes, Chadwick wondered if he had made a mistake by giving Valerie so much leeway. Though he wanted to encourage her, he didn't want to do it at the expense of his most intimate confidants. But, he had to admit, the more she talked, the more he liked her interpretation. It converged nicely with his sense of the thing, the mysterious nature of the feeling that had consumed him since Saturday evening.

Was it possible that God was using Valerie as a kind of Joseph—to interpret His dreams? Maybe so. God had used women in the most surprising ways in the past. Why not now?

As Valerie's explanation came to an end, the men turned to Chadwick. He eased to the edge of the table and sat down.

"What she says makes sense," he said. "But I've got to admit, it scares me some."

"That's right," Kent said. "It's downright dangerous."

"Way too dangerous," chimed in Boggett. "You couldn't hire enough security to make a thing like this work. And even if you could, the cost would go through the roof."

"It's a spiritual problem over there," Ted added. "Let's continue to pray for them. We'll—"

With a wave of his hand, Chadwick cut off the discussion. "All of you are right," he nodded. "Lots of reasons to dismiss this. Still . . ." He paused and closed his eyes. The light overhead hummed softly. Leather creaked as the others shifted in their seats. His eyes still closed, Chadwick began to talk, his voice barely a whisper.

"I started preaching in 1948," he said. "I was barely twenty years old and had less than two years of college. I started in tents; had sawdust floors and pianos hauled in on the back of pickup trucks. One night, about four months into my preaching ministry, a black woman and seven kids—must have been between ten years and six months old—came trooping into the tent. But she didn't stop at the back like all the other blacks did. No, she marched her brood right up the aisle, turned to the left, and sat down right in the front row.

"I watched her as she came in. Though her dress was plain, it was ironed and clean. And her kids—six of them were boys—were clean too. Their blue jeans and T-shirts were a bit frayed, but clean. Those babies plopped down in those hardback chairs like soldiers at attention. That mama held the littlest child in her lap."

Chadwick paused and a touch of moisture crawled to the edge of his right eye. "But then, just as they all got settled, one of my ushers walked up beside her, touched her on the elbow—I can still see it as if it were yesterday—that usher touched her and whispered into her ear. She shook her head. He grabbed harder on her elbow. She shook her head. That usher put his other hand on her elbow and tried to haul her up. She gritted her teeth and closed her eyes, and for a minute, I swear to you I think she was praying. But then she stood up and slapped that usher's hand off her arm. She threw her baby girl on her hip and took the boy to her right by the hand. All her kids joined hands then—all seven of them—and that mama turned that whole brood around and marched them to the back of the tent.

"But she didn't stop there, where we let all the black folks sit. No, she kept right on, marching herself and her babies right out of the tent, the sawdust falling off the heels of her shoes as she left."

Chadwick looked at his crew. "That woman never looked back," he said. "She never looked back, and I didn't do a thing about it. I knew I was wrong, but I let her go. I sat up on that platform about to preach about a God who loves everyone, a God who calls us to love others as Jesus himself loved us, but I didn't do a thing to stop that woman from walking out of that tent." He stopped and propped his head on his hands.

"But you integrated your services long before Jim Crow ever died in the South," Ted said, obviously hoping to alleviate Chadwick's guilt. "You told us that story when you made that decision. You took a lot of grief over that integration and lost a lot of money from supporters who disagreed with your stance."

Chadwick rose from the table. His left leg buckled slightly, but he caught himself before anyone saw it. He walked to the window, stood a second, then pivoted back and faced his troops.

"I saw that woman's oldest boy just over a year ago," he said.

Boggett's mouth fell open.

"I never told you that. I saw him in a state prison in Raleigh, North Carolina. Remember we did a service there on Christmas Eve? That boy is serving a life sentence for murder. He pulled me aside after the sermon. Said his mama took him to hear me preach one time back when he was a boy. But we told them to sit in the back of the tent. His mama hauled him out of the place. He decided right then and there that Jesus was only for white folks."

Rubbing his eyes, Chadwick sat heavily on the table corner. "So I have to do something," he said. "Maybe it is crazy, but I swore last year when I saw that boy that I'd never let something like that happen again. If I've got a choice between sitting around and doing nothing or acting and making a difference, I'm taking the second option. I'm too old to do anything else."

He turned from Boggett to Kent to Ted. "If you want to talk me out of it, I'm willing to listen." A long minute passed in the room. No one said anything.

"Good," Chadwick said. "Then I take it everybody agrees we need to think about this a little deeper." No one spoke. Chadwick's face brightened as he considered what to do next. "Now," he said, "I can't do what Valerie suggests all by myself. I'll need some help, someone who commands the respect of the Catholic world. For this to work, I'll need the pope involved. That's the only way I can do anything."

"But that ain't gonna happen!" Boggett said. "You don't know the new pope . . . he won't—"

"We don't know what we can do until we try," Chadwick said, once more cutting off the debate. "Valerie, what's your best guess? Will the pontiff get involved in something like this?"

A look of confusion flooded Valerie's face. "I . . . have no clue," she said hesitantly. "I knew his predecessor—a wonderful man. But this new guy—Clement Peter? Who knows? I wouldn't count on it if I were you. He's going to have his hands full getting a grip on things in the Vatican, consolidating his power. Guess it depends on what you want from him."

Chadwick walked to the window and stared out at the skyline. "I don't have a clear sense yet of what I want him to do. But that shouldn't stop us. Faith is the substance of things hoped for, the evidence of things not seen. If God's people had waited until they had a clear vision of everything, they'd never have done anything." He turned back to Valerie. "Do you think he'll talk to me?"

She seemed to shrink at the table. Remembering her recent experience involving the Vatican, Chadwick almost left her alone. The assignment at the embassy hadn't been pleasant, at least not at the end. People had died, and Valerie had been right in the middle of all the carnage. A man she had come to love had disappeared without a trace, and a cloak of grief still hung over her from all she had suffered.

Chadwick stepped to Valerie and touched her shoulder.

"You okay?" he asked.

She nodded, but not convincingly. Chadwick gently rubbed her shoulders. He knew her well, knew how tough, how absolutely fearless she had always been. But the last year had wrenched her to the core, tested her faith in ways she had never imagined possible. To some extent, he had offered her a job so she could take a break from the rough and tumble of the real world. Maybe he should just leave well enough alone, not press her over something like this. He turned to Boggett.

"Boggs, you take the lead on this," Chadwick said. "Contact the folks at the State Department. I want to talk to the pope—"

"I'll do it," Valerie interrupted, lifting her head. "I'm the one with the contacts."

"You sure?" Chadwick asked. "Don't do it if you're not ready."

"I'm the one who suggested this," she said, a bit of her old spunk momentarily returning. "It's only fair for me to follow through. What do you want me to do?"

Glad to see that she hadn't lost all her courage, Chadwick smiled. "I'm not sure exactly," he said. "But I want to talk with the pope by phone first, then in person if his schedule permits. And I need to do it soon. Something tells me things will deteriorate even more in Northern Ireland if we don't hurry."

Valerie stood with him, and her five feet seven inches seemed larger in the room as she stretched to her full height.

"You're one of the most beloved men in the world," she said. "Clement would be irresponsible not to visit with you at the first opportunity."

"Can you set up a meeting?" Chadwick asked, his legs steadying as he contemplated his next move.

"I'll take a shot at it," she said. "I still know some people there."

"Then do it," Chadwick said. "Let's see if we can make this happen." He pivoted to his men. Boggett dropped his eyes, but the others nodded, even if a bit hesitantly.

Pleased, Chadwick brushed his hair back with his fingers. These were good men. If he said, "Do it," they would act whether they were thrilled with his plan or not.

SEVEN

TUESDAY
ATLANTA

Her gym bag packed, Valerie checked herself in the mirror one last time. Nothing fancy—off-white turtleneck sweater, black wool slacks, simple gold earrings. Blotting her lipstick, she grabbed her coat, a waist-length tan cashmere jacket, and scurried out of the locker room and out the front door to the street. Slipping on her coat, she hustled over the concrete sidewalk, headed to her office. Three blocks away, she pushed through the front door, checked in at the security desk, and stepped to the elevators. Climbing on, she hit the button for the tenth floor and relaxed against the wall.

Though weary from her workout, she felt better today than she had in weeks and appreciated again the fact that her uncle's building sat so close to a state-of-the-art health club. Having decided after her near-escape from death less than a year ago that she needed to strengthen her body, she spent at least four sessions a week under the guidance of a personal trainer.

In the last nine months, her legs and arms had toned up from some weight lifting, and her aerobic conditioning had never been better. Admittedly, her mental and spiritual state still needed a ton of work, but her physical condition had improved dramatically. In fact, she had almost become compulsive about her workouts. Pushing herself to more and more difficult exercises and heavier and heavier weight routines, she had lost eleven pounds in the last three months. Her face had thinned and her clothes hung loosely on her body. But she felt safer when she exercised—almost as if pumping the StairMaster and pushing up the weights would drive away danger, death, maybe even despair.

When the elevator doors opened, she hustled to her office, a corner suite of two rooms that overlooked the interchange of interstates 85 and 285. After speaking for a moment to her secretary, she stepped inside to a closet, dropped her bag, and collapsed into the seat at her desk. For several seconds, she just waited, letting her heart settle. Staring around the plush surroundings, she noted her diplomas all lined up in a row and an eleven-by-fourteen family picture over a sofa directly across from her desk—her dad and mom smiling at her. Four different plants sat in the corners of the room—each of them real, and each of them vibrantly healthy—no fake plants for Valerie Miller.

These four plants, rescued from her mother—who seemed to kill anything green within a week of its appearance at her house—had almost succumbed before Valerie rescued them. But now here they sat—living testimonials to her green thumb. Standing, Valerie walked to the closest plant and gently rubbed one of its broad leaves. She didn't even know its name, but that didn't matter. When she cared for a plant it thrived, plain and simple.

Calmer now, Valerie picked up a cell phone and moved to the window behind her chair. A speckle of white clouds rolled in and out across the sky. Her uncle Russell and the rest of his team had left Atlanta for an early morning planning session for the Chicago crusade. At her uncle's instructions, she had stayed behind to gather information on the new pope. Before contacting him, Chadwick wanted a complete dossier on the man—his history, his likes and dislikes, his goals for the future. One thing Valerie had learned quickly about her uncle—though he spoke with a simplicity that reflected his upbringing on an Iowa farm, he didn't make decisions without thorough preparation.

She had spent most of the previous evening digging through the Internet, downloading news clips, looking up biographical pieces, ordering books that detailed the new pontiff's life. A file as thick as a briefcase now lay on her desk, its contents bulging at the edges.

Valerie stared down at the traffic whizzing by. With all the information she currently needed in hand, the time had come to make the first call. But still she hesitated. To make the call meant she had to jump back into a stream that had almost drowned her, a stream whose eddies still washed over her far more often than she cared to admit.

Shuddering slightly, she wondered about Michael—Michael

Del Rio, to be exact, a Catholic priest who had shaken her world to its foundation. A dark-headed, bravehearted priest who had saved her life and taught her to love and . . . well, he had taught her, that's all, taught her more than anyone ever had. But then he had vanished into thin air. Now, almost a year later, no one knew where he was or even if he was still alive.

Valerie stepped from the window and picked up the phone. To make the call she had promised her uncle she'd make meant she had to step back into the vortex of the Vatican and all its mysterious ways. It meant she had to relive all those memories, memories she wanted and needed to bury before she could get on with her life.

Valerie rolled the phone in her hands. To call meant she faced the possibility of resurrecting some buried demons. But if she didn't call, she'd break a commitment to her uncle. And how could she do that?

Resigned to her fate, Valerie keyed in the private number for Arthur Bremer, the United States ambassador to the Vatican in Italy. Bremer had fired her less than eleven months ago from her post in the embassy in Rome, but she held no grudges against him. He had only acted on orders from higher up in the diplomatic food chain.

The call skipped straight through to his private study. Four rings later, the ambassador picked up.

"Bremer here."

"Arthur? Hey, it's Valerie Miller."

"Valerie? What in the world are you doing?"

"Surprised, huh?"

"No question. Where are you these days? I lost track after you left the State Department. You back in Charlotte?"

"Not exactly. I'm working with my uncle, Dr. Russell Chadwick."

"*The* Russell Chadwick? You're his niece? How did I miss that on your vita?"

"I didn't list it, that's why. But I am his niece, and he's hired me to do media relations. I've been at it about five months."

"You had a great future at State," Bremer said, his tone sad. "Sorry things didn't work out, and that I was a part of that. You got a bum deal, that's all. I still feel guilty about it."

"Look, Arthur, I appreciate your sentiments. But I'm not calling to rehash past issues. I'm calling for Reverend Chadwick. He's all broken up about the situation in Northern Ireland."

"Aren't we all?" Bremer grunted. "The place is a disaster and getting worse by the minute."

"Reverend Chadwick wants to do something about it."

"He can join the club. The State Department has been be-tween the cross hairs for years over that mess. If he's got an idea, I'm sure everyone in Washington will be glad to hear it."

"He doesn't want to go through Washington," Valerie said. "He sees no progress there. He wants to try something else."

"I'm all ears, but I don't see how that's got anything to do with me here in Rome."

"The Reverend Chadwick wants to talk to the pope before he says anything to anyone else."

"What's the pope got to do with it?"

Valerie exhaled. "I don't know all the details. But I wanted to touch base with you before I went to anyone at the Vatican. Are you still in touch with Cardinal Roca?"

"Sure, I see him pretty often."

"I need his private number."

Bremer hesitated and Valerie knew why. A man didn't become or remain an ambassador by giving out highly secretive phone numbers without due cause. Cardinal Severiano Roca served as the Secretariat of the Curia, a man second in importance only to the pope when it came to Catholic politics. Many, in fact, thought Roca himself should have succeeded the beloved pontiff who had preceded Clement. But in a twist that surprised everyone, Roca had thrown his weight to the man who had been Vittoré Vincen-zio, formerly the head of the Congregation for Divine Worship, an important but surely lesser office within Vatican power circles. Yet, with Roca's behind-the-scene support, Vincenzio won the election on the morning of the fourteenth day, and white smoke drifted up from St. Peter's Basilica. Vittoré Vincenzio became Pope Clement Peter, the first Vicar of Christ in the new millen-nium. Anyone who knew anything about Vatican politics knew Roca carried enough clout to sink a cruise ship. You don't write the private number of a man with that kind of power on the bath-room walls.

"Roca won't mind if you give me the number," Valerie sug-gested, hoping to help Bremer. "He's Michael Del Rio's uncle. You remember, don't you?"

"The disappearing priest?" Bremer asked. "Any word on him from anybody?"

A sharp pang of grief seized Valerie just below the throat, but she choked it back. "Nope, none. Everyone did their best with the search—the CIA, FBI, the pope, well, not the new one, but the deceased . . . you know, everybody tried, but no one found him."

"That's tough. You knew him pretty well, didn't you?"

A flood of memories overcame Valerie, and though she tried, she couldn't push them back. An archeologist had found a manuscript—supposedly the story of Jesus as told by Mary, his mother—in some caves near Ephesus, Turkey. Bremer had sent her to investigate its authenticity. She had teamed up with a priest named Michael Del Rio, a professor from Notre Dame, the nephew of Severiano Roca. She and Michael found the scroll and Michael read it. But mercenaries seeking to steal the scroll attacked them just as an earthquake hit.

Though no one quite knew what happened, Michael disappeared. In all the confusion—guns firing, the ground cracking, everything falling apart—he just vanished. The house sat on some cliffs overlooking the ocean. The authorities said the earthquake might have thrown Michael over, either that or one of the men who had attacked them had killed him and thrown him into the sea. Maybe he died. She didn't know. Or maybe he took the manuscript and fled with it, keeping the document hidden for reasons of his own. In the months since, she thought he had contacted her once. But that had been months ago. Her hopes of ever seeing him again had dimmed since then.

Biting her lip, Valerie forced herself back to the present. "Look, Arthur, Reverend Chadwick is in a rush here. I can reach Roca through the Vatican, but it could take weeks. I'm just trying to save a few steps, that's all. If you don't want to help, I can go another—"

"Don't get huffy," Bremer interrupted. "I've got the number. I'm just thinking through all the implications. You know me. 'Cautious' is my middle name. Here it is."

"Thanks, Arthur," she said, jotting it down. "Reverend Chadwick will appreciate this. He's a friend of the president you know."

Bremer laughed. "Anything to make the Big Boss happy," he said. "Let me know if I can do anything else. I'm still not square with you. I feel bad about that stuff last year."

"Thanks, Arthur, and don't worry about it."

"You keep in touch. I may want you back someday."

Hanging up, Valerie studied the number. Calling Roca pulled

her right back in. Though she didn't know if she was ready for it, she had made a promise to her uncle.

Thinking once more of Michael Del Rio, she keyed in the number to Cardinal Severiano Roca.

EIGHT

Toweling off his beefy arms, His Holiness Clement Peter eased out of the shower and onto the white tile floor of the bathroom of the papal quarters in the Apostolic Palace. Though normally an early riser, the rigors of the papacy had made the pontiff feel less vibrant than usual at 5 A.M. His body felt heavier even than its normal two hundred and fifty-five pounds, weighted down with the burden of the office.

Straining the towel to hook it around his wide frame, the pontiff slipped into a pair of black leather sandals and a white bathrobe and squeaked over to his closet. Two chamber assistants trailed him, but he kept confusing their names. Tito was the bald one, and Felipe, the ancient man with gnarled hands—or was it the other way around? Not yet accustomed to the constant attention and still quite nervous with it all, Clement didn't know. He had so many new faces and names to memorize and so much protocol to follow.

Sighing, the pope gazed into the mirror at his soft white flesh. A large person since the coming of his puberty, he had never liked his body. His legs seemed as thick as the stone columns that fronted his childhood church, and his face sagged at the edges and under the chin. The only things small about him were his eyes. They were narrow, with pupils that reflected little color. In Anselmo, the small village in southern Italy where he had grown up, the children had always made fun of him—calling him "boy of dough" or "pig face." Too heavy to run without gasping for air and too slow to catch anyone anyway, he sat on a wooden stool by the street and watched as the other children played.

Clement slipped into his undergarments and lifted his arms. Tito (was that his name?) eased a white gown over his wrists and up his shoulders. Behind him, Felipe snapped up the buttons of the garment. Clement tilted his head and Felipe took a brush, his gnarled fingers guiding it through the few wisps of white hair left on the pontiff's extra-large head. Clement smiled ruefully. As an opera singer treasured and loved his voice, so Clement loved his head in spite of its size and baldness. His head had carried him all his life, made him all he had become.

While the other boys kicked soccer balls and chased girls, he read books, moving over the years from the children's stories his mother brought from the school where she worked as a secretary, to biography, philosophy, theology, and political theory. As his energetic brain developed, his studies gave him a place to excel and he took every advantage of it. By the time he reached sixteen years, his boyhood priest had noted both his abilities and his social isolation and suggested that the priesthood might fit him as a future vocation.

A thin smile on his lips, Clement left the closet and entered the bedroom of the papal suite. Those who had made fun of him those long years ago now stood in shock when they saw him, their taunts frozen in their throats. Little doughboy Vittoré Vincenzio had risen steadily through the ranks of the Church—deacon to priest to monsignor to bishop to archbishop to head of a congregation. Then, quite amazingly to everyone, even himself, God had seen fit to choose him as pope, one of the most powerful men in the entire world. Who would dare call him names now?

Clement moved to his desk, motioning for his attendants to follow. Breaking his normal routine, he skipped the private Mass he usually took in the papal chapel a few yards from his bedroom and eased into his seat. Taking the phone that Tito offered, he rubbed his massive head with a thick hand and thought for a moment of the man with whom he would now speak, the man to whom he owed the office he now held.

Going into the holy enclave to elect a new pope, no one had mentioned the name of Vittoré Vincenzio as a potential wearer of the papal crown, and he had harbored no ambitions toward that end. Yes, like every man who ever slips into the cardinal red, he had imagined the possibility, but not in his most lucid moments. To all who knew him, he wasn't *papabili,* or "pope-able" in modern parlance. But, somehow, the enclave had found itself deadlocked over two men—Cardinal Severiano Roca and Gustavo

Medico, the powerful archbishop of Milan. Neither man had the two-thirds-plus-one vote needed to get elected, but both had too many supporters to easily give up their claim to the chair of the Vicar of Christ.

For twelve days, the conclave saw almost no change in status. Yes, a man here or there picked up a few votes, but for the most part the blocks for Roca and Medico stayed entrenched.

At just past midnight of that thirteenth day, a young cardinal whose name Vincenzio barely knew came to him and made him an extraordinary offer.

"We need you as a compromise candidate," the cardinal said. "You are well-known by all of us, trusted by most, a man of much respect among the conclave. And, most importantly, you have no genuine enemies, unlike both Roca and Medico."

Not willing to believe his ears, Vincenzio chuckled at the suggestion. "I'm seventy-two," he said. "I am overweight, and I have elevated blood pressure and high cholesterol. Though I hate to say it in these terms, I've served the Lord willingly but with no particular distinction. Who will vote for me to become pope?"

The young cardinal shrugged. "You sell yourself short. One does not have to bark loudly for others to hear him."

Vincenzio liked the understated flattery but held his tongue.

"You have many significant supporters," the cardinal said, his voice a whisper.

"Name me one," Vincenzio said, still unconvinced.

The cardinal looked left and right as if making sure that no one heard him. "Roca will support you," he whispered.

"Roca? Did he send you?" Vincenzio asked, his mind suddenly reeling with the notion.

The younger cardinal stared into his eyes without blinking. "Yes, Cardinal Roca sent me," he said.

Vincenzio started to protest that it was not possible, but then it came to him—Roca's motivation was quite understandable. The good cardinal knew he couldn't get elected. But he wanted to ensure his own standing in the Vatican, his own power. What better way to do that than to throw his weight to one he thought could gather the necessary votes? If Roca couldn't become king, then he wanted to serve as kingmaker. A brilliant stroke of politics! What's more, if the man he supported was already seventy-two, chances remained high that he might get another shot at the papacy in the not-too-distant future.

"So Roca wants me to stand for the papacy," Vincenzio said softly.

The cardinal nodded again, his eyes twinkling. "Cardinal Roca will work through me," he said. "I already have a number of the younger men ready to follow my lead. The rest of the conclave knows nothing of this, and Roca wants it to stay this way. If anyone learns of Roca's support for you, they may become negative. But he wants you and believes he can deliver his caucus into your column. After that, well, the Spirit of God must work in enough of the others to get you to the needed number."

Vincenzio's head began to throb and his hands shook. It was possible! He might indeed sit on the throne of the Holy See! The old saying, "He who enters the conclave the pope comes out a cardinal, and he who enters a cardinal comes out a pope," had once more proven true! Miracle of miracles!

And so it happened exactly as the young cardinal had suggested. Vittoré Vincenzio received nomination on the morning of the fourteenth day. No one rose to speak against him. Several uncommitted cardinals shifted to his side. Momentum built. The rest of the 104 electors, either too wearied to resist or moved by the Spirit of God, sensed the surge toward his candidacy. The trickle became a groundswell, and when the second vote of the day was taken just before lunch, the impossible had happened. Vittoré Vincenzio, the boy once thought too fat to play soccer in the streets, had become Pope Clement Peter, the newly elected Vicar of Christ.

And though the notion now bothered him more than he dared to mention, Clement knew he owed it all to Roca.

He punched the keypad. Ten seconds later, Cardinal Severiano Roca answered, his low voice easily identifiable to all that knew him.

"Good morning, Your Holiness," Roca said. "You slept well?"

"Not really, I've always been a bit of an insomniac. And I had a touch of the headache through the evening. I think I'm not yet comfortable in these quarters. I feel like an interloper."

"That will end quickly enough, I'm sure," Roca said. "I predict you will soon find the place to your liking."

Clement grunted, recognizing the truth of Roca's words. Though not at all secure in the role, being pope agreed with him, perhaps too much. In spite of his nervousness, he liked the constant attention of his assistants, the adulation of the crowds whenever he stepped into the public arena. What man wouldn't like such power? It intoxicated him with a sense of accomplishment, a feeling he had experienced little during his previous years in the Vatican.

After his ascent to the directorship of the Congregation for Divine Worship, his career had dramatically leveled off. He and others came to view his talents as tapped out—an upper-level organization man, but nothing more. As a result, he had spent the last twenty-two years in quiet service. Yes, his position had its rewards—but not the same as the papacy by any stretch of the imagination.

"I'm returning your call from last evening," Clement said, focusing on the matter at hand.

"Thank you for your quick response," Roca said.

"Forgive me for not meeting you face-to-face," Clement said. "But I am somewhat indisposed this morning. The headache— quite unpleasant."

"Don't trouble yourself with that," Roca said. "Take care of your health. Perhaps you should see a doctor. You are too valuable to us to go long without relief."

"How can I serve you this morning, my friend?" Clement asked, not rising to Roca's compliment.

Roca cleared his throat, and Clement pictured the man on the other end of the line. Roca served as both the Secretariat of the Curia and the director of the Congregation for the Doctrine of the Faith, the most powerful division in the Catholic Church outside the office of the pope. No taller than a chest of drawers and almost as wide, Roca had spent most of his adult life involved in this mysterious maze known as the Vatican. Scraggly lines crisscrossed his nose and fenced in his eyes, sure signs of too little rest and too much conversation oiled with wine. Age had thinned his hair on top, and Roca always combed it crossways, left to right, to cover as much bald space as possible. He had eyes the color of black olives, and more than one rival in the upper echelon of the Holy See had buckled under the pressure of Roca's frozen gaze— a stare known in the Curia, the Vatican's ruling council, as "the black ice."

Clement felt a certain appreciation for the man because of his role in his election, but he also feared him, and that fear made him jealous.

"Have you ever met the Reverend Russell Chadwick?" Roca asked, his tone guarded.

"No, never. But I know his reputation. Isn't he in poor health?"

"Quite so, I think, but he's still amazingly productive. An aged lion, much like yourself. But still full of vigor."

Clement cleared his throat, hoping to indicate his disregard for such statements, but inwardly he felt pleased.

"And what about him?" Clement asked.

For a second Roca hesitated, and Clement heard caution in his voice when he spoke.

"He wants an appointment with you."

Now it was Clement's turn to hesitate. Not that he was surprised by the suggestion. People of importance from all over the world had wanted to meet with him over these first months of his tenure, and he had obliged many of them. If he recalled correctly, Chadwick had sent him a congratulatory letter soon after his election. For two such well-known religious leaders to sit down and talk over matters of mutual concern made excellent sense—except for one thing. Clement wasn't sure he wanted to do it, and he had a couple of reasons for his reluctance. But he didn't want Roca to know that, at least not yet.

"Has he said when he wants this meeting?" he asked, masking his hesitancy.

"As soon as possible," Roca said. "He says he'll fly here. Or meet you at a place of your choosing."

"But my schedule is quite full for the next several weeks. Is there a specific purpose for this conference? Other than the standard 'shake and smile' opportunity?"

Roca chuckled slightly and Clement grimaced. Maybe that last phrase sounded too flippant for a pope, too much like a progressive European politician. His head throbbed more intensely.

"Indeed there is. He's concerned about Northern Ireland."

"As are we all."

"Chadwick thinks he needs to do something there."

"An evangelistic crusade, perhaps?" Clement asked, immediately regretting the cynicism in his remark.

"Not exactly," Roca said.

"Then what?" Clement asked, his impatience undoubtedly noticeable in spite of his desire to stay dispassionate. "What does he think he can do that the diplomats cannot accomplish? And how am I involved in this?"

"I don't know all the details. That's what he wants to discuss with you."

Clement rubbed his forehead, hoping to wipe away the dull ache that rose up from behind his eyes. Decisions like this bothered him. Breaking into a schedule that he had worked diligently to construct upset his rhythm, bothered his sense of order. A man given to much precision, he liked to make his plans and then stick by them. But how could he refuse Chadwick? On the other hand, how could he accept?

He knew how he would come across to the press that would engulf such a summit. Short, bald, and fat. A terrible image compared to Chadwick with his towering height and full head of hair. Even worse, a joint appearance would remind everyone of their relative careers—Chadwick a prophetic voice for God for over fifty years, while he had come onto the world stage almost overnight and carrying no significant portfolio. Before he met someone like Chadwick he needed the chance to do something, to make some impact, to etch his name onto some accomplishment. Otherwise, he'd lose face and that possibility made him queasy.

"Who else knows about Chadwick's invitation?" he asked, hoping to stall.

"I don't know," Roca said. "But few, I'm sure."

"What's your advice?" Clement asked.

Roca hesitated but only for a moment. "I'd meet the man," he said. "But tell him you want to do it in secret. I see no reason for the press to get involved at this point. If Chadwick wants something that you can deliver, then the two of you can issue a joint statement. This way, you're immediately seen as his equal, two great men of God trying to further the work of the Lord in our world."

"The downside?"

"Well, nothing happens. You and Chadwick reach no agreements and you both fly home, no one the wiser, but no one hurt."

Clement rubbed his forehead. He wanted to act correctly, even unselfishly and without regard for his own concerns. But that came hard for him. Even though he now sat in the chair of St. Peter, deep inside he still felt like a child who needed to protect himself at all costs. He felt so torn—a most disquieting dilemma.

"Set it up," he said, making a hasty decision. "But I like your idea to keep it secret. Do you think Chadwick will agree to that?"

"I don't see why not. I'll get in touch with him. We'll make all the arrangements."

"Good." Clement placed the phone on his desk and sat still in his seat. The headache that seemed to have started the day he became pope intensified. It felt like someone swatting him in the skull with a tennis racket. Being pope was complicated, far more so than he had ever expected.

NINE

Ian O'Fallon sat behind a round table in the corner of a bar with two other men, each of them almost identically dressed in black turtleneck shirts, olive slacks, and dark brown boots. The bar had no windows, and dark wood covered all four walls. A haze of cigarette smoke hung over the place, and the smell of dirty ashtrays seemed grafted into the dark walls. Three other men and one woman made small talk with the bartender thirty feet away, but other than that the place was empty.

O'Fallon took a drag off the cigarette in his hand, thought about snuffing it out, then decided against it and took another drag instead. Having recently rediscovered his nicotine habit after five years off, he couldn't control himself any longer. Might as well smoke himself to death. He propped his elbows on the table and leaned in closer to his companions.

To his right the leader of the trio, a rotund man named Reginald Murphy, held court, his pale green eyes staring out from behind a pair of wire-framed glasses, his auburn hair falling down over the rims.

"You're lookin' thinner there," Murphy said, pointing to O'Fallon. "Clean-shaven and all."

"Yeah, well, seemed time for a bit of a change," O'Fallon said, his eyes constantly shifting around the bar, his guts nervous that someone might recognize him. He'd stayed home under the excuse of illness since Sunday, but he'd finally run that excuse to its conclusion. Now, even though he'd heard nothing about his presence at the City Hall building on the night of the explosion, he still didn't feel safe.

Murphy leaned closer. "It's a mess with these casualties," he whispered, leaving the small talk.

"The fortunes of war," said the man to Murphy's left, a man so pale and skinny he looked like a candidate for a wax museum. "Thank the good Lord all the dead were Catholics, and none of ours."

O'Fallon studied the ashen face of David Sheehan, the man who had spoken. Sheehan was almost fifty years old and had no family and no job that anyone could identify. In one way or another, he had been a veteran of the Irish conflict for over thirty years. For Sheehan, the strife was his reason for getting up in the morning.

"But four of ours were hurt," Murphy said, his hawkish nose twitching under his glasses. "Not what we planned."

"But the IRA still took the blame," Sheehan countered. "And that's exactly what we planned, right down to the media reporting the phoney anonymous phone call we made." Sheehan tossed back the shot glass he held in his hands, his thin lips eagerly welcoming the brown liquid.

O'Fallon gazed at his cigarette and thought of Heather. He had again left her with his mum, but he felt strange about it, afraid that the next time he went out, he'd disappear and never see her again. Either the coppers would arrest him or someone from the IRA would shoot him, and he'd never again hold his precious Heather in his arms.

He stared at Murphy, then Sheehan. He hadn't told them, hadn't told anyone about his effort to go back to City Hall and remove the bomb. What would these men do if they knew? Would they disown him as a coward? Or would they see him as a dangerous traitor and harm him, maybe kill him?

"Both sides seem intent on keeping the peace talks alive," he interjected, "in spite of our efforts to sabotage them. The telly reports that the negotiators will meet again soon."

"That's always the story," Sheehan said. "No one wants to admit they've been intimidated. It's all a feint, their way of trying to keep us off our stride."

"I'm not too sure," O'Fallon said, refusing to give ground. "Seems to me the Brits are looking for a way to make the peace accord work. And our lads won't go far without their support. Whether we like it or not, the people seem to *want* peace this time. The sentiment in the countryside has changed."

Sheehan and Murphy stared at him, each of them a part of

the Orange and each with his own motivation for this most recent campaign of violence. Reginald Murphy was an auto mechanic, married and father of five, four still living. One, a son, had died at the age of thirteen, the victim of an IRA attack on a schoolyard. Murphy kept the boy's picture in his wallet, an ever present reminder of what he had lost to the Unionists from the south.

Sheehan had never had any family so far as anyone new. But he did have grudges, like all those in the swirl of this civil unrest. A man of keen intellect and at least two diplomas on the walls of his small grungy apartment, Sheehan had once owned a trendy bookstore in the heart of the city. But a bomb had detonated in his store one morning at 6 A.M., reducing it to rubble and ashes. The bomb hadn't killed anybody, but it had destroyed Sheehan. With no money to replace what he'd lost, he drifted down and out of respectable circles and landed in the midst of those who wanted nothing more than revenge for what the IRA had taken from them.

"You may be right," Murphy said, holding a glass of ale to his lips. "But we can't give up that easily. The people need us now more than ever, need us to remind them of the evils of those we fight, the vile nature of their deeds."

"The people are tired of all that," O'Fallon countered. "They're weary of the anger, the hatred. They want to put it all behind them and find a way out of the carnage."

"It's the problem of short memories," Sheehan said, pouring another shot of whiskey. "People forget too easily for my liking."

Murphy nodded, then looked over his shoulder to make sure no one but his allies could hear. "We'll have to give them something they can't forget," he said, his voice quieter than ever. "Something so . . . so devastating it'll stick in their minds like the day they were married."

The conspirators drew their chairs closer, their eyes hollow. Murphy began to outline a new scheme to make sure the peace talks failed. Listening, O'Fallon sucked on his cigarette as if to pull it straight into his lungs. The embers touched his fingers, burned them for an instant. But he didn't pull away. The pain felt good somehow, purging even, and for a moment, he wished for more of it, more of the pain, the cleansing it could bring. What Murphy suggested made him want to go to the bathroom and throw up all over the floor. But he didn't leave. How could he? To do so violated the pledge he had made to Rebecca to avenge her memory, to defend the love they had felt for each other.

Out of nowhere, he remembered again the first few days after her death, the awful black depression that wrapped itself around his heart. Eaten up by grief, he knew he had no reason to live anymore. The men who had killed Rebecca had taken all his joy away. But then, almost a month after her murder, he suddenly discovered a new purpose for existence. Revenge—malice against those who had killed his wife. It grabbed him by the throat and refused to let go. That malice kept him alive. Without it, he had no clue what fuel he would use to pull his eyes open every morning. When they destroyed what he loved, he had nothing left but that which he hated. So he couldn't walk away from Murphy and Sheehan and all the evil they planned to do in the name of a God in whom he no longer believed. To do so was to walk away from life itself. And for Heather's sake, he couldn't do that.

TEN

Sitting in a plush, peach-colored wingback chair in the corner of an opulent meeting room, Valerie Miller told herself to calm down. Licking her lips, she surveyed the room—an ornate suite in the Cosmopolitan Hotel in Paris. Magnificent flower arrangements sat in huge multicolored vases in every corner, and a chandelier that looked as if it came from some ancient castle dangled from the heavily molded ceiling. An incredibly tailored gold and maroon rug covered three-quarters of the hardwood floor, and the furnishings were all antique.

Valerie heard voices in the hall outside and stood nervously, smoothing down the front of her navy pinstriped skirt and jacket. The only woman in the room, she felt somewhat conspicuous.

Having agreed beforehand with the pope to bring only three aides apiece, Russell Chadwick had asked Lester Boggett to wait in the central suite they had rented for the occasion. Lester had acquiesced, but not happily.

Valerie glanced at Rodney and Ted. They looked as displeased about the conference as Boggett had been, their faces tensed as if they were in a dentist's chair awaiting a root canal. For a second, she wondered what was going through their minds. Was Ted angry because Russell had told him not to bring his wife, who usually traveled with them, on this trip? Or did he just not like the fact that they were meeting the pope? And what about Rodney? He didn't have a wife. So what was his problem? Did Ted and Rodney just hate her? Or was that her paranoia—a constant companion since the last time she had talked to a pope—acting up again? Frustrated, she faced her uncle Russell, the only man in the room who seemed happy.

Valerie studied her uncle. Though a public figure for almost fifty years, no scandal had ever touched him. A friend to kings and presidents, the man walked the earth unrivaled in terms of his integrity, generosity, and humility. He always looked for the best in people, and Valerie had never known him to get discouraged. She felt blessed to stand in the same room with him, much less to serve on his personal staff. He made her feel safe—an unusual sensation for her over the past few months.

The door to the meeting room opened, and a square-jawed man in a navy suit even darker than Valerie's stepped in, breaking her focus on her uncle. His eyes busy looking left, right, left, right, the man seemed to ignore the group in the room, including Chadwick, scanning the twenty-four by thirty-two feet area as if expecting an ambush. Valerie immediately recognized the man as a security officer of the Swiss Guard, the elite troop of just over one hundred men who protected the pope at home and abroad. These men, born in Switzerland and trained in modern arms and martial arts, had all sworn themselves to die in the defense of the pontiff if necessary. Though an earlier contingent of officers had already made a thorough canvas of the entire hotel, the man with the square jaw acted as if it had never happened.

Apparently satisfied that no danger lurked anywhere, the guard stepped back to the door and bowed at the waist as if welcoming an approaching king.

Valerie heard a light swish. Her pulse rate notched up and she found herself holding her breath. The guard backed up against the wall and stood at attention. A wave of white entered the room, the swishing sound moving through the door with it, and Clement Peter walked into the conference room and ran his gaze over the occupants.

Russell Chadwick stepped toward him and bowed slightly. The pope also tilted at the waist. Two other men walked in behind the pontiff, but no one seemed to notice. The pope held out his hand and Chadwick took it, his long fingers swallowing up the stubbier hand of Clement Peter. Chadwick bowed again and kissed the top of the pope's hand. To Valerie's surprise, the pope waited until Chadwick had straightened back up, then bowed in similar fashion and returned the gesture.

"So good of you to see me," Chadwick said, his blue eyes

gleaming as he stepped back a couple of paces. "And on such short notice."

Clement waved his hand as if shooing away a fly. "I was already coming to Paris," he said, his English pure and refined. "And your offer to meet pleased me. Such men as you and I need to know each other, especially in quiet, less formal circumstances such as these. I believe much can be accomplished when people of goodwill get to know each other without the interference of the ever present media."

"I couldn't agree more," beamed Chadwick. "I knew your predecessor well. Forgive the informality, but he and I once agreed, in private, of course, that we'd be 'buddies'."

Clement laughed slightly, but the mirth appeared strained to Valerie, maybe even false. She didn't know why, but it suddenly dawned on her that perhaps Clement Peter suffered from a degree of insecurity when he compared himself to his predecessor, a man adored for over twenty years by millions of fawning constituents. No one followed such a man as that without some questions about his ability to manage it. Add to that the fact that many saw this new pope as no more than an interim in the job and maybe he had reasons for a lack of assurance.

"That's not exactly pontifical language," Clement said. "But I'm sure it was appropriate for the both of you—given your long friendship."

Chadwick started to speak but then paused. Clement turned slightly and indicated the two men behind him. For the first time, Valerie glanced at the pope's companions.

"I believe you've met Cardinal Roca," Clement said to Chadwick.

Valerie's neck tensed.

Chadwick took Roca's hand and pumped it energetically. "Yes, yes, on two or three occasions. I thank you, Cardinal Roca, for the role you've played in setting up this meeting. I know you and my aide, Ms. Miller, have really steered this thing, taken care of a thousand details. You know her, I understand." Chadwick dropped Roca's hand and turned to Valerie.

Her eyes watering against her will, Valerie walked slowly to Roca, her memory working overtime. Roca took her in his arms and hugged her, his thick shoulders comforting as she leaned into them. For several seconds, they stayed that way, momentarily forgetting their surroundings, two old friends who had loved the same person—Roca because he was Michael Del Rio's uncle and

Valerie because . . . well, for all the reasons that a woman loves a man. Valerie bit her lip and raised up from Roca's shoulder.

"Are you doing all right, my friend?" the cardinal asked, his dark eyes searching her face.

"I think so," Valerie said. "You know how it is . . . I miss Michael."

"As do I," Roca said. "Perhaps we can visit later, just the two of us, and talk of him some more."

Nodding, Valerie smoothed her jacket and glanced back to Chadwick and Clement. A slight scowl rested on the pontiff's face, and she realized she and Roca had kept him waiting. As if reading her thoughts, Clement cleared his throat.

"Perhaps we should begin the official part of our gathering," he said, his nose slightly elevated and a hint of impatience in his voice. "All of us know the value of time."

Either unaware of the pontiff's pique or deliberately ignoring it, Chadwick smiled, pulled a chair from the table, and indicated to Valerie that she should sit. She turned to Clement.

Neglecting to introduce his other aide, Clement moved to the table, his white robes swishing around his ample girth. The security guard pulled out a chair and Clement eased into it, folding his robe around his legs. To her left and right, everyone else also took seats, Chadwick directly across from Clement, and Kent and Shuster on either side of their leader. Roca sat to Clement's right, the second aide to his left. The security guard took up a position directly behind the pontiff.

Valerie focused on the pope. Though plenty bulky, he seemed thinner than what he appeared on television. His head seemed unusually large, but his eyes were piercing, and she knew from her research that great intelligence lay behind them.

"This is Cardinal Lech Zolinska," Roca said, indicating the ruddy-faced man whom no one had introduced. "He's a special assistant to His Holiness, a native of Poland, former archbishop of Warsaw."

Zolinska nodded, rubbed his hands together, blinked his eyes, and licked his lips. Studying him quickly, Valerie watched him go through several other quirky mannerisms. A brush of his nose, a tug at his left ear, a wiping of his chin, and then back to rubbing his hands together. For a second, she wanted to giggle. The man looked like a third-base coach flashing signs at a baseball game. But she pushed back the laughter and listened to Chadwick introducing Rodney and Ted.

"This is Rodney Kent and Ted Shuster, two of my closest aides," Chadwick said. "And you've already met Valerie Miller." The aides leaned over the table and shook hands with one another.

Valerie marveled at the informal nature of it all. Not exactly what people saw when dignitaries met with cameras rolling. The men settled back into their seats. Roca cleared his throat. Valerie understood the protocol. As the pontiff's chief lieutenant, Roca would lead the conversation from the Vatican side. Clement would observe at the beginning, then ask questions or make comments when appropriate. Roca placed both palms flat on the table, then looked at the group.

"We're here at the invitation of the Reverend Russell Chadwick," he began quietly. "A man most respected around the world for his faith in the Lord Jesus Christ. We have come because of a common concern over the continuing destruction and loss of life caused by the hostilities in Ireland." He paused and swallowed. "The Reverend Chadwick has suggested that he has a plan that might alleviate some of those hostilities, and he wants the office of the Holy See to consider joining with him in his efforts. We're here to listen and see if there might be divine wisdom in his ideas." Roca stopped and brought his hands together under his chin. "Reverend Chadwick," he continued, "His Holiness is ready to hear what you have to say."

All eyes turned to Chadwick. The evangelist leaned back, paused a second, then pushed up from his seat. Valerie saw that his right hand shook as he moved, but he quickly pulled it to his side to still the quivering in his fingers. No one else seemed to notice, and Chadwick smiled hugely, his six six frame a tower of confidence.

"Again, let me say how grateful I am that we could meet," he said. "I do know how valuable your time is." He left the chair and strode to the head of the table. "And whether what I have to say contains any divine wisdom . . . well, only God can know that." He pushed a loose strand of hair from his eyes.

"Just over two weeks ago we all saw another act of violence in Northern Ireland. It broke my heart. Like millions of others, my friends and I"—he glanced to his side of the table—"have prayed diligently over this awful situation. But recently I started to think we had to do more than pray. The night after the explosion in Donegal Square, I went to bed deeply disturbed. I didn't sleep well. That is most unusual for me, I can assure you." He paused and Ted and Rodney smiled knowingly.

"Anyway, I tossed and turned all night. Then sometime late, I started to dream. Also unusual for me. I never remember dreams. But this time I did. I saw a lion and a bear in a desert. . . ." He continued to talk, describing what he had seen.

Roca and the pope appeared impassive, their expressions giving away nothing. Zolinska twitched and touched, and Valerie thought his look approximated a smirk.

Chadwick finished with his story. "When I woke up, I had this strange sense that I needed to do something, something . . . well, something personal. I didn't know what that something was, but the next morning I took my dream and my impressions to my advisers," he waved his hand over his side of the table. "I asked them what it meant. And Ms. Miller . . ." He smiled at Valerie. "Well, Ms. Miller gave me an interpretation. She suggested that maybe I should go to Northern Ireland."

He placed his hands on the chair before him, and Valerie noticed that his knuckles were bleached white. She studied his face and saw that it too seemed bloodless, pale and drawn. Was he okay?

"But that's obviously quite dangerous," Roca said, his face blank.

"My people immediately recognized the same thing," Chadwick said. "As do I. But Ms. Miller makes an interesting case. Perhaps it is worth the risk."

"And just what is her 'case'?" Zolinska asked, his hands tugging at his ears. "What is she asking you—and the pontiff, I might add—to do?"

"She didn't suggest that His Holiness do anything," Chadwick said, his tone just a touch defensive. "That was my idea. If what she proposes has any chance of working, I believe I need the involvement of the Vatican."

"Then the next question is obvious," Zolinska pressed. "Just what is it she proposes?"

"Why don't we allow her to tell us?" Chadwick said.

Valerie's spine went rigid as all eyes turned her way. For a second, she sat transfixed, unsure what to do. Chadwick hadn't told her she would do any talking here. Her eyes implored him to take her off the spot. But he did just the opposite.

"Her idea has the ring of the Old Testament to it," he said extending his hand to her, palm up. "Nathan stood before King

David and confronted him with his sin with Bathsheba. Quite dangerous."

Struggling to gather herself, Valerie took his hand and stood. Chadwick guided her to the head of the table as he continued to speak. "Elijah challenged the false prophets of Baal in defiance of Ahab and Jezebel. Quite dangerous."

Valerie stood in the center of the room as Chadwick finished, his voice firm and steady. "Daniel prayed to the Lord in express contradiction to King Darius's command and faced the lions because of it. Quite dangerous. I could go on and on. You know the stories. Seems to me it's time for us—or at least it's time for me— to do something not quite so safe, something on the edge of my faith, something that's truly prophetic, truly risky for God. Maybe the reason the world's in the mess it's in right now is because men"—he glanced at Valerie—"and women of God haven't taken enough risks, haven't stepped into enough dangerous places. So I'm ready to do something about that. I'll let Valerie, er, Ms. Miller tell you the rest."

Chadwick retreated to a seat to Valerie's right. His right hand shook violently as he eased down, and she wondered if anyone else had noticed. But it didn't seem so. All eyes were on her.

Catching her breath, she stared down at the table. Chadwick hadn't left her a choice. And she didn't want to let him down. She raised her eyes and set her jaw. Though her voice sounded thin to her, she hoped it sounded strong to everyone else.

"I'm not sure I even like my own idea," she began, "but I made the mistake of saying it before I had considered the implications. Reverend Chadwick took it from there." She looked again for help, but he had his eyes on his hands. "Anyway," she continued, "I wondered what would happen if Reverend Chadwick, a man loved by the Protestants of Northern Ireland, went to Ireland and placed himself in the middle of the controversy? Like the lamb in the dream. What if he moved around at random to a variety of public places, places where the radical Protestants—the Orange, for example—might most likely retaliate for what the IRA has just done to them?"

She felt stronger as she talked. "With Reverend Chadwick on the scene, maybe they'd think twice before they did anything. Maybe they'd take more care about their actions. Who knows? Maybe the power of his faith, the willingness to put himself in direct danger would impress on them the need to negotiate, to find a peaceful way out of their dilemma. The two sides have been so close over the last few years. Maybe they need just one more push, one more reason to back away from their hatred of each other."

She dropped into a seat as she finished and glanced around the room. Cardinal Zolinska was the first to respond.

"I appreciate your motivation," he said, tugging at an earlobe. "But I have to tell you I'm at a loss as to what all this has to do with His Holiness. What the Reverend Chadwick does or doesn't do has no effect on—"

Clement raised his hand and Zolinska instantly shut up. "It's quite obvious," Clement said. "Reverend Chadwick wants us to assist him in his project."

Zolinska's mouth fell open and Valerie noted a set of crooked teeth. She glanced at Roca, saw that he looked quite poised, obviously having seen the implications of her idea as quickly as the pope. Clement stared at Chadwick.

"Am I right, my friend?" he asked, his hands folded in his lap. "Two lambs are better than one?"

Chadwick nodded. The two men continued to stare at each other, and though nothing overt suggested it, Valerie suddenly thought of two stags facing each other in a forest, competitive yet respectful of each other. Clement broke first, glancing down at his stomach.

"I can't do it without your assistance," Chadwick said. "The IRA won't take a chance on hurting you with a terrorist act, just as the Orange won't take a chance on hurting me."

"But that's preposterous!" blurted Zolinska, his hands working the air. "To even suggest that His Holiness place his life in such danger is the height of arrogance. How dare you—?"

Clement raised a hand again and Zolinska's mouth ceased to move.

"Let me make sure I'm clear on this," Clement said. "You want to put your life and mine in the midst of the Irish conflict. You want the moral authority of my office and your organization to stand up against hundreds of years of hatred. You want us to use our influence as bargaining leverage to get the two sides back to the peace table."

"That's the drift of it, yes."

"But what about the authorities? Your government? The Irish? Will they allow us to do such a thing?"

"How can they stop us?"

"They can deny a visa to enter the country," Zolinska interjected, his jaw set.

"What country is going to turn down a pope's request to visit?" Rodney Kent countered, automatically defensive of his leader's position, even if he personally disliked it. "Or Reverend Chadwick's? That's politically untenable."

Clement grunted and leaned back, his chubby fingers once more crossed over his ample stomach. The room fell quiet. Valerie found herself holding her breath. A bulb in the chandelier overhead suddenly dimmed, then blacked out. Zolinska coughed and rubbed his nose, and Rodney Kent pulled on the hair at the back of his neck. Nothing else moved.

Valerie wondered what Clement was thinking. Did he realize what such an act could do for him? The man was nothing more than a caretaker pope, according to the news media, and he no doubt knew that little was expected of him. But an alliance with Chadwick might change public opinion, give him immediate status as an equal to one of the most famous religious leaders of the last hundred years. Even better, if the plan actually worked, then Clement automatically had his legacy inked into history. Headlines would trumpet him as a peacemaker, a man of true faith. He and Chadwick might share a Nobel Peace Prize. But if it didn't work? Well, at least he had shown great courage in trying.

Valerie shifted and stared at the pontiff. When Clement grinned, she knew he had figured it out.

"The two of us won't be enough," he said. "Too many places to cover."

"No way can we cover every spot," Chadwick said. "It's more symbolic than anything else."

"Let's make it more than symbolic," Clement suggested.

"How so?"

"I'll take five cardinals," Clement said. "Move them around the key cities of Northern Ireland, place them in the most prominent places. A terrorist won't know from one moment to the next where they'll be. That should give them pause, don't you think? Think of the international outrage that will fall on the perpetrators if any of my cardinals gets hurt."

"And you want me to use people from my organization?"

Clement rubbed his hands. "Maybe you can get some other prominent Protestant ministers to join your crusade," he suggested.

"But I can't make any other Protestant do anything they don't want to do," Chadwick said. "Unlike the power you wield, we Protestants are too independent for that."

"A great weakness of yours," chuckled Clement. "At least in my opinion."

Chadwick laughed too, but Valerie noticed that no one else in the room seemed too gleeful. In fact, everyone else seemed downright glum.

"Then we are in agreement?" Chadwick asked, his grin still present.

"Indeed," Clement said. "We have an agreement."

"I'll start making some calls," Chadwick said. "See who else I can get on board."

"For the plan to work, we'll need to make the public aware of it," Clement said. "Two religious leaders bound and determined to forge an alliance for the greater cause of peace. Putting themselves in mortal danger, daring the terrorists to harm them and bring the wrath of the world upon their heads. Sounds like a movie."

Chadwick faced Valerie. "You're my media specialist," he said. "Put a strategy together to get this out."

"Cardinal Zolinska will work with her," Clement said. "Keep the information coordinated."

"Then let's do it," Chadwick said, standing from the table and reaching over to Clement. The pope, also standing now, grasped his hand.

"Some will say we've lost our minds," Clement said, "placing ourselves in mortal danger as a result of a dream."

"And they may be correct," Chadwick said. "But at our age, there's not much left to lose."

"Of the mind or body," agreed Clement.

Valerie's heart raced. The dread that had dogged her since Michael's disappearance suddenly rose up again, a massive wave of dark water, a wave so deep, so heavy that no one in its wake could survive. She wanted to shout at Chadwick and Clement, to tell them to stop, to warn them of the wave hovering over her head ready to crash and drown them all.

But she knew she couldn't do that. Regardless of what she or anyone else in the room thought, the only two who counted had reached an accord. Lots of details had yet to be worked out, but the basic idea had taken root. The Reverend Russell Chadwick and Pope Clement Peter were going to Ireland. They thought they knew the dangers and were prepared to handle them. But she knew better. She knew that no matter how prepared a person thought he was, danger had a way of throwing unforeseen darts into a life, unexpected pitfalls into a path. She knew that no matter how much security a person thought he had, it was never enough. Death hid behind every door to ambush even good people.

Hugging her waist, she felt the room become colder, as if chilled by a glacier. Shivering, she prayed that her crazy notion didn't get Chadwick and the pope and a whole lot of other people killed.

ELEVEN

Her hair whipping in the autumn wind, Valerie hopped out of her four-year-old Volvo, tucked a brown leather folder under her arm, and hustled across the parking lot to the huge double doors that led into the foyer of the Centennial Broadcasting Company foyer. The building was huge—a modern structure filled with glass and chrome and men and women wearing gray or navy suits, white starched shirts or blouses, and stylish silk ties or scarves. Already fifteen minutes late for an appointment with Casey Sterling, she quickly signed in with the security desk, punched the button for an elevator, stepped in, and hit the light for the seventeenth floor.

Brushing her hair into place, she leaned against the wall and tried to catch her breath. The last three days seemed like a blur, a rush of meetings and phone calls and emails, a dash here and a dash there. One thing about Russell Chadwick—when he made up his mind to do something, he moved heaven and earth to get it done. He had assigned her to work with Cardinal Zolinska to pull together a media blitz that would announce to the world their unprecedented initiative. But that work hadn't been easy. Though he had delegated his own work to an aide, Zolinska seemed to take pleasure in questioning everything Valerie did. Time after time over the last couple of days, he had made her revise her plans. Though not liking the constant nitpicking, she stayed patient, forcing herself to silence.

Even worse than Zolinska's micromanagement, she had to deal with her own mood. It had gotten worse in those three days, sinking lower and lower until she wondered if it could ever drag

any deeper. Except for the nights when she gave in and took the
sedatives prescribed by her doctor, she slept little. And the food
she ate—mostly takeout and quick-order greasy stuff—did nothing to help. Worse still, she had almost given up her spiritual
discipline—time every morning when she prayed, kept a spiritual
journal, reflected on Scripture. When she combined all that with
her deep-seated fears, she felt as though she had fallen into a
bottomless black pit. Not wanting to fail her uncle, though, she
refused to give in to the mood and forced herself to keep working.

The elevator bell dinged and the door swung open. Valerie
trudged off and turned left, looking for 1715. A row of glass-
encased offices ran to the left and right, one square cubicle after
another, the numbers of the offices and the names of the occupants stenciled in black letters in the middle of the doors.

A clump of people poured out of an office at the end of the hall,
and Valerie spotted Sterling amid them, a blond-headed man
whom she knew from her research as a thirty-seven-year-old
graduate of the University of South Carolina School of Journalism and a twelve-year veteran with CBC. Having covered everything from the Oklahoma City bombing to the Senate impeach-
ment trial of Bill Clinton to the NATO war against Yugoslavia,
Sterling had already established himself as one of the most recognized faces in news. Today he wore blue jeans, an open-collared
forest green shirt, a navy blazer, and brown hiking boots. Not exactly the same image he portrayed while on the air. He held a
sheaf of paper in his hands, and a pair of reading glasses perched
on the end of his nose.

Sterling and his group pounded down the hallway, a moving
wave headed right at her, jabbering away without looking up.
Without thinking, Valerie tucked her folder under her arm and
smoothed down her tan skirt and white blouse. Though she knew
it was silly, she felt nervous.

Sterling glanced up from his papers and saw her but didn't
stop. Valerie straightened her shoulders, and as the group
reached her, stepped to Sterling and stuck out her hand.

"Excuse me," she said. "I'm Valerie Miller. I'm sorry I'm late.
We had an appointment at three."

Sterling glanced at his watch but didn't stop walking. "You're
twenty-three minutes late, Valerie Miller," he said. "I'm on to
something else." The group moved past her, a series of quick
glances in her direction but nothing else. Up against the wall,
Valerie scowled at Sterling's rudeness.

"You want to talk to me," she called, her voice more confident than she actually felt.

Sterling twisted back but kept walking. "Call and make a new appointment. I'll talk to you then. If you make it on time."

"Don't think I'll do that," she called out more loudly, her anger at his arrogance overcoming her hesitance. "Instead, I'll make an appointment with CNN. Maybe they'll want to hear what the Reverend Russell Chadwick plans to do to bring peace to Northern Ireland."

Sterling stopped dead in his tracks and pivoted back to face her. His group stopped too, a couple of the people bumping into each other.

"*The* Reverend Russell Chadwick?" Sterling said.

"I told your assistant I was his representative when I called two days ago."

"You didn't say anything about Ireland."

"I thought I'd keep that until I actually saw you."

The group parted and Sterling walked slowly in her direction. "I waited five minutes for you," he said. "But that's my limit."

"And I'm sorry I was late. I said that already. Traffic—you know how Atlanta is."

Sterling smiled, and for the first time, Valerie sensed some of the warmth he exuded so easily while on the air.

"Atlanta people always blame their tardiness on traffic," he said, stopping less than an arm's length away.

"Sometimes they're telling the truth," she countered, her voice instinctively dropping lower at his close proximity.

"My office is the last one on the left," he said, almost whispering. "Give me ten minutes and I'll join you there." Before she could respond, he pivoted away and marched down the hall, his entourage trailing.

Slightly flushed by the power she sensed in the man, Valerie watched him for a moment, then turned, walked to his office, and stepped inside. To her surprise it wasn't very big—no more than twelve by fourteen or so. A standard wooden desk sat in the center, complete with a computer terminal on top. A leather swivel chair and an upholstered wingback, both of them a subdued gold, sat on opposite sides of the desk. Stacks of paper covered the desk, and dozens of tan file folders lay on the floor at its side. The wall opposite the door was all glass and overlooked the downtown center of Atlanta.

She walked to the window, glanced out, then faced the office

again. She saw six pictures, all of them five-by-sevens, framed
behind the wall of paper on Sterling's desk. The pictures showed
Sterling in six different poses with six different women. Though
feeling disappointed for some reason she couldn't immediately
identify, Valerie leaned closer to study the pictures. In the first,
Sterling held a fish the length of his forearm and stood by a gorgeous blond woman. Both of them were dressed like the stars of
a Saturday morning fishing show. In the second picture, he wore
a pinstripe gray suit and a blue shirt with cuff links while a short
redhead looked up at him as if staring at a deity. In the third,
only a pair of yellow swim trunks covered his darkly tanned mus-
cular body. This time a brunette in a green bikini had an arm
looped around his waist. Hearing the door open, she jumped in-
voluntarily and looked up.

"You should have been a reporter," Sterling said, nodding toward his desk. "Snooping around like that."

"I'm not snooping," Valerie countered, feeling the heat of embarrassment rising on her neck. "Just using my time wisely."

"Don't worry about it," Sterling said. "I'd have the desk drawers open by now, maybe even the wall safe, and the email on the
computer. To me, curiosity is a virtue, a key that unlocks opportunity. And opportunity unlocks achievement if the person is
driven enough to take advantage of it. So I take no offense at
your snooping."

He motioned to the wingback chair. "Have a seat."

Her face still warm, Valerie obeyed meekly.

"They're models," he said, pointing to the pictures. "All but
one, that is."

Valerie waved him off. "You don't need to explain," she said.
"It's none of my business."

"But you are curious."

She shrugged. "Sure, why not? One man, six women."

Sterling picked up one of the pictures and brushed off the
glass on his pants. "I did commercials in another life," he said.
"Before the CBC gig. Any way to make a buck. I did some mod-
eling in college. You ever try that? You've got the looks for it."

She dropped her gaze. "Nope, not my style." Was he trying to
flirt with her?

"Well, anyway, I just kept it up as my career in journalism got
started. Fishing gear, bathing suits, menswear. It paid good
money and attracted plenty of women."

His voice carried a tinge of an accent, but Valerie couldn't figure it out. Years of voice training, she suspected. Wipe out all those regional accents if you want to star on national television.

"You said one of them wasn't a model," she said.

Sterling smiled and took a seat on the corner of his desk. Valerie noticed his dimples, more visible in person than on television.

"That's right. One is special, the one I love."

For some reason she again couldn't identify, Valerie felt disappointed but she quickly shook it off.

Sterling turned the picture and showed it to Valerie. The woman in the picture wore a black evening gown, a string of pearls around her neck, a pair of earrings that matched the pearls. She was elegant and beautiful. But she had to be at least fifteen years older than Sterling.

"She's gorgeous," Valerie said, trying to hide her surprise.

"She is that," Sterling said, obvious love in his voice. "I've known her all my life. She's my mom."

Valerie laughed out loud, then threw a hand over her mouth. The laugh sounded odd, the first time she had laughed in what seemed like months.

"What?" Sterling asked.

Valerie laughed again, her whole body shaking.

"Wait, you didn't think. . . ? You did! You thought she was a girlfriend, maybe my wife!"

Her laughing stilled, Valerie nodded. Sterling grinned and handed her the picture. She wiped her eyes. She had come here on serious business. What did she care either way?

Studying the picture more carefully, Valerie instantly saw the resemblance. Same thick hair texture, slightly square forehead, deep set dark eyes, perky nose, and full lips.

"You favor her," she said, handing him the photo. "A lot."

He placed the picture on the desk. "That's a high compliment. She's the prettiest woman I've ever known. At least until now."

"What about your dad?" she asked, ignoring the last phrase.

Sterling averted his eyes, and Valerie sensed immediately that she had asked the wrong question.

"Nothing to tell," Sterling said, pushing off the desk and walking to the window. "Just boring stuff, and you didn't come here to talk about my genetic makeup. Am I right?" He faced her again and she spotted something in his eyes, something a bit anxious. She started to ask him about it, but then knew she couldn't invade a strange man's privacy just because he seemed so . . . well, so vulnerable somehow. Smoothing down her skirt, she nodded.

"Yeah, that's right," she said. "I came to talk to you about the Reverend Russell Chadwick."

"I'm all ears." He took a seat and leaned over his desk, his elbows planted like the legs of a wheelbarrow on the top.

Valerie lifted her folder to her lap. Extracting a manila envelope, she placed it in front of Sterling.

"Read this," she said.

Looking puzzled, Sterling opened the envelope, slipped on his reading glasses, and focused on the three sheets of paper inside. Watching him read, Valerie found herself liking what she saw. But then a wave of guilt washed over her and she shifted in her seat.

As Sterling laid one sheet on his desk and started to read the second one, Valerie told herself to relax. No reason to feel guilty about finding a man attractive. Michael Del Rio had disappeared over ten months ago. For all she or anybody else knew, he was dead. Though she thought he had once contacted her through email, she now wondered about that. Maybe she had misinterpreted that message, had taken the email that had no return address and imagined it to be something it wasn't.

Sterling laid down the second sheet and moved to the third. Valerie stared at her hands. She had loved Michael once, but the two of them had never made any kind of commitment to each other. Tragically, they never had the chance. And, even if he hadn't died, the man was a priest, for goodness sake! Better for them both that he had disappeared. If he hadn't, no telling what might have happened. But how could she have any future with him? The man was a priest and she was a good Baptist girl, and that kind of relationship presented more than enough obvious problems. . . .

Sterling laid down the third sheet of paper, took off his glasses, and chuckled. She centered her thoughts on the present.

"Now, there's an Odd Couple if I ever did see one," he said. "The Reverend Russell Chadwick and His Holiness the Pope. And the two of them are going to bring peace to Northern Ireland?"

"You disapprove?" Valerie asked, not liking the smirk.

"I don't know if I'd say I disapprove. I'm skeptical to be sure, but still impressed, very much so. They're laying a lot on the line."

"They believe in what they're doing."

"And they've got some other guys . . ." He picked up the papers and studied them again.

"Yes, five pastors have agreed to assist Reverend Chadwick. All of them are reputable Protestant ministers, men of high regard in their countries. All of them are committed to peacemaking. Pope Clement named five cardinals."

"I saw that. And they're going to move around like interchangeable parts."

"With no one ever knowing exactly who's going to be where."

"Human shields."

"What?"

"Oh, you know. Like Saddam Hussein tried to do in the Persian Gulf War back in 1992. He put civilians in the spots where he thought the Allies might bomb, using them as human shields to protect his assets."

"Only we're not trying to protect anything but the Irish people," Valerie said. "The innocents who get caught in the crossfire of this awful civil strife."

Sterling stood and walked to his window again, his face staring out over the city. Valerie noticed a slight thinning of his hair at the crown of his head. His only physical flaw, so far as she could tell. She shook her head, clearing her mind.

"What's in it for your guy?" Sterling asked, twisting back around.

"That's pretty cynical," Valerie said, instinctively clenching her fists against the implication of the question.

"I've been around too long to take everything at face value," said Sterling. "When a guy lays his life on the line he wants something. I can understand the pope's motive. Clement is following the most charismatic leader the Catholics have had for centuries, maybe forever. But he's no dummy. He knows that people don't expect anything from him, maybe don't even want anything. Just maintain the status quo, serve out his six to ten years, then go on to his great reward in the sky. But now this comes along, a chance to fill out a few pages in the history books. I mean, if this works—not that I think it will—but if it does, the good pontiff becomes a man for the ages, a guy flying in coach who now gets to step up to first class."

Sterling brushed his hands through his hair and sat on the edge of his desk again, leaning close to her as he had in the hallway. "But Chadwick . . . I don't see it. He's already done it all, nothing else for him, since he's too old to run for the presidency. So what's his angle?"

Valerie fought against a surge of anger. Casey Sterling had cute dimples and a wonderful voice and great hair, except for the little thin spot on the crown, but if he thought he could talk about her uncle this way, he had another think coming. She started to give him a piece of her mind, but then another idea came to her and she nipped her initial response and shifted directions.

"Are you a man of faith, Mr. Sterling?" she asked, inwardly glad that his insolence had pushed her buttons enough to stir some strength in her spine.

He grunted, then wagged his head. "What's that got to do with the price of gas in Gwinett County?"

"Should I take that to mean no?"

"That means it's none of your business."

Not able to hold back any longer, Valerie lit into Sterling. "Well, you may be right that it's none of my business, but if you don't know anything about faith, then you can't understand Russell Chadwick, because he's a fanatic about faith, a faith-is-everything kind of man. And that mean's he's got no angle.

"Did you ever consider the possibility that maybe Chadwick's just a good and godly person who wants to find a way to bring peace to a troubled world? That he's a man of prayer who believes this idea came from God? That he's got enough faith to go forward in spite of skeptics like you, people who want to see him fail so they can feel good about their own faithlessness?" She took a quick breath but didn't stop talking.

"Did you ever think that maybe God really is in this and will pull off a miracle and bring peace to a place that the best politicians have admitted seems to have no hope for peace? Did you ever think that Chadwick might just possibly be a man who's not afraid for his life because he believes in a heaven yet to come and he's not concerned with his legacy because the only one he wants to please is Jesus? Did you ever consider any of that while you were thinking through all the angles?"

Sterling threw up his hands, palms out. "Easy there," he said, smiling. "Don't blow a gasket. I'm just checking. Being a skeptic comes with my job description."

"Well, you're doing a good job of it," Valerie said, her blood still boiling. "They ought to give you a raise."

Sterling picked up the folder. "Maybe when I pop this story on tonight's six o'clock news, they will."

"That's what we want you to do," she said, calming down a little. "You and all the other news outlets. We want the whole world to know what we're doing, and we dare someone to do something about it."

Sterling walked back to the window. "I don't know much about faith," he said, talking to the street below. "But I do know about guts." He twisted to face Valerie again. "And your guy has got more than most."

"Guts and faith can go a long way."

Sterling laughed. And Valerie couldn't help but smile, too, her heart suddenly lighter than it had been in months.

TWELVE

His slender fingers busy, Ian O'Fallon lifted five sticks of Tovex dynamite from the locker at the foot of Heather's bed and slipped them into a beaten-up suitcase the size of a big pillow. The explosives, stuffed like hot dogs into six-inch plastic coverings, were dicey to handle, but he felt no fear. Having already forfeited his life to the need for revenge, what could it do to him that Rebecca's death hadn't already done?

Beside the Tovex, he placed a cheap clock. The clock and the Tovex were wired to an electric blasting cap and a nine-volt battery. Leaving the bedroom, he stepped to the kitchen and grabbed five mason jars full of gasoline off the shelf under the sink, wrapped the jars in paper towels, and set them in a cardboard box that was just large enough to hold them all. With the box under one arm, he pulled five plastic cups from the cabinet over the sink and carried the cups and the mason jars to the kitchen table. After unscrewing the jars, he carefully pushed the cups into the jars, re-tightened the lids, and placed them back in the box.

Back in the bedroom, he packed the jars in the suitcase with the dynamite and clock. Standing, he wiped his hands on the front of his denim jeans and licked a rim of perspiration off his lips. In just a few hours, the timer would explode the Tovex, and the gasoline and cups in the jars would ignite a raging fire. The doorbell rang. Ian shut the suitcase, gingerly set it on the bed, and closed the trunk.

In the living room, he glanced at the television as it played quietly in the corner, then stepped to the door and opened it.

"Come on in," he said, stepping back for Murphy to enter. "I'm almost done here."

"Heather at your mum's?" Murphy asked, easing into the room and taking a seat in the plain straightbacked chair that Ian usually occupied.

Ian wrinkled his nose. "Yeah, since six. She's sleeping the night there. I told me mum I had a date. It pleased her no end."

Murphy laughed. "Mums are the same everywhere, aren't they? Get their children married off, have a roomful of grandbabies to kiss and hug. Makes them quite happy."

"You got mine pegged. Are things in order?" Ian eased to the sofa and sat down. His eyes wandered to the telly, where a news anchor smiled out at him.

Murphy picked at a fingernail. "Aye, shipshape. Sheehan's on go. I'm geared up. And you're primed. All we have to do is choose the locations, deliver the packages, and wait for the fireworks display."

Ian studied his shoes for a moment. They were plain brown tie-ups with thick soles, the shoes of a tax clerk, not a terrorist. He looked at Murphy again. "So what's going up?" he asked, wondering about the targets.

Murphy grunted, worked at a fingernail again. "Not sure. But I'm thinking the Lancer Hotel, the locker area of the airport or St. Jude's Cathedral."

"The church? You're going to—?"

Murphy threw up a hand. "It's not decided yet. But it's on the list. What better way to remind the pope lovers that we're never going to accept their godless practices on good Irish soil? We hit them where they'll hurt the worst I say and never mind the consequences. This is war, Ian O'Fallon, or have you forgotten that? You don't win a war playing parlor games."

Ian stared at his friend and felt his stomach sink. After all his parents had taught him, it had come to this. He was a murderer, and there was no way to deny it. For a second, he thought back to his childhood, to the solid if unspectacular life he had enjoyed. Helping in the cobbler's shop after school, going to the Regent's Presbyterian Church every Sunday. The sermons there, though delivered in a stern and uncompromising tone, majored on the need to love God and care for God's people. Little was said about the "popers," as he had come to call the Catholics in the last few years. Certainly he knew of the ancient troubles between the Catholics and Protestants. No one grew up in Ireland without an awareness of the animosity between the two groups. But his Presbyterian religion hadn't preached that hatred. And neither had his parents, they had—

A picture of City Hall came onto the television screen and Ian picked up the controls and raised the volume. Casey Sterling was reporting.

"The bombing of the Belfast City Hall has spurred an unusual effort to get the peace talks back on track," Sterling said, his tone calm and direct. "According to our sources, the offices of the Reverend Russell Chadwick and Pope Clement Peter, the two most prominent religious leaders in the Christian world, have come together in a unique and unprecedented alliance to do something about the ongoing carnage in Ireland."

Ian sat up straighter and Murphy stopped chewing on his fingers.

"The plan, according to what we've been told here at CBC, calls for Chadwick and Clement and ten of their closest allies to go to Northern Ireland. These twelve leaders will rotate in and around the country in unknown places, in effect daring any terrorist group—either the IRA or the Orange Brotherhood or any other splinter group from either side—to hurt them in any way. As the offices of Reverend Chadwick and the Vatican said in a joint statement, and I quote, 'We're putting our individual lives and the power and moral authority of the Protestant and Catholic faith on the firing line of history. If one of the terrorist groups wants to risk the fury of the world community by hurting one of us or one of our allies, then so be it. Let them live with the consequences. By the power of the Living God and in the name of the Father, the Son, and the Holy Spirit, we will prevail in this struggle against the forces of evil.' End quote."

Sterling took a breath, then started speaking again. But Ian didn't hear him anymore because his eyes were on Murphy. Murphy stuck a fingernail into his mouth. For several moments, the room stayed quiet except for the sound of the television.

"Well, what do you think of this?" Ian asked, a hand pointing at the television.

Murphy chewed his nail a second longer. "I say it's a complication to be sure. But maybe it doesn't matter."

"Doesn't matter?" Ian sputtered. "It means we'll have to change everything. How in the name of all that's holy can you say it doesn't matter? The pope is coming here and he's bringing the whole Catholic Church with him. We'd be more than lunatics to

do anything to harm a hair on his fat head. Every law enforce-
ment agency in the world will come down on us if we do. And
they'll know it's not the IRA this time. None of them would dare
do anything against the pope."

Murphy stood and took the television controls from Ian. Turning up the volume, he listened for several more seconds. Sterling
named the five Protestant ministers who had joined forces with
Chadwick. Ian recognized only one of the names—a South African who had won some international acclaim for his work against
apartheid before the black government came to power in the
early nineties. Sterling listed the five cardinals. Ian had never
heard of any of them. For some reason he couldn't identify, he
suddenly remembered the lemon smell that always overwhelmed
him as his mum hugged him just before he left for school. The
smell came from her soap, and when she wrapped her plump
arms around his neck, he felt snug and secure. He had always
loved that smell.

"This may actually make it easier," Murphy said, his voice
eerily calm as he faced Ian and muted the television. "I mean
what is it we're after? More than anything else, what's our final
goal in this awful mess?"

Ian started to say "revenge," but then realized that was *his*
goal and not the goal of the war itself. "We want freedom," he
said. "Freedom to plot our own destiny, freedom from the Catholic
Church and those who want to unify the island and cut us off
from all ties to the British Crown."

Murphy nodded his agreement. "I agree with you on one
thing," he said. "We do need to change our plans. But not to avoid
harm to the pope or his cardinals. Just the opposite. We want the
pope, plain and simple, we—"

"But that's . . . that's suicide!" Ian sputtered.

"What difference does that make?" Murphy shouted, his eyes
now frantic. "We've been dead for years—me since me boy died
and you since you held Rebecca's head in your lap and watched
her take her last breath! Who wants to live after that? This is
better, I tell you! We take out the pope, and the whole world will
know that we'll stop at nothing to achieve our ends. Our enemies
will know they can never defeat us. They'll know that we'll give
up everything, do anything, stop at no risk, no obstacle. They'll
know the full depth of our resolve, and then and only then they'll
give up their ridiculous belief that they can outwait us or outfight
us! I tell you this gives us our last and only hope to put a stop to

this mess once and for all! It's almost as if the sweet Lord Jesus has dropped this opportunity into our laps!"

He paused for a moment and stood from the sofa. "Even if we don't get the pope," he continued, his hands in his pockets. "Even if he manages to escape somehow, we'll still have shown our colors, the colors of the Orange, and the whole world will take note and give us what we want. We'll have our freedom—no, not you and me or anyone else they find and execute for this. But our land, Ian, our beloved country will have the freedom it has dreamt of for so long. Can't you see that?" He stood over Ian now. "Can't you see? If it's freedom we want, someone will have to make it happen. And someone will have to pay the price for it." Murphy's voice dropped lower and he touched Ian's shoulder.

"We're the ones," he said softly. "You and me and Sheehan and a few other desperate souls like us. We're the ones who can bring freedom to our land."

For a long time, Ian stayed still. He thought of Heather, saw her bouncing into her grandma's arms, her red curls bobbing up and down. He thought of his parents and all their hopes for him. Those hopes had stayed on track for so long, nothing fancy, mind you, but hopes nonetheless. But with the explosion in McGinty's Restaurant and the blood on Rebecca's face had come the anger that had begun to eat away at his liver. Then came his commitment to the Orange and the gradual move into more and more serious crimes. Next came the bombs he had planted, the ones that hurt no one. But then, finally, as if slumping down a long line of stairs to the very pit of hell, he reached the night of the bombing of City Hall. Three men had died. Yes, the men were his sworn enemies, but maybe those men had wives of their own and maybe little girls too like his own Heather. What kind of monster had he become?

Leaving Murphy, and walked to the only window in his apartment. Staring out, he saw a low cloud hanging over the small playground where Heather often played. The sliding board was wet with rain from the cloud.

He had become a monster, a man unworthy of a daughter like Heather. What could he offer her as she grew up? Hatred? She was better off without him, better off in the arms of his folks, the smell of lemon against her skin as she headed out to school. Better off in the care of a shoe cobbler than in the care of a murdering terrorist.

He thought of the man in the raincoat at City Hall. The man

wanted to find him, he felt sure of it. Why not let him? Why not
end it all as soon as possible? Let Heather live her life without a
murdering father in her memory?

Ian faced Murphy with a vacant stare. "I'm with you," he said.
"Why not?"

Murphy crossed the room and placed a hand on his shoulder.
"For our country," he said. "For the Orange and our freedom."

Though he nodded, Ian didn't answer. And in his mind, he
shook his head. In his mind, it was for Rebecca. Always and only
for Rebecca.

THIRTEEN

SATURDAY, NOVEMBER 15
BELFAST, IRELAND

Her shoes off, Valerie looked up from the screen of her laptop computer, laid her head back against the sofa, and took a swig of bottled water. To her left sat Lester Boggett, his tie loosened, his face flushed with exhaustion. Across from Boggett, Ted Shuster held a telephone to his ear as he checked to see what had happened to their food order from room service. Rodney Kent lay stretched out on the hotel room bed, a *Business Weekly* at his side, his shoes still on, his eyes closed. They were all worn out.

For several seconds, Valerie studied the three men, men whom she knew little about in spite of the fact that she had spent an increasing amount of time with them over the last few months.

Once an accountant with an insurance company, Lester had met Russell Chadwick at a crusade in Macon, Georgia, in 1969. Thirty at the time and fresh out of the Marine Corps, where he had flown helicopters, he had come on board as a special assistant and organizational leader two years later. He had a wife, three grown daughters, and a temper that Chadwick had warned Valerie about early in her time with them.

"Lester's got opinions," Chadwick told her. "And he's not shy about sharing them." No kidding.

She glanced at Ted, the only one of the three with a seminary degree. Educated at Southwestern Baptist Seminary in his hometown of Fort Worth, Texas, the superintelligent Ted did an excellent job as the backup preacher for Chadwick and all-around strategy planner for the crusade team. His work with Chadwick began right after his seminary graduation. Of the three, Ted was the youngest at forty-nine, seemed devoted to his family, and often brought his wife on their trips. He also talked often to his son and daughter, both in college. An attractive slender man just over six feet tall, Ted had dark hair and deep-set blue eyes. Many people had concluded that he would replace Chadwick when he retired and rumors said that should happen within the next three years.

Valerie clicked her computer off and closed the top. Of all Chadwick's men, Rodney Kent remained the most mysterious. An incredible voice even now at sixty-seven, but not much for general conversation. For the most part he spent his spare time with his nose buried in a finance magazine or on the computer buying and selling stock through the Internet. Though she didn't know it for sure, it was rumored that Kent had become quite wealthy. Not married, he seemed to have few friends other than Lester and Ted, and even they didn't talk with him that much. A strange man at the center of a strange group if she ever saw one.

Putting down the phone, Ted exhaled heavily. "Food should be here in five minutes," he said.

"I don't think I can lift my hand to eat," Kent said, eyes still closed.

"You're a wimp," Boggett said. "We've only been up thirty-four straight hours. What's your problem?"

"My problem isn't the hours," Kent said. "It's the company I'm keeping. You two"—he raised his head and pointed at Boggett and Ted—"are wearisome to a man of refined tastes such as myself."

"And me?" Valerie asked, eager to feel included in the banter.

"You're . . . well, there's just no word for you." He collapsed back onto the bed.

"She's the one who got us into this mess," Boggett said, an unfriendly edge in his tone.

"Easy, Lester," Ted said. "She didn't talk anybody into anything. If Chadwick hadn't bought into her idea, it would have died quicker than a possum in the middle of an interstate."

Lester grunted. Valerie started to defend herself but then backed off. If Lester wanted to persist in his dislike for her, then okay. She would just deal with it. Ted was right—Russell Chadwick had run with her idea only because it fit his own thoughts.

But Lester would never accept that, and in the last few days, he had kept up a constant litany of complaints. He blamed her for the exhausting work of planning for and then transporting themselves and the other five pastors to Ireland. He blamed her for the complete upheaval of their calendar—the cancellation of the London crusade; the postponement of their plans for a two-week vacation; the rescheduling of their advance trips to Chicago to get ready for the February crusade. He blamed her for the unending meetings, the stack of messages that reached to the ceiling, the steady diet of hotel food. He blamed her for his elevated blood pressure and Ted's backaches.

She accepted all of that, even if it did make her feel even lonelier than normal. But one thing made her mad. Lester had made it plain that if anything happened to Chadwick, if he so much as stubbed his toe on this wild-goose chase she had concocted, he would blame her for that too.

Valerie heard a rap on the door.

"Food's here," Ted said.

"Thank the good Lord," Lester said, jumping from his seat. "Another minute and I'd have starved to death."

"Don't think so," Ted said, opening the door to let the waiter in. He pointed to Lester's ample stomach. "You've got enough excess there to feed a small army for a month."

"You're a funny man," Lester said, lifting a lid off a plate. "Give the man a tip for his troubles." He grabbed a French fry and gobbled it up.

A minute later the four of them were munching on hamburgers, the sounds of their chewing the only break in the quiet of the room.

"Who's got the TV controls?" Boggett asked, his mouth full.

Kent, now sitting on the bed, tossed the remote to him.

Boggett hit the power button and the television screen flickered, then steadied. He searched the channels until he found CBC. Though they had already seen the taped report several times that day, he let the face and voice of Casey Sterling flood through the room once more.

"The unprecedented efforts of Pope Clement Peter and the Reverend Russell Chadwick to bring peace to Ireland will begin in earnest tomorrow evening at 6 P.M. Belfast time. They will come together at the Prestwick Presbyterian Church to consecrate themselves to this, as they call it, 'holy task of peacemaking.' Joining them will be five Catholic cardinals and five Protestant ministers . . ." The pictures of the ten appeared on screen as Sterling continued to speak. ". . . who have joined with Clement and Chadwick to form a religious cabinet unlike any the world has ever seen."

Sterling took three steps to the left, and the outline of a stone church with heavy green vines climbing the side came into view over his right shoulder. "The service will include short homilies by both Chadwick and Pope Clement, music by the Holy Spirit Children's Choir from New York City, and a sharing of communion, the reenactment of the Last Supper as recorded in the New Testament.

"Amazingly enough," Sterling continued, "security for the joint worship is at a minimum, from all we can tell. As Valerie Miller, spokesperson for the Reverend Russell Chadwick, told me only yesterday, 'We are trusting in God for protection. If the Lord is in this, then security is not an issue. If not, then let evil have its day.' "

Sterling stopped and tilted his head, a bemused look in his eyes. "Late tomorrow afternoon, we'll get a chance to see faith in action," he said. "And, for what it's worth, this reporter hopes it works. If it does, who knows? Maybe we'll all start to believe in miracles. This is Casey Sterling, reporting to you live from Belfast, for CBC news."

His fingers hitting the mute button, Lester turned to Valerie. His flushed face seemed to have gotten hotter.

"I still say this is a mistake," he mumbled.

"Too late for that," Ted said. "It is what it is."

"I got a call from Bill Stricker," Lester continued. Rodney and Ted straightened up. Valerie looked puzzled. The name sounded familiar.

"Who's he?" she asked.

"Only one of the richest men in America," Kent said, a tinge of awe in his tone. "He's the founder and chief officer of Applied Automations and Dynamics. Reportedly worth twenty billion dollars."

Recognizing the name now, Valerie tugged at her collar. She knew about Applied A&D, an electronics firm with a finger in a lot of pies—wireless and cable communications, computer software and hardware, just about everything related to modern technology. Stricker showed up on a lot of talk shows.

"What did he want?" Ted asked, chewing a French fry.

"He wanted to know what was going on," Lester answered. "Said he'd tried to reach Chadwick but couldn't get to him."

"That's a mistake," Kent said. "Anybody who's given you over fifty million dollars in the last ten years ought to get to talk to the top dog whenever he wants."

"And he's promised another big gift for the college we're buying," Boggett said.

"Who's buying a college?" Valerie asked.

"Chadwick is, or at least he's thinking about it. A private school that shut down about three years ago. The buildings are still good. It's just north of Rome, Georgia, on a hundred acres. The Reverend wants to start the school up again, make it a Christian campus for eight hundred to a thousand kids, give everyone who comes a tuition-free education."

"And Stricker has promised money for it?"

"Yeah, I've heard as much as two hundred million."

Valerie swallowed. "Two hundred million?"

Boggett wagged a finger at her. "That's right, two hundred. And he's not sure he's happy about all this nonsense over here. He told me he wanted to talk to Russell, find out what's going on."

"We'll tell Russell soon as today is over," Ted said. "We don't want to keep a man like Stricker waiting."

"Exactly," Boggett said, still staring at Valerie. "If anything happens to that gift he's considering . . ."

"Easy, Boggs," Ted said. "It's not her decision. You know that."

He shook his head. "She just better hope nothing happens to her uncle. If it does . . ."

His words landed on Valerie like a hammer on an anvil, and the sense of dread she had felt for months now intensified even more. Something dark and threatening hovered over her head, a cloud of anxiety she couldn't erase, no matter how much she tried to reassure herself. From her recent experience, she knew that nothing ever turned out quite as good as hoped. Troubles came, no matter what anyone did to prevent them, and whether she wanted to admit it or not, she knew that if anything did happen to her uncle, she'd blame herself far more than Lester ever would.

———

Less than ten miles away from the Prestwick Presbyterian Church, Ian O'Fallon held Heather in his lap, his fingers playing absentmindedly with her soft curls. Watching cartoons on the TV, she had fallen asleep, and her sweet eyes were now closed as she breathed deeply. Sitting on the floor to his left was Reginald Murphy. David Sheehan rested on the sofa by Murphy's head.

"I can't believe it," Murphy said, his tones soft. "It's like they're inviting us to destroy them. Nothing beyond normal security, no extra precautions . . ."

"Can we do the pope without harmin' Chadwick?" Sheehan asked. "I rather like the Reverend."

O'Fallon twisted a strand of Heather's hair in his fingers.

"We're not marksmen," Murphy replied. "We're demolitions men. There's no way to discriminate."

"So the Reverend goes down with the pope."

"If he's there, he's in harm's way," Murphy said. "That's what he gets for making an alliance with the devil himself. The friend of my enemy is my enemy."

O'Fallon glanced at Heather to make sure she was still sleeping. The scheme was set. A fellow Orangeman had once been a member of the Prestwick Church and a volunteer steward of the grounds. But he had arrived at his work more than once with too much whiskey in his blood, and the rector had kindly asked him to refrain from coming to the church in such a sorry condition. The man, however, had not taken well to the rector's admonitions and had stopped both his volunteering and his attendance at Sunday services.

To his surprise, the rector had never asked for his set of keys, and he had never willingly taken it back. Now he had given the keys to Murphy, thus insuring them access to every door in the place whenever they wanted it. Everything else fell easily into place.

They would wait until the security teams had finished their canvas of the whole building. With so many visiting dignitaries, including politicians and religious leaders, the police agencies would surely go over the church with bomb-sniffing dogs, infrared scanners, and metal detectors. Unless something happened out of the norm, that would take place around five. But that still left Murphy, Sheehan, and Ian O'Fallon about an hour and a half to do their dirty work and get out.

Dressed in brown overalls, they would come into the church disguised as extra janitorial help. The materials for their bomb were already in the building, just not assembled. Well hidden in a spot most unlikely to be searched—a small safe in the rector's living quarters—the materials would be gathered and carefully mixed. Then, still in the guise of cleaning men, they would place the explosives in cleaning buckets and haul them to the bell tower directly over the sanctuary.

Ian knew it wasn't a perfect plot. If a security officer questioned them, they'd have no proper identification, and if one stopped them between the rector's study and the bell tower, they'd have the explosives on their persons. In that event, they had agreed that Murphy would detonate the bombs on the spot. Death would come instantly, one flaming "whoosh" of incineration for everyone in the place.

Heather stirred in his lap, and Ian gently ran his hands over her forehead. Her skin felt cool. Would he ever get to touch it again? Would he *deserve* to touch it again after tomorrow?

Gritting his teeth, O'Fallon forced himself to pay attention to Murphy. With Chadwick's well-publicized pledge to take no more than normal security measures, he had a reasonable chance of surviving. And if he didn't? Well, war always brought certain risks.

By 6:15 the explosives would be set. The bomb would detonate at 6:30. Unless something providential occurred, Pope Clement Peter would meet his end by 6:31, and the whole insane notion of peace in Ireland would end again for a hundred years.

O'Fallon ran his fingers through Heather's hair. Unless something providential occurred, he'd be dead by then too, as least as far as his daughter was concerned.

FOURTEEN

Valerie Miller stood in the back of the church, her arms folded over her chest. Barely breathing, she waited for Clement Peter and Russell Chadwick to enter the sanctuary. To her left stood Ted Shuster. A battery of cameras ringed the stone walls on either side of them, and an intertwined mesh of cables snaked in and out around her feet. The organ played "A Mighty Fortress Is Our God" in the background. Over four hundred people packed the church to capacity and then some, every one of the plain wooden pews stuffed, every aisle lined with folding chairs, every space along the gray-stone walls jammed with worshipers. Outside, several thousand people craned their necks trying to catch a glimpse of the political and religious dignitaries who had gathered for the unprecedented service.

Scanning the crowd, Valerie spotted the vice president of the United States on the left front row. Beside him sat two senators and three congressmen, all of them claiming Irish ancestry, of course. On the right front pew sat ten of the most important religious leaders in the world—Clement's five cardinals, including Roca and Zolinska, and Chadwick's five fellow Protestant ministers. With Chadwick and Clement, the cardinals and ministers added up to twelve men, the perfect biblical number for those who paid attention to such things, as Valerie certainly did. Behind the front pews, diplomats, government officials, and dignitaries from at least thirty other countries studied their worship bulletins and waited for Clement and Chadwick to enter. Valerie toed the floor beneath her feet and leaned toward Ted.

"Quite a day, isn't it?" she whispered.

"Unprecedented," he said without looking at her.

"Who would have thought it?"

"The whole world is watching."

"I'm nervous," Valerie said.

Ted smiled. "I know, I see the red on your neck."

Valerie tugged at the collar of the white blouse she wore under her navy jacket. Tension always painted her neck red.

"I wish we had more security," she said, her eyes raking the crowd like a Secret Service agent. "If somebody wants to cause trouble . . ." her voice trailed off.

"We've done all we can," Ted said, touching her elbow. "The standard stuff. But Russell insisted that we do nothing more. 'Trust in God,' he said."

A wave of dread washed over her and she tugged her collar again. "Well, trust is fine, but the last time I had any dealings with the Vatican, a better security detail would have helped too."

Ted smiled thinly. "I heard something about that," he said. "You'll have to tell me more later. Now relax and stop being so jumpy."

The organ volume increased a notch and Valerie told herself to calm down. Everything was okay. To her right, she heard the shuffling of feet and knew that Clement, Chadwick, and their entourage had reached the vestibule of the church and now awaited the beginning of the processional. She glanced at her watch—6: 21. The organist played still louder, and Valerie recognized the tune as "O God Our Help in Ages Past."

She sensed someone watching her and automatically looked to the front of the church. To her surprise she spotted Casey Sterling in a seat on the floor to the right of the pulpit, his eyes focused her way. The warmth at her throat moved to her face. She turned from Sterling and focused on the movement in the vestibule. The crowd stood as if on signal, each person in the sanctuary straining to see Clement and Chadwick.

A stooped man in the simple black of a local pastor marched in first, and Valerie recognized him as the host rector of the Prestwick Church. Two children—a local boy and girl dressed in white robes and holding lit candles—followed. Valerie smiled—Chadwick had insisted that people from the local church play a part in this service. Behind the children stepped a Catholic priest holding a large open Bible. Next in line came the Holy Spirit Children's Choir from New York, each child dressed in purple and white, their hands at their sides as if glued there. Valerie counted them as they marched by—forty-four of the most talented children in the world.

Valerie caught her breath as she saw Clement and Chadwick. They walked in shoulder to shoulder after the choir, Clement in a brilliant white cassock and tiara—the pontiff's formal headgear. He held the staff of St. Peter in his right hand, the symbol of his power as shepherd of the Catholic Church. Beside him, Chadwick wore a simple black robe with red stripes on the sleeves, a robe given to him as a token of an honorary doctorate from a small Lutheran college in Minnesota. Though taller than Clement, he looked a bit frail, and Valerie thought for a second that his right arm was shaking. The two men stopped for a moment as they reached the back of the sanctuary, and Valerie caught Chadwick's eye. She smiled at him and he, ever so slightly, winked at her. Her smile widened then and she felt a tear come to her eye. She had helped make this happen, she realized. Her fears were out of place, her cautions unnecessary. She stood up straighter, her heart soaring as her concerns about safety momentarily disappeared.

The organ fairly roared now and Valerie checked her watch. 6:25—only ten minutes behind schedule.

Clement and Chadwick started moving forward now, their robes swishing at their ankles, their eyes raking over the crowd. Valerie's eyes followed theirs, up one pew and down the other. Near the middle of the congregation she saw a man step through the door that led off the side of the church to the small offices down the hallway. Her eyes moved past him but then stopped. Something about the man startled her. She inspected the man carefully. Wearing brown coveralls, he had a shaved head and a thin chin. He looked like a cleaning man. He held a broom in his right hand and his fingers gripped it as if trying to choke it to death. His left hand was in his pocket and he moved quickly toward the front of the sanctuary, his eyes glued on Clement and Chadwick.

Valerie grabbed her throat, then leaned toward Ted.

"That man!" she whispered, pointing at him. The man kept moving, stepping past the chairs in the aisle, his fingers white in their death grip on the broom.

"He's maintenance," Ted said, undisturbed.

Unconvinced, Valerie began to walk forward, her stride quick. The man's movements disturbed her, the way he kept one hand in his pocket. Did he have a gun hidden there?

The pastor of the church reached the front, then peeled off to the left to a seat on the rostrum. The acolytes stepped to the center of the aisle and touched their burning candles to the unlit ones sitting on either side of the communion table. The man in the overalls eased past the acolytes. Valerie spotted a security agent moving from the front of the church toward the man in the coveralls. Only the priest holding the Bible separated the intruder from Clement and Chadwick.

The organ paused between hymns, and as if on cue, a hush fell over the congregation. The security agent moved slowly, apparently unsure what to do, whether or not to interrupt the proceedings.

Valerie began to run, her black heels clicking on the stone floor of the church. The security agent stepped in front of the man with the coveralls, but the man lurched suddenly to the right and threw a shoulder into the agent's stomach before he could react. The agent crumpled to the floor, and the man in the coveralls charged forward, smacking the priest with the broom. The priest fell to the floor and the congregation groaned in unison. A woman screamed. The man's hand jerked out from the coveralls. The guard on the floor pulled a weapon and pandemonium broke out.

Valerie lost a heel and almost stumbled as she reached Chadwick. The man in the coveralls threw himself at Chadwick, who tottered backward, his angular frame dodging away from the man grabbing at him. Chadwick's shoe caught in the folds of his long robe and he tripped and fell. Valerie grabbed for him but couldn't catch his fall. His head banged against the floor and his eyes flickered, then closed. Valerie heard screams coming from the panicked crowd as it pushed its way toward the exits.

The man in the coveralls jumped at Chadwick, his broom gone now, his eyes frantic. Valerie threw herself in his path an instant too late as he landed on her and Chadwick, his face near hers, his hands apparently reaching for Chadwick's throat. Someone stepped on Valerie's back and she banged her head on the floor, but she ignored the pain and sank her fingernails into the attacker's wrists.

"You've got to get out of 'ere!" the man shouted. "You've got less than two minutes!"

Valerie dug harder into the man's flesh, her mind not registering his words.

"I'm not 'ere to hurt you!" the man shrieked. "You've got to get everyone out!"

Valerie's brain focused then and she heard the man's words, and though they didn't make sense, she released her grip on his hands long enough to see what he'd do. From behind him, the security guard suddenly reappeared, his weapon poised. He grabbed the attacker by the back of the neck and jerked him off Chadwick. The two of them scuffled and tumbled against the wall. Someone knocked the candles off the communion table and they lay burning on the floor.

On her knees, Valerie shook her uncle, but his eyes remained shut. Frantically, she looked around for help and spotted Clement with Cardinal Roca at his side, the two of them already at the back door of the church. Searching left and right, she saw that the church was emptying fast. She and Chadwick were almost alone. The attacker said she had less than two minutes! Until what? She didn't know and didn't have time to find out. Now less than one minute!

Standing and kicking off her shoes, she braced herself, grabbed Chadwick under the shoulders, and hauled his head up to her waist. She took two steps toward the side door of the church, then another two. Chadwick's legs dragged along the floor, and she pulled as hard as possible and moved as fast as she could, but she knew she wasn't moving fast enough. She had less than a minute!

From behind, she heard a door open, then felt someone moving her way. She didn't take the time to turn around. But then Casey Sterling stepped past her and grabbed Chadwick's torso and lifted him out of her arms and half carried, half dragged him out the door of the church and into the hallway. Four steps down the hallway, they reached a second door, this one leading to the outside. As she pushed open the second door, the explosion came, a thunderous roar that blew through the top of the sanctuary of the Prestwick Church, tossing its rubble up and out on anyone in its path.

A piece of rock the size of a football rained down from the sky on Valerie, its ragged edge striking her left shoulder, just behind her ear. Collapsing, Valerie felt herself losing consciousness. As her eyes blinked and dimmed, her last thought was of the man in the coveralls who had tried to save her uncle's life.

FIFTEEN

Somewhere in the distance Russell Chadwick heard voices, a low mumbling of conversation, but he couldn't make out any words. Everything sounded muffled, as if everyone spoke through a knitted scarf. He couldn't see either—everything was black. His head throbbed a steady *thump, thump, thump*, and his back felt as stiff as an ironing board. For several minutes he lay dead still, trying to figure out where he was and why he couldn't hear. But no answers came to him. He tried to open his eyes, but they felt glued together, and he couldn't manage it. For a second he wondered if he was dreaming, if all the hurt in his head and back were imaginary. But then he told himself to wake up and turn over, but when he tried, the movement felt as if it would kill him. Groaning, he decided to stay as still as possible for as long as possible.

Someone touched him. A warm wet cloth sponged across his forehead and over his eyelids and cheeks. He liked the way the cloth felt. The moisture from the cloth loosened some of the glue from his eyes. He tried again to open them and succeeded this time.

Staring up, he saw Mildred at his bedside, her hands gently guiding the washcloth down to his neck. Chadwick smiled and a flood of peace rushed over him. Mildred had always been there, never complaining about his long trips away from home, the things he didn't do with his kids, the way he left her to do so much all by herself. Before the children came, she played the piano for his crusades. He'd met her that way. She was sitting on the piano bench in Omaha, Nebraska, one night when he stood

up to preach. It was as if God just tapped him on the shoulder
that night and told him that the hazel-gray beauty with the long
fingers on the piano keys was to be his spouse. Two months later
they walked down the aisle, her mother playing the organ, and
tied the knot. So far as he knew, neither of them had ever had
one day of regret. That didn't mean they didn't have their moments. As Mildred liked to say, "We never argue, but you can
sometimes hear our debates three blocks away." He patted her
hand.

"He's awake," she said, turning to the three men grouped behind her. "Thank God!"

The men rushed to her side, ringing the bed like guards.

"Where am I?" Chadwick asked. His tongue scraped over his
lips.

"Atlanta, West Cobb Hospital," Ted said. "We flew you here
yesterday."

"Got any water? My mouth feels like the inside of an old
cave."

Boggett rushed to the sink, filled a cup, and handed it to Mildred. She touched the cup to Chadwick's lips and helped him
drink.

"What happened to me?" Chadwick asked, touching the wrapping that covered his head. "I'm hazy on everything after I
walked into the Prestwick Church."

Mildred looked at Ted. He nodded and she stepped back a
pace.

"A terrorist," Ted said. "Actually, a group of them. They had
placed explosives in the church. It's . . . well it's a heap of rubble.
Everything is destroyed." He stared at the floor.

"You've got a concussion," Mildred said, taking his hand. "And
a couple of cracked ribs. You won't throw any horseshoes for a
while, but the doctor says you'll be fine after a couple of weeks."

Chadwick smiled thinly at his wife and touched his right
index finger to the left corner of his mouth, their secret signal for
a kiss.

"The press has had a field day," Boggett interjected. "Said this
is what happens when amateurs get involved in diplomatic matters."

Chadwick turned his face to the window. A gray sky greeted
him, and a heavy weariness made his head hurt even worse.

"It wasn't your fault," Mildred soothed, sitting down on the
bed. "You tried to do a good thing. It just didn't work out, that's

all. Don't go blaming yourself for things you can't control."

"How many people got hurt?" he asked, not wanting to know the answer.

"Don't concern yourself with that right now," Mildred said. "You did all you could to—"

"But it was my idea!" he insisted, facing them again, his jaw firm. "I did this. I caused all this carnage."

"I don't mean to argue with you," Kent interjected, speaking for the first time. "But technically, it was Valerie's idea."

"Yeah," Boggett added. "She's the one who—"

Chadwick tried vainly to rise. He had forgotten about Valerie! "Where is she?" he demanded. His head felt like it was exploding. "Is she okay?"

Mildred looked away. . . .

———

A bandage on his right wrist and a paper-encased box in his left hand, Casey Sterling eased out of his Mercedes 480 SL and entered the West Cobb Hospital from the back entrance. Ignoring the elevator, he took the stairs two at a time and quickly reached the landing of the fourth floor. Pushing through the door, he tugged his New York Yankees cap down over his face and hustled down the hallway. To his relief, no one recognized him, and he reached room 415 without interference. At the door, though, stood a security guard.

"I'm here to see Valerie Miller," he said. "She's in 415?"

The guard shrugged. "Not for me to say," he said.

Sterling placed his hand on his hip. "I've just got a few minutes," he said. "I brought her these." He held up the box and opened it. A dozen roses lay inside.

"Pretty flowers," the guard said. "You her boyfriend?"

"Not for me to say," Sterling said, grinning. "You letting me in to see her?"

"Can't keep a man from delivering roses to a pretty girl," the guard said. "Wouldn't be right. Show me some identification."

Sterling flipped out his wallet and handed his driver's license to the guard.

"You're that reporter, ain't you?" the guard said, studying the picture.

Sterling shrugged.

"You need a shave, man. But I guess you can go on inside. She's been sleeping, mostly."

Nodding, Sterling pushed by the man and into the room. He saw a single bed, a rolling table beside it, a pitcher on the table, a sink at the foot of the bed. At least three different flower arrangements sat on the sill of the window just past the bed. But none of them were roses.

Valerie lay in the bed in the center of the room, the light from the window playing on her face. A bandage the size of a computer disk covered her left ear, and her left eye was almost black. But other than that she looked okay, remarkably well in fact for a woman who had come so close to death. And, maybe even more amazingly, she looked pretty too, even in a hospital gown and without makeup.

His roses at his back, Sterling walked to the bed and leaned over.

"Ms. Miller," he whispered. "You awake?"

Her eyes flickered, then opened. For a second she stared out as if not recognizing him, but then her eyes cleared and she smiled weakly. "Hey," she said. "What are you doing here?"

"Slow news day. Came by to check on Chadwick, thought I'd look in on you too."

"You look awful."

"Thanks for the encouragement. Haven't taken the time to clean up since I flew back in."

"A nurse told me it was Wednesday."

"Yeah, you got back yesterday."

"I vaguely remember it. You okay?"

He smiled. "Sure, a few bruises, a sprained wrist, but nothing serious. What about you?" After getting his wrist wrapped in Belfast, he had flown back to Atlanta as quickly as possible.

She waved a hand at him for a second, then dropped it to her side. "Not bad, considering everything."

"Heard you got a few stitches."

"Four, I think." She pushed up, and Sterling stuffed her pillow under her shoulders. "How long have I been asleep?"

"I don't know. I just got here."

"What's in the box?" She pointed weakly at the package.

Sterling pulled out the roses. "For you," he said, looking for a glass but seeing none that would work. "A dozen."

"Three for each stitch. How romantic."

"I hadn't thought of that, but if you think it's romantic . . . I'm okay with that." Sterling placed the roses on the table and eased closer to her.

"I'm glad you're okay," he said. "I've been worried about you."

"Thanks for the concern, but I'm all right." She closed her eyes. "How's my uncle Russell?"

"Got a concussion, I think. And a cracked rib or two."

"But he's okay?"

"Yeah, so I'm told."

"Anyone else hurt?"

"Nope, not seriously and none killed. If I were a religious man, I'd say that was miraculous."

She opened her eyes again. "It might be more miraculous for you to think about being a religious man."

He grinned. She pointed to his wrist. "Does it hurt much?"

"Nope, not really. Doc says it'll be good as new in a couple of weeks."

"Good, good." She reached over and touched his hand. "Thanks for coming back for me at the church," she said softly. "I'd never have managed without your help."

"You were doing fine," he countered, staring at her hand on his wrist.

She shook her head. "That's bad reporting," she argued. "Uncle Russell would be dead now, maybe me, too, if you hadn't come back. You saved us, both of us, you—"

"Shussh," he said, touching a finger to his lips. "Don't tire yourself. I did what I had to do."

She nodded and closed her eyes once more.

"I'm going to Rome in the morning," Sterling said. "I want to do a follow-up on the pope and the Vatican's reaction to all this."

"Rome's a long way."

"True, but if a man's going to climb the ladder these days, he has to pay the price. I wanted to see you first and bring you the roses."

"They're beautiful," she said, ignoring the more personal part of the remark. "Tell Cardinal Roca hello for me."

Sterling pushed back the baseball cap and stood still for a long minute, trying to work up his courage. For some reason he felt shy, like a teenager asking for a date for the first time. In some ways, the brush with death at Prestwick Church had made him feel like everything was new, fresh, and alive in ways he hadn't felt for years. A momentary reaction to surviving, he guessed. It would probably wear off, given a few weeks back in the grind. He took off his baseball cap and twirled it in his hands.

"Look," he said, his voice soft. "I know this isn't the time, but when I get back I want to see you again. You think that would be okay, dinner maybe?" He waited for a response but none came. He waited some more but with the same result. Valerie's breathing had become low and slow, and he realized she had fallen asleep. Pushing his Yankees cap back on, he smiled to himself. Not many women fell asleep while the famous Casey Sterling asked them out on a date. But then again, Valerie Miller was not just any woman. The way she had rushed forward at the Prestwick Church and thrown herself over Reverend Chadwick to protect him had impressed him more than anything he had seen in a long time.

He studied her face. Strange the way he had gone back to help her. Not that he didn't think he had that kind of courage. His stint covering the Persian Gulf War had proven he had plenty of guts. But in all the confusion, he had automatically looked around for her, automatically thought of her over everyone else, even himself. A strange reaction for a guy better known as one who'd knock over his own grandmother if she stood between him and something he wanted. Maybe he had changed. Was that possible? Or had he responded the way he did simply because Valerie Miller was a good-looking woman who intrigued him? Who knew?

Confused, Sterling kissed his fingers, then touched them to Valerie's forehead. She was beautiful and she was brave and she was smart and she was religious. Except for the religious part, she was everything he had ever wanted in a woman.

As Casey Sterling eased into the hallway, Valerie pulled herself into a fetal position and moaned into the gray light of the room. Inside her drug-confused head, ghostly images reared up and rushed at her. She tried to wake up but found herself helpless to do so. The images in her head, shrouded in inky blackness, bounced and rumbled, and she squeezed her knees to her chest in fear. The images shifted, then changed. They became a swirling cloud of black dust, a cloud reaching to the sky, a sky now bright with a dawning sun. Out of the black cloud a herd of horses suddenly thundered, a herd furious in its rush. The nostrils of the horses flared, the neighing was unbearably loud, and the hooves were sharp and deadly as they churned across the earth.

Valerie wanted to scream at the horses to stop their charge, but she couldn't. Her mouth opened and closed in her sleep but emitted no sound. The horses plowed forward, ever forward, the cloud of dust growing thicker as the herd thundered toward the nothingness of a black abyss that materialized out of nowhere.

Sweat broke out on Valerie's forehead as she watched the horses in her dream. They were running, running, running headlong to the cliffs. She felt as if she were falling, falling into the abyss, falling to her death even before the horses. But then she didn't fall. She found herself on the edge of the cliffs, the horses pounding toward her, the dust from the herd choking out her breath.

She screamed at the herd to stop. She waved her arms to warn them. But still they came.

Beside her, a singular horse appeared—a stallion the color of coal dust. On her other side, she saw a second horse, a white one with a flowing mane as white as cotton. Then a paint stood by the white and a palomino by the black. A roan reared up by the paint and an appaloosa by the palomino. The herd thundered toward them all—millions of horses now completely hidden in a murky cloud of black dust. Six horses and her standing against them all, the last line of defense. Somehow she knew she and the six had to stop the rest. They were the last hope, the last barrier to the herd rumbling over the cliff to its gruesome end.

Without warning, she disappeared from the dream, an apparition snuffed out in the dark of night. In her place, in the middle of the six horses, a donkey now stood—a plain gray donkey, its head low, its tail nothing more than a stub. A man sat on the back of the donkey—a faceless man.

But still the herd rumbled and the cloud swirled, and she could hear the hooves of the millions approaching the cliff. Her heart thumped with the rhythm of the horses, and then the cloud dissolved. The horses disappeared and the dream frittered away into the nothingness that eventually captures all dreams. But in her sleep, Valerie Miller stayed afraid.

———————

Six time zones to the east, Cardinal Lech Zolinska scratched his ears, then brushed his hands over his nose and plopped himself into a chair in the private quarters of Cardinal Severiano Roca. Though he had demanded a meeting the day after they returned from Northern Ireland, Roca hadn't agreed to see him until tonight. Furious at the Secretary's tardiness in responding to his demands, he twitched even more spasmodically than usual.

Though he glanced around the room, he hardly noticed the art-
work on the walls—all of the pieces portraying Jesus in one pose
or another—or the delicacy of the antique furniture—all of it intricately carved.

Rubbing his head, Zolinska jerked his breath in and out, in
and out, and inwardly resented Roca's calm. The man seemed
completely at ease, sitting in a straight wooden chair, still
dressed in cassock, sash, and zucchetto, in spite of the late hour,
his countenance as still as a sphinx.

"Tea?" Roca asked him, his voice smooth as he indicated a silver tray on the small table between them.

"No, none for me," spewed Zolinska. "I'm not here to social-
ize."

Roca arched an eyebrow. "You move quickly to the point, my
friend. A trait for which many admire you."

Zolinska rubbed his knees with the palms of his hands. "This
silliness with His Holiness has to stop," he growled.

"To what silliness do you refer?" Roca asked, sipping from a
black cup, a gold ring at the top and bottom of it.

"You know what I mean," Zolinska pressed. "He's not ready to
make decisions on his own. This trip to Northern Ireland almost
resulted in his death."

"He is the pope," Roca said, his cup in his lap. "He makes his
own decisions."

"You know better than that! He's pope for one reason and one
reason only. Neither you nor Medico could gather the necessary
votes. He sits on the Holy See by virtue of that standoff—nothing
more."

Roca reached to the silver tray, dipped a spoon into a sugar
dish, dipped the spoon into his cup, and stirred the sugar into his
tea. "Perhaps God ordained the matters in the conclave to unfold
as they did," he said. "At least that's what I choose to believe."
He sipped from his cup.

Zolinska momentarily ceased his twitching. "You surprise me
with such talk of God," he said.

"You see it differently?" Roca asked, a bemused look on his
face. "God did not ordain the election of our beloved pontiff?"

Zolinska swallowed hard. He walked on thin ice here. One did
not openly say anything that called into question the election or
leadership of a pope. "You know what I mean," he said. "Of course
God ordained it. But God embodies the divine work in human
beings, men such as you and me. And we need not couch our

deeds in the cloak of such holy talk. It is assumed."

"Perhaps we need to verbalize the assumed from time to time," Roca offered. "Remind ourselves of what we believe."

Zolinska wrinkled his nose. The conversation had not taken the turn he wanted. "Indeed," he said, deciding to agree to move the matter back on track. "You have done me a service by such a reminder. I thank you for it."

Roca sipped from his tea, and Zolinska had the distinct feeling that the man was toying with him. Furious at the thought, he decided to become aggressive again. No more capitulation to Roca's word games!

"The pontiff is inexperienced," he said, choosing a softer edge to his criticisms. "He needs counsel until he gains his stride."

"I agree with you," Roca said. "I offer him my advice when he asks for it."

"Perhaps we would do well to confer before we advise him," Zolinska said. "Especially on the most crucial matters."

Roca arched an eyebrow again. "You're suggesting that we caucus on certain issues?" he asked.

Zolinska brushed his ears. "It seems reasonable. Two of his most trusted confidants, striving to give the best of their wisdom to the pontiff, conferring beforehand as to the proper course of action."

Roca set his cup on the silver tray, then leaned back in his chair and folded his hands in his lap. "Let me think on this," he said. "Perhaps it has merit. I will inform you of my decision within the week."

Zolinska ground his teeth. How dare Roca treat him so disrespectfully! As if he had nothing better to do than stand around and wait on the great Secretary to "inform him of his decision." Such unmitigated gall!

Standing, he bowed slightly, then twisted and stalked out of the room. He would not wait on Roca. He would do what he had decided to do—and when he wanted to do it.

SIXTEEN

November 21

Though protesting vehemently that she could take care of herself, Valerie finally gave in to her parents' wishes and flew home with them to Charlotte, North Carolina, on Friday. She still sported a bandage on her head, her body was still wracked by an occasional bout of dizzy spells, and she carried four different kinds of pills in the pockets of her blue jeans.

Her dad Tyrone flew the plane, a ten-passenger Cessna owned by PrimeAmerica—a multinational bank he served as CEO. Her mom hovered over her like a hen over a baby chick—a blanket, a pillow, a question every few minutes. "You okay? You need anything?"

Fully reclined in a leather seat in the passenger compartment, Valerie waved off her mom's incessant attempts to help and tried to rest. But sleep refused to come, and she made the mercifully short trip in a confused daze. The ride from the airport passed in a similar fashion—her dad driving his sleek black Mercedes, her mom in the backseat with her, holding her hand, treating her like a child.

Staring out the window at the overcast sky, Valerie snuggled down into the waist-length black coat she wore and inwardly chastised herself for her attitude. Her mom only wanted to take care of her, nothing wrong with that. God had apparently rigged her DNA that way.

A petite woman with tastefully dyed blond hair and eyes the color of chocolate, Sarah Miller had never met a good deed she didn't like. An art teacher prior to Valerie's birth, she still dabbled with her paints, served on the board of a museum, taught

English in a Hispanic community center, gave away clothes at the church clothes closet, and took annual mission trips to remote jungle countries.

As her dad turned into the driveway of their two-story white brick home, Valerie tried to make herself feel better, but it didn't help much. God had given her every advantage—a dad who made enough money to provide this fifteen-room house on five acres of prime residential real estate. An education in the best schools America offered. Connections to people who opened doors for her career. A healthy body, a better than decent physical beauty. Parents who not only taught her Christian values but who usually lived them out themselves. But in spite of that she had failed miserably.

The car stopped and her mom jumped out and ran around to open her door. Staring up at her, Valerie suddenly realized why she felt so upset by all the attention. For the second time in the last year, she had come home with her life in shambles. She had been dismissed from her position in Rome the first time. Now she had botched her work with her uncle. Thirty years old and the recipient of every advantage imaginable, she felt like a dismal failure, and the fact that she had to depend on her parents again pointed that out in the most poignant manner. The truth was, she wasn't mad at her mom and dad. She was mad at herself.

Taking her mom's hand, she slowly followed her into the house and up the stairs to her bedroom. Sitting on her bed as her mom unpacked the suitcases that Tyrone had deposited there, Valerie pulled off her coat and inspected the space she had occupied before she left home for college. A collection of one hundred and three stuffed cats stared back at her from the white built-in shelves that lined the back wall of the room. Resting atop an elegant mahogany desk with curved legs and balled claw feet were at least fifty different pictures of her, taken in high school, college, and graduate school. Above the desk, more shelves lined the walls. These shelves were made of the same fine mahogany as the desk and were filled with books.

Standing, Valerie walked over to the desk and picked up one of the pictures. She and a man named Rudy Stone—a doctor in Raleigh. She placed the picture back and walked to the arched window overlooking the side yard of the house, a yard filled with trees—two oaks, three different types of pines, and a towering magnolia.

Wrapping her arms around her waist, Valerie thought about

Rudy. She had actually been engaged to him for a while—the only man who had ever asked her for her hand in marriage. Others would have, she felt sure. But she had been too busy with her schooling, then the beginnings of her career. But for what? To what end? So she could end up back home, alone and lower than a catfish at the bottom of a murky pond? Her career a question mark? The only man she had genuinely ever loved missing and probably dead? What a fiasco!

She wondered what Rudy was doing, how his life was going. It had to be better than hers. He was probably married by now, maybe some children, a successful doctor living the American dream.

"You need anything?"

The sound of her mom's voice jolted Valerie back to the moment. "No, nothing. I'm fine."

"Okay, I've got to get some dinner started. If you need anything, just call. The intercom's right here." Her mom pointed to the speaker over the bed.

Valerie smiled in spite of her mood. She knew where to find the intercom. "I'll come down in a while," she said.

Her mom nodded, then left as Valerie turned back to the window. Rain splattered against the pane. She stared at the clouds. More rain was coming. She moved away from the window, stared at the pictures again, then picked up another one and sat down on the bed. Her right arm hung in a sling in the photo, and a small bandage covered a spot on her neck below her right cheek.

As her heart flooded with memories, Valerie pressed the photo to her chest. She had fallen out of the magnolia tree! Tears came to her eyes. The sadness that had hovered over her for months now seemed unbearable. What she had thought so right had turned out so wrong. Her stupid interpretation of her uncle's dream had almost gotten a lot of people killed.

Who did she think she was anyway? She was nothing but an interloper in Chadwick's circle, a newcomer—and a female to boot—who had waltzed her way into their midst and sent the most important religious leader in the world off on a misguided mission that had nothing to do with his calling to preach the gospel! What arrogance! Just like the day she thought she could climb the magnolia! She thought she could do anything. No barriers, no limits to the great, the all-mighty, the "always right" Valerie Miller! Well, circumstances had proven that all wrong. The blessed had become the cursed; the silver spoon had fallen out of her mouth. If the last year had shown her anything, it was simply this—sometimes trees shouldn't get climbed, couldn't get climbed!

Tears flooding her cheeks, Valerie doubled over at the waist, the picture still clutched to her chest. For the first time in her life she realized her own frailty, her own weakness. She understood that sometimes things happened in such a way that no one, not even someone like her, could count on success. Like everyone else, she could lose. She was a loser!

Valerie gritted her teeth. Loser! The word tasted like rotten meat on her tongue. She squeezed the picture tighter. Her tears slowed and her grief shifted slowly toward anger. She didn't like losing. Never had, never would. If she had heard her dad say it once, she'd heard him say it a thousand times, "Only failures fail." He hadn't achieved the position and responsibility he had by giving up just because a few things went wrong. And he hadn't taught her to toss in the towel without a fight either. To do so cut against the grain of everything in her soul. Sure, everyone lost some battles, but that didn't mean you gave up on the war!

Wiping her eyes, Valerie suddenly stood, threw the picture onto the bed, and rushed from her room. Hustling down the stairs before her parents could stop her, she ran to the front door and out onto the porch. The rain fell harder now, and though she wore only a light sweater, a pair of jeans, and a thin pair of casual shoes, she didn't hesitate. Off the porch, she turned left and then left again. The rain pelted down on her head, soaking through her hair and sweater, but she kept moving. Without conscious thought, she somehow knew that what she was about to do was pivotal, crucial to what would happen in her future.

Sliding on the wet grass, she stopped at the base of the magnolia tree. It towered at least fifty feet into the sky, its ancient branches clattering as the rain pelted down on its broad green leaves. Raising her eyes to the almost dark sky, Valerie opened her arms as if embracing heaven and stuck out her tongue to catch the rain as it fell, the cold moisture jolting her body and mind. For several seconds, she stood that way, the rain washing over her like a cleansing shower.

Her hands at her sides again, she stepped to the magnolia, hoisted a leg to the lowest branch, and pulled up. Getting her balance on the first branch, she laid her forehead against the trunk. It felt so comfortable, so much like she remembered from her childhood. She had climbed this tree at least a thousand times. No reason she couldn't do it again! And tree climbers weren't losers!

Raising her face, she reached for the second branch. Her hands slid across the slick wood. She lifted a foot, placed it on the limb, and pulled up, her leg acting as a brace for her weight. She moved to the third branch, this one spaced farther up, almost six feet off the ground. Her left foot secure on the lower branch, she hooked her right foot on the third one. Her hands grabbed the stem of the upper branch. She lifted her weight higher. A chill suddenly wracked her body and her eyes clouded over. A wave of dizziness crashed through her head and she wobbled on the branch. She realized she was still too weak for this, but it was too late. For a split second, she hung suspended between the second and third branch, her teeth grinding as she fought to hang on, her eyes rolling and fluttering against the dizzying imbalance that had attacked without warning. A gust of wind pushed through the magnolia and Valerie lost her footing.

Tumbling backward, she momentarily lost consciousness, and her back crunched into the limb she had just climbed. Bouncing off the limb, she thumped to the ground, the wet grass slamming into the stitches on her head. In less than twenty seconds, the cold rain jogged her back to consciousness. Though groggy, she managed to pull herself up. Leaning on the tree, she caught her breath and gave herself a minute to regain her balance. Then, her hair muddy and her body soaked, she stumbled back to the front door, up the stairs, and into her room. Collapsing on the bed, she fumbled for the covers, jerked them over her weary body, and closed her eyes.

Her body shaking against her cold clothing, she started to cry again. She had tried her best, but she knew now what she had tried to deny—her tree-climbing days had ended forever.

SEVENTEEN

Pulling off the snappy brown fedora that he wore low over his forehead, Casey Sterling slid onto the back pew and laid the hat in his lap. Shivering, he wished he had worn a coat heavier than his brown leather aviator's jacket. His throat hurt and his shoulder blades ached as if someone had removed all the lubrication from his joints. The cold damp weather and jet lag had combined to give him the beginnings of what felt like a monster of a cold. But he couldn't let any of that slow him down.

Pushing aside his feelings, he coughed slightly and surveyed the dimly lit sanctuary of the church he had chosen for this meeting. Less than fifty people scattered around in a sanctuary that could no doubt seat close to a thousand. Row upon row of pews made of dark wood, images of the apostles carved onto the ends on both sides. A marble floor stretched out beneath the pews, a sea of cold, sterile sound enhancement. Around the sides of the pews a number of grottolike areas served as chapels. Scores of candles burned on altars built into the grottos where a scattering of people knelt and prayed. The people in the pews kept their heads down, and a few mumbled into the open air. At the front of the sanctuary an intricately carved pulpit jutted into the air, its bow at least ten feet above the pews, a striking reminder of the power of the man who stood in it each week to offer the homily.

Sterling laid his hands in his lap and gritted his teeth. It had been years since he had sat through a church service—twenty-eight years for those who liked exact numbers.

Remembering the distasteful experience of that Sunday morning, Sterling pulled at the bill of his hat. His mom had visited the preacher of the Swansboro Community Church that Friday, her right eye already turning yellow from the latest of his dad's drunken outbursts. During the counseling session, she had suggested that maybe she needed to leave her husband.

Sterling lowered his head as he waited in the pew. He knew the story because he had waited in the office while his mom stepped into the pastor's study. He remembered the sound of the pastor's door closing in his face, the sight of the pastor's young secretary at her desk popping a bubble from her gum. He thought it quite amazing at the time—a somber place like the church and a woman who barely looked old enough to drive worked in the office and popped bubbles.

His mom came out about an hour later, her eyes red, her hands holding her black purse as if she wanted to strangle it. The pastor followed her, his hands in his pockets, his wire-rimmed glasses perched ever so perfectly on his nose.

One look at his mom's face and he knew she'd kept nothing a secret. The pastor knew about his abusive, shiftless father, his mother's tirades at him, the whole awful situation that he had hoped and prayed would just disappear. But it hadn't and now the pastor knew.

Two days later Sunday dawned. He and his mom walked four blocks to the church—an interdenominational congregation that met in a plain white building sitting in the middle of a grove of pine trees not more than four miles from one of the white sandy beaches of Swansboro, South Carolina. He sang the hymns, listened to the prayers, even tossed in a quarter from his hard-earned paper route money when the offering plate passed under his nose. The sermon started—a sermon on staying faithful. He listened sporadically—tuning in and out as the singsong voice of the pastor winged its way through the message.

"Stay faithful," the pastor coaxed. "Faithful to God, faithful to each other, faithful to your commitments, your oaths, your word, your vows. Why, only this week, a woman came to my office, a woman with problems in her marriage."

Casey sat up straighter in his pew. The preacher's wire-rimmed glasses seemed to stare right at him and Lacy Drew. "She's praying, she told me. Praying about what to do, whether to go or to stay."

Casey glanced at his mom. Her eyes were down, her face red, the yellow spot on her right eye as bright as a caution light.

"But I want you to know, she doesn't need to pray about this," the pastor continued, his voice rising. "Her marriage vows said 'till death do us part.' That's her commitment."

Casey reached over and grabbed his mom's hand. He felt it shaking in his small palm.

"She made that commitment," the preacher shouted. "And she needs to stay faithful to it! Jesus said, 'Let your yea be yea and your nay be 'nay.' That goes for all your commitments. . . ."

The preacher continued to preach but Casey no longer heard him. His mom had started to weep quietly, her whole body shrinking inward. His face turned crimson with embarrassment.

The preacher had told about his mom! Had spoken openly of her struggles! Had publicly chastised her!

Casey stared around the church to see if anyone had noticed, but they seemed oblivious to everything, oblivious to his shame. Maybe they didn't know, he decided, maybe—

He felt someone's eyes on him and he glanced to the right. Then he saw her, the secretary, her tongue on the end of her lips as if she had gum hidden inside her mouth ready to blow a bubble at any second. She held her eyes on him and he squeezed his mom's hand. Though too young to understand everything, Casey sensed enough to know that the pastor had breached some code, had violated a trust his mom had placed in him.

His teeth ground together and his embarrassment changed to anger. The preacher had no right to hold his mom up to public ridicule! He felt like standing up and shouting at the man or taking a hymnal and throwing it at him. But he did neither. He sat with his mom through the rest of the service, and then he stood up and stalked out, his anger sinking like black ink deep into his soul, a stain that nothing since had ever washed out. He and his mom never again walked through the doors of that or any other church. From that day forward, he decided he couldn't trust religious people.

Now, squeezing the bill of his hat, he smiled grimly. Meeting his informant in a church had been an act born of necessity—the price of his increasing celebrity. To meet an informant and keep it secret, he had to hide out in the last place anyone expected to see him—a Catholic church. A good place for such a meeting, really—dark and quiet. And, best of all, not a likely hangout for anyone who might recognize him. He checked his watch— 7:14—plenty dark outside.

He heard footsteps on the marble, then felt someone slide in beside him from the opposite end of the pew. He glanced over. A man with a salt-and-pepper mustache, shoulders as wide as a small tractor, and dressed from head to toe in black slid closer. Sterling held up a hand, palm out, and the man stopped sliding. Sterling started to speak, but a woman with two teenage girls stepped past him and plopped down in the pew directly in front of his. He jerked his head at the man in black, then picked up his hat, eased out of the pew and over to an empty grotto. A statue of a man in a tunic and sandals stood before him, a row of burning candles arrayed around the marble saint. The black clad man moved to Sterling's side, his eyes down.

"Good evening, Guisseppe," Sterling said softly from the corner of his mouth. "Long time, no see."

Guisseppe smiled, displaying a gold-capped upper front tooth. "You no come to Italy in a long time," he said, his accent quiet but lilting. "You don't like us?"

To his surprise, the woman with the two teenagers suddenly stood and moved toward them. He gritted his teeth, left the grotto, and walked to the front vestibule of the church. Guisseppe followed, his black boots clicking on the marble.

Alone with Guisseppe again, Sterling picked up the conversation. "I was here less than a year ago," he reminded his informant. "When the last pope died. Quite a spectacle—more pomp and circumstance than a queen's coronation. I stayed until Clement's election, almost three weeks in your blessed Rome. You ought to make me an honorary member of the Catholic Church."

"Honorary member?" Guisseppe asked, obviously not understanding the term.

"Yeah, 'cause I . . . oh, never mind."

"You mad at me last time I see you," Guisseppe said, his face turning sad. "That makes me feel bad."

Sterling studied his man for several seconds. He had known Guisseppe for almost three years, had met him the first time he came to Rome. The previous pope had taken ill, and most of the world thought he had but days to live. He had flown over to make sure that the American public had a front-row seat through the good and faithful cameras of CBC. An old hand at CBC who had once served as Rome Bureau Chief for the Associated Press had given him Guisseppe's name.

"Guisseppe's well-connected," said the former bureau chief. "Got a brother who's an administrator for one of the cardinals. Some say he's tied to the Italian mob too. Not a choirboy, but if you need information, Guisseppe's your man."

Sterling stared down at his hat. His friend at CBC had steered him well. Guisseppe had delivered more than once. But the one time he hadn't delivered had been the most crucial.

Sterling faced the Italian. "You didn't get me what I needed last time," he said, though not really angry anymore. "I'm not pleased when I don't get what I want. Especially when I pay top dollar for it."

Guisseppe shrugged and his stout shoulders almost covered his ears. "What you ask is impossible," he said. "Nobody knows the name of next pope. The cardinals vote in secret. Security very tight. Nobody talks until white smoke comes from the chimney."

Sterling twirled his hat on his index finger. He knew the tradition. The cardinal electors go into sequestration. The Swiss Guard confiscates all communications devices—no phones, no faxes, no email. The electors vote twice a day. Then they burn the pieces of paper on which they marked their choices. If no pope receives the two-thirds majority necessary for election, a cardinal's assistant adds a chemical to make the smoke from the ballots black. The smoke floats up from the chimney above the Sistine Chapel. Seeing the black smoke, the crowds waiting outside know they will wait at least one more day to greet the next pontiff. But if the electors choose their man, the assistant adds a chemical to make sure the smoke burns white. The white smoke shows that God has worked and that the new Vicar of Christ will soon make his appearance.

Sterling stopped twirling his hat. All a bunch of religious hocus-pocus, in his opinion. Different from the stuff he experienced in his boyhood days in Swansboro, but still a bunch of useless superstition. Suddenly anxious to leave the church, he cleared his throat and stared at Guisseppe again.

"Let's walk," he said, heading for the double wooden doors that fronted the church.

"But it's cold outside!" Guisseppe protested.

Slipping on his hat, Sterling never slowed. Guisseppe tagged along behind him, his thick body clomping down the concrete steps of the church.

"What's Clement's condition?" Sterling asked, his head down into the wind. "The Vatican tells us nothing."

"No one says much," Guisseppe said. "It's quiet like a tomb."

Sterling suddenly stopped and faced Guisseppe. "Don't give me that nonsense," he spat. "Cardinals talk more than a bunch of farmers at a barbershop. They're worse than preachers."

Guisseppe scowled, looking confused. "I know nothing about this 'barbershop' talk," he said. "But everybody stays silent at the Vatican. I still listen, but so far nothing, I tell you. The press men from the Vatican say pope is resting, that is all I know."

Though not happy, Sterling recognized he had pushed as far as he could. If Guisseppe knew anything more, he would have told him. Grunting, he started walking again. His throat ached as if someone had dragged a broken bottle across his tonsils. Guisseppe tagged along at his side.

"Keep your ears open," he said to his informant. "You know how to reach me."

"I do my work good. You can count on Guisseppe."

Sterling turned right at the next corner and Guisseppe went left. As he walked toward his hotel, Sterling coughed again. His whole body hurt. He was far from home, and he felt lonelier than he had ever felt in his life. But he had a story to report, and so he kept his head down and his jaw set.

EIGHTEEN

Snuggling into the leather seat of the black limousine that she shared with Russell Chadwick, Valerie pulled her tan trench coat closer to her shoulders and shivered. Outside the car, the day was slate gray and pouring rain. Not exactly weather to lift the spirits.

The last few days had been some of the worst of her life. The weekend had passed slowly—her mom and dad fussing over her as if she had less than a month to live. But that kind of attention had gotten old fast, and she flew back to Atlanta on Monday morning determined to get a grip. This self-pity had its limits! But then things became even bleaker. With Chadwick still at home recovering from his injuries, the rest of the crew drifted in and out of the offices all day Monday and Tuesday, their attitudes frosty when they saw her. She tried to talk to them, but to little avail. Even Ted, usually civil at least, kept his eyes down and said little in her presence. No wonder! Her big idea had almost gotten Chadwick and a lot of other people killed. Ted and Lester and Rodney hated her and she couldn't blame them. Trying to ignore their silence, she puttered around the office each day, her mind blank, her body still tired and emotionally spent.

Casey Sterling had called once from Rome, but that had only confused her. Was he actually interested in her? But why? Other than the fact that they both had a background in media and had survived a terrorist attack together, they had absolutely nothing in common.

She found his roses, faded and still in the box, in her bedroom when she came back to Atlanta. The other three arrangements were also there—one of them from her uncle, a second from her mom and dad, and a third with a card that said, "That's my story," but had no name to identify the sender. Puzzled, she studied the flowers and the card for several minutes but came to no conclusions about their origins. The words on the card seemed vaguely familiar but she couldn't say from where. Telling herself she'd worry about it later, she took one more whiff of the arrangements, then placed them all, including Sterling's roses, in the trash can.

Growing more and more depressed, she begged off her parents' invitation to come back home for Thanksgiving and spent the whole day in her apartment eating ice cream and Coke floats and watching television. If not for the fact that her uncle had surprised her with a phone call late on Thursday, she might have remained there for days, her hair in a dirty bun, her bare feet on the coffee table, her eyes glazed from too many hours of useless television. But then the call came. And though it hadn't solved any of the deeper issues churning around in her gut, the assignment he had laid out for her had snapped her out of her funk, at least for the time being.

So now here she was with Chadwick two days after Thanksgiving, just past the airport in Belfast, headed to the Central Correctional Institute of Northern Ireland. She glanced over at her uncle. The man really was remarkable. Ignoring both his doctor's advice and his wife's pleading to rest up for a few more days, he had left all the crew but Valerie and his security team and flown back into Belfast. She marveled once again at his physical stamina and spiritual depth. Not only did he seem fully recovered from his concussion, but he had insisted that he had to return here as quickly as possible so he could personally meet and forgive the man who had caused his injuries in the first place.

That man, one Ian O'Fallon, had done more, of course, than give Chadwick a concussion. By coming back into the church, he had also saved Chadwick's life and the lives of hundreds of others. But, quite obviously, he had forfeited his own freedom by doing so. The news media, led by Casey Sterling, had chronicled the details of O'Fallon's confession so thoroughly that everyone in the world knew the story.

Thirty-four years old, with a preschool daughter named Heather, O'Fallon worked as a tax clerk in Belfast's City Hall. After his wife was murdered by terrorists three years earlier, he became part of a group that had planted bombs all over Northern

Ireland in the weeks just before the attempt at Prestwick Church. The goal of his terrorist band had been straightforward—hurt no one but blame the bombings on the Irish Republican Army. Even the deaths at City Hall had been inadvertent.

The attack on the church, though, had been different. There, in a twisted effort to demonstrate their resolve to never give up, they wanted to kill as many as possible. But, for reasons no one could yet fathom, O'Fallon had disrupted the plans that day. Instead of killing, he became an angel of mercy. The man was a terrorist. He was also a hero. Now he awaited trial in Northern Ireland's courts.

The limousine turned left, and Valerie wondered if O'Fallon's actions at Prestwick would help him when his case came to trial. Would he get the death penalty for his actions before Prestwick? In spite of the fact that he saved so many lives and had given the authorities the names of his companions in the attack? Did Northern Ireland even have the death penalty? Other than through the bars of a jail cell, would he ever get to see his daughter again?

The street came to a dead end and the limousine stopped. Putting her thoughts on hold, Valerie piled out behind Chadwick as the driver opened the door. The wind jerked at her face and a fresh torrent of rain washed down on her head. She touched the spot behind her ear where her stitches had been. At least those were gone.

A trio of prison officials greeted them briefly, then led them inside.

"We don't get many visitors like you," said the man who was introduced as the director of the Institute. He indicated Chadwick.

"I'm grateful for your cooperation," Chadwick said, his face serene. "And thank you for keeping the press out of this."

The director nodded, then stepped back and indicated Chadwick should follow him. Without another word, he turned and led them down a dingy hallway, his two assistants peeling off as they passed an office about forty feet down.

"The wages of sin," Chadwick mumbled to Valerie. "Places like this."

Valerie studied the place as they were led into an inner office. A number of secretaries looked up but didn't say anything as they passed. The office walls were as bleak as the day outside—the tan paint peeling, the furniture sagging and stained, the light

hazy and full of shadows. Valerie's spirits sank. Two days after
Thanksgiving and she, the only one of Chadwick's inner group
other than Kent without a spouse and children, had willingly accepted his invitation to accompany him on this trip. Now she
wished she had found a reason to stay home. Her work history
hadn't exactly prepared her for this kind of thing.

The director led them through a security checkpoint, the
heavy steel doors clanging hard behind them as they walked
past. "Your request was most unusual," he said.

Chadwick shrugged. "Seems the right thing to do. Like the
Scripture says, 'If you come to the altar and remember that your
brother has ought against you, then leave the altar and go to
your brother and be reconciled to him. Then come back to the
altar to worship the Lord thy God.' "

"Don't get much Scripture here," the director said, leading
them into a small interview room.

"Maybe you should," Chadwick said.

The director pointed them to a single square table that sat
alone, except for three straight chairs, in the center of the room.
"I'll get O'Fallon," he said, leaving them before they could respond.

Valerie took a seat beside Chadwick. He laid his hands on the
table. She noticed his left one quivering. He saw her watching it.

"I've got Parkinson's, you know," he said.

"No, I didn't know," she said.

"Diagnosed about a year ago. It's advancing pretty fast."

"You're still strong as an ox. Men half your age can't keep up
with you."

Chadwick laughed. "The Scripture says, 'thou shalt not lie,'
young lady. Don't you forget it."

The room fell quiet again. Chadwick reached over and took
Valerie's hand. "You okay?" he asked.

She smiled briefly, then lowered her gaze. "I guess. It's just
. . . well, I thought my time with you would get me away from
some of the ugliness I've experienced in the last year."

"That mess with the Ephesus scroll hurt you, didn't it?"

Valerie closed her eyes and replayed, for what must have been
the ten-thousandth time, the most terrifying episode she'd ever
faced. "More than I realized," she said. "I've been pampered all
my life. I used to tell people I lived a 'Norman Rockwell' life—the
perfect American family. Then all that . . ."

"So you came to me expecting nothing more exciting than an ice cream social?"

Valerie laughed. "Well, I wouldn't exactly put it that way."

Just then a door opened and the Institute's director stepped in, an assistant trailing, and a prisoner at his side. Wearing gray overalls, a white sweatshirt, and black sandals with white socks, the prisoner walked with his head down. At first Valerie didn't recognize the man, but then he glanced up at her and she saw it was O'Fallon.

Valerie started to stand and extend her hand but then remembered the conditions of their visit. Though they had thirty minutes with O'Fallon with no glass walls between them, they couldn't touch him. She stayed in place.

"Sit," the director commanded, pointing O'Fallon to the chair across from Valerie and Chadwick. "You have twenty-nine minutes. If you need less, I'll be at the door. Knock and I'll come."

Chadwick kept his eyes locked on O'Fallon. Valerie watched him too, barely noticing as the two officials left and closed the door. O'Fallon kept his head lowered, his hands in cuffs resting on the table. For almost a minute, no one spoke.

"I'm sorry for what happened to your wife," Chadwick said, breaking the silence. "Things like that are wrong."

O'Fallon didn't move.

"I can understand your desire for vengeance," Chadwick continued. "The awful hatred you must have felt."

O'Fallon still didn't respond. Valerie felt herself holding her breath.

"I'm here to thank you," Chadwick said. "To thank you for all the lives you saved, including mine. That was a noble thing you did, the way you gave up your own life to save ours."

Valerie thought she noticed a small nod of O'Fallon's head, but she wasn't sure. She took a breath.

"I hear you have a daughter named Heather," Chadwick said.

O'Fallon lifted his head and Valerie saw black circles under his eyes.

"Is she the reason you saved us?" Chadwick asked. "You saw the children in the choir, children like your own Heather, and you didn't want harm to come to them?"

O'Fallon lowered his gaze again.

"Is that the reason?" Chadwick pressed.

After several seconds, O'Fallon shook his head. "Not really."

"Then why?" Chadwick asked.

"You should know," O'Fallon said, his voice as small as his hands. "You're the preacher."

Chadwick glanced at Valerie. "What's that got to do with it?" he asked.

O'Fallon raised his head and stared at him. "Your preaching . . . what you believe. I'm a . . . well," he hung his head again. ". . . I believe too . . . Least I did as a lad. Me mum taught me right."

Chadwick stayed quiet.

O'Fallon bit his lip, then continued. "I . . . well, I knew from the beginning that what I had done was wrong. It tore me up inside, the people dying and all."

He studied his sandals but kept talking. "At first, when we did the buildings, when no one was hurt, it was okay, a harmless bit of skullduggery, a way to make the popers look bad. But then City Hall came and people showed up when there weren't supposed to be any, and innocent people died. So, after that, what difference did it make to kill a few more? I was already a murderer, already doomed to hellfire. So I went on with me pals' plans, the Prestwick Church with all you high officials to be present." O'Fallon's fingers interlocked in his cuffs, and he worked his thumbs in circles around each other.

"I figured why not? A few more bodies on top of the ones I'd already laid out." He stopped and stared at the dingy walls. His thumbs stopped twirling.

"But then something happened," Chadwick whispered. "Something happened to you in the church?"

"I did what I was told at first," O'Fallon said, his voice also soft. "I entered the church with me mates, pieced the bomb together, placed it in the bell tower." He seemed to have lapsed into a trance, his eyes wide and vacant, staring at the wall, his hands still. Valerie held her breath again. The shadows in the room seemed to dance, and she felt something, something eerie, the strange sensation of another presence in the room. For a second she wondered if the director had come back but then knew he hadn't. What she felt was something different than human. She strained her ears as O'Fallon's voice dropped even lower.

"Me mates left the church. I decided to stay, to stay and ride out the explosion with all the other doomed ones, to meet death head on. I knew Heather would be better off without me . . . living with me folks."

He licked his lips but his eyes never blinked. "Then the

church organ started up. I checked the time. The music was beautiful, like I used to hear when I was but a wee lad. I waited for the explosion. But the organ kept playing . . . and the music was beautiful and something clicked in me head."

Valerie felt the presence again, the eerie sensation of an unseen quivering. But it didn't scare her. Instead, it gave her comfort, a feeling she hadn't experienced much over the last few months. O'Fallon continued.

"All of a sudden I knew I couldn't do it. Couldn't go through with the awful plan, couldn't ignore the teachings of me mum any longer. Here I was about to murder hundreds of people—and not because I believed that deeply in the cause of the Orange, but because I hated those who had killed me dear Rebecca."

He stopped and stared at his hands as if seeing them for the first time. Tears came to his eyes. "She was lovely, you know," he said. "Far too pretty for the likes of me. And kind too, the kindest woman God ever gave breath."

Chadwick placed his hand over O'Fallon's wrists. "Was she a believer too?"

"Aye, a better Christian than any ten others. I knew she didn't want me to hurt anyone else."

"So what happened then?" Chadwick asked, obviously sensing that O'Fallon needed to express the experience, to speak it out and make it real.

O'Fallon lifted his head again. His tears made thin rivers down his cheeks and into the corners of his mouth. "It's like that man . . . that man in the Good Book," he sobbed. "That prodigal man . . . the one who left his family for the country afar away. He realized . . . saw his awful ways."

"The Bible says he 'came to himself,' " Chadwick whispered.

"Aye," O'Fallon agreed. "I came to meself." His tears eased off as he explained. "I realized that you were innocent, you and the pope and all the other priests and preachers with you. You had come there to worship God, to try to help us out of our own mess of killing. I knew you had no motive but to love us. . . ."

"And that's when you rushed to the sanctuary to warn us?"

"Aye, something snapped in me and I knew I couldn't kill anymore. I ran as fast as I could." His voice weakened. "I knew I couldn't disarm the bomb in time, so I ran to you to tell you to get out, to leave before it was too late."

"The Lord changed your heart," Chadwick said.

O'Fallon nodded. "Aye, I'd say that. All of a sudden, me heart flipped over, like a light switch turned on. It wasn't exactly a conversion but a rememberin', a turn back to what me mum said was right and true. I didn't want any more blood on me hands."

Chadwick turned to Valerie. "If any man is in Christ, he is a new creation," he said.

She nodded. "Miracles still happen."

"I guess I'm proof of it," O'Fallon agreed, wiping his face.

Chadwick faced the terrorist again. "We've had no more bombings," he said. "From the IRA, the Orange, or anyone else. And the peace negotiators are back at work. With more momentum than ever."

"Word in here says there won't be any more attacks," O'Fallon said. "Me group was one of the last cells intent on prolonging the hostilities. People are tired of the killing. They want peace."

"Prestwick shocked the world," Valerie said. "The very notion that someone might actually try to murder the pope and the Reverend Chadwick made millions of people realize what they've done to one another. It helped everybody see that the madness has to stop."

"And maybe a few others have remembered what their mums taught them," Chadwick said. "Maybe that's at the bottom of all the recent quiet."

"If God can touch me black heart, then others are certainly possible," O'Fallon agreed. "I hope it's so."

"Do you believe it can last?" Chadwick asked, his eyebrows arched.

"I'm prayin' it will," O'Fallon said.

"In either case you've done what you wanted to accomplish," Valerie said to Chadwick. "Brought the violence to an end. Jumpstarted new peace talks."

"All I did was show up for an explosion," Chadwick said.

"Aye, but it seems that's all it took," O'Fallon said. "A grand gesture."

"The authorities asked me to sit in on the peace negotiations," Chadwick said, staring at the tabletop. "The pope as well. But we agreed that wasn't our work. We can't personally settle the issues that have plagued Ireland for 800 years."

"But you've brought everyone else back to the table," Valerie said. "Mission accomplished."

Chadwick nodded. Valerie checked her watch. They had five more minutes. She indicated the time to Chadwick. He faced O'Fallon again.

"I thank you again," he said. "For saving my life."

"I don't deserve your thanks," O'Fallon said, twirling his thumbs again. "I need your forgiveness."

"But you didn't hurt me."

"I hurt so many . . . so many others."

"Then you need their forgiveness," Chadwick said. "And the Lord's."

"Can the Lord forgive a murderer?"

"You know the answer to that. The Lord can forgive anyone."

O'Fallon stared at his handcuffs. "It's a hard thing to believe."

Chadwick patted his wrists. "You can believe it," he said. "The Bible says it's so."

O'Fallon sighed. "I want that forgiveness. Can you tell me how to get it?"

Chadwick stood and eased around to O'Fallon's side of the table. Placing a hand on the prisoner's head, he said, "Close your eyes, my son. Close your eyes."

O'Fallon obeyed, bowing his head to the table surface.

Valerie clasped her hands together and bowed too.

"We come to you as unworthy people, Lord Jesus," Chadwick started. "All of us stained by sin, none of us righteous, no not one. So we ask for your forgiveness, the power of your Holy Spirit to wash away the blood of our sin. Forgive me my sins, even as I forgive those who sin against me. And forgive my brother's sins too, the sins of Ian O'Fallon. Nail his sins to your cross and burn them away in the white-hot heat of your eternal love for him. Remind him of this wondrous truth, 'Christ showed his love for us in that while we were yet sinners, Christ died for us.' You know his heart, the repentance his actions have shown. Provide for him the grace he has requested, provide for him . . ."

Valerie heard the door open and knew without looking that the director had entered the room.

"You're not supposed to touch the prisoner!" His voice cut through the prayer. "I have to ask you to step back . . ."

Valerie opened her eyes and saw Chadwick stretch his free hand over to the director's shoulder. The man stopped talking as Chadwick's big palm landed on him. Chadwick concluded his prayer. "Give us all your grace, Lord Jesus," he said. "Because we all need it so desperately. Amen."

Finished, he turned to the director and hung his head. "Sorry I broke your rules," he said. "It's not usually my way. But I had to touch this man," he indicated O'Fallon, "because he had already touched me."

Chadwick faced O'Fallon. "If there's anything I can ever do for you or your little girl, don't hesitate to let me know," he said.

"Thank you," O'Fallon said, his eyes moist again. "And thank you for coming."

Five minutes later, Valerie and her uncle checked out of the prison and walked back into the raw outdoors. The limousine driver opened the door and they climbed inside. Exhaling heavily, Chadwick closed his eyes for a moment and leaned back against the seat. The car pulled away from the curb. The rain fell in sheets and the wind buffeted the windshield. Several minutes later, Chadwick opened his eyes and faced Valerie.

"The Lord still touches people," he said, his eyes gleaming.

Nodding, Valerie just sat there. Chadwick grabbed her hand. "O'Fallon said the Lord touched him," he continued. "You heard that, didn't you?"

"Sure, that's what he said."

"Then it can happen to others," beamed Chadwick.

"That's why you do crusades, preach the gospel, lead people to faith."

"But that's not enough!" Chadwick said, obviously not satisfied with her answer. "This whole episode proves we can do more."

"I don't get it," Valerie said. "You almost got killed here. What else are you going to do?"

Chadwick faced the window and stared pensively into the rain. "The news says that the splinter groups in Northern Ireland are laying down their arms. The peace process is on track. We've had no terrorist action since Prestwick. Commentators say something fundamental has changed. They're giving our efforts a lot of credit for that."

"Everyone is grateful," Valerie said. "But your work is done here. No more to do."

He faced her again. "But this isn't the only place," he said. "Kosovo, Rwanda, the border between India and Pakistan, all over the world."

"So?"

"So you heard O'Fallon. If God can touch his heart, God can touch anyone's heart."

"That's what we pray will happen, that God will convert hearts all over the world and bring peace."

Chadwick nodded. "But this time, even though all we did was show up, God gave grace through it. Hearts were changed. If it can happen here . . ."

"It can happen anywhere," Valerie finished his sentence for him.

"You've got it," Chadwick said. "It can happen anywhere."

The limousine plowed through the falling rain but Valerie no longer noticed. Unless she had mistaken his intentions, her Uncle Russell had just decided that Ian O'Fallon was only the beginning, the first step in a journey that would take them further and further into the unknown. Like a storm cloud giving way to other, perhaps even larger and darker storm clouds, Northern Ireland would now recede into the background of the sky to make room for the next conflict to come. And, whether she agreed with him or not, she couldn't back out now. Though she didn't know exactly what he had in mind, she was in this up to her eyeballs with no clear way out. Instead of a place to retreat and regroup, she had found that working for the Reverend Russell Chadwick had become a staging ground for more danger than she had ever imagined.

PART II

Terrors overwhelm me;
My dignity is driven away as by the wind,
My safety vanishes like a cloud.

Job 30:15

The wise man in the storm prays God not for safety
from danger,
but for deliverance from fear.

Emerson, 1833

NINETEEN

The Tuesday after Thanksgiving Russell Chadwick called everyone together again at his retreat center near Big Canoe, Georgia. The center contained twenty bedrooms, a huge kitchen with industrial-sized appliances, and a great room with a fireplace as wide as a garage door that reached all the way to the ceiling. An adjacent building held a workout room, complete with weights, treadmill, StairMaster, and sauna. An Olympic-sized pool provided relief for those who liked to swim. Valerie had been there only once in her life, on a family retreat one summer. Her uncle hadn't even been there at the time. But Valerie and her mom and dad had enjoyed the pool, the hiking trails that ran in and through the sixty-five acres that Chadwick owned, and the five horses that he kept for riding.

Now, dressed casually in jeans and flannel shirt like everyone else in the room, she stood by the fireplace and listened to the crackling of the fire. Her uncle rocked in an oak chair to her left, an afghan on his lap. Lester sat on a tan sofa beside him. Ted lay on his stomach on the floor, his elbows propped under his chest. Suffering from a bad back for the last decade or so, a physical therapist had told him to stretch out this way whenever he could. Just beyond Ted, Rodney sat in a recliner. But he wasn't reclining. He sat on the edge like a bird on a wire, as if anxious to fly if anything bothered him.

Studying the men, Valerie could almost taste the tension. Everyone but Chadwick had arrived by midmorning, and the questions that Ted and Lester and Rodney had popped at her at lunch were endless. But, following her uncle's request, she had refused to say anything about their visit with O'Fallon.

The interrogation continued after lunch. According to the three men, Chadwick came to the cabin only twice a year—for two weeks before and after Christmas and for two weeks before and after the fourth of July. He'd kept that pattern for the last twenty-seven years. So what was up now? Why had he called them here? What had happened in Belfast?

Lester Boggett suggested that maybe Chadwick planned to announce his retirement. Though he never complained, he was obviously losing some stamina. His hands shook a lot. Did he have Parkinson's or something? And maybe he'd name his successor too.

Rodney Kent dismissed the idea. "Everyone knows that Ted is going to take the reins when Russ retires. This is probably about a new series of crusades—plain and simple."

Ted said nothing and Valerie followed his lead, keeping her own counsel and deflecting questions when they asked her opinion. She didn't know for sure what Chadwick planned to do, and that was the truth. But she didn't think it had anything to do with a possible successor.

At five o'clock, her uncle had finally arrived, his two bodyguards in tow. The place felt like opening night of a Broadway play. Something was about to happen but nobody knew just what.

Now Chadwick stopped rocking and cleared his throat. Valerie held her breath.

"I know you're all wondering why I called you here," he began.

"No," mocked Lester. "That's the furthest thing from our minds."

Chadwick smiled, but only briefly, and everyone knew that Lester's banter was out of place. No one else would try that.

"I apologize for the mystery," Chadwick continued. "But the last few weeks have been really tough for me, last week most of all. I went to see Ian O'Fallon—you know that. But you don't know what he told me."

He stared around the room as if waiting for an answer. When no one spoke, he started up again. "He told me he warned us to get out of the church because God changed his heart."

"Wonderful," Ted said. "The power of the Lord is a glory to behold."

For a few moments, everyone stayed quiet. Valerie eased closer to the fire.

Chadwick fluffed his afghan and stared down at his hands.

"I'm scared of what I'm about to say," he whispered. "But I believe God has been speaking to me." He looked up again as if daring anyone to interrupt. "I believe it as strongly as anything I've ever believed."

No one challenged him.

"I believe the Lord wants me to do what I did in Ireland in other places."

Everyone seemed too shocked to counter.

Valerie leaned against the mantel as Chadwick pressed ahead.

"Just think about all the places where human beings do despicable things to one another, where they kill and maim and pillage. It's an abomination, a stench in the nostrils of God." He lowered his gaze.

Valerie thought she saw tears in his eyes.

"None of us argue with that," Ted said, finding his voice as Chadwick gathered himself. "But that's work for diplomats, not us."

"In a sense, you're right," agreed Chadwick. "Our business is to preach the gospel. It always has been. But, like I said before Ireland, maybe the Lord wants us to do more."

"How do you plan to do that?" Lester asked, ever the pragmatist. "You and the pope pulled the last one off. But that was a Catholic-Protestant thing. No one wanted to hurt either of you. But in these other places, some lunatics would like nothing better than to kill off a Christian leader—Protestant *or* Catholic. To them, you and the pope are both infidels. You have no standing whatsoever."

Chadwick propped his elbows on the rocker and started moving again. "I admit it's tricky," he said. "But I've been praying about it. I've had . . . I don't know . . . certainly not a dream this time, but I've had a strange sense of direction on this. I want to be a peacemaker, but I can't go it alone. I need others." He reached into his shirt pocket, pulled out a piece of paper, and unfolded it. Patting it down in his lap, he faced Lester.

"I don't know all of these people," he said. "But I'm going to try to form an alliance of religious leaders from all over the world, men and women of all faiths, people who—"

"You're going to all these hot spots?" Ted asked, off the floor now and on the sofa. "Place yourself in danger again? Take a slew of other people with you?"

Chadwick shrugged. "It worked in Ireland."

Lester exploded from the sofa. "Nothing worked in Ireland," he shouted. "You almost got killed! That's not exactly 'Peace in Our Time,' now, is it?"

"But just going made a difference, you know it did. We accomplished what I set out to do. The bombings have ceased and the peace negotiations have started again."

"But you can't do it again!" Lester continued, his face turning red. "Your life is too important! What happens to your work if you get hurt, or—God forbid the thought—killed this time? And what about your supporters? They'll think you've gone senile! I've already started getting calls, from important people too. How can you even suggest such a thing? Endanger your own life, join forces again with nonbelievers like—"

Chadwick held up a hand and Lester sputtered to a halt. "I'm well aware of the dangers here," he said. "But let me finish. Here are the people I want to consider. They don't represent every major religion, but they almost do, and they're the most prominent religious leaders in the world." He held up the list and began to read.

"Pope Clement, of course. He's vital to all of this. Plus, the Dalai Lama brings in the Buddhists. The Rabbi Yoachim ben Moseph represents Judaism; the Ayatollah Kahil Khatama, the Muslims; Martha Sophia Blevins, the guru for that whole New Age crowd; and Luis Zorella, the Latino Pentecostal. That makes seven of us. Maybe later I'll add a few more if these come on board."

Valerie's knees almost buckled. She had forgotten her dream in the hospital! A thundering herd headed to an abyss, six horses and a man on a donkey between them and death. Her dream embodied through Chadwick's scheme? But how—?

"Sounds like the seven-headed beast of Revelation thirteen," Lester mumbled, cutting off her thoughts.

"Or the number of letters the apostle John wrote to the churches," Ted countered, obviously disturbed by Lester's statement. "Seven is the perfect number in Greek thought."

"Yeah, well, I don't think our people will see it that way," Lester continued. "Four of these people aren't even Christian, much less Protestant. And we're going to join up with them to bring about some kind of universal peace?" He snorted and threw his hands down in a dismissive gesture. For several seconds, everyone became quiet.

Chadwick rubbed through his hair. "I know it's a long shot," he said. "And I know I'll take some criticism for working with non-Christians. But I've given that a lot of prayer. And I think the Lord has given me some scripture. I wouldn't do it if I couldn't find Biblical support for it, you know that. But do you remember the man casting out demons in Mark's Gospel, chapter nine, verses thirty-eight through forty? The disciples didn't like it because the man wasn't one of their group. But remember what Jesus said? 'He who is not against us is for us.' "

"The truth of the matter is that God used nonbelievers to do His work in a number of occasions in the Scriptures. I mean, look at Rahab, a harlot and a non-Jew used by God to assist Joshua when he went in to spy out the Promised Land. And the Chaldeans? According to the book of Habakkuk, God raised them up to punish Judah for their evil."

"It's not gonna happen," Boggett said, dismissing Chadwick's logic. "No reason to even talk about it. These people have their own agendas and organizations. To think they're going to put everything aside and join us in some kind of idiot notion . . ." He stopped and shook his head.

Pushing aside her dream for a second, Valerie admitted to herself that Lester had a point. It was a long shot. Yet she knew not to underestimate her uncle. No one had believed in him in the beginning either, back when he was just the son of an Iowa pig farmer, back when he came out of an independent Bible college and started preaching in the small churches that dotted the Midwest. Though his preaching filled the churches almost from the beginning, it took years before anyone beyond the flatlands of mid-America heard of him. But the amazing thing was, he didn't care if anyone ever did. That was his genius and his gift. He preached not because he cared about the size of the crowd or the applause of the public but because he cared about the saving of souls. He was twenty when he started preaching, thirty-seven the year the national media first put him in its spotlight.

Valerie remembered the night her mom turned on the television and she saw her uncle on screen for the first time. A tornado had ripped through the heart of Oklahoma killing sixty-one people. One of the networks had decided to televise the funeral service of a family—a mom, a dad, and four children—that had perished in the killer storm. The church where the service was held was without a pastor at the time, and the elders had asked the evangelist who had been there for a spring revival to preach the funeral. The cameras framed Chadwick perfectly as he stood at the simple wooden pulpit, his six feet six inches making it appear small next to his height. His strong blue eyes seemed to pierce the very soul of the nation, and his voice laid a spell on the millions who watched, the comforting spell of a best friend offering a shoulder for a country's tears.

The nation fell in love with him as he offered words of Scripture in gentle tones. Valerie could still remember the concluding words Chadwick spoke.

"In fiery trials, God will see us through; in deserts of despair, God will see us through; in thunderous storms, God will see us through. If you live by faith in Jesus—come life or death or success or failure or temptation or triumph—no matter what steps into the path of your life, God will see you through."

"The Reverend Russell Chadwick speaks to us all," said the broadcast commentator as he wrapped up his coverage of the funeral. "God will indeed see us through."

From that night on, Russell Chadwick began his rise to prominence in the consciousness of America. Within five years, he had made the cover of every major news publication in the country. But he had never sought popularity and had never let it go to his head or his heart. Through all those years, he had sought only one thing—the clear voice of God speaking to his soul.

Had he heard God correctly this time? Valerie wondered. Or was Lester right? Was this all too silly to even consider? Had her uncle finally come to the end of his road? Was this notion the insane considerations of a man only a step or two away from senility? Even more to the point for her, did this really have some connection to her frightening dream? Should she tell him what had happened in the hospital? Did God work in such ways anymore? With so many unanswered questions, she decided to say nothing.

His hands shaky, Chadwick took the afghan, folded it neatly, and laid it across the arm of the sofa where Lester sat. Then he pushed up from the chair and walked over to the fireplace by Valerie. Propping a hand on the mantel, he cleared his throat and faced his team.

"I know we've all got a lot of questions," he said. "But I aim to do this. For better or for worse, I'm going to expend my last breath if necessary to make this happen." He began to pace in front of the fireplace. "I also know you didn't sign on with me so many years ago to do this kind of work. You're crusade folks, like me. Deep down, that's what you want to do. Bring the people to hear the Word of God—organize it, plan it, preach it, sing it. That's what God called us to do, and it's what we do best."

He stopped and rested his hand on the back of his rocker. "I may be way off base this time. So I don't expect you to go along with me if you don't want to do this, if you don't believe it's the Lord's will for you.

He stretched to his full height. "I'm pressing on, crazy or not, until the Lord shows me otherwise, and I'm asking you to help me. But, if you opt out now, I've got no hard feelings. We've had a long ride together. But I'm tired now, and sick—"

"You're strong as a—" Lester interrupted.

"Let me finish," Chadwick silenced him with a wave of his hand. "I've got Parkinson's. You've already guessed it, and you're right. I'm on medication but it's getting worse. I don't know how much longer I can keep preaching. So maybe this is the end of the Chadwick crusades. Maybe this is the Lord's last commission for me. I don't know, but I'm willing to find out. We've done some good things over the years. But I think the Lord is in this new thing and I can't say no if I think the Lord wants me to say yes. All of you know that."

They all nodded.

"When this ends, for good or bad, we'll get back together and decide whether we want to start preaching again. But you've got to decide whether you're in or out on this. No matter what you do, I love you. You're the best friends a man could ever have. I just ask you to do this for me, this one thing. If you say you're in, you can't drop out later. You have to go all the way. I'll not have any quitters in this bunch. Just make your choice and stick by it. Okay?"

He looked from one face to the other. For several seconds no one moved. Chadwick held out his right hand. "Who's with me?" he asked.

Valerie heard the fire crackle as the logs shifted and fell in on each other, but she still felt cold. Chadwick's idea, a logical extension of what had happened in Ireland, brought a lot of danger with it. If, by some miracle the other religious leaders actually signed on, not everyone would like it. People who profited from violence wouldn't take kindly to anyone trying to put an end to it.

Chadwick's right hand began to shake. Everyone stayed still. A pall fell over Valerie. She glanced over at Ted, Rodney, and Lester. One of them needed to support her uncle! But none did.

Chadwick dropped his hand and, visibly weaker, staggered to the rocker. Valerie's eyes watered. She didn't want to get into this. It wasn't her fight. She had just come out of an awful situation, one filled with death. She'd lost Michael, the man she had grown to love! How could she jump into this now? She had come to her uncle because she wanted a place of refuge, a haven where she could piece her life back together, a quiet job with no complications and no chance for more hurt. She wanted time to think through her faith and come to some conclusions about her relationship to God. But now this.

In his rocker, Chadwick closed his eyes. Valerie stared at her uncle's trio of friends again. Still, none of them moved to his side. Unable to stand it any longer, Valerie stepped to him, placing her hand on his shoulder.

"I . . . don't know how to say this," she mumbled. "But I had a dream too."

"A dream?" Chadwick looked up at her, appearing confused. "What kind of dream?"

She stepped back a pace. "Well, the night after I came back from Ireland. I was still in the hospital. It was crazy. A whole herd of horses, all headed over a cliff . . ." She described what she had seen. "But then six horses appeared, each of them a different color. And one donkey, with a faceless man on its back." She told Chadwick how the horses and the donkey stood there, a barrier between the herd and the abyss. The room became still, all the men transfixed by her story.

Chadwick seemed stunned—his eyes blank as she talked. When she had finished, he just sat there for what seemed like forever. Then Lester spoke, his derision obvious.

"Well, Lord help us," he said. "Miss Miller here suffers a bad dream while all drugged up in the hospital, and we're—"

Chadwick silenced him with a look that could've cut glass.

"You're with me then?" Chadwick asked Valerie, without commenting on the dream.

"Yes," she said. "Though I don't know what I can do."

Chadwick nodded. Behind her, Kent stepped over.

"Give me your hand," he said. "You're the Lord's man. I can't argue with that." He took the hand Chadwick extended.

"I thought we'd always do crusades," Ted whispered, his eyes studying the floor.

"And you thought you'd succeed me," Chadwick said. "Maybe you will, but I just can't say that right now."

Ted stared over at him. Valerie tried to read Ted's eyes but they were indecipherable. But then, his jaw set, Ted walked over and laid his hand on Kent's. Only Lester held out.

"What'll we do next, read some goat innards?" Lester asked, gritting his teeth. "It's lunacy. A bunch of silly dreams."

"Maybe you're right," Chadwick whispered. "But an ark was lunacy too. Noah built it anyway."

"I can't 'out-Bible' you," Lester said. "No one can."

"I need you," Chadwick said. "You know that."

Lester stepped to Chadwick and placed both his hands on top of the others. Standing in the clutch of men, Valerie listened to their breathing and smelled the fire burning, and a strange sense of destiny overwhelmed her. Maybe God didn't want her in a safe place. Maybe God wanted her right here. Like Abraham of old, she was walking toward a strange land and she didn't know her final destination. Whether God had given her the dream and was therefore directing the trip or not, she didn't know. But she had made her decision. She was ready to head out and it scared her to death.

TWENTY

Sitting in the back of a black town car on the freeway four miles from the Los Angeles airport, Valerie fingered the scar under her ear and tried to slow down her breathing. Ever since Chadwick's announcement of what Lester had taken to calling "The Peace Project," she had been unable to eat much, sleep much, or breathe much. She felt like an engine with the idle set too high. Her wheels were spinning and her mind was clicking, and if someone had told her to paint the face of Mount Rushmore with whitewash, she felt as if she could do it in one day.

In one way, she welcomed all the excitement. It gave her an escape from the depression she had fought for the last several months. As long as she stayed busy, she at least felt alive and useful, a far better feeling than the soggy bread sensation that had gripped her so much lately.

Chadwick had outlined the strategy and parceled out the assignments before the team left his retreat. He would make preliminary contacts with each of the six religious leaders and ask them to receive him or one of his envoys for a meeting. Since he already had personal relationships with the Dalai Lama and Rabbi Yoachim ben Moseph, he would take Lester Boggett and make the face-to-face calls on the two of them if they allowed it. Plus, he'd tackle the Ayatollah Kahil Khatama, probably the most difficult of the six to sign onto the plan.

Since she spoke reasonable Spanish, Valerie and Rodney Kent would go to Mexico City to visit Luis Zorella. And since she was a woman, she would make the personal call on Martha Sophia Blevins. Kent had protested his assignment, arguing that he should stay with Chadwick, but no one argued for long with Russell Chadwick. In the meantime, Ted would return to Atlanta and make contingency plans to transport, house, and accommodate any and all who actually accepted Chadwick's invitation to meet face-to-face and talk about the possibilities.

The town car swerved around a corner and Valerie felt a touch of nausea hit her. Trying to ignore the feeling, she glanced over at Rodney Kent. He had a *Business Week* in his hand and seemed oblivious to his surroundings. To her surprise, he had become even quieter than normal in the last few days as they traveled together. During their time in Mexico City, his demeanor had become more and more aloof, almost rudely so. She had carried the conversation with Luis Zorella, the Hispanic evangelist and faith healer. She had told him how crucial he was to the operation, how they couldn't expect to win the support of many Third World factions without a man of his stature, his ethnicity, his charisma.

———

Zorella was thirty-eight years old but appeared at least ten years younger. His eyes were as black as motor oil, as was the hair he slicked back in thick waves from his square forehead. Not overly tall, he was slender, with teeth miraculously straight and white for a man born in the back streets of Mexico City. One of seven peasant children with an absent father, he had lived on the street, penniless and uneducated. Caught for stealing at the age of nine, he was sent to a church-sponsored school for wayward boys. He ran away from the school the next year. At the age of twelve, he was converted to Christian faith by a stern man who dispensed stale bread, warm milk, the alphabet, and fierce Pentecostal gospel in equal proportions from the front steps of a street-side church.

By the time he was fifteen, Zorella had started to preach in the narrow lanes of Mexico City's back alleys. Picking up bits and scraps of education as he grew into manhood, he became a self-taught success. He spoke English fluently, though his speech was laced with a Hispanic accent. Those who had watched his progress over the last two decades seemed to agree that God had gifted him with an uncanny sense of the dramatic. His fame had gradually seeped beyond the borders of Mexico, and hundreds of thousands of worshipers now flocked to soccer fields all over Central and South America to hear his fiery sermons and watch the colorful spectacle of his crusades. People by the scores claimed that his hands felt warm when he touched them and that the power of the Holy Spirit flowed through his fingers and that ailments of all kinds disappeared into the sea of God's mercy when he anointed them with holy oil and prayed for them. Among the masses of the Third World, he was often called "The Hand of God," and he had begun to get calls from Korea and China and other Asian nations inviting him to come and teach the secret of his work.

Zorella had impressed Valerie in their four-hour meeting. His surroundings weren't fancy—a house no bigger than that of a middle-class American, his demeanor comfortable and not showy, his handshake firm and his eyes steady. He didn't have a big entourage either, unlike so many religious leaders who had taken on the air of celebrity. Just a brother named José and a couple of secretaries.

After listening to her speech, Luis and José had asked for a few minutes of privacy to talk through the matter.

"Of course," she agreed. "Take as long as you need."

Sitting in the small office they kept in a corner room of their house, she watched the two of them leave the room. José looked like a carbon copy of Luis, only three to five years younger, by her guess. A few minutes later, she heard shouting in the next room, the two brothers obviously disagreeing. Though her Spanish was rusty and she felt guilty for eavesdropping, she leaned as close as possible to the wall and listened to their dispute.

"But you don't need Chadwick," José shouted. "You are the new man of God. Everyone knows that. As soon as he is gone—"

"But perhaps this is a good thing," Luis interrupted. "Perhaps a true movement of the Spirit of the Lord."

Their voices dropped a notch and she couldn't make out anything more. But the conversation lasted another ten minutes. When they emerged from the room, however, they both smiled, though José's smile seemed to have an edge on it.

"I am open to more conversation on this matter," Luis said, "though I have to admit I have some concerns."

"Certainly," Valerie said. "I expected as much."

"I have been praying for God to do some great thing," Luis continued. "In this new millennium, we have to end the warring, the killing of the people. If such a miracle as your Reverend Chadwick suggests could take place, we could take the money the nations now spend on weapons and use it for the poor. Money now spent for bullets and tanks and food for soldiers could go for bread and shelter and food for children. If your Reverend Chadwick, a man whom I admire much, has a plan to make such things happen, my ears are ready to hear it."

He looked to José, then back to her and Kent. "When will the Reverend Chadwick announce all of this to the world?"

Valerie looked to Kent. "As soon as we get everyone on board," he said. "Assuming that happens, of course."

Zorella nodded. "My first thought is a positive one," he said, "if the Reverend Chadwick can answer a few questions. Let me know what you want me to do."

———

The town car darted past a line of stopped cars, wheeled off the interstate, and began the climb into the hills outside of Los Angeles. The queasiness came to Valerie's stomach again but it passed almost immediately. For a second, she wondered if she had some kind of virus, but then she forgot it and concentrated on her surroundings. According to Valerie's research, Martha Sophia Blevins lived free of charge in a sprawling contemporary villa donated by a wealthy philanthropist to Blevins' organization, "The Center for Harmonic Prosperity."

The road snaked past a succession of mansions and became much steeper. Palm trees and manicured yards surrounded the homes.

"This one feels funny," Valerie said to Rodney Kent.

He looked up from his magazine. "Why so?" His silence at Zorella's had only worsened on the way to Martha Blevins' place. Now he seemed morose, sullen even.

"Well, it's obvious, isn't it? Blevins isn't even a Christian. She's a New Age disciple—claims she's talked to spirits of the dead. And she believes in reincarnation."

Kent laid his magazine in his lap. "Then let's not go."

"You know we can't do that."

"The whole scheme is pretty loony if you ask me. And Blevins is worst of all. But Russell says we've got to have her on board. Millions of people hang on her every word. She's as popular in England as she is here, and Australia and New Zealand too. Plus, she's a woman. And no offense, but like everything else these days, we can't do this without some 'politically correct' diversity."

Valerie bit her tongue. As the only woman connected to her uncle's inner circle, she often felt out of place. But she didn't want to make an issue of it. She knew she had the credentials to do the

job he had hired her to do, and the fact that she wore a skirt and
high heels from time to time had nothing to do with her capabilities. But credentials or not, the trio would never fully accept her
into the circle. As both a newcomer and a woman, she had too
many hurdles to jump for that to happen.

Stopping at a black wrought-iron gate, the car's driver lowered his window and spoke to a security guard. The gate opened
and the car passed through. A two-story white stone English
Tudor home with ivy growing all over the front stood straight
ahead. When their car reached the front door and stopped, Valerie and Kent climbed out. Before they could ring the bell, the
door opened and a woman with frizzy gray hair greeted them
wearing a tan straight-lined sleeveless dress and low-heeled
brown sandals. At first Valerie thought it was Blevins, but then
the woman spoke and she knew better.

"Please follow me," the woman said, closing the door behind
her. "I'm Daphne Farmer, Ms. Blevins' personal assistant. Ms.
Blevins is waiting to meet you." Without another word, she led
them to an arbor on the side of her house. Some kind of evergreen
vine covered the arbor, and a collection of chairs, swings, and
hammocks awaited occupants beneath it. A sundial rested on a
waist-high stand behind the hammock, and a sculpture in the
shape of a pyramid loomed as tall as a moving van to the left of
the sundial. A small fountain gurgled water through the mouth
of a frog in the center of the chairs.

Martha Blevins rose from her seat and stepped toward Valerie and Rodney. She was bare-footed, had a head of frizzy gray
hair like her assistant, and was dressed almost exactly like her
as well. Was it a uniform of some kind? Or just the simple garb
of the New Age, middle-aged woman—all plain, earth-toned, and
full-bodied? Valerie knew from her notes that Blevins was fifty-
nine years old, had been divorced three times, and had no children that anyone knew about—a most unusual woman.

"Welcome to Harmonic Prosperity," Blevins said, her arms
open as if greeting a favorite family member. "I've felt your presence here for the last hour."

Glancing quickly at Kent, Valerie stepped to Blevins and accepted the hug. Blevins' arms were warm and soft, and Valerie
briefly remembered hugging her grandmother in just this manner years ago. Though resisting the feeling, she liked Blevins'
kind embrace. But then her stomach clutched up on her and a
wave of nausea rolled through it. Taking a deep breath, she

pushed down the sick feeling and stepped back.

Their hostess turned to Kent, her arms still open. Kent kept his distance, offering a hand instead. Blevins pushed a strand of hair from her forehead and indicated they should sit. Kent and Valerie took seats in white wooden chairs on either side of the gurgling frog. Blevins chose a hammock opposite them, perched on the edge, and began to swing. Daphne Farmer took a seat on a bench behind the hammock.

"I love this spot," Blevins said, her bare toes swishing along the top of the grass at her feet. "It brings out the natural quiet in people."

Valerie wondered if the woman's toes were cold. The day, though warm for December, was not exactly what she'd call hot.

"Reverend Chadwick called you a few days ago," Kent said, obviously anxious to get the conversation moving to more practical matters.

"He did," Blevins said, staring at the sky. "The man is such an inspiration. His aura ripples through the whole universe, changing everything it touches. I went to hear him speak two years ago when he came to San Francisco." The hammock picked up pace as she talked. "I mean, the Reverend just glowed. You could see the presence of all that's good quivering in the aura around his head. He's a channel of the cosmos."

She stopped and stared at Valerie as if expecting her to concur. Valerie stared back, alternately attracted and repelled by the woman. On the one hand, she seemed so calm, so at ease, so much consumed by an inner peace, a peace that Valerie now coveted. On the other hand, she wondered what in the world the woman was smoking. She seemed so "other-worldly," almost as if she walked without touching the ground.

She knew about people like Blevins, of course, people who combined their religions like mixed nuts in a can—a bit of this with a touch of that and a smidgen of something else. But meeting such an eclectic person up close felt disconcerting. For the first time since her uncle had mentioned his idea, she truly understood how difficult it would be to merge all these people for one common goal. How could two people as different as Blevins and Chadwick work together on anything, much less something as complicated as what Chadwick proposed? And how on earth could you multiply Martha Sophia Blevins by six and expect the whole group to blend? Only God could make this alliance happen. And even then God had to inspire everyone else to cooperate. If one thread in the garment unraveled, the whole piece came loose.

Another shot of nausea hit Valerie but didn't last but a few seconds. She wrapped her hands in her lap and wondered if she had eaten something sour that morning.

"You seem troubled," Blevins said.

Valerie straightened up. "Not particularly."

Blevins scowled as if to contradict but then relaxed again. "Tell me why you've come," she said.

Valerie turned to Kent but he shook his head as if to say, "You tell her. This wasn't my idea."

Though wanting to protest, Valerie deferred. If Rodney wanted to act snotty, so be it.

"Well," she began, "I guess you've heard about Reverend Chadwick's initiative in Ireland with the pope."

Blevins nodded. "A noble effort. The convergence of such holy substance holds much promise."

"Okay, well," continued Valerie, "that seems to have succeeded—"

"At least for now," Kent interrupted.

Blevins jerked her head toward him. "It's working," she defended Chadwick. "You can feel it in the wind. Peace is flowing outward from Ireland. The cosmos is calmer."

Kent looked as if he was about to snicker but caught himself at the last instant.

"Anyway," Valerie continued. "Ireland is quiet, at least for now. Reverend Chadwick believes God is moving there, changing hearts."

"The heart is the only way to peace," Blevins said, her face toward the clouds again.

"Right, so . . . Reverend Chadwick wants to bring together more spiritual leaders who are respected throughout the world. He wants—"

Blevins suddenly stretched out crossways in the hammock, her arms extending over her head to the other side. "He wants to multiply his channels!" she whispered, her eyes round as saucers. "It's the ancient prophecy coming to fruition! The power of the holiest people of the human race merged into one universal stream of consciousness, arching its way into the universal fountainhead of love." The woman closed her eyes and laid her hands under her head. The hammock rocked out and back, out and back.

Valerie glanced at Kent. His lips curled in a kind of quiet derision. Valerie's stomach suddenly rolled as if it had run into a storm at sea. She wrapped her arms around her waist and leaned forward to keep her stomach quiet.

"It's pure potential," Blevins whispered. "Pure untarnished potential. And the Reverend wants me to participate. He's a man with a wide alpha space . . . one of the broadest I've ever touched. . . ."

"Then you'll meet with him and the others?" Valerie asked, her voice tight against the subsiding nausea.

Blevins popped up from the hammock as if ejected from a toaster. "I didn't say that," she said. "It's premature. Come with me." She stalked away from the arbor without further comment, her assistant right behind her.

Valerie hesitated for a second, but then, not knowing what else to do, followed along. Kent trailed behind. At the back of the house, Blevins opened the door and led them inside. They passed through a wide hallway that had a glass ceiling and was filled with ferns. Valerie spotted several rooms off the hallway—bedrooms, a bathroom, and a study.

Blevins turned left and led them into a huge white space, also covered with glass. Mirrors curved around the room in all directions and on all sides. In the center of the room a clear glass ball the size of a Volkswagen Beetle spun around and around on a rotating dais, its sides turning one shade after another as it picked up and reflected the different colors in the room. For a second, Valerie felt as she had as a little girl when she went to the glass house at the fair. Her reflection bounced back at her from all angles, none of which seemed real or solid. It gave her a sense of quivery movement, and for a moment, she feared she might really get sick.

"It's from Switzerland," Blevins said, calling her back to the moment. "From the home of a holy woman who saw far more than she could ever explain to mere mortals like us. A donor brought it to me five years ago. I'm still trying to learn its secrets."

"You sure the woman who owned it was holy?" Kent asked.

Blevins shrugged. "Who's to say what 'holy' is?" she asked.

Valerie started to say something about the biblical definition of the word but then refrained. No reason to get into that argument here. Knowing Blevins' mindset as she did, she suspected the woman would simply accept her viewpoint, then spin it into something she believed anyway. People like Blevins weren't dogmatic. To them, no person's religion was untrue. But then again, no one person's religion was completely true either. In minds like Blevins', all faiths were relative, all claims to exclusivity provincial and rigid. To be truly religious meant to accept all "truth," to reject the particularity of any one claim to God. For people like Blevins, God was a bit like an oblong ooze—a mix and mash of everything and anything that anyone wanted to believe. Their only dogma was that there was no dogma.

"What does this do?" Valerie asked, pushing away her dislike for what Blevins represented and concentrating on the crystal.

"I think you can answer your own question," Blevins said. "Look at it, see if you don't know."

Valerie stared into the ball. The sun's rays drenched down through the glass ceiling and washed through the sphere. Her reflection looked back at her at a distorted angle. She stared at her face—still fairly wrinkle free at thirty, still clear-eyed. But she knew she had become much more negative in the last year, much sadder and less optimistic.

For a few beats, she continued to stare into the ball. It seemed to mesmerize her, glue her in place. Who knew what her future held? Could she overcome the pessimism that her recent troubles had caused?

She noticed a ring of circles under her eyes, dark rims of worry and doubt reflecting back at her. The crystal seemed to grow black all of a sudden, and the despair she had felt for months seemed to rise up from the ball and reach out at her. Her eyes became blacker still, and a shadow seemed to rise out of them and slide out of the orb. The shadow slid around her neck and covered her shoulders and wrapped itself down her waist and hips and knees and ankles. She tried to move but couldn't. Her body felt like a boa constrictor had gripped itself around her chest, and she found herself unable to breathe. Her face contorted as she stared at the orb, and something as empty as death and as cold as a pond in the middle of winter grabbed at her throat.

"I knew you'd see it," Blevins whispered.

The woman's voice snapped Valerie out of the trance the ball had placed on her, and she shivered suddenly and dropped her gaze. With a quick glance, she looked at Kent to see if he had seen what she saw, but he seemed oblivious to the power the crystal ball seemed to emanate. Stepping back as if escaping a poisonous snake, Valerie turned to Blevins.

"It's your basic crystal ball," she said, her voice sounding thin and shaky. "Only much bigger. You actually believe you see the future through it?"

"No one knows who made it," Blevins said, obviously impressed with that fact but ignoring her question. "It has a diamond the size of a quarter in the center. The heat of the universe radiates inside it, the multiple swirls of all that is. Here, you want to touch it?"

Valerie shook her head, a sense of fear gripping her stomach. But then she felt foolish at her hesitance. What harm could the ball do?

Blevins shrugged, walked to the crystal sphere, and laid her hands on it. Then, as if nuzzling a baby's cheek, she rested her face on its side and closed her eyes.

To her left, Kent stepped back a pace but Valerie stayed still. Blevins' lips moved and she started to chant in quiet tones, her words indistinguishable. Her arms stretched out farther and farther, and now she seemed to have wrapped herself completely around the orb. For a second it appeared to Valerie that the thing had begun to glow even more luminously. An eerie quiet fell over the room, and except for Blevins' chanting, everything hung still and silent in the air. An odd dread came over Valerie, and her shoulders slumped and she put her face in her hands.

As if knocked off by an electric shock, Blevins suddenly bounced back off the ball, her arms still in the air over her head, her eyes round in surprise.

"I see evil in all this," she whispered. "A raging beast that will threaten all that will happen next."

"There's evil in everything," Valerie countered. "It's in the air we breathe."

"But this is stronger than the air," Blevins said. "Not as natural. It's a moving thing, first here in this place, then there in the next, first in this person and then another." She dropped her arms and stared at the ball.

"Sin lies at the door, and its desire is for you," Kent said. "Genesis 4:7."

"The Reverend Chadwick and all who aid him in this undertaking will face the stalking of this evil," Blevins said. "His life is in much danger."

"He's had over a hundred death threats in the last forty years," Kent said. "No danger will deter him when he thinks something is the will of God."

"But what about the rest of those you need?" Blevins asked.

"I don't know about the rest," Valerie interjected. "We're here to find out about you. Will this evil and the danger you say it brings keep you from helping us?"

Blevins grinned slightly. "Oh no," she said. "The evil is what makes me say yes."

"The evil?"

Blevins walked toward her and touched the side of the ball with one hand. "The evil is the opposite of the good," she explained. "As the yin is to the yang, the night to the day, the no to the yes. If I can feel the one, the other cannot be far from it. I will face the evil in order to gain access to the good."

"So you're with us?" Valerie asked.

Blevins smiled again, then touched the globe with both hands. For several moments, she fingered the ball as if caressing a child. "Oh yes, I am with you," she whispered. "I am with you." She laid her head on the ball once more and closed her eyes. Feeling suddenly sick, Valerie knew she couldn't hold back her nausea this time and dashed toward the bathroom down the hallway.

———

Almost ignoring Valerie as she fled, Rodney Kent's gaze never wavered from Martha Sophia Blevins' face. His mouth stayed firm, his teeth grinding. His fists clutched and opened, clutched and opened at his sides. Several seconds ticked away. But then he relaxed his hands and sat down on the edge of one of the white wicker chairs that ringed the walls of the solarium.

"I need to talk to you alone," he said, nodding toward Daphne, who stood in the corner.

Blevins pointed at the door and the assistant left quietly.

Blevins faced Kent again. "I didn't know if you'd recognize me," she said.

"You've changed a lot," he said. "You're much thinner."

She patted her hair. "More telegenic, I'm sure."

"Absolutely. I didn't know it was you for sure until just now."

"You remembered the words about the evil."

"How could I forget?"

"But you have overcome the evil, is that not so?"

Kent shrugged. "It's a daily battle, you know that. No one ever truly overcomes it. You just walk around it as best you can, hoping to escape its clutches one more time."

"Your Reverend Chadwick is a good man?"

"Yes, I believe he is. As good as any who ever lived."

"You stay with him because he keeps the evil at bay."

Kent nodded and dropped his head into his hands. "He's the soldier for all of us," he said. "I think that's why everyone wants to get near him. He knows less about evil than anyone who ever lived."

Blevins smiled, walked over to Kent, and placed her hands on his back. "You are wrong there, my long lost friend."

Kent stared up at her, confusion on his face.

"Your Reverend knows more of evil than anyone else who ever lived," she said. "Only he who knows evil well can defeat it so often." Blevins began to rub his back, her hands moving in a clockwise motion. Feeling her touch, Kent took a heavy breath. All these years with Chadwick and he had still not escaped the clutches of the evil that so often grasped at him.

TWENTY-ONE

FRIDAY, DECEMBER 12
ROME

Lifting a wheat cracker covered with a most delicate cheese to his mouth, Peter Clement leaned back on the bed and looked serenely at Cardinals Zolinska and Roca. His head hadn't hurt since the unpleasantness at Prestwick Church. Though not injured, he had stayed in bed quite a bit since that day, enjoying the attention that such an event brought his way. Messages poured in from all over the world—plaudits from presidents and prime ministers, prayers from millions of the church faithful. Everyone gave him credit for great courage. He had brought peace to Ireland. Yes, Chadwick had suggested the method, but without him nothing could have happened. He popped the cracker into his mouth and waved his hand at Cardinal Roca, who sat on a sofa to his left.

His face unreadable, Roca glanced across the bed at Zolinska. The Polish cardinal moved incessantly as usual, his hands and face as twitchy as a room full of flies. Swallowing his cracker and reaching for another, Clement studied his long-standing friend. Zolinska had been his chief assistant for almost twenty-five years, a plodding bureaucrat who made up in loyalty and zeal what he lacked in sheer intelligence. Few people liked him; his ticks made most nervous. But Clement didn't mind. Zolinska's jerks and twitches kept people from noticing his own flaws. He reached for another cracker and faced Roca. The morning meeting had a most serious purpose, and he needed to move on with it.

"I understand you have news for me?" he asked.

Roca nodded and twisted his cardinal's ring. "Yes, Your Holiness, news from America. It seems our friend Reverend Chadwick has been most busy in the last few weeks."

Clement spread a layer of cheese on his cracker and stayed calm. "In what way?" he asked.

"He's contacting other religious leaders."

Clement shrugged. "So what? He plans his crusades, brings Protestants of all denominations into his coalition. He's done it for years, hasn't he?"

Roca tilted his head. "Well, they're not all Protestants, for one thing. They're world leaders of a number of different religions."

Clement laid his cracker on the table at his knees. "I'm listening." A thin twinge cut through his head but he tried to ignore it.

"Chadwick has contacted Zorella, the Latin Pentecostal, Moseph the Jewish rabbi . . ." Roca called out the list. "My sources tell me he's asking them to attend a meeting near his Atlanta home."

"A strange group."

"Indeed."

Clement rubbed his forehead against the throb that had suddenly appeared there. He felt so ambivalent—angry that Roca had gained such information and he hadn't, yet also grateful that the cardinal had seen fit to come to him with his important news. "Where did you get your information?" he asked, pushing aside his feelings.

Roca shrugged. "I've been cultivating contacts for years. Ambassadors, government officials, church leaders in cities all over the world. It's part of what I do."

Clement nodded. In a way, he was in awe of men such as Roca, men who lived and breathed politics, who loved the intrigue of office, the constant effort to build power, to curry influence, to monitor the pulse of the world's heartbeat and maneuver it to their purposes. The fact that Roca knew such things as he now reported wasn't surprising. But Clement still didn't like it too much. It made him look amateurish, out of touch with events.

"Why didn't these people come to me?" he pouted.

"They asked me to report to you," Roca countered, his eyes studiously lowered. "All of them are loyal to His Holiness."

Clement liked the way that sounded, even if he suspected it as somewhat untruthful and perhaps a bit condescending. But he decided to let it pass. "Any conjecture as to the purpose of this meeting?"

"I'm not sure just yet. But I have my theories."

Clement turned to Zolinska. "What's your thought?"

"I'm unclear," he said, brushing his ears. "I see no evident purpose."

Clement grunted, then faced Roca again, his mind at war with itself—a cable stretched on both ends as he considered Chadwick's scheme.

"The Reverend Chadwick is going to try something bigger than Ireland," he said, figuring it out. "That's all it can be. He's going to expand his scope, go worldwide. Am I right?"

Roca rolled his ring. "That's my conjecture. Why else would he arrange a meeting with such a disparate group?"

"Then why didn't he invite me to the meeting?" Clement asked.

"I'm glad he didn't," Zolinska interjected. "We've had enough of his silliness."

Clement ignored his aide. Roca shrugged. "Who knows? Maybe he didn't want to bother you until he knew something more concrete. He'll invite you to participate then."

Clement rolled off his bed and walked to the row of rounded windows that overlooked the spacious gardens of Vatican City. For several minutes, he stared out, his mind clicking. To his dismay, his headache had returned and he decided he might as well accept it as a permanent part of his new job.

What Roca said made sense. There was no need for Chadwick to contact him until later, after he knew if he could enlist anyone else or not. But that logic didn't make him any happier. Why hadn't he thought of the idea first? Why had Chadwick moved to it and he hadn't? Ireland had been a wonderful success for the both of them. But instead of taking that success and trying to build on it as Chadwick had done, he had relaxed and basked in his glory. What stupidity! No wonder he had spent most of his years in the Vatican in the shadow of others. No wonder his elevation to the papacy had been such a fluke.

Angry at his own laziness, he pivoted back to Zolinska and Roca. "I want constant updates," he thundered. "Find out exactly what's going on. Who's coming and who's turning Chadwick down."

"You're not planning to get involved in this, are you?" Zolinska asked, standing and rubbing his cheeks. "Chadwick is a madman, a Protestant heretic."

"That's not your concern."

"But he cannot and will not do anything without you," Zolinska insisted. "It would be foolhardy to even try."

Clement faced Roca. "What will Chadwick do if I say no?" he asked.

Roca rolled his ring. "Who can say? He's a man of much determination. Though I'm sure he will want you to participate as a co-equal with him, he will not likely give up if he believes he's doing the will of God."

"Ah, the will of God. Just as it was the will of God for me to become pope."

Roca studied his hands. "The people believe it so," he said.

"And you, my good cardinal. What do you believe about the will of God?"

"I believe we see the will of God better while looking back over our shoulders than from any other view. You are the pope, the Vicar of the Lord Jesus Christ. It has to be God's will or you would not have arisen to such a station."

Clement smiled but he wasn't sure why. "You answer well, my good cardinal. Stall the Reverend Chadwick so I can have time to think. And get in touch with his niece. Find out what Chadwick will do next and get the details to me."

"Yes, Your Holiness."

Clement turned to the window again. His heavy body shook with fury. He was such a sluggard! Though he had the power of over nine hundred million Catholics at his disposal, his first tendency was always to do nothing. The manner in which he had come to the papacy had caused him to act tentatively, to hesitate when he should move, to wait when he should step forward. Well, enough of that! He was indeed the Vicar of Christ as a direct result of the will of God. From now on, he would become the one to steer things. No more backseat. He was the primate of Holy Mother Church, and from this moment forward he would take up that mantle and wear it well. If he wanted to lead the Church in this new millennium, he needed to jump feet first into the present moment and do what had to be done.

Sitting in his glass-encased office in the CBC building in Atlanta, Casey Sterling heard the telephone buzz. Quickly checking his caller identification, he dropped the turkey sandwich he was munching onto his desk, wiped his hands on his black socks, and punched the "hands-free" button on his telephone.

"Yo', Casey here. What you got for me?"

"Still puzzling through it," said the voice on the other end, an
informant Sterling had used over and over again in the last few
years. "But it seems we've got some major league religious types
flying into Atlanta over the next few days."

"Like who?" he asked, sitting up straight.

"Well, Rabbi Yoachim ben Moseph for one."

Sterling licked mayonnaise off his fingers. He knew of Moseph. Kind of an in-between Jewish leader. Not orthodox as defined by the ultra-conservatives, but not reformed as defined by
the super-liberal. A conservative, but not angry about it. Willing
to work with progressive people if it helped him accomplish his
own ends. Moseph moved well in secular circles. He had recently
visited New York to raise money for an orphanage he had started
for the children of deceased Palestinians. A man of diverse sensibilities, Moseph wanted no part of any peace statement that
cost Israel any more land, but he worked feverishly to make life
better for the Palestinians already settled in the Gaza Strip. "A
Hawk with a Heart," Sterling had called him in one of his better
moments of off-the-cuff journalism.

"Who else?" he asked his informant.

"Luis Zorella."

"You got me on that one."

"He's a Mexican Pentecostal, just now getting some publicity
here in America."

"Okay, no big deal, maybe he's preaching around here somewhere. Lots of Hispanics in Atlanta."

"Add the Dalai Lama."

Sterling licked his fingers again. "Where did you get all this?"
he asked.

"I'm doing what you pay me to do. Keeping tabs with U.S.
State Department officials. Visas, you know how that goes. A
man or woman comes to the States, they've got to get a visa. I
pay the right people, they tell me who comes and goes. I tell you
and you pay me. It's American commercialism at its best. Makes
the world go round."

Sterling rubbed his hands through his hair. "Anyone else coming?"

"Not to my knowledge."

"They're coming the same day?"

"Zorella comes in today, private plane, Dalai Lama tomorrow
morning, courtesy of an official Indian jet. Moseph is on commer-
cial, also tomorrow."

"How long are they staying?"

"All three are scheduled to leave on Monday morning."

"You know where they're staying?"

"Hey, I'm not a travel agent."

"Okay, just checking. You think they're meeting each other?"

"No way to know, but it seems unlikely. They've got little or nothing in common."

"It's strange though, all three of them here the same weekend."

"I know, coincidence is that way."

"Okay, keep me informed if you hear anything else. And nose around some more, find out where they're staying."

"I assume the check is in the mail."

"Even as we speak." Sterling hung up and leaned back, his hands behind his head. Now what in the world would three men of such disparate religious beliefs have in common that would bring them to Atlanta on the same weekend? Was there a meeting of some kind going on that he had missed? Wracking his brain, he couldn't think of any. Curious.

Leaving his seat, he walked to the window, picking up the picture of his mom as he passed the credenza. At the window, he studied the picture for several minutes. He looked like Lacy Drew, no doubt of that. He lowered the picture to his side. He thought like her too, all logical and precise. Good for some things—studies, work, a neat, clean house. But too narrowly focused for other things—like relationships, for example.

Sterling stared out the window at a jet floating by, headed toward the Atlanta airport. His dad had run off four days after his eleventh birthday. A bad artist with a drinking problem, his dad had more heart than pure natural gift, and his frustrations poured out when he had too much tequila poured into his system. But instead of moving on to something he could do to make a decent living, Carter Sterling liked to sit on street corners and sketch passersby for whatever they wanted to donate to the baseball cap he kept lying on the sidewalk by his feet. Casey's mom nagged him to do something, anything that paid a regular salary, and work on his art on the side. He refused, though, and sucked down more and more booze and became more and more angry. From time to time his anger boiled over into physical abuse.

Casey shook his head against the memories. More than once he had seen his dad slap his mom, heard her scream out her fears and frustrations. Like any child he wanted both to escape it, to run and hide in a corner, and to stop it, to stand between his parents and demand that they stop destroying each other. But like any child, he had no power to do either.

For years, his mom and dad had fought the same battles. Finally, unable to defeat his alcohol problems and not wanting to hurt anyone anymore, his dad moved out, his paints and canvases tossed into the back of an old pickup truck, his small suitcase of clothing beside him on the seat. Casey saw him about twice a year for the first few years after that, but then he had disappeared completely and Casey hadn't seen him in years. His father had moved back to Swansboro about a year ago—a bad liver driving him back to the one place where he knew a few people who'd check in on him from time to time.

Having adopted his mom's work ethic, Casey had done exceptionally well in the eyes of most, better in fact than he had any reason to expect. Only a notch above trailer trash—as the rich kids at school called his kind—he had grown up tough and poor, a kid with quick fists and a sharp mind. His mom had done the best she could, but her job as a secretary at a truck loading dock didn't pay that much and she had barely scraped by.

Sterling had climbed out of that Southern backwater by the skin of his teeth, and he lived every day of his life afraid something might knock him down and throw him back in it. That drive gave him his edge, made him successful. But, he admitted to himself, it also left him pretty empty inside. Hard work and career advancement provided plenty of money for gadgets, plenty of people to say yes to your every whim, and plenty of plaques to hang on the walls. But when you went to bed at night, those things didn't add up to much. And now he was thirty-seven years old and had gone through more than his share of women, booze, and travel. But what difference did any of that make?

For some reason he couldn't explain, he thought of Valerie Miller. What was her story? Why hadn't she married? Or had she? Was she a divorcée? A widow?

Something behind her eyes seemed sad, as though she had seen something others hadn't. Did tragedy lurk behind those sad eyes? A husband who left her? Or died of some unexpected cause?

Pushing past the thought, Sterling turned from the window and moved back to his desk, pressing a speakerphone button as he moved.

"Have them bring my car around," he told his secretary. "I need it in five minutes."

Shutting off the phone, he took a deep breath and headed to the door. A woman as good as Valerie Miller wouldn't have anything to do with him. He might as well forget her and go back to the one thing he did well—dig out the stories that all America wanted to hear, stories that would one day make Casey Sterling an anchor at one of the networks. It had been his ambition since college, and he knew he could achieve his dream if he never compromised on it. Just scoop a few more of the major stories and it would fall into his lap. He would allow no distractions, no shortcuts, and no complications until that happened.

Opening the door, he almost cursed as he felt his hand begin to shake. Before he could stop it, the quivering had moved up his right arm and into his shoulder. From there it invaded his chest. It took him almost a minute to shut it down—the uncontrollable, hated episodes that had overwhelmed him at odd moments for years.

Until the explosion in Belfast, he'd not felt the shakes in over ten years. But now, less than two months later, they had come again. Concerned about the recurrence, but assuming he wouldn't experience them again anytime soon, he headed down the hallway. Leaving the building, he thought of Valerie Miller once more and wondered why he felt so lonely.

TWENTY-TWO

Fourteen people gathered in the main room of Russell Chadwick's lodge on Saturday evening—Chadwick's four aides, Martha Blevins and Luis Zorella with one assistant each, and the Dalai Lama and Rabbi ben Moseph with two others apiece. The Ayatollah Khatama had failed to show. No reason had been given, and Chadwick had been unable to reach his office by phone. Though disappointed, Chadwick had decided to go ahead with the meeting. Extra chairs had been brought in and the group had settled quickly into them. Outside the lodge, the temperature had dropped to less than thirty degrees and a light snow fell.

Waiting for her uncle's arrival, Valerie noticed that other than a brief sharing of small talk, the different leaders stayed to themselves, taking quiet counsel with their assistants. She told herself she should have expected as much. These people didn't know one another except by reputations, and each one had a particular agenda at stake. Why get too chummy with a bunch of strangers whom you might never see again after this one meeting?

For several minutes, she studied the guests, reflecting on her research about each one. Martha Sophia Blevins, known as Jennie before her elevation in pop culture as a New Age guru, was the daughter of a half-Navajo woman from Arizona and a G.I. who had been stationed there. She was fifty-nine years old, but according to Blevins' official web page, she had lived a couple of lives already—one as the queen of a European nation and another as the high priestess of a fertility cult in South America. With no education to mention, no family of record, she made her living doing psychic readings for stars and politicians and writing books on "angelic visitations." One of her titles, *Angels I Have Heard on High*, had sold over fifteen million copies. Today she wore a straight-lined cobalt blue dress, no makeup, a necklace with a ruby pendant, and sandals without socks. Her feet had to be freezing.

Rabbi ben Moseph, fifty-seven, was a small man with a full beard and tiny ears. Though not officially orthodox, he kept the orthodox prescription for a rabbi's hair, ringlets of gray dangling over his ears. He dressed completely in black—shoes, pants, shirt, suit coat, and yarmulke. Educated since childhood in the rigors of Hebrew academia, he had trained as a rabbi from the beginning. Known as a master motivator, some said he could someday become prime minister of Israel if he wanted. So far he had refrained from mixing himself directly in political affairs.

Luis Zorella looked just as he did the last time she saw him, right down to the tan suit and brown tasseled shoes. His brother José—dressed nearly identically—sat beside him, casting sharp and not necessarily friendly glances at the others in the room. Luis seemed ill at ease too, much more so than when she visited him in Mexico. Valerie guessed that perhaps his background made him feel insecure in the presence of so many high-powered personalities.

The Dalai Lama seemed strangest of all. Speaking almost no English, he stayed completely aloof from everyone else and talked only to his two aides, one of them a translator. Even smaller than ben Moseph, he wore an ankle-length orange robe cinched at his waist. His head was completely shaved, and a singular round monocle balanced in his right eye. No one seemed to know his exact age, but he looked to be in his late sixties, maybe older.

Russell Chadwick's entrance interrupted her thoughts, his angular frame filling the doorway. He kept his right arm close to his side as he walked, and Valerie wondered if his Parkinson's was acting up again. Stepping gingerly, he took up a spot by the fireplace, his casual jeans, boots, and denim shirt making him seem as ordinary as a Georgia farmer. The room became quiet except for the crackling of the logs in the fireplace. Chadwick cleared his throat.

"Let me begin by saying again to each of you how grateful I am for your presence," he began. "And I'm equally grateful that

you agreed to keep this confidential for the time being. We don't
want to alert the press just yet."

Martha Blevins lowered her gaze, and the Dalai Lama's interpreter whispered in the small man's ear.

"The Ayatollah Khatama sent me a message just a minute
ago," Chadwick explained. "He offered his apologies for not at-
tending. But matters in his country aren't as stable as he would
like, so he needed to stay there. I will update him after our meeting and let him know what, if anything, we decide to do."

The group nodded their understanding. Chadwick eased to a
sitting position on the hearth and laid his hands on his knees.

"You all know why I brought you here," he said. "I, or one of
my assistants, has outlined the matter for you. So I'll not waste
your time rehashing all of that." Again, the nods came.

"I've thought a lot about how to make this speech," he said.
"And it seems we have to start with what we have in common
rather than what we have as differences." He rubbed his knees.
"We don't have the same beliefs," he continued. "So let's not pre-
tend we do. I'm a Christian, a believer in the Lord Jesus Christ
as the final revelation of God to the human family. But I'm not
here to impose that belief on you."

"But there is at least one thing we all want. We want our
world, this place where we live day in and day out, to attain some
semblance of unity. We want people to speak more kindly to one
another; we want nations to stop spending so much on weapons;
we want peace instead of war. That's the cornerstone of anything
we do."

He smiled gently. "No matter how many matters separate us,
that binds us together." He paused and licked his lips.

Valerie wondered how his words were hitting his listeners. So
far, everyone seemed okay. Chadwick rubbed his face.

"On that simple basis, I want to form an alliance," he said.
"An alliance similar to the one the pope and I formed in Ireland,
only much larger, one that includes all of you, the best-known
religious leaders in the world. I want us to place the moral and
political power of our personal lives and religious followings on
the line in every conflict on the face of the earth. Every time civil
unrest breaks out, every time two countries fight over territory,
every time some bloodthirsty dictator goes on a rampage, I want
us there, right in the middle of it, daring anyone to harm us, daring anyone to keep fighting while we're there."

He paused and surveyed the room. His words had mesmerized

the group, his powerful voice grabbing those who listened. Even as an old man, Chadwick still possessed a charisma unequaled by any but a few in the history of the planet. The Dalai Lama's interpreter lifted his hand. Chadwick nodded at him.

"The good Dr. Chadwick brings much passion to the moment," the interpreter said. "But His Holiness wishes to ask why he should share this passion. Will this alliance come to the places of poverty in the Far East, or in Africa, or the rest of the Third World? Or will it keep its eyes only on the West?"

"We will go wherever the trouble is," Chadwick said. "If it's Christians against Hindus in India, we'll go there. If it's intertribal warfare in Africa, we'll go there. If it's the Klan fighting black gangs in Atlanta, we'll go there. It doesn't matter to me. I care about all God's children, not just those of white skin, not just those who speak English."

The interpreter whispered the response and the Dalai Lama fingered his monocle and nodded slightly.

Clutching the ruby in her necklace with both hands, Martha Blevins stood and looked at the ceiling. "I see the cosmos aligning itself to embrace what you say," she intoned. "But you should know I also see great obstacles to it. Much darkness blocks this astral convergence."

Chadwick smiled and Valerie could imagine what he was thinking. But he didn't let on that he felt anything negative. "I know we've got all kinds of problems to overcome," he said. "But if God is in this, nothing is impossible."

"Many in this room will find themselves in grave danger," Blevins continued.

Chadwick's smile disappeared. "The devil always combats the ways of God."

Valerie sensed a shift in momentum in the room. No one liked danger.

"We will have to outpray the evil one," Luis Zorella said, speaking for the first time. Everyone turned to the young Mexican. He stared into the fire as he continued to speak.

"The Reverend Chadwick came to Mexico City many years ago," he said. "He preached a great crusade. I attended that crusade at the invitation of a believing man who fed me bread twice a week from the back door of his storefront church."

Zorella faced Chadwick now. "I listened to you preach the gospel of the Lord Jesus Christ. Your words confused me greatly, but I could not subtract them from out of my mind. They stayed there, like a beggar on the street corner, entreating me to pay attention to them. My friend the bread man helped me much. He told me to dwell on the words you had given me—and he added a few words of his own. Two weeks after you preached on the soccer field, I sat on the back steps of the bread man's church and felt the presence of the Lord. I too became a believing man. You and the bread man are responsible for this. Did you not know it?"

Chadwick shook his head. Zorella stood and walked over and placed a hand on his shoulders. "If you tell me I have to face the devil all by myself; if you tell me to stare into his black eyes and smell the acid breath from his mouth; if you tell me to go into hand-to-hand combat with him and tear out his bloody heart with my fingers, I will gladly do it. For you or the bread man, I will do anything."

Zorella paused and stared at the others. "I know many details have yet to be learned," he said. "And I know that the danger is real. But can we not at least agree that the Reverend Chadwick has brought us a great hope? That he has given us what may be a God-given opportunity to work together for peace? Who else besides me will help him do this? Who else?"

Martha Blevins dropped her necklace to her chest and walked over to Zorella. "I feel a true harmonic convergence," she said. "I cannot resist it. I too will walk this path with the Reverend."

Rabbi ben Moseph joined Zorella and Blevins by Chadwick. "I am not a believer in the eternal life that you trust," he said. "I am more pragmatic than that. No 'pie in the sky by and by' for me. So this world, this life is the arena for me." He paused and twirled the ringlet of hair over his ear. "I've tried to live up to my responsibility to make life better, to serve others," he continued. "But it grows tiresome at times. So few others want to help. Now you offer me allies in my battle to bring peace and justice to this age. A blessing to be sure. I am in agreement that this is a thing we should try."

With his interpreter whispering into his ear, the Dalai Lama's gaze raked from one person to the next. He said something and the interpreter responded, his voice sounding somewhat agitated. But then the Dalai Lama stood and inched his way across the room, one short step at a time. Reaching the cluster, he placed both hands together, his fingers palm to palm in front of his face. He spoke and his interpreter immediately translated.

"Peace is a good thing," he said. "For peace I am glad."

Chadwick stood in the center of the group. Valerie and the

rest of the assistants held their collective breath. José Zorella clenched his fists and studied his shoes.

"I know it may seem strange to do this," Chadwick said. "But I believe we should pray. Any objections?"

There were none.

"Keeper of the universal quiet," intoned Martha Blevins before anyone could stop her, "hear our entreaties. Bring our consciousness together into one harmonious path; guide our imaginations into one vision of unity. Protect us from the yin of darkness and lead us into the yang of light and peace. For the sake of all that lives we breathe this thought as one. . . ."

As Martha's voice trailed away, Valerie wondered how in the world such a strange mixture of people could ever mesh enough to do any good thing.

———

Outside, the snow began to fall harder as the wind picked up. But the bearded man with the black ponytail hiding in the woods about a hundred feet from the front of Chadwick's lodge didn't mind. Adjusting the listening device that allowed him to hear everything being said inside the building, he snuggled down against the trunk of an oak tree. Beside him lay a pair of binoculars, but he didn't really need to see much more. He knew what was going to happen. In a few hours the group would break up and go their separate ways. Then he would pack his gear and hike back down the mountain through the ice and snow and get ready for the next step in the operation. Yeah, work like this got cold sometimes, but for the right reasons a man would endure just about anything.

TWENTY-THREE

The logs in the fireplace had burned down to cinders, and a noticeable chill had fallen over the room. Perched on the edge of a rocking chair, Ted stared at the floor and wished he had stayed in bed. He glanced at his watch—it was 1 A.M. To his right, Rodney Kent, elfish in red flannel pajamas and bedroom shoes, bit his lip and waited for the meeting to officially begin. It didn't take long. Lester Boggett charged into the room holding a sandwich of some kind in one hand and a cup of coffee in the other. Placing the coffee cup on the fireplace mantel, he faced the two of them and took a deep breath. A dab of mayonnaise decorated his left cheek, and Ted started to say something about it, but then, not feeling too kindly toward Lester at the moment, he held his tongue.

Boggett took a bite of his sandwich, then hitched up his blue jeans. His face, always red, looked worse tonight. Placing the last of the sandwich by the coffee, he began to pace, his chunky legs working like pistons, heavy and steady. Ted braced himself for what he knew was coming.

"I'm sorry we've got to meet like this," Boggett started, his fists clenched. "But one of us had to do something. You know I love Russell, have since the day I met him way back when. He's like a brother to me, to all of us. But this time I can't just stand by and let something happen that I know is wrong-headed, a bad notion from the get-go." He stopped pacing and stared at Rodney and Ted as if challenging them to disagree.

"Russ has never steered us wrong before," Kent countered, his eyes studying the floor. "It's always been all right. Whatever he said always turned out good."

"Well, there's a first time for everything," Boggett said. "Maybe this time he's wrong. No man is infallible, not even him."

"So you're deserting him?" Ted asked.

"Not sure I'd call it that," Lester said. "But look what he's doing. I mean, you were going to succeed him. All of us know that. But that ain't going to happen now. Aren't you mad at him?"

Ted didn't answer.

"He may be sick," Kent said.

"Sick?" Ted asked.

"Yeah, you know . . . he's not as sharp. He's got that Parkinson's—he told us he did. He's shaky all the time. And he's taking medication. No telling what that does to him. I mean, you know him! I've never known him to have trouble sleeping. And that dream? Come on, he's never remembered a dream in his life."

"Yeah, some of these drugs can cause all kinds of screwy things," Boggett agreed.

"But that's got nothing to do with his mental capabilities," Ted argued, unwilling to desert Chadwick just yet. "I admit he's weak, but let's face it, he's in his seventies. I've seen no sign of any mental change in him and neither have you." He came out of the rocking chair and stalked to the window. "So don't come at me with that 'he's losing it' junk, because that's just stupid on your part and you know it!"

"It's Valerie's fault," Kent said, his tiny feet suspended over the floor as he sat on the sofa. "She's the one who put him on the idea in the first place."

"That's right," Lester said. "Before she came in with us, we never had these kinds of problems. We were all together, one accord."

Ted faced them again. "That's the easy way, you know. Blame it on the woman."

Lester laughed derisively. "It worked for Adam," he said.

"That's ridiculous," Ted said. "And you know it!"

"I know what's true," Lester said. "And Rodney's right. Until Valerie Miller started tagging along with us, we were content with doing what the Lord called us to do. Preach the gospel, that's our ministry, no more and no less. But now Russ has lost his focus, and he's all twisted up. I mean, think about it—we've canceled two crusades! I never dreamed he'd do anything like that. And I've gotten some phone calls. More and more people want to know what's going on."

"Did Stricker call you again?"

"He called me too," Kent said. "Sounded angry."

"He said he talked to Russ, but he didn't think he made much headway. He doesn't like this, I can tell you that. Said he's watching us real close. Wanted to know how long I thought this charade would go on."

"What did you tell him?"

"That I had no clue."

"Have you ever heard him talk about his faith?" Kent asked.

Ted laughed softly but he wasn't really amused. "We're not sure he has any faith," he said. "Certainly no church that we know of."

"Then why does he give so much money to Chadwick if he's not a believer?" Kent asked.

"Who knows? Maybe he thinks he can buy his way into heaven. Maybe he needs a tax write-off and figures this is as good as any. Maybe it's public relations, pure and simple. Maybe he's a good man underneath, just doesn't know how to express it."

"Don't matter to me," Lester said. "The Lord can use his money, no matter what the motive. So let's not do something to keep him from giving it." He scowled at Ted as he spoke.

The room fell quiet for a moment. "Russ is right about the Scripture," Ted said. "God did use nonbelievers to further His purposes. No reason it can't happen again."

No one argued. "And maybe it's a witnessing opportunity," he continued, hoping to deflate the tension in the room. "Russ can talk to all these leaders about the Lord. I mean, just think what would happen if Blevins or the Dalai Lama should get converted. Imagine the worldwide exposure such a thing would give to the gospel."

"That's throwing pearls before swine," Lester countered. "They're like Pharaoh—their hearts are hardened. Did you listen to the so-called 'prayer' that Blevins woman offered? I mean, come on, you got no chance of that woman trustin' in the Lord."

"You don't know that," Ted said. "You're not giving God a chance to change them."

"And you don't know otherwise," Lester said.

For several seconds, silence fell again on the room. Lester slugged down more coffee. Ted moved back to his rocking chair but didn't rock.

"What about these dreams?" he asked, trying to find a way to slow things down, give himself time to think.

"Nonsense and double nonsense," Lester said. "Are we goin' to chuck aside decades of work 'cause two people ate spicy food too late at night?"

"But don't you believe God can use dreams?" Ted persisted. "It happened in the Bible. Joseph, Daniel . . ."

"Yeah, God spoke through a donkey too, according to the Bible. We lookin' for that to happen next?"

"Maybe it just did," Ted said, his temper flaring.

"Hey, watch it!" Lester growled. "I might take offense."

Ted shrugged and fell silent.

"So what are our options?" The question came from Kent.

Placing the coffee cup down, Lester glanced at Ted, then continued. "We tell Russ we can't support him in this, that we're out of here if he goes ahead."

"That's pretty drastic," Kent said.

"What he's doing is even more drastic," Lester said.

"But we gave him our word just a few hours ago," Ted said, arguing with himself as much as with Lester.

"Buyer's remorse," Lester said. "He'll understand. He's a forgivin' kind of guy."

Ted wanted to hit him but he also knew he was right. Chadwick would forgive them no matter how disagreeably they acted.

"I'm not too sure about this," Kent said, staring at his shoes.

"I am and it scares me," Lester said. He moved from the fireplace to a table a few feet away. "I mentioned the seven-headed beast earlier tonight." He picked up a Bible off the table and flipped to the back. "You know the passage," he said. "Revelation 13. Listen to this." He cleared his throat as the lights in the room dimmed, then burned bright again.

" 'Then I stood on the sand of the sea. And I saw a beast rising up out of the sea, having seven heads and ten horns, and on his horns ten crowns, and on his heads a blasphemous name. Now the beast which I saw was like a leopard, his feet . . .' "

Ted felt his face getting hot as Lester kept reading. His spine tensed. It seemed like treachery to suggest that Russell Chadwick had any connection to the Beast of Revelation. But who knew? Maybe Lester was right! Maybe Chadwick had gotten twisted by his illness; maybe he had lost connection with what was real or not real; maybe he had gotten confused, missed the will of God.

"That's enough!" he shouted, coming out of his seat, his hands grabbing the front of Lester's shirt before he could stop himself. "I don't want to hear any more of this!" He pushed Lester back against the mantel. "If you're going to leave, go ahead. But I . . . I don't know what . . ."

Confused and unsure, he dropped his hands from Lester's shirt and stepped back a pace. Lester rearranged himself, closed the Bible, and held it up at Rodney as if presenting a trophy. "If I thought of this, you know someone else will when all this comes out. It'll sound like the beginnings of a world government, just like the Bible says, all dressed up in religious garb."

"You don't believe that," Ted said. "You're just using it to stop something you don't like."

Lester laid the Bible on the table. "I don't think that Russ is doing anything bad on purpose," he said. "But he's getting old— tired and worn out. A man makes a lot of mistakes that way. He gets confused and throws in with the wrong bunch. I can't be a party to it. I just can't."

Ted turned to Kent. "Are you with him or me?" he asked.

Kent pulled his knees to his chest and buried his head behind them. Ted walked over to him and placed his hand on the little man's back. Kent was shivering.

"It's okay," Ted soothed. "It's going to be okay." But inside his head, he had no assurances at all that what he was saying was right.

———

At 6:16 A.M. the phone rang in the master bedroom of the eight-room Buckhead condominium that Casey Sterling called home. Rolling over, Sterling grabbed the phone, flipped on a lamp, and sat up in bed.

"Yo', Casey man," said his informant. "Big doings up in Big Canoe."

"Better be for you to call me this early on a Sunday morning."

"You'll give me a bonus for this one, so stop your griping."

Sterling rubbed his eyes.

"They all met at Chadwick's place," the informant said. "The whole posse. More religion up there than you ever saw, wall-to-wall God-people."

Instantly awake, Sterling squeezed the phone and swung his feet onto the floor. "But what's Chadwick doing?" he asked.

"You promise me that bonus?"

Casey grinned. "Always the capitalist, aren't you?"

"Hey, I got expenses like everybody else. And information is costly. You know that."

"You remind me of it often enough. Spill your guts."

"It's Ireland again, but bigger this time."

"Bigger?"

"Yeah, Casey man, wake up here. It's the whole world—anywhere trouble crops up."

Sterling jerked up from the bed and stood straight beside it. "Chadwick wants to put religious leaders in the center of every conflict on the map," he said, getting the picture now.

"Yeah, ain't that lunacy."

"Or sheer brilliance." Sterling pushed his hair out of his eyes and considered the scheme. An alliance of such a magnitude had never been tried. Probably because no one ever imagined such a thing could happen. And why should it? Religious differences kept people apart. What made Chadwick think he could overcome them when no one else ever had?

Sterling remembered a neon sign outside a church that had once caused him to sneer: "The church needs the courage to try something that only God can make succeed." Maybe Chadwick had read the same sign.

"When is everybody leaving?" he asked, focused again on the immediate moment.

"Late this morning," said his informant.

"When's Chadwick going to announce all this to the public?"

"I got no clue," said the informant. "You want me to stay close?"

"Yeah, real close. But don't say anything to anybody yet. I want to pop this, but not too early."

"You know me better than that. I don't say nothing to nobody but you."

"That's 'cause nobody pays you better than me."

"You know me so well."

"Keep in touch."

Sterling cradled the phone back on the hook and sat back on the bed. Though he didn't know how his informant came up with information like this, he knew to trust it. The man had never given him bad facts, not once. But he didn't feel comfortable just yet with such a major story. Some pieces of the puzzle had yet to come together.

He walked to the bathroom and washed his face. Sitting on

such an explosive scoop didn't come easily. If he messed around
and someone else reported it before he did, he'd hate himself for
the rest of his life. But if he went half-cocked and broadcast
something of this magnitude before he had verification, and it
turned out even a little bit false, he'd suffer incredible professional consequences. With his sights on an anchor desk, he
couldn't afford to slip up even once.

Brushing his teeth, he glanced at his watch and wondered
what time he could safely call Valerie Miller. She'd know the
straight skinny on this. Maybe he could ask her to have brunch.

TWENTY-FOUR

His schedule busy and his feelings still hurt at what he saw
as a personal slight, Clement Peter managed to miss the first
three calls that Reverend Chadwick placed to his office. As a result, he didn't talk to the Reverend until almost six on the Monday after the Georgia conclave. When he finally did consent to
accept the call, he took it alone in his private quarters, a tray full
of caviar and other tasty tidbits beside him on a table.

"Reverend Chadwick," he beamed, trying his best to overcome
his own sensibilities and sound pleasant. "So good of you to call.
I hope you're feeling well after all the unpleasantness in Ireland."

"Yes, my friend, I am over those injuries, I think. Doing fine
now. I hope you're okay also."

"Yes, certainly, doing excellent. My injuries weren't nearly so
serious as yours."

"I've had you in my prayers."

"And I you."

"The peace seems to be holding in Ireland," Chadwick continued.

Clement spread a touch of caviar on a cracker. "Indeed," he
said. "Our efforts seem to have borne some fruit."

"I think so. That's why I'm calling you again."

Clement swallowed the cracker, told himself to stay positive,
and waited for Chadwick to tell him what he already knew.

"I want to broaden our emphasis," Chadwick said. "Take it
global."

"I'm listening," Clement said.

"I think people can change," Chadwick said. "I met the man

in Ireland who set the explosives at Prestwick Church. He's a different man now. The Lord has transformed his heart. I want to give others the same opportunity to feel the Spirit of God. If we can just get people to stop long enough to think, to talk to each other—to pray even—I believe we can make a difference in a lot of places. I've invited some others to join me in this effort."

"Others?" Clement hoped the tone didn't sound as irked as he felt. A small throb rose up behind his eyes.

"Yes, other religious leaders. I didn't think you and I could do this by ourselves this time."

"Oh, you've inviting me to participate with you again? How nice of you." Sarcasm. He didn't like it but he didn't seem able to avoid it.

Chadwick paused and Clement knew he had hit a nerve. He took a bite of caviar, then chastised himself for that too. If he kept eating as much as he had in the last few weeks, they'd have to put extra support under the papal bed. He closed his eyes in shame. His headache thumped harder.

"Well, sure," Chadwick said. "I just . . . well, I assumed you'd want to continue our efforts, broaden them . . ."

Clement wiped cracker crumbs from his mouth and waited a few seconds before he spoke. He had backed into this corner and he didn't know exactly how to extricate himself. "I have many responsibilities," he said. "Vatican matters, that sort of thing. I don't know if my official duties will allow me the time I'll need for such a worthy effort as you're proposing."

"But I need you," Chadwick said, sounding surprised. "I know you have incredible demands on your time, pressures I could never understand. But I've reached an alliance with four others. You know them, Luis Zorella, Rabbi ben Moseph, Martha Sophia Blevins, even the Dalai Lama. I see the hand of God in this . . . but . . . well . . . I need you if it's going to succeed. I mean, without the Catholic Church, I don't know what chance I'll have to make this work. . . ."

Though inwardly pleased with Chadwick's predicament, Clement tried to disguise it as best he could. He cleared his throat and took on a solemn tone. "I'll need to talk to my advisors," he said. "After those consultations, I'll contact you again."

"I have a news conference scheduled for this afternoon," Chadwick said. "What shall I tell them?"

Clement licked his lips and weighed the options. In his heart, he knew he should embrace Chadwick's goals, assist him in any way he could.

"I will talk to my advisors," he said to Chadwick. "Then I shall contact you again."

He clicked off the line, looked at the plate of crackers, but decided that his head hurt too much to eat anymore. For a moment, he wondered how Zolinska and Roca would respond to the way he had handled Chadwick. Zolinska would like it, he concluded as he rubbed his eyes, but Roca might not. Closing his eyes, he told himself not to worry about Roca's reaction. He was the pope, after all. Let Roca worry about *him* for a while.

———

Sitting cross-legged on a golden rug on the floor of a simple brick apartment in the center of Tehran, Iran, the Ayatollah Kahil Khatama tucked his black robe around his ankles and smoothed down his beard. On the other side of the rug, his most trusted advisor, the mullah Ali Ruhamen, also cross-legged on the floor, waited for him to speak. Known as a man given to much deliberation before acting, Khatama stared around the room as if seeing it for the first time. The walls were bare of décor and painted with a color remarkably similar to that of his scraggly gray beard. A single bed with plain cotton sheets and a black wool blanket stretched out in the left corner. A simple wooden table with a lamp stood by the bed. Other than a small metal desk and an accompanying chair, the room was otherwise unoccupied. Folding his arms over his chest, Khatama grunted and began to speak.

"I have received another call from the Reverend Chadwick," he began. "He went ahead with his meeting, even though I told him I could not attend. Now the man has called me again. It seems that four religious leaders have reached some kind of accord with him to move ahead with his New Millennium Peace Initiative."

"It's all very strange," Ruhamen said, a tall thin man of sparse beard and a slender neck. "Why should he do such a thing now? The world is much quieter than it has ever been. Though outbursts of violence crop up here and there, fewer people die by hostile means today than ever in history."

Khatama rubbed his beard. "Who can fathom the ways of the West?"

"Or the thoughts of a Christian?"

Khatama nodded. "Perhaps the fact that the world is almost
at peace drives such a man as Chadwick to think he can take it
the final step and create the circumstances through which the
last of humanity's atrocities are eliminated."

"A bold initiative," Ruhamen said. "And a stupid one. No one
but an arrogant American would dare such a thing."

Khatama waved his hand at his friend. "That's old rhetoric,"
he said. "Though I agree with the sentiment. But we can't show
that face to the world anymore. It's too antagonistic. The new era
demands more subtlety."

Ruhamen leaned in closer. "You're up to something, my
friend."

"I think perhaps I will join this new alliance and add my voice
to those crying out for peace. Our young people clamor for this
kind of rapport with the West."

Ruhamen pushed out his skinny chin. His beard pointed forward like a thick pencil. "Our young people don't know the Great
Satan America like we do."

"Too much Western music and too many hamburgers," agreed
Khatama. "Whatever pleases the eyes, the ears, and the stomach,
that's what they want. Promise it to them and they will hand you
their souls."

"I fear for the true faith," Ruhamen said. "Too many think the
five pillars of our heritage are too confining for a modern age."

"But we shall remind them at the proper time. One God,
prayer five times each day, fasting, the pilgrimage to Mecca, the
giving of alms for the poor—such things make us strong."

"So you will actually ally yourself with Chadwick?"

Khatama rolled his eyes. "You insult me, my friend. Of course
my alliance will serve my purposes and mine alone. But it will do
the cause of the great Allah much good in the arena of public
relations for everyone to see our diligent efforts to bring about
peace."

"But how can you work with such men as Chadwick and ben
Moseph?" Ruhamen asked. "They see us as infidels."

"As I see them," Khatama said, rubbing his beard.

For several minutes the room fell silent, but neither man
minded. Khatama pictured Chadwick in his mind. The evangelist
was old and weak. But Khatama had no doubts about his zeal. In
his estimation, only one man's zeal for his cause matched up favorably with Chadwick's fervor for his. And that one man was
none other than himself. Either of them would no doubt die for

his faith if he thought it necessary and valuable to do so.

For a moment, Khatama recalled the death of his father, a glorious leader who had died as a martyr to Allah on a suicide mission into the belly of Israel during the days of open aggression between the Jews and the Muslims. But such days were over now, much to his regret.

"The old ways of military conquest for the Muslim faith worked well in the past," he explained. "But times have changed. Now a man has to use cunning to accomplish his ends. If joining this alliance for peace can advance the holy cause of the great Allah, then I gladly mold myself to the new reality."

"I bow to your judgment," Ruhamen said. "I know that you will do anything in order to make the truths of Allah more available to the masses."

Khatama scratched his beard. "Make contact with Reverend Chadwick," he said to Ruhamen, standing to take his leave. "Tell him I am most pleased to ally myself with him in this holy cause."

Khatama pulled at his beard, his face yielding no clues to his thoughts. "When the time comes I will do what the moment requires."

TWENTY-FIVE

Dressed in a navy pin-striped skirt and jacket, a crisp blue silk blouse, and plain navy pumps, Valerie Miller gripped both sides of the podium as if trying to crush it. She knew her neck had turned red. She took a deep breath and stared out at the throng of reporters crammed into the ballroom of the Sheraton Hotel near mid-town Atlanta. It was 4:12, Monday afternoon. In three minutes, the news conference would begin.

Her mood was somber, due to the seriousness of her announcement. Her gaze steady, she told herself to stay calm. No reason for the media to see her unease. To her left, Russell Chadwick sat in a leather wingback, his wide hands folded in his lap, his eyes as calm as the ocean on a windless day. A lapel mike was hooked to his tie. To her right stood Ted Shuster and Rodney Kent, both of them looking haggard, the price of too little sleep and too much tension.

She marveled at Chadwick's appearance. The morning had been ugly. Though she wasn't in the room when it happened, Ted told her that Lester had bailed out. The meeting in which he informed Chadwick had turned out badly. According to Ted, Lester had gotten angry, shouting all kinds of accusations, including some nonsense about Revelation 13.

Chadwick had stayed quiet most of the meeting, letting Lester take his shots. Near the end, he had hugged Lester and cried on his neck.

"When you're ready to come back," he said, "I'll be here to welcome you." Lester had slammed out of the room.

Valerie blamed herself for the tension among the men. If she hadn't interfered, if she hadn't offered her half-baked interpretation of Chadwick's dream, maybe none of this would have ever happened. She and Chadwick and the pope wouldn't have come so close to death. Hostility wouldn't have arisen between her uncle and one of his closest friends and aides. Lester wouldn't have left. She felt certain that Lester hated her.

Minutes before the news conference, her uncle had tried to reassure her. "Lester just needs some space," he said. "This isn't the first time he's left in a huff, and it won't be the last. Don't worry about it. His temper is his worst sin."

Though she appreciated Chadwick's efforts, it didn't make her feel much better. She had to find a way to get Lester back, had to—

Ted touched her elbow and pointed to his watch. Time to start the news conference. Clearing her throat, she pushed aside her concerns and stared out at the media. At the back of the room on the left, she spotted Casey Sterling. A scowl covered his face. He was probably mad at her too. He had called her all morning, but she hadn't found enough time to return his calls. Fighting to stay calm, she began to speak.

"Good afternoon," she said. "My name is Valerie Miller, and I'm here as spokesperson for the Reverend Russell Chadwick." She glanced at her uncle. He smiled and she continued. "I'm going to read a short statement, and then the Reverend Chadwick and I will take your questions."

The reporters shuffled their feet. They knew the routine. Valerie moved ahead. "We live in a world where the threat of a world war has largely faded. And we're grateful for that. But regional and civil conflicts continue to erupt in places like Kosovo, Pakistan, East Timor, Rwanda, and other places around the globe. These on-again, off-again episodes of violence are displeasing to God and are the source of death and hardship to thousands, even millions of people. They need to stop."

The reporters stared at the floor. They had heard all the religious jargon more than once. Valerie pressed on. "After the bombing in October in Donegal Square, Northern Ireland, the Reverend Chadwick began to pray most diligently about ways to end the destruction. One night, soon after that, he had a dream." Valerie described the dream for the reporters. A few of them stared up at her with renewed interest. Others almost snickered.

"I know some of you don't understand this," she continued after finishing the description. "But Reverend Chadwick believes

God gave him this dream, just as God gave dreams to the biblical Joseph—recorded in Genesis 37—and to Daniel in Daniel 7 and 8. As a result of his dream, Reverend Chadwick decided to go to Ireland. You know what happened there.

"So, gratified by the cease-fire and renewed peace talks in Northern Ireland, the Reverend Russell Chadwick is announcing today that he has reached an agreement with five other world-renowned religious leaders to expand his unprecedented effort for peace in Northern Ireland to the rest of the human family." She paused for a moment as the reporters held their recorders higher, their earlier lack of interest now replaced by an effort to get her every word on tape.

"The Reverend Chadwick wants religious leaders to do what the politicians and military leaders have shown they cannot do—usher in a true season of tranquility to the planet."

The room had grown dead still. Valerie recognized the phenomenon. Her words were so astonishing that even the most cynical in the media had become tongue-tied. She relaxed her hand on the podium.

"The other leaders involved in this alliance are . . ." She read off the names and gave a short piece of biography for each person. The media people began to shuffle. She knew they were anxious to ask questions. She moved to the conclusion of the statement.

"This effort will begin with the first outbreak of the New Year. Anywhere violence happens, anytime it breaks out, in any country, any ethnic group, anytime—night or day—the Peace Project will spring into action. Let the hatemongers, the lovers of war, and the distillers of death go on notice. People of faith, bound together by their common desire for peace, will stand for it no more." She folded her hands and laid them in the middle of the podium and looked out at the media. Some looked stunned. Others were whispering to each other. A few held cell phones to their ears.

"Now," she said, "Reverend Chadwick and I will take your questions."

Hands immediately shot into the air. She pointed to an elderly man at the back whose name she couldn't recall.

"Did the Reverend have a dream that supports this broader effort toward peace?"

"No, I didn't," Chadwick said, glancing quickly at Valerie. "But I still believe the Lord is in this."

Valerie started to add something but then decided against it.

She smiled and recognized Casey Sterling next, hoping to make up for not returning his calls.

"I didn't hear Clement Peter's name in that group you gave us," he said. "Can you tell us why he isn't included? Is there some problem between him and the Reverend Chadwick?"

Valerie bit her lip. Sterling had asked the question she dreaded the most. For some reason she couldn't understand, Clement had backed off. She turned to Chadwick. He nodded at Sterling.

"An appropriate question," Chadwick said evenly. "I and my associates have been in fruitful discussions with the pontiff over this matter. Unfortunately for now, his schedule is most difficult. I gave much prayer to the matter of whether or not I should move ahead without him. I concluded that I should. But let me assure you that the Vatican agrees with us on the need to do all we can for peace, and Clement Peter and his advisors are working to find ways to assist us in our efforts. We were glad to work together in Ireland and believe we will again in other places in the future."

Valerie nodded. All that Chadwick said was true. Roca had talked with her three times over the last day and a half. He wanted the pope on board, but he couldn't push his views any harder at the moment. If Clement needed some time to warm to the idea, he had to allow it.

Chadwick pointed to a female reporter near the front, a blond woman in her midforties named Beth Roper. Valerie recognized Roper from their last crusade. She worked for *The Christian Weekly*, a large religious magazine whose board of directors read like a "who's who" of the evangelical world. Even more importantly, Roper's father owned the magazine, plus a publishing house that produced religious books, and a chain of Christian bookstores and radio stations.

"Yes, Reverend Chadwick, Beth Roper, *Christian Weekly*. Not everyone in the Christian world is likely to be happy with your involvement, indeed your leadership, in this matter. In fact, my sources tell me that some in your own camp are already upset. Can you comment on the controversy, or lack of it, that your efforts are creating?"

Valerie gripped the podium again. Where did Roper get that? Had Lester said something? She wondered how her uncle would handle the question.

Chadwick rose up in his chair but his eyes stayed calm. "Your sources are good, Ms. Roper. Not everyone agrees with my deci-

sion. Some say I shouldn't join in partnership with those who
aren't of the Christian faith. And I give my associates the right
to their disagreements. I'm a Baptist, remember?"

A few of the reporters chuckled.

Chadwick continued. "Anything this monumental will almost
inevitably create some controversy. I expected that. But so long
as I feel at peace with God about it, I have to press on. That's the
way I've always operated and I'm too old to change now."

Roper threw her hand up again. Chadwick nodded and she
offered a second question. "With you and the other five you
named, that makes six leaders. If the pope joins you, that'll be
seven."

Valerie's fingers whitened on the podium. She knew where the
question was headed and she didn't like it.

Roper pressed ahead. "I've heard at least one person suggest
a possible relationship to the beast mentioned in Revelation 13,
who many believe will establish a one-world government and
bring a false peace to the world just prior to the prophesied Rapture of the Church. What do you say to those who suggest that
you're unwittingly contributing—?"

"I'm sorry," Valerie interrupted. "This isn't a theological debate. You'll have to—"

Chadwick pushed up from the chair and stepped to Valerie,
cutting her off in midsentence. She eased back as he came to the
podium and rested his elbows on it. His face looked sad now, sadder than she had ever seen it. He leaned over the podium, and
Roper seemed to back up as if to escape his intense gaze.

For several long moments, no one said anything. Valerie noticed her uncle's right hand shaking, and his face had taken on a
gray pallor. Though she didn't want to think it, she suddenly
wondered how much longer he'd live.

Chadwick braced his shoulders. When he spoke, his voice carried a surprisingly light tone.

"Some say the false peace will come *after* the Rapture," he
said.

A young man wearing a navy CBS blazer held up a hand.
"Some of us aren't . . . well . . . perhaps you could explain about
this Rapture thing for our uninformed viewers."

Chadwick grinned. "It's pretty complicated," he said. "But basically, it's the belief that before the end of time, God will lift all
who believe in Jesus out of the world. Some say a false leader, an
Antichrist, will rise up before that happens. Others say the An-

tichrist will come to power after it happens. Either way, though, all believers will rise up to meet the Lord in the air."

"A kind of spiritual levitation?" the CBS man asked.

"I'm not sure I'd say it that way," Chadwick said. "But God will remove believers from the world, either before or after the Tribulation begins. There is some debate on which timetable is accurate."

The CBS man lifted his hand again, but Chadwick shook his head and winked, as if anticipating the question.

"Don't even go there," Chadwick said. "The Rapture *and* the Tribulation may be too much for you in one day."

The man grinned and Chadwick cleared his throat. "Now," he said. "Let's go back to Ms. Roper's question as to whether or not I'm unwittingly contributing to some evil purpose." He paused and gripped the podium more tightly.

"I'm grieved by those who throw out such statements," he said, his tone serious now. "And I have to admit I don't quite understand them. I've preached for over fifty years, in big towns and small, in countries rich and poor, to crowds of thousands and to groups of no more than I can count on my two hands. I've tried to the best of my ability to do the Lord's will. Yes, I've messed up at times, more than I care to admit here in public to all these cameras." He swept his hands out over the media swarm. "But I've tried to stay faithful, and I think you know that."

He seemed to get even taller now, straight as an arrow, his wide shoulders square, his eyes searching over every man and woman in the ballroom. "I can't answer those who want to see something evil in this. By nature, I'm not one to argue with those who are negative. If people want to suggest that I'm some kind of good-hearted but senile old man being unwittingly used by Satan, then let them. I will pray for any and all who speak evil of me. All I can do is let my life be my defense."

His voice sounded strong now, and Valerie heard the prophetic tones that had shaken a nation for nearly half a century.

"May God strike me dead," he challenged, his arms outstretched toward heaven, "if I am in any way a hindrance to the holy work of the Lord Jesus."

Valerie felt chills run up and down her spine.

"May God strike me dead if I am doing this work in the power of Satan."

The room became as quiet as a tomb.

"May God strike me dead if my alliance with any of these is outside the will of the Almighty."

Chadwick lowered his arms and his voice. "May God strike me dead . . ." His voice trailed off and he turned from the podium and sagged back into his seat.

Another reporter asked a question and then a second and a third, and Valerie mumbled an answer to each of them, but she was too caught up in the power of her uncle's words to pay much attention to what she said. Thankfully, the news conference soon ended, and she stepped away from the podium to watch Chadwick, Shuster, and Kent leave the room. Turning back to scan the empty ballroom, she noted that only one person remained.

"You didn't call me back," Casey Sterling accused, walking toward her.

"I'm sorry," she said, suddenly weary. "Things have been so hectic."

"I knew about the meeting at Big Canoe," he said, beside her now at the podium. "I should have reported what I had."

"You're mad at me."

"Yes, I'm mad. You sent me a fax like you did all the other riffraff. I thought we were friends."

"Are friends obligated to tell each other things their boss isn't ready for them to tell?"

He shrugged. "You could've at least called me to tell me something was up, even if you couldn't tell me what it was."

She leaned on the podium. "I can't argue with you there, but I'm not good with those kinds of subtleties. Any way I can make it up to you?"

Sterling placed his hands on his hips. "Are you teasing me?"

"No tease," she said. "Do you want to have dinner? You said you did. Or was that just pity because I was in the hospital at the time?"

"Guilt more like it. I was pretty slow back at Prestwick Church. Another ten seconds and I might have attended your funeral."

She punched him playfully on the shoulder. "I thought you said I was doing fine by myself."

"Well, true, but a little help never hurts." He brushed back his hair. "I didn't think you heard me at the hospital."

Valerie lowered her eyes. "I heard you but didn't know how to answer."

"Am I that bad?"

She laughed. "You're not bad at all. I've just got some baggage, that's all."

"Do you want to talk about it?"

"Maybe over dinner."

"Are you asking me out?"

"Apparently so."

"Then it's a date. When?"

"What about tomorrow night?"

"You're fast."

"Only when it comes to food."

"Here's my number," he said, handing her a business card. "Home and work. Call me with the details."

"Home number too?" she asked, arching her eyebrows.

"A good reporter is always available," he said.

"And I'm supposed to call you?"

"You asked me out." He smiled at her then, and though she started to remind him that he had asked her first, she decided to play along with his teasing. But then she thought of Michael, and a jolt of guilt hit her and she almost backed out. But then Casey smiled again and she decided to push ahead. Who knew when or if she'd ever see Michael Del Rio again? For that matter, who knew if he was even still alive?

———

Two time zones to the west, billionaire Bill Stricker held a smoldering pipe in one hand and a cell phone in the other. His thick neck was bowed, and a vein the color of grape jelly ran down the back of his left ear and disappeared in the collar of his starched white, cuff-linked shirt. Closing the door of his wood-paneled office, he keyed in a number and strode to a balcony off the top-story suite of the ten-story, one hundred and twenty-room ski lodge that he owned and used as his mountain home. He held the phone to his ear. Two rings later, a familiar voice answered on the other end.

Stricker took a pull off his pipe. "I saw the news conference," he bellowed. "Is the man daft?"

"I . . . I'm working on it," said the man on the other end. "You've got to understand Chadwick. He gets his mind fixed on something, he—"

"You've got to understand something too," Stricker shouted. "I don't like failures. And right now, that's what you are to me. A flat tire, a computer on the blink. You got that?"

"I'm sorry, Mr. Stricker, just give me some time. Nothing can happen until after Christmas. Chadwick said that himself. That gives us a couple of weeks to slow this down."

Stricker studied the Rocky Mountains for a moment. A huge outcropping of rock cast a shadow over his balcony from about noon until dark every day. A ski slope and chair lift, installed for the use of his guests, ran up from the ground below, up the side of the stone and to the top of the mountain crest over a thousand feet over his head. A row of lights that switched on automatically at dusk each day bordered the slope. On the opposite side of the ski slope, just past the huge rock, the edge of a cliff jutted up. Over five hundred feet below the cliffs, a shallow river flowed through the valley, its water crystal clear and cold.

Sucking his pipe, Stricker tried to relax. He loved to stand in the shadow of the rock and stare out at his mountain. He loved everything about it, the barren beauty of the craggy peaks, the sky that stared down at him so blue it seemed breakable, the heat in the summer, and the pure white of the snow in January. He took a puff from his pipe. The only thing he loved more than his mountains was his money. And Chadwick's kooky ideas were potentially at odds with his pursuit of more of that.

"You think Chadwick has a chance with any of this?"

"I don't know. Ireland is still quiet."

Stricker laughed, then sucked his pipe once more. "Do you know what I do?" he asked.

"Well, not completely. You own Applied A&D, I know that."

"And A&D manufactures guidance systems for tanks, planes, missiles, ships—anything that moves and needs a system to make sure it reachs its designated target. World peace tends to lower the demand for things like that. When I can't sell my products, my stock portfolio loses value. A drop of even a few dollars a share costs me tens of millions of dollars. When the stock of Applied A&D drops, my contributions to a lot of worthy causes tend to go down too."

"That's a not-too-subtle threat."

"I'm not a subtle man. The last ten years have been a horror show for men like me. Defense cuts from the United States budget every year. The Pentagon goes begging for new defense systems. Less demand for the biggest moneymakers in my company's line of products. At the same time, I'm having to spend a boatload of cash on research and development just to keep up with all these young entrepreneurs who want to make me road kill on the way to their first billion. The computer industry changes every day. And now this . . . this world peace nonsense— what a joke! Even a few months of it hurts me. So I want this stuff stopped and I want it stopped now. Is that subtle enough for you?"

"I'm working on it."

"You do that."

Stricker hung up, stared up at his mountains, and sucked on his pipe some more. If Chadwick pushed ahead with this stupid idea . . . well . . . he had to make sure that didn't happen.

TWENTY-SIX

ROME

Although it was almost midnight, Clement Peter called Cardinals Roca and Zolinska into his private office chambers within an hour after his Office of International Affairs briefed him on the latest developments from Chadwick's news conference. His stomach felt slightly queasy, and his head felt like someone had used the back of his skull as a soccer ball, but he refused to give in to the pain.

Slamming into a soft chair by the window, he dismissed the two aides that hovered over him night and day and motioned for Roca and Zolinska to sit. A tray on the table next to him was filled with an assortment of edibles and a bottle of water. Though eyeing the food, Clement forced himself to leave it alone. Self-control had to come to him, no matter how difficult he found the task.

Zolinska and Roca eased down across from him. A golden tapestry rug lay between them. Clement stared at both of them.

"You told me Chadwick wouldn't move without me!" he said, trying to control his fury. "And yet now I see the announcement at his news conference. Now the whole world knows! We've had over a thousand calls already, all wanting to know why we weren't included. What am I to tell those people? What?"

"Tell them you don't work with fallen infidels," Zolinska said. "Tell them you make your own decisions, your own peace initiatives."

Clement turned to Roca. "Do you agree?"

Roca rolled the ring on his finger. Clement could almost see his mind at work. The man never spoke without forethought.

Surely he knew the purpose of this meeting. That meant he was prepared for it.

"First, let me say that we have lost nothing to this point," he began. "The Reverend Chadwick left the door wide open for you to join his initiative at any moment you decide. Second, he most graciously gave you an easy excuse for not already aligning yourself with him. Your schedule, he said. Everyone understands that. And third, I did not say that Chadwick would wait on you. Quite the opposite, I reminded His Holiness that the Reverend Chadwick would do what he thought God wanted him to do."

Clement felt his heart rate settle down a little. Roca made such good sense. No wonder the man had achieved so much. But still *he* had become pope and not Roca. God's will? He wasn't so sure.

"The Reverend Chadwick follows what he understands as God's will. Are we back to that again?"

"Precisely. Remember, this is a Protestant thing, this idea that every individual can approach God without benefit of a priest to determine what the Lord wants for him or her to do in life."

"A potentially dangerous idea."

"If taken to an extreme."

"And what is God's will for me in this matter?"

"You know what I think," Zolinska said. "My opinion has not changed. Leave this nonsense alone. Go your own way. You don't need Chadwick. He is an insignificant man compared to you. If you want to call a world summit on peace, so be it. But don't work with those outside the one true Church. To do so is blasphemy."

Feeling his head start to throb again, Clement closed his eyes. Such difficult decisions lay on the shoulders of a pope, such agonizing choices. How did one know the will of God in such a matter? Which voices should he heed? Which counsel should he take? He wanted to do the right thing, but how did one determine it?

His heart heavy, Clement closed his eyes and pondered the state into which he had fallen. Not a pretty picture—torn by choices, insecure in his own abilities, petty with his subordinates, jealous of Reverend Chadwick, selfish to a fault. But what could he do? What course could he take to climb out of the hole into which he had fallen? A sudden notion came to him. He opened his eyes and turned to Zolinska.

"Leave us," he said. "I want to talk privately with Cardinal Roca."

Zolinska opened his mouth as if to protest but then stood silently and stalked from the room. Clement reached for the bottle of water and took a long drink. He looked at the tray of food and started to reach for it, but decided to fight the temptation of his appetites. A man of his position needed better control of such things, better hold of his cravings. He dropped his hand and immediately felt better about himself. But his head still hurt terribly, and his stomach rumbled as if filled with heavy weights tumbling over and over each other.

It occurred to him that just as his craving for food sometimes threatened to overwhelm him, so also had his craving for recognition. And, just as one was unbecoming for a pope, so also was the other. He laid his face in the palms of his hands. He had come to the end of his rope and he knew it. He faced Roca.

"You put me in this office," he said, beginning to perspire. "Whether it was the will of God for you to do so, I cannot truly say. But I am here now in this holy office and no one can alter that. But . . . I hate to say this . . . but I feel like a man adrift. I am afraid I am not up to the task."

"Your humility becomes a pope," Roca said, his tone comforting. "You are simply adjusting to the enormity of the office. Give yourself a chance. Don't expect so much so soon."

Clement nodded, wiping perspiration from his forehead. "I have decided that I want to do the right thing and for the right reasons, but my pride gets in my way. I want the world to see me as a great man, a great pope. But I fear I am neither." He leaned back and tried to get his breath. Such honesty felt good, noble, and cleansing. But his head hurt worse and worse and his left arm began to tingle.

Roca leaned closer. "Greatness is perhaps found in the instant that one gives up the search for it," he soothed. "Do what you see as the good thing, the godly thing, and perhaps you will see that you will find greatness where you least expect it."

Clement gripped his arms around his stomach to squelch the pain. "God's will, my friend . . . are you telling me to do what I see as God's will?"

Roca nodded, and the look in his eyes comforted Clement as he had not been comforted since the day he placed the tiara of the papacy on his head. "I believe that what Chadwick is doing has the potential for much good in it," he said. "My decision to go to Ireland with him wasn't completely a self-indulgent one. I do want the Church to use its power, its spiritual authority, in in-

novative ways. The Reverend Chadwick has offered us just such
a way. Are you in agreement with this?"

"I am in agreement with whatever His Holiness chooses,"
Roca said. "My decision in the conclave to give you my support
was also not completely self-indulgent. I believe you are a good
man, one who will find his way to the right thing if given the time
and the counsel to do so."

Clement studied Roca for several moments, trying to determine the sincerity or the lack of such in his words. But the cardinal stayed impassive, unreadable. "You always find the right
words, my friend," he said, smiling slightly. "Though I cannot always discern the message in them."

Roca's eyebrows arched. "I am always sincere," he said. "Especially when it comes to advising His Holiness about matters of
importance to the Church. Even if I am wrong, I am nonetheless
sincere in my error."

"And your advice in the matter of Reverend Chadwick's invitation for us to join him in his quest for peace. . . ?"

"Do what you believe to be the will of God."

"I will try, my good cardinal," Clement whispered. "I will try."

"That is all a man can do," Roca said. "All that God can ask of
him."

Clement closed his eyes and leaned back in his seat. His head
pounded and pounded, and he tried to open his eyes but couldn't.
He saw soccer balls whizzing at his face and felt himself running
to escape them. But they whizzed faster than he could run, and
they struck him in the head over and over again. Then he saw
his mother. She was on the street where he grew up, and she was
opening her arms for him, and he was running from the soccer
balls toward his mother. As he reached her, she held out her arms
once more and he ran into them. She wrapped her arms around
his thick body, and the soccer balls bounced off her arms and fell
into the street, harmless toys of harmless boys.

A smile crossed Clement's wide face. But then his left arm
became completely numb, and his chest seized up. Before the
smile had a chance to completely disappear, his heart thumped
and lurched and thumped again. Then it stopped, and Clement
Peter, a man who had just decided to truly seek the will of God,
passed from this life into the next.

TWENTY-SEVEN

ATLANTA

Her wet hair in a towel, Valerie wrapped up in a tan robe and padded into her bedroom. Rolling her tired shoulders, she pulled back the bedcovers and plopped down. Switching on a lamp, she took a Bible from her bedside table and flipped it open to the Psalms. Feeling guilty because she hadn't spent much time in devotions lately, she patted down her pillow, leaned back, and tried to focus on the page.

"The earth is the Lord's," she read, "and all its fullness." The phone rang beside her. Fed up with interruptions, she kept reading. "The world and all those who dwell therein . . ." The phone rang again, then a third time. She read another sentence. "For he has founded it upon the seas . . ." The phone refused to cooperate. Slamming the Bible shut, she checked caller identification and recognized the number as an international code. For a second she tried to figure it out. Then it hit her. She dropped the Bible and picked up the phone.

"Hello, Valerie Miller."

"Valerie? It's Arthur Bremer here. Are you sitting down?" The ambassador's voice sounded agitated, almost breathless.

"Yeah," she said. "What's going on? It's what, 3 A.M. there?"

"You won't believe it," he panted, "but Clement . . . Clement died a few hours ago. Just fell right over. Seems like a heart attack, though no one knows for sure."

Valerie sagged back onto the pillow. "Are you sure, Arthur?"

"Hey, Valerie, I'm a diplomat, remember? I'm not given to loose words. I'm telling you he died. I just got word. An insider from the Vatican called less than an hour ago. It's not even out

on the news yet. It will be within the next thirty minutes or so,
but I . . . well . . . I thought I'd call you. I know you're working
with Reverend Chadwick, and I've appreciated what he's tried to
do the last couple of months with the pope. I saw his news conference and I know he wants the pope involved. So I wanted to
let him know before it hit the media. Besides," he paused and
took a breath, "I still feel bad about what happened to you . . .
how we left you high and dry—"

"That's in the past," Valerie said, not wanting to dredge it all
up again. "Let's leave it there."

"Fine. Look, I need to get off. The place is in an uproar, as you
can well imagine."

"You go," she said. "I appreciate your calling more than you
can ever know. We're square now, you hear? Square."

"Take care, Valerie." Bremer hung up.

Pulling the towel off her head, Valerie hustled to her dresser
and pulled out a pair of jeans and a Duke T-shirt. Though not
sure exactly what she planned to do, she got dressed and shoved
on a pair of brown hiking boots. In front of her mirror, she
thought of Casey Sterling. Wonder if he knew? Maybe not. Bremer said the Vatican hadn't made any announcement yet.

Hustling to the phone, she grabbed Sterling's card from the
nightstand and dialed the home number. Seconds later, he answered.

"Hey, Casey, it's Valerie Miller."

"Couldn't wait, huh?"

"No, it's not that," she said, rushing past his teasing. "Listen,
I just got a call. Have you heard about the pope?"

"The pope?"

"Yeah, he just died." She sat down again. "Arthur Bremer
called me."

"The pope's dead? No way!"

"Believe me, it's true."

"Bremer is the ambassador, right?" Casey asked.

"Yeah, an old friend." She pulled a lipstick from the nightstand and opened it.

"And you're sure of this?"

"Sure I'm sure! I'm not an amateur, remember? I worked over
there for almost two years. Bremer wouldn't call me if he didn't
have the facts." She stepped to the mirror and slid on the lipstick.

Sterling became quiet. Valerie blotted the lipstick. Her hair
was almost dry. Though she didn't know exactly what she was

going to do in the next few hours, she knew she wasn't going to stay home. Not with the momentous news she had just heard.

"I've got to call the station," Sterling said. "We can scoop on this one. What time is it?"

"About nine."

"Look, I need to go," he said, his voice revved. "Get on the air . . . make some calls . . ."

Valerie imagined the way he looked. No doubt he had been relaxing for the evening, maybe in gym shorts or sweat pants, no shirt, no shoes. Now he was probably scurrying around, looking for his shoes, grabbing a shirt from his closet.

"I'm sure we can't keep our dinner appointment tomorrow night," she said. "This will consume us for the next few days." She turned away from the mirror, looking for her car keys.

"You're probably right," he said.

She heard rushing water. Maybe he was about to wash his face.

"Why not meet me at the CBC studios?" he asked. "Or will Chadwick need you?"

Valerie stopped moving. Unless she missed her guess, her uncle was already in bed. She should call him—that much was certain. But there wasn't much he could do at this point but watch the news like everyone else. Tomorrow he would surely make a statement, but until then he wouldn't need her much.

"I think I can meet you there," she said. "At least for a while. Though I'm not sure what I'll do."

"It's not social," he said hurriedly. "I can use you. You're a professional, remember? Your expertise with the Vatican—your knowledge of what's going on over there—that's the kind of thing the viewers need to hear in a situation like this. So you'll come?"

She hesitated but only for an instant. "Sure. Let me call Reverend Chadwick. I'll meet you there within the hour."

"Super! See you then."

She hung up and headed to the closet. If Casey Sterling planned to interview her on national television, she didn't want to wear a Duke University T-shirt.

———

Twenty minutes away from Valerie, a bearded man with a black ponytail slipped a lock-pick into a rear door of the office suite of the Reverend Russell Chadwick. After less than ten seconds, the lock clicked, then slipped, the locking mechanism breached. Whistling under his breath, the bearded man slipped through the door, his movements partially hidden by the all-black garb he wore and the black makeup on his face.

The man worked quickly and expertly, his fingers sure and certain, moving from office to office, lamp to lamp, telephone to telephone, desk to desk, computer terminal to computer terminal. Pulling his tools and supplies from a black bag he had slung across his broad shoulders, the man placed listening devices in any and all conceivable places. If someone sneezed in the offices of Russell Chadwick, he and his employer would know it instantly.

Still whistling, the man exited the last office, pausing to take a short glance over his shoulder before gliding back into the hallway. A minute later he slipped back down the stairwell toward the ground floor. Men like Chadwick trusted too much, he thought. A couple of bodyguards, but almost no other security. Yes, a security team patrolled the building, but they weren't sharp. Second-rate at best, no match for a man of his expertise.

Out the back door now, the bearded man stepped hurriedly to the black van that sat by the curb. Inside the van, a wall of high-tech surveillance equipment awaited him. He climbed into the van, took off his black jacket, and started the engine. He would return early in the morning long before anyone arrived in the office.

Chadwick made such an easy target. With his phone lines tapped and his offices bugged, he couldn't do a thing without broadcasting it.

Eight time zones to the East, Cardinal Severiano Roca stepped out of the private chambers of His Holiness Clement Peter and rolled his ring on his finger. His face the color of a concrete sidewalk, he slumped past two members of the Swiss Guard and leaned his head against the wall. Closing his eyes, he exhaled heavily and wished harder than he had ever wished for anything that the last six hours had never taken place. The worst of all nightmares had happened. In office for only a few months, the pope had died. A pope who had finally, in the last hours of his life, shown that he was truly beginning to understand what it meant to sit in the Holy See of Jesus Christ.

Hearing footsteps, Roca opened his eyes and saw Lech Zolinska and another cardinal headed his way. Zolinska's broad chest seemed even broader tonight, as wide as a small truck and equally as sturdy. By his side now, Zolinska's eyes seemed frantic, almost crazed.

"You were with him," he hissed at Roca, a stubby finger poking the air. "You were there when he died."

Fighting to stay calm, Roca straightened and eyed his accuser. "So I was. Do you have a point?"

Zolinska appeared confused but he quickly recovered. "You say he had a heart attack."

"I said nothing of the sort. I don't know what happened to him. I said he grabbed the left side of his chest with his right hand and collapsed to the floor. His doctor said that he had suffered from angina for years and that this appeared to be a heart attack."

"But you were with him," Zolinska said again as if the words had some magical power to make Roca guilty of something.

"The Swiss Guard and his doctors have already quizzed me thoroughly," Roca said wearily. "You can take up your concerns with them." He turned to leave.

"I will do that!" Zolinska raised his voice. "I will insist upon an autopsy."

Roca faced his accuser again. "You know better than that," he said. "Canon law prohibits an autopsy on a pope. It keeps the conspiracy theorists busy." He pivoted and walked away.

"You killed him!" Zolinska shouted. "You killed him because he had decided to fight you and your desire to make alliance with the Protestants. I know his heart on this matter. But you will not get away with this, you will not become pope and pull the Holy Church down that path. I will see to it . . . I will . . ."

Though Zolinska continued to rant, Roca no longer listened. Turning the corner and heading back to his own quarters, he rubbed his forehead and prayed for the wisdom of God upon all that he now had to do.

TWENTY-EIGHT

Her black boots crunching the snow, Beth Roper stepped down from her rented utility vehicle and gingerly tested her footing. Satisfied with her balance, she launched herself through the tall drifts that separated her from her destination—a large A-frame building that sat in the center of a whole complex of other buildings—all of which combined to form a hotel-like ski lodge. The buildings sat about forty yards away in the middle of a huge forest of spruce trees. A curl of smoke drifted up from the chimney of the house, and the smell tickled Beth's nose. The place looked like a postcard of a winter wonderland. She wanted to pause and drink it all in for a few seconds, but she dared not do so. Too much serious business ahead for such personal indulgences.

Breathing heavily, she reached the door, kicked the snow off her boots and knocked. In less than thirty seconds the door opened, and a man she recognized only from his pictures stepped back to let her enter.

"Hello, Ms. Roper," he said pleasantly. "Glad you could accept my invitation and join me so soon after Christmas. Let me take your gear."

Handing the man her yellow parka and gloves, she inspected her surroundings. Though the entryway to the house was small, it led into a spacious room with a cathedral ceiling. Everything was made of wood—walls, floors, even the furnishings. Not many feminine touches here. A huge stone fireplace dominated the left side of the room, and a massive window overlooking a mountain valley covered the back. The head of a bear stared at her from

over the fireplace and that of a moose looked down from over the
window. For some reason she couldn't identify, she shuddered.
From the right, four other men entered, three of whom she knew
personally.

"Hey, Beth," Ted Shuster called, taking her hand. "Hope you
traveled okay."

"Sure, from Chicago to Denver, from rental car to here."

"I see you've met Mr. Stricker," Ted said.

"Well, not officially, but he did invite me here and let me in."

"Forgive me," said the host. "I'm Bill Stricker. You know Ted,
Lester, and Rodney. And this gentleman is Ludwig Roth, a col-
league of mine."

A flicker of recognition hit Roper, but she couldn't place it. She
knew the name Roth, but she didn't know from where. She shook
hands with Roth and gave Rodney and Lester each a friendly
hug.

Stricker watched for a second, then moved matters ahead.
"Now, everyone knows everyone. But since this isn't really a social occasion, and I'm sure you want to head home as soon as
possible, let's sit down and discuss the matter that brings us all
out here."

Eager to do that, Roper followed Stricker's lead as he pointed
everyone to a seat. She eased into a tall dark-stained chair that
had arms wide enough to walk on if she had so desired. Everyone
else ringed around her, Ted and Lester on a black leather sofa,
Stricker in a rocker, and Rodney and Roth in chairs identical to
hers.

Stricker took out a pipe, fiddled with it for several seconds,
then put a match to the bowl. Smoke bubbled up from the pipe.
Stricker inhaled for a second, then faced the group.

"I'm not a beat-around-the bush kind of man," he started. "So
I want to get right to the point. I'm displeased with the Reverend
Chadwick, real displeased. If what he proposed a few days ago
actually succeeds, it'll make my life tough. So I'm here to talk
about how to stop it, plain and simple." He puffed on his pipe and
looked at the group as if expecting someone to challenge him. No
one did. Roper stared at him, not sure what he expected her to
say or do.

"You don't know this one," he said, indicating Roth. "So let me
tell you about him."

Roper stared at Roth, an elfish-looking man with wispy gray
hair and a sharp nose.

"Mr. Roth owns an international chain of car and truck dealerships. Though he's no longer in *Forbes Magazine*'s list of the one hundred wealthiest men in the world, he hasn't fallen too far. In addition to making cars and trucks for folks like you and me, he also makes troop transports, military jeeps, and all-terrain vehicles. You get my drift. Plus"—he pointed his pipe at his friend as if noting the presence of a rare jewel—"he's also what we used to call an oil baron. He's got fields and refineries in such far-flung places as the North Seas of the Atlantic and the dusty prairies of west Texas."

Stricker stopped and puffed his pipe again. Roper mentally clicked through the files of her brain, struggling to place Roth. The information was in the files somewhere, but she couldn't pull it up. Frustrated, she glanced at Chadwick's men, trying to get a read on their purpose here. Had the Reverend sent them to meet with Stricker, to see if they could calm his concerns? But what difference did it make to Chadwick what a man like Stricker wanted?

"I give a lot of money to the Reverend's work," Stricker said, answering her question before she could ask it. "And I intend to keep on doing that. But like I said, I've got some concerns." Pipe in hand, he stood and walked to the window. The room was silent.

Ted Shuster cleared his throat and crossed his legs and stared at the floor, and Roper could see that he felt as uncomfortable as she did. Something didn't feel right here, something she was missing, something hanging in the air like the smoke from Stricker's pipe. From out of nowhere, she suddenly remembered the name Ludwig Roth. Her mouth fell open. The Ludwig and Edna Roth Foundation for Catholic Education!

Three years ago she had written a story about wealthy people who were trying to use their fortunes for benevolent purposes. Though she interviewed their publicists instead of the actual persons, she had come to know over twenty people—seventeen of them men—of various religious traditions and levels of commitment who sought to make a difference with the dollars they possessed. Roth and his wife were two of those people. But what was he doing here? What connection did he have with Stricker? And what about Chadwick's trio? How did they fit into this?

Stricker faced the group again. "We need your help," he said to Beth. "Or I should say we need the help your magazine can give us."

"I'm not sure what you mean," she said.

Stricker gave a dismissive wave of his hand. "Don't give me that," he said. "You know what's going on here. I know the Reverend's plan is noble. Who doesn't want peace? But it's never going to happen, not in the long run. Since it won't happen in the long run, I don't think it makes much sense to do what he's trying to do. It hurts as many people as it helps. So he stops a few skirmishes over the next few years. Then he dies. Everything goes back to normal. War and rumors of war, isn't that how the Bible says it? So I say leave things as they are. Why hurt men like me and Mr. Roth, men who do good things with the dollars we earn?" He paused but only for a second.

"You destroy men like us, and you destroy the means to help those in need: boys and girls who won't have enough to eat, boys and girls who won't have clothes to wear, boys and girls who won't get to go to college. You see where I'm going with this, don't you?"

Roper glanced at Ted Shuster. Did he agree with Stricker? Then it dawned on her. Ted and Rodney and Lester weren't here at the direction of Russell Chadwick! They were here on their own, behind the Reverend's back.

Smelling the rat and not liking it, she leaned forward and gritted her teeth. "I see where you're going," she said. "You want me to use my influence to discredit the work Reverend Chadwick wants to do."

"Oh, it's more than that," interrupted Stricker. "We want you to talk to your father, get him to bring his influence to bear here, to use his publications, his radio stations to call the Reverend Chadwick back to the work the Lord chose him to do—the preaching of the gospel. That's all we're asking here, right, Ted? We just want the Reverend to return to his first love."

Ted lowered his eyes but didn't speak. Roper sensed that he had some real misgivings about the whole situation.

"My dad is pretty much out of the business," she said to Stricker. "He doesn't involve himself too much anymore."

"All the more reason for you to join our efforts," Roth said, intervening in the conversation. "You're the only child, the heir apparent."

"The board makes all the editorial decisions," she said.

"But you can shape the board," Boggett said, his heavy face eager.

"I'm not sure I want to do that," she countered. "Why should I?"

"I reminded you of Revelation thirteen," Boggett said. "You asked the question at the news conference."

Roper stared into the fire—the seven-headed Beast of Revelation. Did Boggett really believe that the Reverend Chadwick had somehow, wittingly or otherwise, become a party to such evil as that? Did *she* believe it? Roth raised his hand as if to ask a teacher a question.

"I'm a novice here," he said. "What's this about Revelation? As a businessman, I know of no such thing as this."

Roper shook her head. "Ted, do you want to take a shot at this?"

Ted stood and walked to the window, wiping his hands on his pants.

"It's the way a large segment of the evangelical Protestant world interprets the New Testament book of Revelation," he began. "They believe a literal man will arise to rule the world and bring in an era of universal peace. Most of the world will view him as a godlike figure. But the truth is, he will be what we call 'the Antichrist,' the very opposite of the Lord Jesus.

"In Revelation, chapter thirteen, we see a description of a beast, a seven-headed beast, a beast with ten horns. In this interpretation, the seven-headed beast is the political equivalent of the Antichrist. It represents a revived Roman Empire, an empire that gave the world peace the first time it existed and will do so again when it comes back to life. But the peace will be a false one, one created by the very epitome of evil, one in which this beast of a man will ultimately seek to destroy everything and everyone remotely connected to belief in the true God, Jesus Christ."

"Quite complicated," Roth said.

"More than you know," Ted said. "Before the twentieth century, many Protestants believed that the Catholic Church, centered in the pope, was the Antichrist."

"And what did the Catholic Church believe?" Roth asked. "Since we obviously didn't agree with the Protestants on the matter."

Ted shook his head. "That's hard to say. Catholics haven't made much of Revelation over the years. They just accepted it as God's word of hope to the people of faith, a promise that in the end God will triumph, evil will receive its due punishment, and the faithful will gain eternal life with Jesus Christ."

"That makes sense to me," Roth said.

Ted shrugged. "The currently popular view really came into vogue after the founding of the nation-state of Israel in the late 1940s. A book called *The Late Great Planet Earth*, by a man named Hal Lindsay, made it accessible to the masses. Now almost everything that happens in international politics gets interpreted through the filter of this view of history. So when Reverend Chadwick asks six other religious leaders to join him in a crusade for world peace . . ." His voice trailed off.

"Millions of evangelicals automatically analyze his actions in light of the book of Revelation," finished Roper. "Which brings us to where we are today."

Stricker stood and chewed his pipe for a moment. Ted moved back to his seat, automatically yielding the floor to the billionaire. Stricker walked over to Roper and stared down over her.

"I need your help," he said. "For the sake of a lot of people. We need your help."

"I don't know," Roper said, her heart beating heavily. "I don't know if I agree with you, for one thing, and I don't know what I can do, for another."

"Will you think about it?" Stricker asked. "Pray about it?"

Though the room was warm, Roper shuddered again. She doubted if Stricker prayed much about anything. From out of nowhere, she suddenly felt claustrophobic. Right now she wanted out of the room, away from the all-male contingent that seemed so bent on enlisting her in their scheme to stop Reverend Chadwick. Standing up, she turned away from Stricker. "I'll see," she said. "But right now, I think I want to go." She moved briskly toward the door.

"Don't rush off," called Stricker. "Stay the night with us."

"I . . . I don't think so," she mumbled, taking her parka from the woman who appeared from out of nowhere. "I just need to be alone to think through all this. I'll . . . call you."

"Yes, you do that," Stricker called as she opened the door to leave. "Call me soon."

Watching Roper leave, Stricker turned to the rest of the group. "Do you think she'll help us?" he asked.

No one answered.

He drew on his now dead pipe, then stepped over to the fireplace, grabbed a match from the mantel, and struck it. "She will," he said, touching the burning match to the pipe. "If she knows what's good for her and the Reverend."

TWENTY-NINE

FRIDAY, JANUARY 2
ATLANTA

Her black overcoat buttoned up against her throat, Valerie leaned into the wind and told herself to think summer thoughts. Hit by a rare ice storm, most of Atlanta had stayed home for the day, avoiding the hazardous roads. Yet, according to the news, the freezing rain had still caused over two hundred fender benders. Amazingly, though, only one person had died in the accidents.

Pushing open the door to the Six Sisters, a stylish but quiet restaurant she liked to frequent, she squinted through the bright lights and saw Casey Sterling waiting in the vestibule, his eyes facing away from her. He wore a tan pullover sweater and navy slacks, and he needed a haircut. Blond curls had begun to twist up on the collar of the sweater.

For a second, Valerie stood there and studied him, her mind racing back over the last two weeks. The days seemed like a blur. With the funeral of the pope as a backdrop, she had appeared on Casey's broadcasts on three different occasions as an expert on Vatican affairs. People on the streets had started to recognize her face, and on two occasions someone had actually asked for her autograph. But the frenzied activity of those weeks had kept her and Casey apart, except for their moments on camera together. The date they had made the night of Clement's death had been postponed three times—first because of the pope's death, second because of the increased work load that followed, and finally, for Christmas.

She'd gone home to Charlotte on the twenty-third and returned to Atlanta on the twenty-seventh. Since then her uncle had kept her busy. Though his Peace Project had gone on hold

and the other religious leaders who had met with Chadwick at
Big Canoe had scattered back to their own lives, her uncle
wanted things ready when the next outbreak of violence came.

Her job was to stay in touch with Zorella, ben Moseph, Blevins, the Dalai Lama, and Khatama, to keep them updated on
events, help them prepare for the joint efforts ahead, encourage
them, stroke them, and make sure they stayed enthusiastic.
Though the Christmas holidays and Clement's death slowed progress down, Chadwick's zeal for his grand alliance had not dimin-
ished.

Handing her coat to a hostess, Valerie stepped up behind
Casey and tapped him on the shoulder. Twisting, he stood and
made a show of staring at his watch.

"It's almost eight," he said, but without rancor. "You're late
again and you can't blame it on traffic this time."

"You hold a grudge a long time," she said, stepping by him
toward a table. "My workout went long."

"You're one of these 'fitness' women, aren't you?"

Her mind flashed back to some unpleasant memories, and
Valerie shrugged. "Like they say, it's dangerous out there. A girl's
got to take care of herself."

"What kind of stuff do you do?"

They reached their table and sat down.

"Oh, aerobics, run three to five miles, some weight training.
There's a Fit For Life Club less than a mile from my office."

"Yeah, I've seen it. You climbed the wall yet?"

Valerie felt herself blush and glanced down. The club had a
climbing wall over seventy-five feet high. She'd always wanted to
try it, but the experiences of the previous year had made her
more cautious than in the past, and she hadn't mustered the
courage to climb anything, much less a wall as high as a six-story
building. "Not yet," she said, facing him again. "I . . . well . . . I've
got a thing about heights. But I'm going to do it one of these days.
I'm determined."

Casey shook his head. "Women like you are scary," he said.

"Sometimes we need to be."

"You don't do firearms too, do you?"

"My dad made me," she said. "I . . . well, I ran into some trouble last year. My dad bought me a gun, a Sauer .25 automatic,
and made me take some lessons."

The waiter appeared, interrupting her explanation. They ordered water with lemon, then studied the menu.

"Did you have a good holiday?" she asked, changing the subject.

"Yeah, I guess so," he said, still looking puzzled. "Didn't do
much. I saw my mom for Christmas Day, then flew to Rome for
the pope's burial."

"I saw you on television. You did a great job covering the funeral ceremony."

"It was amazing," he said. "Open-air Mass in St. Peter's
Square, over a million people paying their last respects. They
buried him in a plain cypress coffin in the crypt of St. Peter's,
right beside his predecessor."

"You were eloquent at times," she said. "You seemed touched
by it all."

He shook his head in an "aw shucks" fashion and changed the
subject. "You went to Charlotte?"

Valerie started to push him back to the pope's funeral but decided against it. "Yeah, home for a few days. Couldn't rest much,
though. Too much going on."

The waiter returned and they ordered. "Vegetable omelet,"
she said. "And a root beer."

"Blueberry pancakes," he said. "And milk, whole."

The waiter disappeared. They made small talk for a few
minutes. A muted television screen flashed its images at her from
behind Casey.

"Glad we could finally get together," he offered. "Outside of
work, that is."

"I'm glad you called. I didn't know if you would." She looked
away to the television.

"Oh, you knew I would," he said. "As attractive as you are,
there's no way—"

"This is my first date in over a year," she blurted before she
could stop herself. "And it's for breakfast."

The waiter appeared with their food, placed it on the table,
and left them to eat. Valerie's face still felt hot. She took a bite of
her food.

"I don't understand that," Sterling said, sipping his milk.

"It's complicated," she said. "I broke off an engagement, then
met a man, and thought I was falling in love. But he disappeared . . ."

Sterling stopped in midbite. "He disappeared? Like . . . liter-
ally?"

"Yeah. Crazy, huh? Like into thin air."

He munched for a few seconds. "I'd like to hear that story, and I bet it connects with the Sauer somehow."

She shrugged. "Maybe it does. But now's not the time to talk about it." She picked at her omelet.

"What about you?" she asked. "You're a wealthy man, famous all over the world. No girlfriend, no wife?"

"Oh, I've had girlfriends. But I don't believe in marriage. Besides, you get a tax break if you just live together."

She lowered her gaze and frowned.

"Hey, I didn't mean to offend you," he said. "It was just a joke."

"I don't joke about something as sacred as marriage vows. Maybe that makes me a prude, but I'll live with that."

"Oh, I wouldn't say you're a prude. You've just got some convictions. I like that."

She took a drink of root beer. "What about yours? What do you believe in?"

Sterling stared at his plate. "Oh, I don't know. Dark beer, steak sandwiches, convertibles—except on days like this. Beach sand between my toes, hard work, Mom."

They stayed quiet for a second.

"Your father?"

"You're nosy," Sterling said.

"You said once that you admired curiosity."

"Yeah, well, my dad made a bad bargain with a bottle of tequila somewhere back in the 1960s and never put it down. Haven't seen him in a while. He was a tumbleweed for years—here, there, wherever the wind blew. He showed up back in Swansboro last year, his liver eaten up by the booze. Pretty useless, if you ask me." He swallowed a bite of pancakes.

"That's sad, not having a dad around."

"Yeah, well, no one promised us a bed of roses."

"Why'd he do it? Leave you, I mean?"

Sterling shrugged. "Who knows? Maybe being without me and Mom made him happy."

"You think that's true?"

"Who knows? Who knows what makes anyone happy? What about you? Are you happy?"

"Now who's being nosy?"

"Just curious."

They ate for a couple of minutes. Sleet clicked against the

windows to the right of their table. Valerie set her fork on her plate.

"I can't honestly say I'm happy right now," she started. "I'm a mess, really, more confused than I've ever been. A lot has happened to me in the past year, and it has 'rocked my world,' as the saying goes."

"But you don't want to talk about any of that."

"No. Maybe someday, but not now."

Sterling drank some milk. "Maybe we're not supposed to feel happy," he said. "Maybe that's not the way we're made, not the way the world is made. Maybe we just drift through it all, one big bundle of stuff. No reason, no purpose."

"That's pretty pessimistic."

He wiped his mouth. "Yeah, well, my mom and dad split when I was a kid. I wasn't happy then, and though I've accomplished a lot since then, I learned that happiness isn't promised. Fun, maybe, but happiness . . . I don't know about that." He took another bite, then abruptly changed the subject. "So who's going to replace Clement?"

She ate a minute before answering, deciding whether or not to go back to the happiness discussion and tell him that she did believe in it, that she believed that God gave happiness, deepseated peace to those who lived by faith. But she had just admitted that she hadn't experienced much of that lately, so maybe she should just stay quiet lest she come across as a hypocrite.

Feeling slightly guilty for allowing the opportunity to pass, she nonetheless took a drink of her root beer and shifted her thoughts to the papal conclave. It had gone into session on the second day after the required *novendiali*, the nine-day waiting period after Clement's funeral. Right now one hundred ten cardinals were sequestered in quarters in the Sistine Chapel, charged with the sworn duty to elect the next leader of the Catholic Church. Following historic custom, all the officers of the Roman Curia, the ruling body in the Vatican, except the Dean of the Cardinals, had lost his position. Everyone entered the conclave as one among equals, each of them a candidate, but none of them a favorite.

The Dean of the Cardinals had called the conclave to order. Guards had sealed the doors. No one could enter and no one could leave until a pope had been elected. The cardinals bunked in the St. Martha Guest House, a new one-hundred-fifty-room hotel just a few hundred yards from the Sistine Chapel. Though the quarters were stripped of telephones, faxes, and any other communications devices, they were a vast improvement over the austere conditions endured by cardinals before them.

"You know the saying," she finally answered. "He who goes into a conclave as pope comes out as a cardinal."

"But you've got some ideas," he said.

"I know the characteristics they'll want," she agreed. "Probably an Italian again, like Clement. A man over sixty, maybe close to seventy. Though everyone wants someone who'll last longer than Clement, no one wants a pope who'll go on forever like Clement's predecessor. He'll have to have a lot of international experience too—and an ability in multiple languages. And he'll have to be a traditionalist, someone who won't make wholesale changes, or take the Church in too liberal a direction."

"You think it'll take long?"

She chewed on a forkful of egg. "Who knows? Most of the conclaves before Clement took four days or less. But now, if an absolute majority of the electors favor a specific candidate on the first ballot, all they have to do is hold firm through the next twelve days—about thirty elections on average—then the rules change to simple majority vote. They can elect their candidate without compromising or moving to a consensus figure. It's a process made to order to elect a man of great principle, but not necessarily to elect a man acceptable to the whole body of the Church."

"But that didn't happen with Clement."

Valerie shrugged. "It's all unpredictable," she said. "There's no way to predetermine it."

"Sounds complicated."

"You have no idea."

"So who are the most likely candidates, the *papabili*?"

She held up her hand. "Is this an interview or a date?"

He took a bite of a pancake. She stared at the television. An image of St. Peter's Square flashed onto the screen. She faced Sterling again. Maybe she had sounded too harsh.

"Look, I'm sorry," she apologized. "But I've had a lot of work lately. And not enough sleep. I didn't mean—"

"Hey, don't sweat it," he said. "I do that too much. But I'm interested, that's all. Remember what I said about curiosity. I promise you I'm not asking you these questions as part of the job. I . . . well . . . you didn't want to talk about personal stuff, but I like to hear you talk. So I ask questions. So what do you want to talk—?"

"Casey, look!" Her eyes were glued to the television screen. Tom Brokaw's face filled the airwaves. The scene had shifted from Brokaw to Rome, to the makeshift chimney on the Sistine Chapel. Smoke from the chimney drifted into the air, the historic sign that another vote had been taken. She studied the smoke carefully to determine the color. It was white!

"They've elected a pope!" Sterling said, instantly sliding out of his seat. "Let's get to the station!"

The television picture switched to the crowd in St. Peter's Square. Over a hundred thousand people waited below the balcony of St. Peter's Basilica to hear the name of their new Supreme Pontiff.

A step behind Sterling, Valerie motioned to the waiter.

"We need a check," she said. "In a hurry."

The waiter hustled away. At the cash register, the hostess grabbed their coats. The waiter brought the bill.

"Wonder who it is?" Sterling asked, handing money to the waiter and slipping into his gray overcoat.

"Wait a minute," Valerie said as she slipped her fingers into her gloves. "The *carmerlengo* will make the announcement from the balcony of St. Peter's."

She ran to a television in the lounge and turned up the volume.

The portly figure of Cardinal Peroni Fellucio filled the screen, his face wearing a comforting smile. "I announce to you a great joy!" he intoned. "We have a pope!"

The crowd roared, their prayers answered. Then they hushed to hear the name.

Apparently enjoying his moment in the spotlight, Fellucio paused and drew out the announcement, the syllables of the name. "The new pope is Cardinal . . . Severiano . . . Roca."

The crowd burst into cheers again, and a picture of Cardinal Roca flashed onto the screen, but Valerie and Sterling didn't hear the crowd or see the picture because they had already dashed out of the restaurant, their coats still unbuttoned.

"Leave your car!" Sterling shouted. "Ride with me."

Obeying quickly, she jumped into his Mercedes.

Sterling reached over and squeezed her hand for just a second as he accelerated away from the curb. "Never a dull moment when I'm with you," he said. "Never a dull moment."

———

Sitting alone in his private quarters, the man formerly known as Severiano Roca rolled his cardinal's ring on the third finger of his left hand and tried to get control of his breathing. Though never one to get overly emotive, his face had turned splotchy from tears and he felt himself close to hyperventilating. In the last six hours, a truly miraculous event had transpired. Having entered the conclave with no plans and no hopes to stand as pontiff, he had just been elected the Vicar of Christ, the prelate of Rome. Only an hour or so ago, the carmerlengo of the cardinals had officially asked him the ritual question: "Do you accept your canonical election as Supreme Pontiff?"

His throat tight, he had said, "Accepto," and announced the name he had chosen: John Peter. In accordance with historic practice, he had chosen one of the names of his predecessor.

After the singing of the *Te Deum* of thanksgiving, the electors had escorted him to the sacristy to put on his temporary papal robes—a white cassock with a shoulder-length cape and a high white sash.

Back in the Sistine Chapel, he had taken a seat on a throne erected in front of the altar, and each of the cardinals had approached him one by one to embrace him and kiss the papal ring.

To his great amazement, the deed was done.

His chin in his hand, he pondered the mystery of it all. Months ago, he had entered a conclave as the odds-on favorite to become pope. But the unforeseen had occurred and his efforts failed. But this time he had entered the conclave with a genuine peace that someone else should wear the tiara of Rome. But again the unexpected had happened. By doing nothing on his own behalf, he had done exactly the right thing. When seeking the office, he had not found it. But when glad for it to pass to someone else, it had fallen to him. Somewhere in that, surely he could learn a great spiritual lesson. Perhaps popes are indeed chosen, he decided, rather than elected. Perhaps his decision to support Clement in the last conclave had truly been the will of God. But now that was over. His time had come.

Standing, he walked to a row of simple square windows that overlooked a small garden below. Night covered the ground and he could not see far. But that did not matter. With so many weighty matters on his mind, Pope John Peter wasn't much interested in viewing the gardens.

THIRTY

Her eyes scratchy from a lack of sleep, Valerie vigorously shook her head to stay awake, and though not normally a coffee drinker, chugged down half a cup of the stuff—black, no sugar. To her left at the conference table sat Ted Shuster, to her right, Rodney Kent, his laptop computer on but not active. The two men didn't appear any happier than she felt. In fact, they looked downright depressed. Ted's black pin-striped suit was wrinkled and his tie knot off center, and Rodney's slender frame seemed to have wasted away to almost nothing, his cheekbones now sharp points poking against the skin of his face. The events of the last few days had definitely affected their holiday season, and from what she could see, not for the better.

She glanced at her watch—7:32. Her uncle Russell had requested their presence at 7:30 A.M. She tried her coffee again, but it had already grown cold. Placing the cup down, she started to say something to Ted but then decided against it. Neither he nor Rodney had made a sound since their initial greeting five minutes ago. Valerie sighed. She'd attended wakes with more noise than this.

Apparently holding fast to his decision to bail out, Lester Boggett had failed to show. Her uncle would feel terrible about that. He took everything to heart.

Valerie rubbed her eyes and checked her watch again. 7:40 and still no Chadwick. It wasn't like him to come in late. She thought back over the last day. Sterling had asked her to work with him through the day, filling him in on what she knew about the personality of Cardinal Roca, now known as John Peter.

At 10 P.M.—the end of prime time—Sterling invited Valerie to dinner. Seeing no reason to say no, she joined him back at Six Sisters. The meal was uneventful, both of them too pumped about the day's work to talk much about anything else. At the door of the restaurant after dinner, Sterling asked her to take a walk.

"It's a touch cold for that, don't you think?" she asked.

"You're wearing a warm coat," he countered. "And a scarf and gloves and boots. You put on anything else, they'll declare you a clothing store. Just a short walk. Come on, I need to burn off some energy."

"Okay," she said, not really ready to sleep herself. "We walk until my nose turns red, then we come back."

"Agreed."

They walked out of Six Sisters and turned right toward Olympic Park. The streets were quiet; it was too cold for anyone else. Halfway down the first block, Sterling lightly laid a hand on her back. Her alarm bells sounded but she didn't say anything.

"So what happens now?" Sterling asked.

"Related to what?"

"The new pope. Will he throw in with the Reverend and the rest of his new buddies?"

"Don't you ever take a break?" she asked, perturbed for some reason she couldn't readily name. "I mean, we've been at this all day. Give it a rest."

He dropped his hand from her back and shoved his hands in his pockets. "Look, I'm tired, that's all," she said, regretting her outburst. "I'm ready to think about something else."

He nodded. "Forgive me, I'm just a one-track guy."

Valerie stopped and faced him. The streetlight poured white light on his handsome face. "You're ambitious," she said. "I know something about that."

"You were a climber with the State Department, weren't you?" he asked.

She started to walk again, deliberating whether to tell him anything or not. "Yeah," she said, deciding it didn't matter what he knew. "On the fast track. But not for long."

"What happened? You obviously know your stuff. You relate well to people, have the right family and political connections. What made you step off the ladder?"

She tucked her scarf under her neck. "I almost got killed," she said. "An archeologist found a manuscript in some caves near Ephesus, Turkey. The ambassador to the Vatican, Arthur Bremer, sent me to investigate. I joined up with a priest named Michael Del Rio, a professor from Notre Dame, the nephew of Severiano Roca—"

"The new pope!" Sterling interrupted. "No wonder you know so much about Roca."

Valerie stepped over a chunk of ice. "I know him pretty well," she agreed. "But more from my work in the Vatican than personally—though he and I have talked about Michael a few times. Anyway, Michael and I found the scroll, and Michael read it. But . . ." She hesitated and stopped once more, her hands in her coat pockets.

Sterling stepped closer, put a hand on her side. "What happened, Valerie?"

"We had the scroll," she said. "Or at least Michael did. We met in Costa Rica, at a mansion there owned by Willard Madden. He died a few months ago."

"The media billionaire," Sterling said.

"Exactly. Anyway, we were on the island when a group of mercenaries and an earthquake hit at the same time. Somehow . . ." She turned her face to the sky. "Somehow . . ." Her voice trailed off and she didn't finish.

"What happened to him?" Sterling persisted, a hand on both her elbows now.

Tears pushed into Valerie's eyes but she fought them back. "He . . . he disappeared," she stammered. "In all the confusion, the guns firing, the ground cracking, everything falling apart . . . he just disappeared. No one knows what happened. Maybe he died, we don't know. Maybe he disappeared deliberately. . . ."

"Why would he do that?"

"The scroll . . . it told the life of Jesus . . . supposedly from the eyewitness account of Mary, his mother."

"Wow!"

"Exactly. I think Michael was afraid of what would happen if scholars said it was authentic, of what it would mean to the Christian faith."

"So maybe he took the scroll and ran with it."

"Maybe, I don't know. That's the hard part. These cliffs . . . the house sat on these cliffs . . . maybe he . . . maybe the earthquake threw him over, or maybe one of the men who attacked us . . . We just . . ." Her hands covered her face and the tears refused to stay still and she couldn't talk anymore.

Sterling stood beside her while her grief poured out. The tears kept coming, and then her body trembled in the frigid night. Sterling stepped even closer and hugged her, his arms encircling her waist, his body warm against hers.

"Did you love him?" Sterling asked.

Valerie trembled even harder. Sterling hugged her tighter, and the alarm bells rang again in Valerie's head, but she hurt too much to resist. No harm in a hug on a cold January night when her heart ached so bad it seemed that it might crack and splinter into a thousand pieces. So long as Sterling knew it could never lead to anything, it didn't matter.

The sound of an opening door shook Valerie from her memories, and she looked up to see her uncle stepping into the room. Pushing away her thoughts of Casey Sterling, she glanced at Ted and Rodney. They looked like men headed to the firing squad. She sat up straighter and smoothed down the front of her sweater. Chadwick took a seat at the head of the table. He looked haggard, but his jaw was firm. He laid a manila folder on the table, then folded his hands in front of him.

"I'll not waste time with preliminaries," he said soberly. "I know things feel strange right now. I've canceled our spring crusades until we see what happens with this peace initiative. I've run Lester off. I've caused our supporters to ask a lot of questions. I've raised concern in the entire evangelical world. Have you seen this?" He opened the folder and slid three magazines across the table at them. Valerie grabbed a copy, then pushed the others over to Ted and Rodney.

The Christian Weekly. Though not the lead story, a sidebar insert on the cover contained this headline: RUSSELL CHADWICK: PROPHET OR PAWN? Editorial on page thirty-two.

Her heart jumping, Valerie flipped to page thirty-two. The byline said, "Beth Roper." She quickly read the editorial.

In the December 18 issue of this magazine, I reported the news story in which the Reverend Russell Chadwick announced to the world his plans to ally himself with six other religious leaders in an effort to bring peace to the world. In that article, I introduced my readers to the six with whom Chadwick hoped to work. Of these, only two others are Chris-

tians. The others, as I reported, include a Muslim, a Jew, a
Buddhist, and what can only be described as a New Age guru.
At the time, however, I made no editorial statements regard-
ing my opinion of the merits of such an initiative by Reverend
Chadwick, a man most of the world respects and loves. Today,
though, I want to speak briefly to the matter of the proposed
alliance.

Within the last couple of days, I have heard discussions
about the Reverend Chadwick that I never thought I'd hear.
These discussions have suggested that he has somehow fallen
into league with Satan, that his efforts toward peace are connected to the seven-headed Beast of Revelation, that he's now
an unaware pawn of the power of evil. I'm no theologian or
Bible scholar, but I do know a thing or two about people. And
this I think I know about the Reverend Chadwick. He's a
godly man, a man full of the Spirit of the Lord Jesus, a man
who has been a prophet to our world for almost half a century.
If this peace initiative isn't of God, he'll figure it out soon
enough. But if it is, I can't imagine anyone I'd rather see leading the charge.

For now, I propose to wait and see. Withhold judgment.
Maybe Reverend Chadwick is a pawn. But maybe he's still
our prophet. So let's give peace a chance. Pray for Reverend
Chadwick. And yes, pray for those with whom he seeks to
work. Who knows? Perhaps he can tell them all about Jesus.
Wouldn't that be a miracle?

Valerie laid the magazine on the table and stared at her
uncle. His shoulders slumped and his eyes seemed glazed. She
felt sad for him, sad that a man of his stature had to deal with
the kind of trash that Roper mentioned in her editorial. On either
side of her Ted and Rodney finished the article.

"I'm listening," Chadwick said, his hands in his lap. "Who's
having these discussions?"

Ted hung his head. Rodney stared past the room to the sky
outside the window. Valerie felt like crying.

"I've heard these discussions," Ted admitted, his voice
guarded. "Lester suggested it first."

"He's told some others," Rodney added, "though I'm not sure
he really believes it."

Chadwick weighed their words. Valerie had the sense that
Ted and Rodney weren't telling all they knew. But she had no
basis for the feeling and so didn't comment.

"It doesn't matter if Lester believes what he's saying or not,"

Chadwick said, the first bit of anger edging into his voice. "Just speaking a story gives it life. The tongue is a raging fire, and you can't control the word once it's spoken."

"Roper didn't side with the naysayers," Valerie said, hoping to accentuate the positive. "She told people to wait and see."

Chadwick smiled but it wasn't a happy smile. "She did what every careful journalist does," he said. "She left herself an opening either way. But she communicated the message that Lester has apparently already started. I might be in league with the Devil; I *might* be connected, *unwittingly*, of course, to the Antichrist. You don't have to say whether I am or not. You just put the notion in play, and people all over the country receive the message. Plus, who knows how many people will hear this idea over their radio stations? Roper has almost one hundred fifty outlets scattered across the country." He took a deep breath and shook his head.

"So what's next?" Ted asked. "Do you want me to resign?"

Chadwick stared at him for several seconds.

"No, Ted, I don't want you to resign. Nor you either, Rodney." He faced the soloist. "We've been through too much together. I don't know what I'd do in your place. Maybe I'd think the guy was off his rocker too, the things I've suggested."

"Does this mean we go back to crusades?" Rodney asked hopefully. "I mean, if people think this, they won't support us if we press on with this peace thing. It'll kill everything, all we've built all these years."

Chadwick stood and walked to the window, his steps slow, his right arm trembling. The sunlight washed in over his head and Valerie saw the lines in his face. He looked old and tired and uncertain, and for the first time it really dawned on Valerie that her uncle was gravely ill and terribly weary. But when he turned to face them again, it seemed that a new energy infused his entire body.

"No, we don't go back to the crusades," he stated. "We may never go back to the crusades. People think they can stop me with a suggestion that I'm senile? With the notion that I'm a pawn of Satan? They threaten to cut off their contributions? Shows how little they know. I don't do what I do for the size of the check someone throws in the offering plate or sends in the mail. I started off with a ten-year-old car and a suit out of my dead uncle's closet, and I can go back to that if necessary. You know when I'll go back to the crusades, Rodney? Do you know?"

He moved back across the room faster than Valerie thought possible and stood at the head of the table again, both palms flat on the surface, his eyes sharp and focused.

"No . . . I don't know," Rodney stammered.

"What about you, Ted? Do you know?"

Ted shook his head, his eyes down.

"I'll tell you when," Chadwick said. "I'll go back when I believe the Lord wants me to go back. I'll go back when the Spirit rushes over these old bones of mine and moves me in that direction. I'll go back when I hear the voice of God, when I feel the tap of the hand of the Almighty on my shoulder." He paused, but only for an instant.

"I told all of you one other time," he said. "Leave if you want, if that's what you think the Lord wants from you. Lester did, and I admire his conviction. Right or wrong, he's doing what he thinks he should. So I'm saying it again—don't stay if you've got doubts. I'd rather you leave now than do something halfheart-edly.

"I'm making contact with the alliance again tomorrow morn-ing. If you haven't seen the rest of the newspaper, things have erupted in Kosovo all over again. The place is a mess. The United Nations troops are trying to get control but they're scattered. There aren't enough of them and they don't have enough author-ity. I'm making arrangements to go there with any member of the alliance who wants to join me."

He stood up from the table. "I need you with me. I don't mind saying it. But I'm not begging. You decide today. I'm giving you until noon. Pray about it. Let me know what you choose."

Without another word, he pivoted and left the room. Her heart breaking, Valerie dropped her head into her hands. She knew she'd stay with her uncle. But she had no idea what Ted and Rodney would do. But if they left, she couldn't help but feel that she had caused the breakup of the most effective evange-listic team the world had ever known.

Strolling through a garden just outside his private quarters inside Vatican City just over two hours later, Cardinal Lech Zo-linska heard his cell phone ring. Flipping the phone from the pocket of his black jacket, he edged up against a tree and spoke in little more than a whisper.

"Yes, this is Cardinal Zolinska. I've been expecting your call."

"It seems that the Reverend Chadwick will move forward with his silly peace initiative," said the caller, "in spite of our best efforts to dissuade him. I'm calling to ask what you believe your new pope will do?"

Zolinska brushed at his nose and resisted the temptation to curse the fates that had put Roca on the throne of St. Peter.

"I fear the new pontiff will look favorably upon the Reverend Chadwick's efforts," he said in disgust.

"Sorry to hear that," said the caller. "Do you think he will actually place his life in danger as Pope Clement did?"

"I cannot judge at this point. But if he does, it cannot happen anytime soon. He has much to handle here first. Matters of Church."

"Can you slow him down some, or keep him in place there for a while?"

"That is my plan. I will work with my caucus to see that it happens."

"Excellent, we need time to deal with Chadwick."

Two priests walked past Zolinska and he shielded the phone against the tree.

"Does anyone suspect foul play with Clement?" the caller asked.

Zolinska squeezed the phone tighter. "I think not. But you know how people talk."

"Talk will not hurt us," said the man. "And the lack of an autopsy means the talk can never advance past the conspiracy theory stage."

"Indeed," Zolinska said. "What will you do about Chadwick?"

The caller hesitated and Zolinska blew on his fingers. The late afternoon sun had dwindled, and the dusk felt like a frost would soon descend.

"I shall do whatever is necessary, you can rest assured of that. Meanwhile, keep me informed about events in the Vatican. I'll call again on the prearranged schedule."

Zolinska scratched an ear. The night fell deeper. The caller hung up and Zolinska walked back into the warmth of his private apartment. Fixing himself a cup of tea, he took a sip and pondered his next move. He hated the notion of his pope working with religious infidels and pagans, and he would do whatever it took to see that Mother Church had no part in doing so.

THIRTY-ONE

The back of her white silk blouse damp with perspiration, Valerie hung up the phone and eased herself off the corner of her desk. Having spent most of the last three days on the telephone, her left ear hurt. Rubbing it, she plopped into her office chair and took a deep breath. What a zoo!

She had spent hours and hours making arrangements for Chadwick's excursion into Kosovo. First, she had talked at length with representatives of the six religious leaders Chadwick had invited to accompany him. Luis Zorella, Rabbi ben Moseph, the Dalai Lama, and the Ayatollah Khatama had made firm, positive commitments. They would meet her uncle in the small village of Sophia, Macedonia, on January 10 to make final preparations for their foray into hostile territory. Unfortunately, Martha Blevins' mother had fallen ill and she regretfully had to decline for the time being.

Valerie had called the Vatican and left messages for Roca— she had difficulty remembering to call him John Peter—and an official had warned her it might be days before anyone on the pontiff's staff could return her call. She had expected as much. Clement Peter hadn't seemed too cooperative after the near tragedy in Ireland, and the new pope's advisors were surely warning him to stay away from anything having to do with the cockeyed plans of Reverend Russell Chadwick.

After the Vatican, Valerie had called some friends at the State Department to inform them of her uncle's timetable and to get the proper authorizations. At first, the State Department balked.

Too dangerous, they said. A private citizen shouldn't get involved
in diplomatic matters.

"But we're not involved in diplomatic matters," she insisted.
"We're not necessarily talking to heads of state nor to their representatives. We're just going there to stop the violence and call
everyone to sit down and find a way to make peace. If they want
us involved, we'll consider participation, but that's not our real
purpose."

"I'll get back to you," said the official.

A day later, he called her back. He sounded even less happy
than before.

"You've got us over a barrel here," said the official. "Your man
Chadwick is more popular than any ten politicians. We say no to
him and we make millions of people mad at us. But he's putting
himself in harm's way. Confidentially, you need to know the president has talked about more strategic bombing to wipe out the
last of the armed enclaves. We need to say no to Chadwick for his
own protection."

"You can't keep an American citizen from leaving the country," she reminded the diplomat. "You don't have the power unless he's committed a crime, which of course, he hasn't. I only
called as a courtesy to let you know what Reverend Chadwick
was planning."

The man sighed. "I know all that," he said. "But we can't necessarily protect him either. If your guy gets in too deep over there
and runs into trouble, we'll do what we can, but we may not have
the capacity to help him. Just know that up front. And if the president decides to bomb again, then all bets are off."

"I'll relay all this to Chadwick."

"You do that."

She did. But it didn't slow Chadwick down, not even a little
bit. "Let them bomb," he said, his jaw set. "That'll take his poll
numbers down a notch or two."

Finished with the State Department for the present, Valerie
burned even more hours dealing with the media. Reporters from
every major market in America had contacted her in one way or
the other—phone calls, emails, faxes, or personal appointments.
Trying to answer all their questions at once, Chadwick had held
another news conference, this one dealing specifically with his
plans to go to Kosovo. As usual, the press fluctuated between bla-
tant cynicism and hero worship. Though it seemed they all respected Chadwick for his years of scandal-free leadership, they

had a hard time buying into his simplistic explanation for his decision to plunge headlong into international diplomacy.

When Chadwick insisted, "I believe God is leading me in this," the reporters shook their heads and wondered. *Time, Newsweek, The Christian Weekly,* and *U.S. News and World Report* all had major stories planned on his efforts. *20/20* and *60 Minutes* had called to schedule television interviews.

Valerie checked her watch—11:52. She thought about lunch and wanted to call Ted or Rodney but knew that was hopeless. Though they had decided to stick with Chadwick, she didn't really know about their level of enthusiasm. In the last seventy-two hours the two of them had treated her as if she had a bad case of bubonic plague. They blamed it on a heavy schedule, but she knew it went deeper than that. Like Lester, they obviously blamed her for what they saw as her uncle's lunacy. She had tried a couple of times to talk to Ted, but both times he had mumbled something incoherent and walked away.

Her heart heavy, Valerie decided she'd eat alone. Maybe in a few days, when things calmed down some, she could try again to talk with Ted and Rodney. Deciding to squeeze in a short workout before she returned, she grabbed a gym bag from behind her desk, threw it over her shoulder, and headed for the door. Turning into the hallway, she almost bumped into her uncle.

"Hey, young lady," Chadwick greeted. "I was just coming to see you. You eating lunch?"

"Sure, headed that way."

"By yourself?"

"Just me and my lonesome."

Chadwick glanced at his watch. "You want some company?"

She looped a hand through his arm. "If it's you, absolutely."

"Great, let me get Curtis."

Chadwick headed back to his office to inform his bodyguard. Waiting for him, Valerie heard her phone ring. She ignored it through two rings. But when her uncle didn't reappear immediately, she darted back to her desk, dropped her gym bag to the floor, and picked up the phone.

"Valerie Miller," she said.

"Casey here. Got a minute?"

"Just about one. What's up?"

"Well, a couple of things. One, I'd like to see you again soon. I know you've been busy, so I haven't called. Any hope in the next couple of days?"

"I'll need to check my calendar. The second thing?" She hoped she didn't sound too short.

"I'm hearing some things about this trip to Kosovo. Scary things."

"What do you mean?"

"I'm hearing that Reverend Chadwick is upsetting some powerful people. People who don't like the idea of peace."

"You got names?"

"Not names, necessarily, but groups. Zionists, for one."

"Zionists?"

"People who don't like ben Moseph. The more rigid orthodox Jews. They think he's about to sell them down the river. They're afraid if he and Chadwick succeed in places like Kosovo, they'll try the big enchilada—Israel. They don't want that, not at all."

Valerie pushed back her hair. "But what are they going to do?" she asked. "No one has said a thing about Israel."

"I don't know that they've thought that far. I'm just telling you that Chadwick's notion won't go unchallenged. And some of these people don't mind using violence. I just want you to keep your eyes open. Don't take anything for granted."

She heard a knock on her door, then saw her uncle poke his head inside. "I appreciate your call," she said. "I really do. I'll tell Reverend Chadwick what you said."

"Good, do that. Shall I call about the other thing?"

She hesitated, but only for a second. "Sure, call me later today. I'll know more then."

Hanging up, she slipped on a coat, stepped to Chadwick, and looped her arm through his. "Where are you taking me?" she asked. "Somewhere expensive?"

"I'm a simple man," he said, smiling. "So don't get your hopes up."

Minutes later, the two of them pushed through the revolving door in the lobby, the bodyguard at their heels.

"I know a new place," Chadwick said, slipping a scarf around his neck to protect against the chilly air. "It serves the spiciest wings I've had in a while. And the sweet tea is unbelievable. It's only a block or so. Let's just walk."

Valerie started to ask him if he felt up to it, but realizing that might hurt his feelings, she refrained. Still holding his arm, she stepped off the curb and crossed the street. A car horn screeched somewhere a block or so away, and a jackhammer blasted away at the concrete not more than fifty feet from where she stood.

"We have to go through this construction," Chadwick shouted over the jackhammer. "Then a quick left at the corner and we're there."

A metal fence ran along the sidewalk to protect the pedestrians on the traffic side, and a wood covering formed a tubelike passageway straight ahead. A huge crane worked about sixty feet to the left of the sidewalk, a steel girder in its teeth high above their heads.

Staring up at the girder, Valerie shook her head. Construction seemed as much a part of the Atlanta scenery as the ever present advertisements for Coca-Cola. With the bodyguard leading the way, she and Chadwick entered the wooden passageway.

"You doing okay these days?" Chadwick asked. "Not overworking yourself?"

"I'm great," Valerie said with a little more enthusiasm than she really felt. "Gearing up. Only five days until Kosovo. I've got a lot to do before then."

They stepped out of the passageway. The steel girder in the jaws of the crane quivered in midair, eleven stories high. The glint of the girder bounced off an office tower to Valerie's right. She glanced upward. The crane opened its teeth and the steel girder fell out.

Valerie screamed. The steel beam ripped down toward them, its reach more than forty feet across, its weight over a thousand pounds. Jerking Chadwick back into the passageway, she stumbled and fell. On her knees, she pulled her uncle again, and the two of them rolled backward. The steel beam landed, its front edge jamming through the passageway like a mammoth arrow and burrowing itself more than three feet into the concrete sidewalk. The passageway collapsed above her head, and Valerie threw herself over her uncle, her body a shield against the falling debris. Chunks of wood and metal slammed into the ground on all sides, and an eruption of dust and dirt boiled up from the sidewalk. She wanted to scream again but didn't.

Within seconds, everything became suddenly still. A siren sounded somewhere in the distance, and Valerie hoped it was headed their way. Staring at her uncle, she saw his eyes open, his face blank.

"Are you okay?" she whispered, almost as if to hide from some unknown enemy.

He nodded but said nothing, and she wasn't sure if he had actually heard her or not.

Suddenly, to her left, she heard a moan. She turned and saw Chadwick's bodyguard less than ten feet away. A piece of concrete the size of a computer printer lay on his chest, and the edge of the steel girder rested on his legs. His eyes were open, but blood covered the left side of his face, and Valerie knew instantly he was badly hurt. The siren screeched closer now, and she eased her uncle's head to the ground and moved toward the bodyguard. By his side, she took off her coat and pulled it over his chest. The siren scratched to a stop at the curb and emergency personnel ran her way, their hands full of equipment.

Stepping away from the bodyguard, Valerie began to sob. Without looking up, she knew in the deepest parts of her soul that the falling girder hadn't been an accident. Someone wanted to stop her uncle—someone who cared so little for human life that he would kill to stop one man's effort for peace.

———

Pope John Peter stared down at the folder lying flat on his desk, his head in his hands. The folder contained a transcript of a phone conversation between Cardinal Lech Zolinska and some unknown man from an untraceable number. It had not surprised John Peter that the head of the Swiss Guard had such a transcript at his disposal and that it had been taken after a cell phone monitor had caught Zolinska at his devious schemes. A man much educated in the intrigues of Vatican politics, John Peter found it entirely reasonable that papal security had such techniques at its disposal. But he had postponed reading the transcript for over a day. But now, after hearing the news of Reverend Chadwick's close encounter, he knew he could put it off no longer. Bad news could wait for a while, but not forever.

His hands trembling, he opened the folder, pulled out the transcript, and began to read. It didn't take but a couple of minutes. Rolling his ring, he eased back into the comfort of his thick leather chair and thought long and hard about what he should do. Zolinska hadn't technically done anything wrong. To have a difference of opinion with a now-deceased pope and a suspicion about what the new one might do was no crime and no sin. And to try to steer the new pope toward a particular policy also violated no oath or commitment. When he was only a cardinal, John Peter had done the same many times.

He stared at the walls of his office. Such pristine paintings, such elegant pieces of holy art. He steepled his hands under his chin. What troubled him most about the transcript was the reference to the death of Clement Peter. Though neither Zolinska nor his phone confidant had admitted anything, the inference was that perhaps Clement's death had not come as the result of natural causes.

John Peter considered his options. Confront Zolinska? Ask him about Clement's death? He tossed aside the idea. He had no proof of anything and no way to gain any.

Standing, John Peter walked to the window and stared out over the Vatican complex. The last rays of the sun were about gone. An illuminated fountain pushed a white spray of water into the air, and a bird the color of a dark church pew fluffed its feathers, splashed in the water for a moment, then flew off to make its bed for the night. John Peter pivoted away from the window.

An old adage skipped through his head. "Keep your friends close to you," advised the sage, "but your enemies even closer." A grim smile on his face, John Peter walked back to his desk and picked up the phone. Not a bad plan, he thought, not a bad plan at all.

THIRTY-TWO

On Monday morning at 7:30, Valerie Miller, Russell Chadwick, Ted Shuster, Rodney Kent, and a score of other aides noisily climbed aboard a chartered 747 at Atlanta's Hartsfield International Airport, buckled themselves into their seats, and took off for Macedonia. Her body as exhausted as her mind, Valerie chattered aimlessly for a few minutes with a couple of Chadwick's aides, then quickly leaned back and decided to rest. Dressed comfortably in blue jeans, a cobalt blue fleece top, and tennis shoes, she snuggled down into the seat, pulled a blanket over her shoulders, and closed her eyes. Thankfully, she had two empty seats beside her. She yawned and stretched her legs but found rest impossible. Too much to think about, too much to handle. The last five days had passed faster than any she could remember.

She had spent the first day after the girder fell almost exclusively with an accident investigator from the police department. After rehashing every last second of the experience for what seemed like a hundred times, the investigator handed her off to a detective who allowed that the accident might have been a deliberate attempt to kill someone.

So she told the story a few more times. The detective listened intently, jotted a few notes, nodded wisely, then left. A day later, he showed back up to tell her that his investigation had pretty much come to a quick dead end. As he explained it to Valerie, Chadwick, and the rest of the crew, a dark-skinned man in khakis, with appropriate identification and obvious skill, had reported to work on Wednesday morning as a crane operator, the normal man at home sick. But when a construction crew supervisor rushed to the crane within a minute after the beam fell, the man had disappeared. In the days since, no clues had surfaced as to his identity or present whereabouts. Yes, the construction company overseeing the building project had recently employed a man named John Ruiz as a roving substitute for their crew of crane operators, but he had since disappeared, and his phone number now answered as disconnected.

"We'll keep looking," said the detective. "But since no one was killed, it'll fall pretty far down the list."

"You think it was deliberate?" Ted asked, his eyes wide.

The detective shook his head. "Hard to say. Maybe this Ruiz guy made a mistake—then didn't want to deal with all the hassle, cleared out before anybody caught up with him. Maybe he was an illegal alien and thought he'd get deported."

"Or maybe he purposefully tried to kill Reverend Chadwick," Valerie insisted. "And he's on the run from his failed murder attempt."

The cop shrugged, then stood to leave. Valerie wanted to protest but she knew better. Though Chadwick's bodyguard had suffered three broken ribs, a fractured cheek, and a smashed left knee, that didn't register too high on a list of investigations that included up to three hundred homicides a year. She let it drop.

The next day became a sprint to tie up loose ends before the departure for Kosovo. Though shaken by the near escape from death, Chadwick remained undeterred about the peace effort. Having previously alerted the U.S. State Department, the appropriate officials in Greece, and his allies, he reconfirmed by phone his commitment to go and plowed ahead as if nothing had happened.

On Saturday, Valerie caught a plane home to Charlotte and spent the night and all day Sunday with her mom and dad. After church, her mom fixed a feast of fried chicken, mashed potatoes, green beans, hot biscuits, and banana pudding—all washed down with sweet tea—and they all stuffed themselves to the gills.

Sitting by the fire afterward, her dad became serious. "We're the ones who suggested you go to work with your uncle," he said, his gray eyes somber.

"Yes, we thought it would give you a chance to deal with a few things in a quiet, safe place," her mom said.

Valerie smiled. "Yeah, right!"

"So we can't try to talk you out of going to Kosovo," her dad said.

"But if you don't want to go—"

"I gave him my word," Valerie interrupted. "He told us all to leave if we wanted, no hard feelings. Lester took him up on it, but I told him I'd stay. So that's it. I can't back out now. You didn't raise me to quit when things got a little tough."

"But you've been through so much," her mom said, moving to the sofa beside her and taking her hand. "I mean . . . before . . . with all that business with the scroll and the danger you faced. And now this too. Almost getting killed with that crane . . . it's just too . . . too much!"

Her mom looked close to tears and Valerie wanted to comfort her. "I'm okay, Mom," she said. "I'm scared some, sure. I guess everyone is. But I trust Uncle Russ, and you do too. You know that. If he thinks God wants him to do this, how can I walk away? He's so . . . well, you know how he is . . . so peaceful about it all."

"Are you peaceful?" her dad asked, standing by the fireplace, his hands at his back.

Valerie stood and walked to him, took his hands in hers. "No," she said. "Not peaceful, not yet. I've felt shaky for almost a year. I'm skittish, almost paranoid at times. But I think that's normal. You don't go through what I've been through and bounce back like you've spilled an ice cream cone." She dropped her dad's hands and wrapped her arms around his waist. "So I'm not peaceful. I don't know . . . maybe I'll never be like I once was, so naïve, so innocent."

She faced her mom. "You remember how I was—never a cloud in the sky, never a dark moment. 'Miss Sunshine,' my friends called me."

"We called you that too," her mom said, dabbing her eyes. "I liked Miss Sunshine."

Valerie smiled. "I liked her too," she said. "But I don't think Miss Sunshine can live forever."

She lowered her hands and slid back onto the sofa. "Hey, let's not dwell on sad things," she said, wanting to change the subject. "Let's watch some basketball." She grabbed the television controls, flipped on an NBA game, and left the talk of Kosovo behind for the rest of the afternoon.

That evening she kissed them good-bye at the airport and flew back to Atlanta. Now, trying to sleep, she listened to the drone of the plane engines and wondered what would happen once they landed.

According to the agreement with the allies, they would meet

at a small hotel in the city of Sophia, the major city of Macedonia, at 11 A.M. on Tuesday morning. After final briefings, they would take a truck convoy to the Kosovo border. There, UN peacekeepers would escort them to their drop-off points—Luis Zorella to the capital city of Pristina, Chadwick to Kosovska Mitrovica, Rabbi ben Moseph to Prizren, Ayatollah Khatama to Zitinje, and the Dalai Lama to Gnjilane. With the five of them moving around like chess pieces in these key cities, the ethnic Albanians and their Serbian enemies might find it more difficult to continue their blood feud without endangering one of the religious leaders.

Valerie shifted in her seat and stared out the window. She knew the plan had holes in it. Many of the Serbs and ethnic Albanians hated each other, and hatred often destroyed any sense of reason. Perhaps they wouldn't care what the world thought of them. So what if they killed a famous religious leader?

"You asleep?"

The voice startled her and she sat up with a jerk. Opening her eyes, she saw Casey Sterling standing in the aisle of the plane. Like her, he wore casual clothes—a pair of khakis, a navy and white golf sweater, a pair of brown hiking boots.

"Casey? How in the world—?"

"I stowed away," he said, smiling. "Can I sit a minute?" He looked at the two empty seats beside her.

"Sure, here." She slid over and he took the aisle seat.

"I didn't know you were flying with us," she said, still surprised.

"I talked to Ted Shuster. He said you had plenty of room. I told him I'd pay normal fare. He said 'no problem.' I sneaked in the back door and here I am."

Valerie snuggled into her blanket. "You show up in a lot of surprising places," she said.

"Like used chewing gum. Can't get rid of me."

She smiled, inwardly pleased to see him.

"You're all excited, I'm sure," he said. "Seeing all this happening, your uncle's hopes moving to the next level."

"Yeah, excited, nervous, all of that. Can you really believe it's happening?"

He shrugged. "It's a crazy world these days. Anything seems possible."

"But did you really think you'd see this?"

He laughed and crossed his arms. "Well, no, not really. But your man Chadwick seems awfully stubborn."

"Fearless is more like it. I mean, he survived the explosion at Prestwick Church and the steel beam falling on his bodyguard, and more than a few of his most active supporters have advised him to give this up, but he pushes ahead anyway."

"I'm glad," Sterling said. "People like him keep me in business."

"That's the only reason you're glad?" she asked, perturbed by the tone of the statement. "The fact that he makes news? Keeps ratings high?"

He faced her more directly. "Well, sure," he said. "Plus the fact that he gives me more exposure. I mean, let's get real here, Valerie. The chances that he'll actually lead the world into a new era of peace are slim to none. You know that as well as I do."

"So you're not here because you think—"

"I'm here to cover the story, plain and simple," Sterling said. Do I want his scheme to work? Absolutely. Do I think it will? Well, I've already answered that. But regardless, I do my job. I communicate whatever happens—the good, the bad, and the ugly—to the world. If peace comes, amen, praise God. We'll bury the AK–47s, shut down the F–16s, and I'll take you right to the ceremony, front-row seat. But if it doesn't—if blood covers the streets and bullets and bombs rain from the sky—well, I'm your faithful bird's-eye view there too. Your man on the spot, Casey Sterling. My smiling face is in your living room, either way."

He leaned back, his speech ended, a look of contentment on his face. Valerie felt her stomach turn a little queasy. She didn't know if it was the stale air in the plane or the sentiment Sterling had just expressed.

"Then this is just work for you," she said, loneliness hitting her again.

Sterling leaned closer, his voice a whisper. "Nothing is 'just work' for me," he said. "No such thing as 'just work' exists. It's *life* for me."

He placed his hands on his knees. "Let me see if I can explain this. I've worked since my ninth birthday. I started with a paper route. At twelve I moved to a neighborhood grocery store—stock boy, sales clerk, bagging groceries. At sixteen I took a job in a local mill on the swing shift. I drove right from school to the mill, got home at midnight, studied for an hour or so, then hit the bed. In college, I became a part-time reporter with a newspaper. Round the clock, when they wanted me to cover a story, I showed up, regardless of classes, dates, anything. I'm thirty-seven now, and I've taken less than ten vacation days a year for the last fifteen years."

"Aren't you tired?"

Sterling ran his hands through his hair. "I don't think about it."

"Don't you miss things? Don't you want a family? Time to enjoy some of the things you can buy, some of the things you can do with the money you've made?"

He shook his head as if to eliminate the idea from his brain. "You don't understand," he said. "I'm this close to my dream, to the reason for my existence."

"And what is your dream?"

He faced her, his eyes wide. "I want an anchor desk," he whispered. "Like Brokaw, Rather, Jennings. All three of those guys are getting old. They can't go on forever. I'm this close"—he held his thumb and forefinger a half inch apart—"this close to making it. I just need to break one more story, a major one, a Princess-Diana-crashes-in-the-tunnel story. Let me get the exclusive, the first camera, the first report on one like that and I'm there, I'm right there."

Valerie suddenly felt sorry for him and she put her hand on his. "That's a big dream," she said. "What happens if you don't get it? Does your life just end? Is it all or nothing—anchor desk or bust?"

"Oh, I'll get it," Sterling whispered. "One way or the other, I'll get it. I've never failed in anything in my life. I don't plan on starting now. No matter what it takes, I'll do it to make it happen."

Valerie removed her hand as a disturbing notion came to her. "Is that why you're . . . you're hanging around with me? So you can stay close to Chadwick. You think this is your story, the big one to push you over the top?"

Sterling licked his lips but didn't answer.

"That's it, isn't it?" Valerie pressed. "You're here for what you hope I can do for you!"

Sterling shook his head. "I'm sorry if that's what you think of me," he said. "Maybe I need to go back to the back."

"Do what you want," Valerie said, her anger rising. "You paid your fare."

Sterling stood and turned to leave. She noticed a tremor in his right arm, an almost imperceptible movement of palm and fingers. She grabbed his hand. It shook against hers for an instant, then held steady. "You okay?" she asked, concern for him overcoming her anger.

Sterling pulled his hand away and leaned back over, his eyes sad. "I know you don't understand," he said, ignoring her question. "You grew up with a maid, rode around in a luxury car, took family vacations in Acapulco, watched movies in your home theater. I ate canned applesauce sandwiches, bought clothes at Goodwill, watched my mom cry because she didn't have enough money to rent me a new tuxedo for my senior prom. So don't judge me because I want to make something out of myself. Until you've walked in my shoes . . ." He sighed and walked away before she could respond.

Watching him leave, Valerie wanted to cry. Casey had hit the nail on the head. She didn't know what drove a man like him. How could she? But at the same time, she couldn't condone his "no matter what" attitude either. It scared her, made her question his motives about everything, even his relationship with her. And what about his shaking? What did that mean? What vulnerability did it signal? What fear?

She pulled her sweater close to her chin. But really, what difference did it make? She had no business getting interested in a man like Sterling. His religious convictions were zero. No faith, no church background, and apparently no plans to establish any. He had no interest in even talking about such things.

She snuggled back down in her seat. Don't even think about it, she told herself. A man like Sterling made no sense for someone like her, no sense at all. Which was exactly the kind of man she always seemed to go for. Listening to the plane drone on, she wondered to herself why that had always been the case.

His pipe cradled in his hand, Bill Stricker tightened the belt of his black and burgundy house robe and walked from his bedroom into the den of the private section of his Colorado ski lodge. In the den, he saw Roth already dressed and standing by the fireplace, a huge blaze roaring away.

"You sleep well?" Stricker asked, stepping to the fireplace.

"Like a baby," Roth said.

Stricker nodded and stared out the window. The sunlight bounced back off the white of the ground and momentarily hurt his eyes. "More snow fell last night," he said. "Looks like four to six inches."

"You need to open this place to the public," Roth said. "You could make a bundle."

"I'm going to need it," Stricker snorted, facing him again. "The share price of A&D took another three-dollar dip yesterday. All this talk of peace makes my portfolio as shaky as an elephant on ice." He moved to a table by the window and picked up a newspaper lying there.

"I guess you saw this. Chadwick's headed to Kosovo."

"With all the rest of the lunatic crowd," Roth said. "Not good, not good at all. Did you ever manage to reach him?"

Stricker chewed on his pipe, studying the paper. "Yeah, I talked to him a couple of times. It didn't seem to help much." He tossed the paper on the table and stalked back to the fireplace. "Did you talk to your contact?" he asked.

"Just like we discussed. I think it'll make a difference. I just don't know when."

Stricker turned and stared into the fire. "I already warned Chadwick," he said. "In more ways than one."

"Maybe we can't threaten him," Roth said. "He seems fearless."

"I heard an old saying once," Stricker said. " 'Better to face a hundred German musketeers than one lone Calvinist armed with the will of God.' "

Roth chuckled, but only for an instant.

"Chadwick won't back off," Stricker continued. "I'm sure of it. You can't buy him because he doesn't care about money. He lives too clean a life to find anything to blackmail him with. Believe me, I checked. And he's not afraid for his own life."

"He's old and has Parkinson's," Roth said. "Every day is a bonus already. So how do we get to him?"

Stricker placed both hands on the mantel of the fireplace, his back to Roth. "I'm thinking on that," he said. "Maybe it's time we took this up a notch."

"We haven't done enough already?" Roth asked. "What more can we do?"

Stricker faced his guest. "We can stop him dead in his tracks," he said. "And I will do everything in my power to do just that."

THIRTY-THREE

JANUARY 13
SOPHIA, MACEDONIA

With most of the hotels already filled, Russell Chadwick had rented the only one available in Sophia—a clean but rather drab establishment that had only thirty-eight rooms, no restaurant, and a central meeting area not much bigger than a couple of racquetball courts strung back to back. When Valerie Miller followed Chadwick into the room at 10:55 A.M., the place had as many people jammed into it as possible. Though none of the "Holy Seven"—as the news media had taken to calling the group—had more than ten aides present, that group alone filled up the available space.

Most of the media people—almost a hundred of them by Valerie's last count—waited outside. But six representatives—elected by the contingent from among their number—stood to the left of a small, upraised platform that the hotel had found somewhere and shoved into place. Each of those six had placed cameras against the wall and held tape recorders in the palms of their hands. Not surprisingly, Casey Sterling had gotten elected as one of the representatives. She spotted him almost immediately as she entered the room but quickly looked away.

A low hum of conversation filled the room as she and Chadwick made their way to the front. Though cool outside, she suddenly felt flushed and claustrophobic. A fan whirred slowly overhead but it didn't help much. Too many people and too much pressure squeezed into this place.

Staying close to Chadwick, Valerie reminded herself to stay calm. There was no reason to panic now. Her uncle knew what he wanted. He had managed all this so far, and he could handle it

right through to the end. Stepping onto the platform, she walked
to the microphone, waited for Chadwick to take a seat, then
looked at Rodney Kent. He nodded and she leaned into the mike.

"Ladies and gentlemen," she began, her voice shaky. "I'm Valerie Miller." The crowd fell quiet as everyone stared up at her.
She felt terribly out of place. Sitting in a folding chair in the front
row was Luis Zorella, his brother José directly behind him. Beside Zorella, Rabbi ben Moseph stared at her, his posture erect.
On his left waited the Dalai Lama, his dark eyes serene, the left
one covered with a monocle. Finally came the Ayatollah Khatama. He scratched his beard and his body language seemed
rather indifferent, as if he cared little for the proceedings before
him.

How in the world had she ended up here? Halfway across the
globe from her childhood home, in front of the most mismatched
group of people anyone could imagine? The fan overhead suddenly stopped, and she looked up at it and remembered she had
a job to do. She focused on the crowd again.

"The Reverend Russell Chadwick has asked me to call this
historic meeting to order," she continued. "I have talked with
many of you by phone in the last few days, and I'm glad to finally
meet you." Nods of recognition came from the crowd. Gathering
her courage, she continued.

"We're here today because of a decision that contains within
it the potential to change our world. As you know, Reverend
Chadwick invited all of you, and several others, to join with him
in this endeavor. Pope John Peter is unable to be here for obvious
reasons. We have hopes that he will cast his lot with us as this
project moves ahead to other venues in the future. And Ms. Martha Blevins informed us that her aged mother has recently fallen
quite ill. We ask you, in your own way, to remember the pontiff
and Ms. Blevins in your prayers."

She faced Chadwick and he winked at her. Feeling even better, she pressed ahead. "Now we come to the last details. As previously indicated, we will head out in a truck convoy at 7 A.M.
tomorrow. The trucks contain all the supplies that you will need
for a couple of weeks: large military-style tents, food, generators,
utensils, water. If necessary, we will resupply when the time
comes. As agreed, each of you brought your own aides—including
a maximum of two security people—to make your stay as pleasant and efficient as possible. NATO has provided each of us a
translator.

"Remember, we don't want to become combatants in this situation; we must avoid that at all costs." She hesitated, as if to give the group an opportunity to contradict her. No one did.

"If all goes well," she continued, "we will arrive in Kosovo by tomorrow. Each of you has your assigned location. You will establish a headquarters there. We will keep in contact through cell phones. Once you've set up your base camp, use it as a center to disperse humanitarian aid—food, clothing, blankets. But do not stay in one location. Make periodic, but not consistent, visits to key places in your city. Come and go in sporadic patterns. Remember our purpose—to stop the violence that still plagues this country. We cannot stop the hatred. Only God can do that. But perhaps we can cause the ethnic Albanians and the Serbs to think twice before they attack each other again. Perhaps we can prevent more NATO bombing. Perhaps our example can encourage peace in this troubled place."

She stopped and turned to Chadwick again. He pushed himself up from his chair. "Now, it gives me great pleasure," she said, "to introduce the man who brought us all together, a man whose vision sees possibilities when others only see problems, a true man of God—the Reverend Russell Chadwick."

For a moment, she expected applause, but none came. Chadwick moved to the microphone and she noticed a limp in his left leg. Had that started recently? Unsure, she took a seat.

Chadwick wasted no time with preliminaries.

"It's now time to do this thing," he said, his voice steady. "But we need to make sure we're all of one accord. If any of you have any hesitation, now is your opportunity to make it known."

Staring out at the four allies, Valerie saw José Zorella place a hand on his brother's shoulder. Luis shook his head almost imperceptibly. Ben Moseph and the Dalai Lama stayed dead still. The Ayatollah smiled slightly, but for some reason it didn't seem pleasant. Valerie wondered about him. He appeared almost smug, as if he knew something no one else knew. Her sense of paranoia kicked in again and she gritted her teeth. The bias she had first experienced when a Muslim group had almost killed her and Michael had raised its ugly head again.

Chadwick gripped the microphone and Valerie focused on him again. "I'm going to take your silence as consent," he said. "Consent that we're in this thing together. We're in it because we believe it's right, that we can make a difference."

He let go of the microphone and stepped down to the floor. "I know we come from different faiths," he said. "But I'm going to ask you to do something that might feel a bit uncomfortable at first. I want us to stand and hold hands. Can we do that?"

He moved toward Zorella and motioned for him to stand. Zorella complied and his entourage followed suit.

"Everyone," encouraged Chadwick. "Let's all stand and join hands."

Valerie, Ted, and Kent stood. Slowly, everyone else obeyed too. Within seconds, the entire room had joined hands—the news media included.

Standing between Ted and Kent, Valerie searched for Casey Sterling, then saw him to her right, one hand connected to another member of the media, the other in the grasp of one of Zorella's group. She wondered how he felt, whether this kind of moment made a difference to him or not. Without knowing why, she suddenly felt sad for him. He had so many talents, yet from his own words, she knew his insides were empty.

"I'd like for us to pray," Chadwick said. "And I'd like the honor of leading us." He bowed his head. Zorella fell to one knee. The Dalai Lama leaned sideways to listen to his interpreter.

Chadwick began. "O God of all that exists, we ask thy holy presence in this moment. We ask thee to guide us in this endeavor. If we have misunderstood thy will, make us aware of it in ways we can understand. But if not, then give us thy blessing. Pour out upon us thy power. Grant us thy grace. Make our efforts successful in accordance with thy holy purposes. Bring peace to this troubled land and use us as humble instruments to fulfill thy divine will, we pray. Amen."

For several moments, no one moved. As Valerie opened her eyes the room seemed suffused with a bright glow. She felt lightheaded, almost faint. She glanced at Chadwick. Overhead the fan started to whir again. Someone coughed. Valerie glanced at Sterling, whose head remained bowed, his eyes closed.

The spell was broken when the Ayatollah moved, pulling his hand from the man beside him. Hands released other hands and the moment passed.

"We leave tomorrow," Chadwick said. "God go with you."

Spilling from the room, the crowd began to hum with talk again, but Valerie stayed still for several more minutes. In spite of the good spirit created by her uncle's prayer, she had a bad feeling about all this. Though she trusted Chadwick, something seemed eerie, and she suspected that before this Peace Project

ended its Kosovo stage, something dramatic and dangerous
would almost surely take place.

———

At 10 A.M., Beth Roper drove up to a freshly painted blue and
white horse stable outside Nashville, Tennessee, parked her
pickup truck, and climbed out. Filling her lungs with fresh clear
air, she took a quick look around. A barn for almost fifty horses;
a white fence as far as the eye could see; a white house with a
porch running across the front, a horse-and-jockey weathervane
on top, and eleven oaks taller than the house in the front yard.
This was a place steeped in history and tradition and the smell
of old Tennessee money.

Her western boots clicking across the concrete drive, she hustled to the stable doors and pushed inside. Letting her eyes ad-
just to the dim lighting, she took a deep breath and enjoyed once
more the smell of the horse farm on which she had grown up.
Fresh hay stacked high in the loft, the pine scent of the cleaning
fluid used to keep the floors and stalls clean, the unmistakable
aroma of horses, all brawny and thick.

A horse neighed and broke the spell. To her right, she saw her
dad, a simple wood cane in his hands, sitting on a bale of hay.
Beside him waited Bill Stricker.

Beth stepped toward her dad and gave him a hug. He accepted it without getting up. She shook Stricker's hand but felt
clammy doing it. She stepped back and took a seat on a hay bale
near her dad.

"I'm sure you watched the news from Macedonia," her father
said, his gruff voice dispensing with any more preliminaries.

"Yeah," Beth said. "Got up at 4 A.M. to catch it live. Quite a
spectacle."

"I read your column on Chadwick's peace idea. It gave us all
something to mull over."

Bill Stricker snorted. "A lot of good it did," he said. "Stocks
are down another—"

"We're not here for that," Charley said, cutting him short.
"What she did was right—for the time."

Beth looped one ankle over the other and stuffed her hands
into the pockets of her brown leather flight jacket. Obviously, her
dad had done some thinking about all this.

Charley touched her knee with his cane. "This is all getting
serious, child. People are upset. They love Reverend Chadwick,

but maybe he's past his day, confused, used by someone else."

"Some would say that about you," Beth said, not willing to concede the point.

Her father grunted. "Yeah, well, maybe they're right. But I'm not out trottin' all over the world, gangin' up with heathens, making speeches about world peace."

Beth started to say something but decided against it. There was no reason to fight her dad on every point. "What do you want me to do?" she asked.

Her father poked at the ground with his cane. "Tell me what's on your mind," he said. "You buy what Chadwick's doin'?"

Beth placed her elbows on her knees. "I'm studying it," she said. "The whole Revelation 13 thing confuses me."

"Not me," Stricker grunted, his bad mood obvious. "Chadwick's a tool, a good man in the hands of someone else."

Beth stared hard at Stricker. Even if she did agree with him, Stricker's distasteful personality made her mad. She wanted to ask Stricker why he didn't attend church. How did he come by his sudden knowledge of Revelation? Why did a man with such deep biblical insight end up married three times? What difference did it make to him what Chadwick did or didn't do? But, remembering her manners, she bit her tongue.

"I think we should wait," she said to her dad. "Why rush to conclusions? Chadwick almost died in Northern Ireland, and it shocked the negotiators back to the bargaining table. Why get all worked up now? See what happens in Kosovo. It's not like peace is breaking out all over. There are still plenty of trouble spots."

Stricker shook his head and gazed at the ceiling, and Beth suddenly understood why he cared so much. The man didn't want peace—not in Kosovo, not anywhere. Peace threatened him because his company made a ton of products that sold best when people practiced the art of war.

She felt so disgusted she wanted to spit. He didn't give a rip about Revelation 13! She faced her dad, her face hot. "I don't like this!" she started. "You called me down here like I'm a child or something. I run the business now. You put it in my hands. Either you trust me to do it right or you don't. Just let me know, one way or the other—I don't care! But I'll not have the likes of this . . ." she paused and pointed toward Stricker, "this man giving me advice on spiritual matters!" She rose from the hay bale, but her father tapped his cane on the ground and motioned her back down.

"You're just like your mom, God rest her soul," he chuckled. "A live spark, no doubt about it." His smile turned grim. "Look, child, even a bad apple can have a good spot or two on it. Why don't you just hear him out?"

Beth turned impatiently toward Stricker. "Well?" she asked.

"I've got certain contacts in high places," Stricker said. "And they've been telling me some pretty interesting things about Reverend Chadwick and the president."

"Like what?"

Stricker lifted his eyebrows. "I suppose you've noticed the president's response to all this peace talk. He's promised to support Chadwick any way he can."

"Big deal! What would you expect him to say? I'm not following."

Stricker smiled but didn't seem amused. "Let me spell it out. If Chadwick succeeds, even in a small way, the president suddenly appears, arms around Chadwick's shoulders in front of the cameras, one great man with another, helping bring peace to the world."

"But if he fails?"

"That's where it gets good," Stricker said. "According to my sources, the government *wants* Chadwick to fail. In fact, they may assist him just a bit toward that end. But then, just in the nick of time, the cavalry will arrive. An army tank or two, a contingent of troops, a squadron of Apache helicopters. They'll rescue Chadwick—the most popular man in America today, according to most polls—guns blazing. Old Uncle Sam, protecting the rights of every free American citizen from all enemies. The president will come off like a hero, saving the beloved pastor. Both of them will be all smiles, live for all the world to see."

Beth pulled a strand of hay from the bale where she sat. "Now that's a kooky idea," she said. "Do you really believe it?"

Stricker shrugged. "I'm only reporting what I heard. Politicians do crazy things."

Beth faced her dad. "Papa?"

"The president is no friend of mine," he said. "The most godless man we've elected in a century."

"But what am I supposed to do with this?" she asked. "We're a Christian organization. We can't get political."

"But we don't want Chadwick giving the president's ratings a boost," Stricker said, his tone softer.

"Well, it's too late to do anything about Kosovo," Beth said. "He's already there."

"But we can stop the next move, wherever he goes."

Beth shook her head in disbelief.

"I'm going to speak out against this," her father said, "no matter what you do. I'll hold a news conference if I have to, to stake out my opposition to what Chadwick's doing."

"But who's going to believe what you just told me?" Beth said.

"You're right. I'm arguing it using Revelation 13."

Beth stood up. "You're using the Bible for political purposes?"

Her father quickly shook his head. "Oh no, that's not it. I think all this fits together. No matter how you look at it, Revelation 13 connects. When you're dealing with evil, you can't ever underestimate its reach. Remember what the apostle Paul said: 'We're not battling flesh and blood, but against principalities and powers and the rulers of the darkness of this age.' Who's to say the president's not a part of the scheme? And Chadwick is a pawn, an old man caught up in something past his ability to handle. When I refer to Revelation 13, I'm as sincere as a heart attack."

Charley Roper stood then and leaned on his cane with both hands. "I'm tired," he said. "It's time to finish this up. Here's what I want. Beth, you put together a scenario by which we take a stand against Reverend Chadwick. Nothing directly attacking him as a man or as a believer. Just call into question those who advise him. Go after them. They make easier targets. Put all the radio stations, all the journals, everybody in the organization on notice. Don't tell them yet what we're doing. But get it ready. If Chadwick is doing the bidding of the president, and maybe the devil, we can't let that happen. Not on my watch."

Finished, he tottered toward the door, leaving her standing with Bill Stricker. Cold chills tickled her spine as her dad pushed through the barn door, and she didn't know if they came from the air outside or the company beside her. Grinding her teeth, Beth Roper left the barn, climbed into her truck, and scratched out of the driveway. She loved her daddy, but sometimes he made her furious.

THIRTY-FOUR

Valerie woke at exactly 5:34 A.M. on Sunday morning, within fifteen minutes of the time she'd awakened every day of her four-day sojourn in Kosovo. Climbing out of her bunk, an army-style cot covered with olive drab blankets and a pillow as hard as a boiled egg, she flicked on a battery-powered lantern and picked her clothes off the metal chair that sat by her bed. Sniffing the olive-colored slacks, black turtleneck, and brown flannel shirt, she decided she could wear them again. She didn't have the luxury of changing every day in her current circumstances.

Slipping into the clothes, she shoved her feet into a pair of clean white socks and hiking boots and stood to stretch. Her arms hurt as she lifted them over her head, sore from handling the thirty-pound bags of flour, rice, and beans they handed out every day.

Staring into the mirror, she brushed her teeth over a metal bowl sitting in the corner of her side of the tent. Her hair looked awful, as though someone with a rake had started the job but not finished it. She ached for a shower, but then remembered she took one yesterday. Camp rules allowed only three per week. Lathering her hands, she washed and rinsed her face, toweled off, and shoved a Braves baseball cap over her hair. She grabbed a black jacket from a trunk and slipped into it. Taking a pair of gloves from the coat pocket, she pulled back the blanket that hung on a string between her and the rest of the group—the only concession anyone made to her gender—and stepped out of her cubicle.

For several seconds, she stood and watched as the men who

shared her tent continued to sleep. The last few days had taught her a lot about them. Ted snored like a warthog snorting. Rodney slept in the same spot without moving, his covers appearing unwrinkled every morning—as if someone had slipped him under the blankets with a spatula. Beside those two, Russell Chadwick rested peacefully, refusing to sleep in quarters any nicer than those allowed his team. Beside Chadwick, one of his bodyguards also slept, his face buried in his pillow while his partner kept watch outside.

Walking lightly, she eased over to her uncle's side. Gently shaking his shoulders, she woke him. He stared at her with blank eyes for an instant, then smiled sweetly.

"Hang on a minute," he said. "I'll be right with you."

She nodded, left the tent, and stepped into the gray predawn of another day in Kosovo. She and Chadwick had started this routine their first day in the troubled country. They awoke early, took a thirty-minute walk to loosen their muscles, ate breakfast with everyone else, spent a half hour or so in private devotions, then headed off to the distribution tent for a day of tough but rewarding work. Today, they would substitute a joint worship time for the private devotions before they took off to work, but other than that, everything remained the same.

Valerie slipped on the gloves and stretched again as she waited for her uncle. Her breath hovered in front of her face, a gray stream giving evidence of the cold. Overhead, the sky was turning lighter, a clear blue showing up from the east. The landscape sloped slightly upward from where she stood to a line of tree-covered mountains in the distance. Though ripped by the ravages of war, the place still displayed a rugged beauty. She tucked her gloved hands into her coat pockets.

For the most part, the time in Kosovo had passed uneventfully. They spent several hours a day handing out food and clothing. When not working, they made sporadic tours of the city, visiting the burned-out houses, the rubble of the schools, the town center, the sites of the graves where the Albanians said the Serbs had buried those they slaughtered. Everywhere she looked, whether in Pristina or Kosovska Mitrovica, Valerie saw devastation and despair. The people gratefully accepted the aid they brought them, but they looked at her with vacant eyes, and Valerie wondered if they would ever know lasting peace. The entire region had suffered so long under so many different flags with so much racial and religious hatred. It really would take a miracle for anything resembling peace to take hold.

She heard the tent open and turned to see Chadwick and one of the guards walking toward her. The guard walked with them every day. As if on cue, their NATO translator also joined them from a nearby tent.

"Morning," Valerie said.

"You ready to go?" Chadwick asked.

Nodding, she started down the road, a gravel thoroughfare marked by scores of potholes. They had made camp only a mile or so from a bridge that ran over the Ibar River, a bridge that the Serbs and Albanians had established as a kind of no-man's-land of demarcation. The remaining Serbs—only a couple of hundred people—lived on the far side of the bridge. The ethnic Albanians, now the majority in the city, lived on the near side.

A stray black-and-white dog of questionable parentage appeared from the remains of a burned-out house beside the road and began to tag along. Chadwick clicked at the dog and it wagged its tail. They turned right and walked up a steep incline, the rocks from the road scratching under their boots. Their walk carried them past a score of houses, some of them the blocky squares built under Tito's communist regime. Others, the older ones, featured stucco walls and window boxes for flowers. Almost half the homes were burned out, though, their window boxes holding nothing but charred ashes.

Their route this morning carried them up to the bridge, then twisted to the right and wound its way back to the base camp.

Her hands stuffed into her coat pockets, Valerie wished she had worn a heavier cap. She inched deeper into her coat. A toothless woman waved at her from the porch of one of the few houses that had managed to survive the war. Valerie returned the gesture.

Though she knew not to get careless, Valerie felt fairly safe. A healthy contingent of the thirty-five thousand NATO troops in Kosovo regularly patrolled the area, and the multinational police force that NATO had trained did a reasonable job of keeping petty crime under control. The same situation existed in the cities that hosted the four other peace groups. Though the Kosovo Liberation Army still operated in the area, to this point no one in their contingent had run into any trouble.

"Did you sleep well?" Chadwick asked.

"Sure, I'm so tired I could sleep a week, no matter how bad the pillow."

Chadwick nodded. "Any news from back home?"

She smiled. Chadwick depended on her and her wireless Internet connections to keep him up-to-date on events in the States. "Right before I went to bed. An article in *The Christian Weekly* claims you're a good man, but you've taken bad advice."

"Godly people of good intent can and do sometimes disagree," he said. There was a momentary flash of anger in his eyes, but it disappeared quickly.

Valerie started to reply but thought better of it. They fell silent again. Over the last three days, she had become accustomed to her uncle's morning quiet. "Prayer," he told her when she asked about it on the first day. "Quiet is a time of prayer for me. I find so little silence in my normal day." Determined to learn from his example, she fought her natural urge to talk and kept her mouth shut.

Stepping past a crater, she thought of Casey Sterling. He had stopped by a couple of times since their arrival in Kosovo, but they were both far too busy to do anything more than say hello. Just as well, she figured. She kept getting funny vibes from him—all warm and cuddly in one minute and professional and calculating the next. She liked him, no question about that, but he seemed intensely focused on his career, and she didn't feel quite sure that his motivation for seeing her was strictly personal.

Someone shouted up ahead on the road.

Focused on the present again, Valerie rounded a curve and saw the Ibar River bridge about fifty yards directly ahead. The bridge—a solid structure of concrete and rusty steel arches—spanned a stretch of muddy water. An old convoy-style truck sat on the near side of the bridge, rust spots the size of phone books on its sides, a driver in a tattered brown hat at the wheel. At least seventy-five men stood beside and behind the truck, their bearded faces fierce in the early-morning light, their weapons drawn. A green jeep with a crushed left fender sat behind the men, its engine running, heavy smoke pouring out of the exhaust. A bearded man whose shoulders seemed as wide as the hood of the jeep sat in the passenger side, a machine gun poised in his arms, his black beard flecked with gray.

On the other side of the bridge stood at least thirty armed men, their faces equally fierce. In the center of the bridge waited a group of ten French NATO troops, their uniforms clean and pressed, half the contingent facing one way, half the other.

"Looks like trouble," said Chadwick's bodyguard, stepping between the evangelist and the bridge. "Let's mind our own business, go quietly back—"

"It looks like the Albanians are trying to cross to the Serbian side," Chadwick interrupted.

Valerie quickly understood, the persecuted had become the persecutors. Now that the NATO bombing had stopped, the Albanians had returned to their ransacked homes from the refugee camps. But, furious at their enemies, they wanted to cross the bridge and destroy what remained of the Serb district on the other side. NATO peacekeeping forces had prevented more than one such episode on this bridge over the last several weeks.

The Albanian in the jeep shouted something and his men surged forward a few steps. The French troops advanced a couple of paces in both directions, their weapons at the ready. Valerie saw instantly that if a firefight broke out, the French would take fire from both sides. They were too few to hold off the confrontation if either the Serbs or the Albanians insisted on it.

The passenger in the jeep jumped out, a long black coat on his stumpy body, a cigarette in his lips. He shouted and his men surged forward once more. They now stood a fourth of the way onto the bridge, all bunched up like a contracted muscle about to explode. On the other side the Serbs also advanced a few steps. The French raised their weapons and everyone froze expectantly, waiting for someone to twitch, for a leader to give an order, for the first bullet to rip out the heart of the morning.

Everything fell silent on the river. No one moved. A crazy notion flashed through Valerie's head. Is this how death felt? As peaceful as a hospital hallway in the middle of the night? The dog at her side barked. Several of the men on the bridge glanced in her direction, then back to their enemies. Valerie shivered.

Chadwick broke the silence.

"In the name of Jesus Christ, I command you to halt!" he thundered, his feet planted firmly on the road, his right hand extended as if pronouncing a benediction. Several of the soldiers glanced at him, their expressions confused.

Valerie cringed, expecting shots to ring out any second. Before anyone could stop him, Chadwick started walking toward the bridge, his long legs moving faster than Valerie had seen in weeks. He held his hands in the air like a policeman halting traffic. The men on the bridge stayed still, obviously shocked at the intrusion.

By the time Chadwick reached the bridge, Valerie, the translator, and the bodyguard had caught up to him. The commander of the French troops shouted in English for him to stop, but he ignored the command and plunged forward, pushing his way past the jeep, past the stunned Albanians, past their leader with his black coat and smoldering cigarette.

Within seconds, Chadwick reached the center of the bridge where the French troops stood. He towered over everyone on the bridge, his presence awesome in its fearlessness.

Valerie jumped as she felt something brush her leg, but then realized that her dog friend had joined her, its head pushing against her knee. She held her breath, her heart thumping wildly.

Chadwick raised his arms, one toward the Albanians, one toward the Serbs, and glanced toward his translator. "Translate," he said.

Chadwick's voice thundered across the bridge. "I am your friend," he began. "I am here because God loves all people—Serb and Albanian." The translator hesitated. Chadwick stared at him, his eyes as fierce as those of the men who surrounded him. The man swallowed, found his voice, and called out the translation, turning first toward the Albanians, then toward the Serbs.

The Albanian leader in the black coat snorted and moved forcefully through his men toward Chadwick.

"How can . . . can God love men who butcher children?" he shouted, his English halting but understandable.

"God hates the sin but loves the sinner," called Chadwick, his voice softer but just as firm. "God loves all people because God created all people."

Silence fell on the bridge again as the message was translated. Chadwick waited an instant, then spoke again.

"These men," he said, indicating the Serbs behind him, "are your brothers."

"I no . . . brother to these butchers!" shouted the Albanian leader, his weapon bouncing in his hands as he stood in front of his troops. "I kill the butchers . . . burn their houses . . . as they burned my house!"

The Albanians shouted their agreement and the mob edged farther onto the bridge, a tidal wave of anger about to crash. The truck driver gunned his engines and the truck bolted forward, the Albanian leader right beside it.

The Serbs on the opposite side also rushed forward, their

voices screaming out their hatred of the Albanians. A shot rang
out, then another. The dog at Valerie's side began barking. Valerie fell to her knees. The French commander grabbed Chadwick,
but Chadwick pushed him away and stepped toward the truck, a
hand out, palm extended toward its hood.

The shooting stopped quickly, and the Albanians' truck
screeched to a stop at Chadwick's knee. Behind him the French
troops were hemmed in by the Serb advance, and now the antag-
onists faced each other with only a few feet of the bridge between
them, a seething mob of desperate men stoked by fear and hatred.

A spot of red appeared near Chadwick's right collarbone, and
Valerie realized he'd taken a bullet! Forgetting the danger, she
pushed through the Albanians to her uncle's side, but he held out
an arm, eased her away, and faced the Albanian leader again.

Up close now, Valerie saw the Albanian's eyes. They stared
out black and steely, no hint of compassion anywhere in them.

"They butcher . . . my family," he stammered, jabbing his gun
toward the Serbs. "Two babies . . . my wife and son. I have . . . no
one. Now I . . . I butcher . . . them."

Valerie felt her heart sink. How could such cruelty go unpun-
ished? Could she forgive someone if the same thing happened to
her, or to her family?

"And then what?" Chadwick asked, his eyes searching the Albanian's face. "The kinsmen of those you butcher, will they come
for you? You can't sleep at night because you fear their coming?
And because you are haunted by the faces of those you killed. Is
that the way you want to spend the rest of your days? Is it?"

All fell still on the bridge again. The red on Chadwick's neck
and shoulder had spread outward now, down onto the front of the
tan sweater he wore under his brown coat. On both sides of Chadwick, the opposing forces stood ready. But somehow they seemed
to sense that the encounter between Chadwick and the Albanian
leader was the key. What happened between them determined
the fate of those on the bridge, whether they lived or died.

The hair on Valerie's neck stood to attention. She sensed
something else happening too—a larger conflict—a battle between good and evil—black hatred pulsating against the power
of a holy God. She prayed silently.

The Albanian spat on the bridge. "I . . . want my revenge," he
said.

"God will take your vengeance," Chadwick said. "Leave it to God."

"God take too long," growled the Albanian. "I want vengeance today!"

Chadwick nodded. "I have children too," he said. "If someone harmed them, I would want the same. But that would make me no different from the murderers. Are you no different than the ones who killed your family?"

The Albanian paused. "I *am* different," he insisted, tossing his cigarette to the ground.

"Then show that," Chadwick said. "Show them you are different." He indicated the Serbs over his shoulder. "Show them you are not a butcher!"

Chadwick shouted the words for all to hear, and the NATO translator's voice was equally forceful.

The Albanian ground his teeth.

"Show them!" Chadwick shouted. "Show them you are a man big enough to leave death behind, a man big enough to choose peace over destruction, a man big enough to leave his vengeance on this bridge. A man who will teach his people a new way of life, a way that gives them all a chance to leave this hatred in the past."

He stepped closer to the Albanian. The man's finger twitched on the trigger of his weapon.

Valerie's dog whined and she touched its head, holding her breath.

Chadwick moved again. The Albanian cursed. Chadwick laid his hand on the man's shoulder. "Go back to your home," he whispered. "Leave your vengeance on this bridge. In the name of Jesus Christ, I command you to do this!"

The Albanian raised his weapon and pointed it at Chadwick. The evangelist froze. The troops on either side tensed, their fingers playing with the triggers of their weapons.

The dog at Valerie's side barked as a vehicle approached from the Serbian side, skidding to a stop on the far side of the river. To Valerie's astonishment, Casey Sterling jumped out of the jeep, a cameraman right behind him. For an instant she wondered how he had gotten there.

"Make your peace with your God," the Albanian whispered to Chadwick. "It is your day to—"

"Hold it!" Casey Sterling shouted.

The crowd shifted as Casey headed onto the bridge, a gangly, emaciated boy at his side.

"Prikova!" Sterling shouted. "Drop your weapon!"

Valerie recognized the name. The man facing Chadwick was the leader of the KLA! She twisted to face Sterling, who had the boy by the elbow.

"I have your son!" Sterling shouted. "Your son is alive!"

Prikova's black eyes rounded into saucers but he didn't lower his weapon.

"Bring him to me!" he shouted. "Show me the proof of what you say!"

Sterling pushed the boy through the parting crowd. Now he stood by Prikova, the boy in front.

"Look at him," he urged. "This is your boy. I found him in a refugee camp in Macedonia."

Prikova lowered his weapon slightly, his eyes inspecting the boy as if examining an apparition. The youngster stayed quiet, his face and hands covered with sores. Prikova stepped toward him, his gun halfway to his side.

"Is it you, Rajeen?" he asked, his voice trembling. "Is this miracle possible?"

The boy nodded. "It is me, Papa."

His eyes filling with tears, Prikova lowered his gun, turned its muzzle away from Chadwick, and handed it to him by the stock. The troops on both sides exhaled as one and Valerie began to breathe again.

Chadwick took Prikova's weapon, then stepped back as the Albanian threw his arms around his son's shoulders, tears the size of pennies rolling down his face.

Valerie started to cry too, her heart soaring. Whether anyone else understood it or not, she knew she had just stood on holy ground, in the midst of a miracle. Something touched her elbow and she turned to see Casey Sterling at her side, his cameraman right beside him.

"Incredible," Sterling whispered. "Simply incredible."

Overcome with gratitude, Valerie opened her arms and hugged him.

"A son belongs with his father," Sterling whispered, his whole body shaking.

Valerie hugged him tighter. That shaking again! Her face flushed and for some reason she felt that she had to protect him, that even as strong as he appeared, he had ghosts around him, powers that made him shudder and tremble, even in the midst of his most triumphant moment. His quivering stopped suddenly and she felt him steel himself.

She stepped back, and as she did she saw his cameraman hard at work, the lens aimed at her. But she didn't mind. In fact, she felt so good that she still didn't mind when she found out later that millions of people all over the world watched her hug Casey over and over again as the scene on the bridge played back across one television screen after another over the next twenty-four hours.

PART III

The rattling thunderbolt hath but his clap, the lightning but his flash, and as they both come in a moment, so do they both end in a minute.

John Lyly, 1579

*There is no fear in love
But perfect love drives out fear . . .
The one who fears is not made perfect in love.*

1 John 4:18

THIRTY-FIVE

The charter jet touched down in Atlanta five days later, and Valerie and the rest of the crew climbed wearily off, their bodies worn out from dealing with the results of Chadwick's most improbable accomplishment. With Prikova's amazing turnaround, the whole cycle of retaliation in Kosovo faltered.

Within half a day everyone in the world within reach of a radio, computer, or television set had seen what happened on the Ibar River bridge, and all of Kosovo seemed to exhale with relief. If Prikova could give up his hatred, perhaps others could also.

By Tuesday, leaders in Kosovo—both Serb and ethnic Albanian—had agreed on a preliminary plan to restart peace negotiations. Though clearly the problems weren't over, that agreement satisfied Chadwick, and after conferring with the others in his alliance, he agreed they should each return home. The hostilities that had forced him into Kosovo had ended. That was his goal—not to sit in on negotiations to impose his will on the involved parties, but to dramatize the need for peace and to make plain the world's insistence upon it.

To everyone's relief, Chadwick's wound turned out to be a superficial injury. One of the shots had creased his collarbone at a side angle, cutting through his flesh like a knife but not penetrating his body. An American army doctor sewed in nine stitches, congratulated him for his good luck, and suggested he stay out of such situations in the future. Chadwick thanked the doctor, told him he didn't believe in luck, and instructed Ted to send the man a Bible with Deuteronomy 32:39 marked in it.

Valerie watched it all and marveled. Chadwick seemed indestructible—a colossus striding a world of mere mortals.

Now, a bag thrown over each shoulder, Valerie reached the doorway that led into the airport terminal, intent on driving straight to her apartment to sleep for a week. Chadwick and the rest of the group trailed her slowly. She heard a rumble, then saw a throng of people jammed into the space around the door. Stopping instantly, she eased up against the wall, hoping no one had seen her. She peered out. Someone had roped off a narrow walkway through the crowd for her crew to pass. From what she could estimate, the crowd numbered in the hundreds, maybe a thousand. It stretched as far down the terminal as she could see. Scores of people on both sides of the ropes carried posters covered with hand-scrawled writing. The ones on the right were flattering, the ones on the left the opposite. Two policemen stood in the center of the two groups as if holding back a flood.

"God's Man With God's Plan," read one of the posters. "A Prophet, a Peacemaker," offered another.

"God's Man in Satan's Hand," said a counter argument. "Jesus Yes, Infidels No."

"We have a crowd," Valerie said, turning to face her uncle. "Bigger than we expected."

Chadwick appeared thinner than a week ago. The rest of the gang paused with him.

"I knew we'd have some press," he said. "But not much else. Guess *The Christian Weekly* article stirred up the opposition. Let's take a look."

Staying close to the wall, Chadwick walked almost to the door. Valerie followed, her fatigue now forgotten. She saw a number of cameras pointed toward the door from which Chadwick would emerge, and a score of eager reporters waited to pounce. She scanned the group for Casey Sterling but didn't see him.

Her uncle studied the crowd for several seconds, his eyes weary, his shoulders stooped. Moments like this reminded her of his fragile condition.

"We've got some protesters," he sighed. "And some supporters. So now we've got a mess." He ran his fingers through his hair. "Here's what we're going to do. Valerie and I will go meet the crowd. The rest of you will wait here. I'll make a short statement, then leave with everyone except Valerie. She'll stay behind to talk with any press that wants further conversation. That'll be it. Any questions?"

Valerie looked immediately to Ted and Rodney, but they appeared too tired to argue. For a second she thought of her appearance—wrinkled khaki slacks, a simple burgundy pullover sweater, her hair brushed but uncurled, worn-out makeup and no earrings. Not exactly what she wanted the whole world to see.

"Okay," Chadwick said, "let's get this over with." He headed to the door, his stride long and purposeful.

Valerie tagged behind, focusing on what she would say to the press. As she followed Chadwick through the door, the crowd responded immediately, a chorus of cheers on the right battling an equally loud chorus of boos from the left. Trying to ignore the yelling, she pushed through the mob with her uncle. A policeman hurriedly stepped over, his arm out to push back the crowd. When they reached the clear spot in the center of the ropes, Chadwick stopped and raised his arms.

"You're being used!" someone shouted from the left.

"Used by the Lord!" shouted a woman from the right.

Chadwick waved his arms, signaling the crowd to quiet down. After a few seconds, they obeyed, even the protesters. Clearing his throat, Chadwick faced first to the left, then to the right.

"I'll make a short statement," he began.

"We don't want to hear it," shouted a man to the left. "We've heard enough!"

Chadwick closed his eyes, obviously gathering himself. The crowd fell silent for a second. He opened his eyes again.

"After my statement, my press agent, Miss Valerie Miller, will take questions from the media."

"We don't want to hear her either!" shouted the same man, his tone hate-filled. The policemen stepped toward the man, obviously intent on keeping order.

Chadwick spoke again. "I know some of you don't agree with what I'm doing," he said. "Or the way I'm doing it, working with people of other faiths. But I ask you to consider the results. In two places, peace has returned. People are alive today who would be dead if my allies and I had not intervened. We don't have the same beliefs, that's true. But I can't help but think that our work has pleased God. And I've not compromised any of my convictions about the Lord Jesus Christ."

Chadwick paused and studied the crowd, meeting as many people as possible eye to eye. "You know me," he continued, his tone softer, more personal. "You've known me for years. Some of you trusted Jesus for the first time at one of our crusades. So I ask you to trust me now, not because of who I am, but because of

who Jesus is, who Jesus has led me to become. I ask you to examine your hearts, test this in your prayers. I believe if you do,
you'll accept this, embrace it." He stopped, glancing at the floor
now, his hands in his pockets.

"You're going forward?" shouted the loud man from the left.

Chadwick nodded slowly, looking up. "Yes," he said firmly.
"I'm moving ahead. In fact, I'm going to expand the effort one
more time. I've asked each of my allies to invite four other leaders from their circles to join us. I'm holding a summit with them
in two weeks."

The crowd began to murmur. Chadwick's voice rose as he
spoke over the rumble. "At that time we will make plans to go
into every corner of the world where violence erupts, every nook
and cranny, large or small, where hatred breaks out. We will
bring peace . . ." He had to shout now over the roar of the mob.
"With God's help, we will bring peace!"

He walked away then, his bodyguards clearing a path down
the hallway. The crowd trailed after him, their posters bouncing
in the air, half of them convinced they were following a man of
God, the others sure they were trailing a man in league with the
devil.

Mouth ajar, Valerie watched Chadwick go. The press hustled
after him, none of them staying to talk with her. She exhaled and
turned back to wait for Ted and Rodney, wondering as she did
whether they knew of the plans Chadwick had just announced.
She suspected not. The expansion of the alliance probably came
as much of a surprise to them as it did to her.

———————

Following the police down the airport hallway, Russell Chadwick kept his eyes straight ahead. Though people called out from
all sides, he kept his mouth shut. The vehemence of the opposition surprised him, but he had learned from past experience that
he never won when he argued with someone whose mind was already made up.

The officers turned left and walked out of the terminal and
Chadwick followed, much of the crowd still with him, the media
included. Ten seconds later he waved to the crowd, climbed into
a car waiting at the curb, thanked the police for their courtesy,
and told his driver to head home. His bodyguards settled in too,
one in the front by the driver, the other beside him in the backseat. The car pulled slowly away from the terminal. A man hold

ing a poster banged his fist into the side of the car, snarling at
Chadwick. "A Wolf in Sheep's Clothing" said the sign, the words
written in black marker below a newspaper photo of Chadwick.
The car moved past the man, cleared the crowd, and turned right
toward the interstate.

Chadwick laid his head against the seat. People like that last
man confused and depressed him. What had he done to make
people so unhappy? Did his alliance with nonbelievers negate the
good they had done? Certainly, all his allies weren't Christians—
he never claimed they were. Didn't people see that majoring on
differences led to problems? That majoring on commonalities
solved some of them? He closed his eyes, suddenly aware of an
ache in the small of his back. He heard a phone ring, then saw
his driver pick up the mobile unit from the front seat console.

A second later, the driver passed the phone back. "For you,
sir," he said.

Chadwick took it, expecting to hear Mildred's voice on the
other end.

"Hey, Reverend Chadwick, glad you landed safely. You're
doing well?"

It took a second for Chadwick to recognize the caller. "Oh,
sure, Bill," he said, surprised to hear from Bill Stricker. "What
about you?"

"Fine. Excellent. Doing great. I'm sure you're worn to a frazzle."

Chadwick nodded. "I'm an old man," he said. "Getting up in
the morning wears me to a frazzle."

Stricker laughed but Chadwick didn't know whether it was
genuine or not. Bill Stricker hadn't exactly supported him
through all of this.

"Hey, I won't keep you but a minute," Stricker said. "I know
you're headed home. But I just saw you on television, heard your
statement when you got off the plane. I want you to know I've
been thinking about all this, trying to figure it out. I've not liked
it so far, you know that—not one iota. I want you to preach, do
what you do best. But, well, what you did on that bridge made
me stop and reconsider. I've been waiting for you to come home
so I could tell you."

"Glad to hear it," Chadwick said, his defenses still up. "I need
all the help I can get."

"Yeah, exactly. And I want to do my part." Stricker paused,
but then continued. "Look, I heard you say you're expanding your

alliance, calling everybody together to make preparations for your future work."

"That's right."

"So, anyway, that gave me an idea. You'll need a place to meet all these folks, am I right? You haven't settled on a spot yet, have you?"

"No, not yet. My people will talk to some hotels, but nothing is definite."

"Well, let me save you the trouble. There's no reason to rent a hotel and spend a ton of money. I've got a ski lodge out here in Colorado, rooms for a hundred and twenty people, another seventy-five or so in ten cottages right by it. You can meet here. I've got all the staff you'll need—kitchen, maids, security—you name it, we're set up for it. It's easy to reach too. You fly to Denver, then head toward Breckenridge. It's only forty miles or so to my place. They've got a good local airport too. Lots of celebrities fly right in here. I'll give you the place for free as long as you like. What do you say to that?"

Chadwick hesitated. What Stricker offered made sense. He needed a spot to house a lot of people. And why spend money on a hotel, money that he had less and less of these days? But something about Stricker made him nervous. The man had contributed millions of dollars to his ministry—he didn't know exactly how many millions because he never asked. But he had seemed so adamant against this peace idea. He'd even threatened to withhold any more funds, including the dollars he'd considered giving to the school in Georgia. So why had he changed his mind?

The car passed a truck and sped by the Braves baseball stadium. Why did anyone change his mind? Why had Ian O'Fallon changed his? And what about Prikova on the Ibar River bridge? What caused him to hand over his weapon and turn away from his hatred? If people like O'Fallon and Prikova could experience transformations, then why not Bill Stricker? Sure the man had tried to use his money as leverage to stop him from going to Kosovo in the first place. But so what? People used what they had at their disposal. Stricker wasn't the only supporter to oppose him. Good people sometimes had differences. He needed to believe the best about Stricker and give him the benefit of the doubt as he did everyone else.

Chadwick focused on the phone again. "I think you're awfully generous," he said. "Though I have to tell you it surprises me some."

"Well, like I've heard you say, 'The Lord works in mysterious ways his wonders to perform.' "

"It's not original with me."

Stricker laughed again. "Do you know the dates yet?"

Chadwick rubbed his forehead. "Yeah, I've been thinking about the first weekend in February, Friday through Sunday afternoon. Better block it out through Monday. Is that workable?"

Stricker paused but only for a second. "I'll make it workable," he said. "Anything you need, let me know. Anything at all."

Chadwick thanked him and hung up the phone. His car sped by the 285 loop and headed north, and he told himself to relax. But, try as he might, he couldn't push away the notion that Bill Stricker had more than generosity in mind by offering the use of his ski lodge. He'd need to keep his eyes open on this one, he decided. He'd have to be "wise as a serpent and as gentle as a dove."

Laying down the phone, Bill Stricker walked to the massive window that overlooked the valley opening up below his lodge. A fire burned in the stone fireplace to his left. He held his pipe in his left hand, the bowl cradled in his palm. For several seconds, he stared out at the snow-covered slopes. A shadow from the rock formation above the lodge spread out on the white landscape, giving it an eerie, gloomy look in spite of the bright sunshine. Puffing his pipe, Stricker turned back and faced the men in the room with him.

"He accepted," he said. "He's bringing the whole lousy crew out here to Colorado."

"I hope you know what you're doing," Ludwig Roth said, his hands on the mantel as he stared into the fireplace.

"I didn't hear any brilliant ideas from you," Stricker said.

Roth nodded meekly.

Stricker puffed on his pipe and stared back out at the snow. He wasn't sure if he knew what he was doing or not. But one thing was certain. If he had to make a mistake, it'd be a mistake of action rather than inaction. A man didn't attain the heights he'd attained by standing around with his hands in his pockets. He might mess this up, but if he did, he'd mess it up on his own terms. Given his past successes though, he had no reason to think he'd fail this time either.

THIRTY-SIX

MONDAY, JANUARY 26
NORTH OF LOS ANGELES

Dressed as always in a tan, ankle-length, straight-lined dress and soft brown sandals with white socks, Daphne Farmer, personal assistant to Martha Blevins, New Age guru to the multitudes, walked into the garage of Blevins' earth-toned house at just past 8 A.M. Climbing into her employer's favorite vehicle—a black Suburban that a contributor from Arizona had given to her three years ago, Daphne pushed her frizzy gray hair from her eyes, tugged the brown sweater she wore around her shoulders, and backed out of the driveway. Once on the road, she pushed in a CD and leaned back to enjoy the sounds of a cascading waterfall as she drove to the grocery store.

Checking to make sure she had her list in her sweater pocket, she eased the Suburban up the hill by the house, steered around a curve, and hit the automatic window button to let in the morning air. What a gorgeous day—blue sky overhead, a blue ocean down to her right, the temperature about fifty-eight degrees. She took a deep, relaxing breath and reached the summit of the road. The highway began to descend. Farmer slid her foot off the gas. The incline dropped more quickly as the road swerved left, then right along the top of the precipice. The Suburban picked up speed. Farmer tapped the brake. Nothing happened. She pressed harder on the brake. The Suburban picked up more speed. The road straightened up for half a mile and she kept the vehicle under control, working the brake with her foot, hoping, believing that it would catch at any moment and give her the traction she needed. But nothing happened.

Daphne's brown eyes widened. Knowing that a sharp curve

waited just past this straight stretch on the highway, she jammed her foot toward the floorboard again. The brake hit the floor of the vehicle and the Suburban kept gaining speed. The speedometer read "80," and the only straight part of the entire road was about to run out!

Frantic now, Farmer's eyes darted to the right and left. The cliffs dropped off at least four hundred feet to her right. A thick wall of mountain rock blocked her on the left. She pounded the brakes again and again, hoping that she could reverse the Suburban, stop it in its tracks, or slow it down at least a little.

She saw the curve reaching for her at the end of the straight road. She grabbed the emergency brake and pulled it back, slowly at first, but then with more and more pressure. The brake squealed and she smelled smoke. The vehicle swerved and skidded and headed toward the cliffs. One arm fighting the steering wheel, Daphne let go of the emergency brake and shifted the automatic transmission to a lower gear. But the incline was too steep and the Suburban had too much momentum. The curve bent to the right.

Jerking the gearshift down another notch, she pulled on the emergency brake one more time, but the speed of the vehicle and the incline of the road had burned up the brake, and she knew she had just one more chance.

Choosing the mountain over the cliffs, she steered the Suburban to the left, across the lane and into the side of the rocky plateau. Still fighting, she jammed down on the brakes one more time. But then the vehicle crashed into the guardrail and her head hit the steering wheel. The air bag inflated and popped into her face and she lost consciousness. Her hands fell from the steering wheel and the Suburban ricocheted off the rail and bounced to the right.

The Suburban cleared the cliffs and hung in the air for a second, appearing almost to climb for a beat. Then it plummeted toward the ocean, its wheels still spinning against the backdrop of the clear blue sky.

The hood of the Suburban plowed into a mass of jagged rocks at the edge of the ocean. A loud crunch broke the rhythm of the waves as water sprayed upward.

The Suburban exploded. Fiery scraps of metal cascaded up and out over the ocean. Flames fizzed in the water and a plume of smoke joined the water spray. Inside the Suburban, Daphne Farmer never felt a thing.

GARY E. PARKER

Valerie heard about Daphne Farmer at about 1 P.M. Eastern
time. Though she didn't remember much about Farmer, she did
recall her remarkable resemblance to Martha Blevins, right
down to the clothes she wore and the way she pinned back her
frizzy hair.

Sitting in a meeting in the conference room with Ted and Rodney, she followed Ted's lead when they heard the news, pausing
for a time of prayer for Blevins and for any family that Farmer
had. When they finished praying, she suggested calling Blevins
while Ted and Rodney made sure that Chadwick knew about the
tragedy. Walking to her office, she found the number and dialed
it. Within seconds Blevins answered the phone.

"Martha Blevins?"

"Yes."

"Valerie Miller here. I'm with Reverend Chadwick."

"I remember you well, Valerie. Thanks for calling."

"I'm so sorry to hear about Ms. Farmer," she began. "And I'm
speaking on behalf of Reverend Chadwick and everyone else
here. Things like this don't make much sense sometimes."

Blevins sighed. "It's so sad. Daphne loved life so much."

"Does she have family?"

"A brother somewhere. We're trying to reach him. She came
to us from a prison. I guess you didn't know that. I met her there
five years ago. I make periodic visits to a facility near here. My
good deed, you know."

"Any idea what happened? I heard she had a car accident."

"We're not sure of the details. But they hauled the Suburban
out of the ocean a few miles from here. A policeman said the
brakes might have failed. I don't know. We just had the thing
serviced a couple of weeks ago. It should've been me, that's the
worst part. I drive to the store every morning. I usually stop at
the top of the hill for thirty minutes or so and enjoy the ocean. I
do it every day, first thing after I get up. There's a farmers' market that sells the best fresh vegetables. But I woke up today with
a headache—not like me to have a headache, but this morning I
had a screamer. I sent Daphne. Now she's dead."

Valerie walked to her window, studying the traffic speeding
through a gray rain. She knew something about unexpected tragedy. It happened far too often for her liking.

"Any plans for the funeral?" she asked, pushing away her own issues.

"We'll cremate the remains, then do a memorial, probably on Thursday afternoon, assuming we can find her brother."

Valerie did a quick calculation, then made a decision. "I'd like to attend the memorial," she said, "on behalf of Reverend Chadwick."

"That's nice of you," Blevins said. "Real nice."

"We have to stick together," Valerie offered. "None of this is easy."

"It should have been me," Blevins said again.

"I'll pray for you."

"You do that. Your prayers will help."

Valerie hung up and studied the traffic for several more minutes. The miracle on the Ibar River bridge had momentarily given her a respite from her almost-year-long depression. But now the sadness fell over her again, a blanket of gloom as bleak as the weather outside. No matter what good came of her uncle's efforts, she still hadn't made much progress on her own struggles. Even if he managed to usher in a new era of peace for the human race, she still hadn't managed to find peace in her own soul. She needed a Peace Project for herself.

Leaving the window, she plopped down at her desk and laid her face in her hands. She was too old to call home and cry on her parents' shoulders and too busy to have kept up with many friends. She suddenly felt lonelier than she had at any point in her entire life. Ted and Rodney tolerated her, but their relationship went no deeper than that. And her uncle Russell had so many other problems on his mind, she didn't feel she should burden him with hers. Bottom line? She had no one. Not family, not friend. Not even God. Her spiritual life felt as dry as Death Valley dust. Yeah, she still believed in God, but that belief carried no flesh on it, no warmth. For the good it did her, God seemed as remote as a distant star and twice as cold.

Sighing, she forced herself to get busy. After instructing her secretary to call the travel agent for flight arrangements for California, she stood again and walked to the window. The rain fell in sheets now, a good old January soaking. Nothing like a chill winter rain to drag down the spirits. She hugged her waist. Poor Daphne Farmer.

She thought back over the past year. Daphne wasn't the only one to die. Maybe Michael was dead too. And a score of men she

had never met had died in the search for the stupid scroll that
Michael had tracked down and read!

People died all the time, she decided. As regular as birth,
death also came.

Chadwick had Parkinson's. How much longer before that or
something else took his life—like that steel beam that almost
killed them both?

And what about Clement Peter? One of the most powerful
men on Earth one minute, but dead the next. He had been no
different than any pauper. Poof! As suddenly as that—it all ends.

Now Daphne Farmer, headed to market one morning—Valerie's eyes widened. She stared down at the traffic but didn't
really see it. Martha Blevins said it should have been *her*! *She*
drove to the store every morning, not Daphne! The police said
maybe the brakes failed, but the Suburban had recently been
serviced. Did that make any sense?

Clement dead of a heart attack, according to the reports, but
Vatican law allowed no autopsy. A few Internet sites suggested
something more sinister than a natural death. Most people dismissed the conspiracy notions as nonsense. But what if the theories were right? Had someone murdered the pope?

A steel beam almost killed Chadwick. Was that an accident?
She certainly had her doubts. Now Daphne Farmer—though it
should have been Martha Blevins.

Back at her desk, Valerie told herself to forget it, to leave her
paranoid notions out of things. But she couldn't escape the idea.
What if the brakes on Blevins' Suburban hadn't failed by themselves? What if someone had helped them along in a murder attempt?

But why would anyone want Blevins dead? Simple—not
everyone liked Chadwick's plans for peace. Clement Peter—dead.
Chadwick—almost dead, a missed opportunity. Now an attempt
on Martha Blevins.

Valerie rubbed her eyes. Had she finally reached the desperate end of her paranoid delusions?

She stood and walked to the window again, her mind skipping
from one notion to another. She kept telling herself to drop her
suspicions, but she just couldn't do it. Too much had happened in
the past year, too many bad things to just assume the best about
all this. But where could she turn? What could she do? Assuming
that any of her suspicions were right, how could she prove them?
More importantly, how could she stop this?

She thought about her options. Her uncle would listen politely—he did that for everybody—but he'd dismiss her ideas. He believed the best about everybody. No way would he swallow something so unlikely as this. And even if he believed her, he'd probably not stop his work. He'd say something like, "Trust the Lord, Valerie. If God wants this to happen, He'll take care of us." But if not Chadwick, then who would help?

Not her parents. They'd just insist that she resign her position and come home to safety. Besides, how could a grown woman go running back home every time she faced a problem?

Valerie sighed. She didn't have many options. The police didn't believe her about the steel beam, they'd made that clear. And U.S. officials had no jurisdiction to investigate the death of a pope.

Stumped, she left the window once more and slumped back to her desk. Picking up the television remote, she pushed a button and the screen across the room brightened. Flipping through the channels, she stopped on CBC. Then she twisted back to her phone, dropped the remote, and searched through her Rolodex for a phone number. She knew who would help her! Casey Sterling! If the man thought he'd find a story at the end of the trip, he'd walk barefooted across a thousand miles of broken glass.

Her heart soaring, Valerie keyed in the number. With Casey's energy and her paranoia, no telling what she'd find out.

———

Pope John Peter stepped through the gardens carefully, his stride slower than normal to prevent dragging his white cassock along the top of the grass. The winter air chilled his face and he curled his arms up under his white cape to keep his hands warm. Accompanied only by two Swiss Guards and Cardinal Lech Zolinska, the pontiff moved gracefully amid the well-manicured beauty of the Vatican grounds. The place felt like a quiet cathedral, the branches of the trees forming a canopy over his head. A soft stream of water gurgled up and out of a fountain to his right. A statue of the Virgin Mother stood beside the fountain, her face serene, her eyes wide. John Peter loved the spray of the fountain. It helped calm his mind—a difficult chore this evening, even for the most active of fountains.

Over the last few days, his chief of security had brought him copies of four more conversations held between Zolinska and an unnamed associate at the other end of the phone connection.

Each conversation outlined a similar theme—Zolinska distrusted John Peter and disliked the process that led to his election.

Though it surprised John Peter that Zolinska expressed his views so blatantly, that sentiment in and of itself provided no basis for any disciplinary action. Hadn't he also held similar thoughts about some of the actions of both popes for whom he had labored? Unlike himself, however, Zolinska had also expressed in no uncertain terms his plans to do everything in his power to sabotage any peace initiative that the pope adopted in conjunction with the Reverend Russell Chadwick. Even worse, the verbal assurances to this effect that Zolinska had given to his unknown accomplice had been followed by a number of key and traceable acts.

Zolinska had begun to whisper his discontent to a number of members of the Curia. In addition, he had compiled a substantial paper with arguments against the pope's action if he should choose to join Chadwick. He had also fed the rumors that Clement Peter might have died of suspicious means and that John Peter himself—unhappy that he hadn't won the papacy in the earlier election—had actually contributed to Clement's death.

Grieved by Zolinska's actions, the pontiff stopped at a pond formed by the runoff from the fountain, picked up a small pebble, and tossed it into the water. Zolinska stared at him but said nothing. Most amazingly, the man who always twitched stayed still, obviously sensing the gravity of some upcoming announcement.

Studying the pond, John Peter reassured himself that he had made the right decision. Now all he had to do was announce it to Zolinska. He picked up another pebble and rolled it between his fingers. He kept his eyes on the pond, his back to Zolinska.

"I will go to the Reverend Chadwick's summit," he said softly. "I will cast all the power of the papacy into the effort to bring peace." He reared back to throw the pebble, but Zolinska grabbed his wrist. The two guards moved toward Zolinska, but John Peter held up a hand and they halted. John Peter faced the cardinal, his black eyes grim. He glanced at the cardinal's hand, still clutching his wrist, then stared into Zolinska's eyes.

"You forget yourself!" he whispered through clenched teeth.

"You are inviting disaster," Zolinska hissed, his fingers tight on the pope's wrist.

"That may be so," John Peter said. "But it will be a disaster of my own making, not yours."

"You think you can succeed in this?" Zolinska arched his eyebrows.

"If God so wills it."

"You speak of God's will as if you think you know it."

"I have sought it these last few days. That much I know to be true. Whether I have found it or not, I cannot say. But one thing I do know . . ."

"And what is that?"

John Peter calmly but firmly pulled his hand away from Zolinska's grip and nodded to his guards. One of them stepped forward, a small tape recorder in his hand. The pontiff took the tape recorder and punched the play button. Zolinska's voice sounded in the garden. The cardinal's shoulders slumped and the light in his eyes seemed to go out. He stared blankly into the fountain.

"I know you will cease and desist in your efforts to stop me," John Peter said. "If not you will find yourself serving a small parish as close as I can find to the North Pole. Are we clear on that?"

Zolinska said nothing. John Peter stepped to him and clamped a hand on both his wrists. The pontiff's fingers turned white from the grip. "Are we clear on that?" he repeated.

Zolinska nodded, his eyes still glazed.

John Peter released his grip and stepped back a pace. He tossed his pebble into the air once more, then threw it into the fountain. As the pebble sank to the bottom, he turned and headed back to his quarters. Zolinska followed after him, his head down, seemingly defeated. But John Peter knew better. Zolinska would not give up so easily. But that didn't matter. It didn't matter because after days of prayer and contemplation, John Peter had indeed concluded that God had truly directed him to the path he had chosen.

THIRTY-SEVEN

TUESDAY, JANUARY 27

Valerie met Casey Sterling in the lobby of the Fit For Life Club after she finished her noon workout. As usual, he looked great—navy sport coat, light gray slacks, white button-down shirt, no tie, a tan briefcase in his hand. She hoped her own appearance—tailored tan skirt, burgundy blouse, hair recently cut and styled, gold earrings—belied the fact that she felt worn out since her return from Kosovo.

"You all pumped up?" he teased, stepping past her to the door that opened to the main exercise area.

"I think I can handle you," she said, hefting her gym bag and following him.

He pointed to the climbing wall on the other side of the spacious room. "You climbed it yet?"

She shrugged, biting back the annoying sense of failure that hit her every time she thought of the wall. "Nope. The height thing, remember?"

He faced her, his eyes bright. "Don't worry about it. Are you ready to eat?"

"I'm starving."

"Then follow me."

At the restaurant, a hostess led them to a table by the window and seated them. A few seconds later a waitress appeared, lit the candle in the center of their table, and took their drink orders—tea for her, coffee for him.

"Thanks for calling," Sterling said, scooting his chair back. "I've wanted to see you."

"It's been hectic," she said, studying her hands. "And you've been as busy as I have."

"It has been wild," he agreed. "That scene on the bridge was unbelievable."

"Unbelievable that you showed up when you did. And with Prikova's son too."

Sterling dropped his eyes. "Well, I'd worked on that since Ireland. Had two people searching all over Central Europe. One of my guys found him in a makeshift hospital in one of the last refugee camps down in Macedonia. He was all drugged up, about dead. I had him delivered to me. Then, since I pretty much knew where Prikova operated, I headed that way with the boy. The rest of it was just plain dumb luck. Getting there when I did was a coincidence, that's all."

"I don't believe in luck," Valerie said, her response automatic. Sterling shrugged. "Whatever."

"I believe in God," she said, realizing as she said it that in spite of all she had experienced in the past year, the miracle on the Ibar River bridge had truly made a difference in her faith. Yes, she still had to deal with her grief in losing Michael, but that didn't necessarily minimize the reality of her relationship to God.

"I know," Sterling said. "But that's way past my expertise. If I don't have film, it's a non-event."

"Lots of things are real that you can't get on film," she said, determined to voice what suddenly felt incredibly real to her again.

"Like what?"

She leaned forward, her hands on the table. "The most important things: joy, anger, contentment, love, all the inner things that make life worth living. I mean, take Prikova. What made him put down his machine gun? You can't capture that on film, the wild joy he felt when he saw that boy of his, the—"

The waitress suddenly appeared with their drinks.

Sterling picked up his cup, drank from it. "I give you that," he said. "But that doesn't prove anything about God."

Valerie sipped her tea. "I'm not trying to prove anything," she said. "I'm just telling you what I believe."

"I thought you were struggling with some of that."

She hesitated, studying her tea. "Sure. That happens to many believers at one time or another. But ... I don't know ... I've made some progress lately. I've been in a grief spiral, sure. But maybe I shouldn't expect to handle everything all at once. Maybe a recovery from what I've experienced works in bits and pieces, stops and starts, not all at once. At least that's the way it feels to me. And I'm finally beginning to move through it all. The scene on the bridge—it jump-started something in me. A miracle if I ever saw one."

"No miracle," Sterling countered. "Hard work and dumb luck."

Valerie started to argue, but Sterling had his jaw set, and she felt an immediate resistance to anything further on the subject. Though determined to come back to the matter later, she let it drop for the moment.

"I heard the ratings for your coverage went through the roof," she said.

Sterling grinned, immediately more relaxed. "We teased it all afternoon, then showed it the first time at 6 P.M.," he said. "Over four hundred million people saw it worldwide, over one hundred twenty million in the United States alone."

"You're on the way," she said. "An anchor desk, no doubt about it."

The waitress reappeared and they both ordered. Chicken salad with avocado and a bowl of broccoli soup for her, grilled salmon and house salad with Italian dressing for him.

"I'm not counting any chickens," he said. "Not until I see them hatch."

Valerie sipped her tea. "But that's what you want, you told me that. And everyone says it'll happen sooner or later."

"There's no sign anybody's retiring, though," he said, his eyes on his coffee. "Fact is, I hear that Rather and Brokaw have recently signed new deals, five to seven more years for both. By the time they finish those contracts, who knows what'll happen? That story on the Ibar River bridge? Who'll remember it five years from now? No one, that's who."

Valerie bit her lip, surprised by Sterling's response. The man should feel ecstatic right now. Everywhere she turned, she saw his face, heard his name. Hotter than anyone in the media, he had every reason to enjoy some of the fruit of his hard work and natural talents. But he seemed anything but joyful. She remembered the hug she had given him on the bridge, the shaking in his shoulders. What caused that? Excitement? Fear? Insecurity? What?

The waitress appeared with their food, laid it on the table, and disappeared.

Sterling changed the subject before she could respond to his pessimism. "Too bad about Martha Blevins," he said, nibbling at his salad. "Her assistant, I mean. You just never know, do you?"

A spoon in her hand, Valerie nodded and sipped the soup.

"Is Blevins still going to join you and Chadwick out in Colorado?"

"She's not indicated anything to the contrary."

"What about the pope?"

"We're still waiting to hear."

Sterling laid his fork down and wiped his lips with a napkin. Placing both hands on the table, he interlocked his fingers and stared at Valerie. The candle flickered across his handsome features, and Valerie felt more and more drawn to him in spite of his obvious indifference to matters of faith. He had some problems, sure, but who didn't? She certainly did, more than she liked to admit. What if everyone she met dismissed her because she didn't have life all figured out yet?

"You really think Chadwick can do this?" he asked.

"I don't have a clue," she said. "But he's determined to try."

"It could get dangerous."

"More than it already is?"

"You've got a point there." He began eating his salad again.

She swallowed two more spoonfuls of soup, then laid down her spoon.

"Look, Casey," she began. "I didn't ask you here for purely personal reasons."

"Oh?" He put down his fork.

"Right. You see, I'm confused about something . . . well, Daphne Farmer's death, for instance. Martha Blevins said the brakes on the Suburban failed."

"So?"

"She'd just had the thing serviced. No sign of problems at the time."

Sterling took a bite of salmon. "No big deal," he said. "Things like that happen all the time. Maybe the people who worked on the vehicle never checked the brakes."

Valerie took a breath. "I know," she said. "You're probably right. But there's something else. Martha said she always took that drive, every morning. I just thought . . . maybe the brakes didn't fail by themselves. Maybe someone wanted to kill Martha."

Sterling rocked back, obviously stunned. His brow furrowed.

"There's more," Valerie said. "A few days before we left for Kosovo, a construction crane dropped a steel girder that barely missed Chadwick and me. It injured one of my uncle's bodyguards."

"I didn't hear about that," Sterling said. "But I still don't see your point."

"I don't think the steel girder dropped by accident."

Sterling grunted, shifting in his seat. "Did the cops check the crane operator?"

"They tried, but here it gets more curious. They couldn't find him. He disappeared. He was a temporary worker, an immigrant. The detective said the man probably didn't have his papers in order, didn't want trouble with immigration."

"That makes sense." Sterling rubbed his chin.

"You don't think it's possible that someone wanted to kill Chadwick, hired a crane operator to do it, then got him out of there?"

"Anything's possible. But not everything's likely." He leaned toward her. "Look, you're telling me someone tried to kill Chadwick, then went after Blevins. Missed both times. I assume you've thought of a motive."

"That's pretty evident, don't you think?"

"To stop Chadwick's peace initiatives?"

"Exactly."

"But you've got no proof of anything, not a trace of evidence."

"What about the pope? Rumors say his death might have been due to foul play."

Sterling laughed, leaning back again. "You've been on too many Internet chat lines," he said. "A conspiracy behind every bush. That's what you're thinking now?"

"You don't think it's possible?"

"Asked and answered," he said. "Look, it's true all this seems more than a touch odd. And you know better than anyone that if I thought you had a shred of evidence, I'd jump on this with both feet. But you walk into any police station in the country and lay this out, and they'll hoot you out of the place. You got nothing, zip, nada. End of story." He took a bite of salmon, then sipped his coffee.

Valerie tried to focus on her food, too, but found it impossible. She knew that the facts agreed with Casey's assessment, but she still couldn't throw off the feeling that he'd missed something here, something crucial to the whole picture. A sensation of fear suddenly gripped her, and she knew that if she didn't convince

him to help, she'd have to go it alone, and she didn't know how
she could do that. Feeling panicky, she grabbed Sterling's wrist.

"Come to Farmer's memorial service with me," she said. "We'll
find the Suburban and get someone to check the brakes for us to
see if anyone tampered with them."

Chadwick glanced at his wrist then back at her. "You're a determined woman," he said.

"I'm . . . well, I'm scared," she admitted, dropping his wrist
and staring at her food. "I've seen too much in the past year.
Maybe I do see a conspiracy behind every bush, something sinister in everyone."

"Even Chadwick?"

"Well, he's the exception. But everyone else, that's for sure."

"So who's your suspect?"

Valerie licked her lips. "I haven't taken that step yet. No
clue."

Sterling picked at his salmon. "You must have a thought or
two. Who gains the most if Chadwick fails? Who's got the clearest
motive?"

Valerie sipped her tea. "A number of people. Fanatics on either side of the religious divide. You mentioned Zionists yourself.
Muslims too. Who knows what the extremists there might do?"

"Who else? Those are too obvious, too easy."

"I don't know. When you think about it, a whole lot of people
have motives—even some closest to him. I mean, I don't think
there's a chance, but even someone like Ted Shuster has a motive. He's always thought he'd succeed Chadwick. But if Chadwick never goes back to preaching, then there's nothing to succeed. If Chadwick fails . . ."

"Then he goes back to what he was doing, and when he dies
or leaves the scene in a couple of years, Ted slips back into the
role of successor."

"But I don't think he'd kill for that."

Sterling shrugged. "People have killed for a lot less."

Valerie shook her head. "I don't know where to start," she
said. "There're too many suspects. That's why I want to go to California. I'll attend the funeral, then check on the vehicle to make
sure no one tampered with those brakes."

"Don't you think the police are already doing that?"

"I want to guarantee it."

"And you want me to come with you?"

Feeling uncomfortable all of a sudden, Valerie hesitated.

"Promise you'll be a perfect gentleman?" she asked.

Sterling grinned. "Do you suspect I'd be anything else?"

"I just want it clear from the beginning," she said, her voice firm. "We're there to nose around some and see what we can find out. Nothing else."

"That's what I do best," Sterling said. "I'm a pro, remember."

"I saw the pictures of all those women on your desk," Valerie said. "I'm afraid you're a pro at more than one thing."

"You've got a suspicious mind. Don't you trust me?"

"Like I told you, right now I don't trust anybody."

Sterling leaned to his left, pulled his briefcase from under the table, and laid it in his lap. Flipping open the case, he pulled out a sheaf of papers and laid them on the table.

"Read these," he said without explanation. "I don't trust anybody either."

Valerie picked up the papers and began to read. To her surprise, Casey Sterling had already started his investigation, and the papers from his briefcase gave her more reason to fear than anything she had ever read in her life.

THIRTY-EIGHT

Thursday, January 29
Near Leucadia, California

Her body weary from jet lag, Valerie climbed behind the wheel of her rental car and started the engine. Beside her, Casey Sterling—dressed in a black pinstriped suit, blue silk shirt, and yellow tie—kicked beach sand off his tasseled wingtips and sighed heavily.

"I'm not good at funerals," he said. "Even New Age ones."

Valerie pulled onto the highway. "It was strange, wasn't it?" she asked.

"Strange ain't a strong enough word," Sterling said.

Valerie glanced over, then back to the highway, her mind a jumble. Sterling was right. The memorial service for Daphne Farmer had stretched her emotions in a zillion ways. A crowd of about a hundred people—at least half of them dressed in white gowns, the other half mostly in all black—gathered just past daybreak on the beach below Martha Blevins' villa.

———

Standing barefooted at the edge of the ocean in a white ankle-length robe, her frizzy hair blown to all angles by a steady wind, Blevins presided over a ritual marked by an eclectic mix of religious symbols. A man in a ponytail and all black clothes played "Morning Has Broken" on an acoustic guitar. A woman in white with a shaved head read a passage from *The Celestine Prophecy*. Blevins lit incense and waved it in the air as she walked in and out among the crowd. A teenage girl told of a time when she had been a runaway and Farmer had found her on a street corner and offered her shelter and food.

That offering had introduced her to a new way of life, said the
girl, one in which she had found harmony with everything that
existed. As she said it, "Daphne Farmer led me to the nexus of
the eternal."

When the girl finished the guitarist played again, a piece Valerie didn't recognize. Next, a man identified as Farmer's only living relative took a white dove from a cage, held it in his hands
for a moment, then released it into the air. As the dove circled,
then disappeared overhead, Blevins produced a silver urn and
held it up to the sky as if making an offering. Opening the urn,
she pulled out a handful of ashes and held her fist over her head.

"From the dust Sister Daphne came," she called to the wind.

"From the dust," responded those in black.

"But to the sky we now offer her," intoned Blevins.

"To the sky and the seas," said those in white.

"Freely she gave," Blevins said.

"Freely we give her back," said those in black and white.

Blevins walked to the ocean and opened her fist. The ashes
fell toward the water. The breeze caught them and scattered
them over the waves. The people in white moved toward Blevins,
their faces somber. Blevins offered them the urn. They each took
small bits of the ashes and tossed them over the water, and
Daphne Farmer was no more.

The crowd dispersed, Valerie and Casey Sterling with them.
Though wanting to talk with Blevins about Farmer's accident,
Valerie resisted the urge to interrupt her grief. Maybe later.

———

Valerie pulled off the highway and onto the interstate. The
morning sun beat down through the windshield, warming her
face. Martha Blevins' Suburban was at a junkyard about six
miles away. A mechanic she'd called planned to meet them there.
She settled back into the seat and tried to sort through her tan-
gled thoughts. The folder that Sterling had shown her on Tuesday had kept her up late for two nights now, the information in
it acting like a weed eater chopping away at her stomach. . . .

Always the cynical reporter, Casey Sterling had started gathering information the day he heard of Chadwick's plan to go to
Ireland.

"I know a monster event when I see one," he had explained,
"and it didn't take a rocket scientist to figure out that somebody
would take issue with a project like Chadwick proposed. If Chad-

wick wants peace, someone else will want the opposite."

"And you immediately started investigating both sides?"

"I'm a professional," he shrugged. "It's what I do."

"It's more than that," she said. "You're the most driven man I've ever met."

"I do like to stay one step ahead of everybody else."

"One step?"

"Okay, as many steps as possible. My goal is to anticipate a story," he said. "Not just show up after it happens, but actually report it as it takes place." His eyes took on a strange gleam as he talked.

"That's the ultimate high for a newsman," he continued. "So much of what we do happens after the real action ends. We report on what has already passed. But the guys who make it—those at the top—report on what's happening right now—in the present. They lay it out live on camera. That's the best."

"You're serious about this," Valerie said, not sure if it was a compliment or not.

"It's my only religion," he said.

Watching him out of the corner of her eye, Valerie hesitated, unsure whether to say anything. But then she felt an odd fear. If she shut down the desire to tell Sterling what she believed, she might choke off the resurgent sense of God's presence she'd felt since Kosovo. In spite of the fact that she hadn't nailed down all the loose ends, that didn't mean she shouldn't say what she *did* know. For some reason Sterling's shaking came to mind, and she spoke quickly before talking herself out of it.

"You shake," she said, her tone neutral. "I've seen it."

Sterling faced the side window and Valerie knew she had hurt him somehow. She touched his elbow. "I know what it feels like," she said. "Something out there, something you don't know, can't control."

"You think you've got me all figured out, don't you?" he said, still staring out. "Just like that, you talk to a guy a few times, see him here and there, and you're the expert on what he's feeling."

Valerie touched his hand. Sterling faced her now, his jaw set. "My shakes are my own business," he said. "Mine and mine alone."

Valerie started to protest, but she could tell from his demeanor that it wouldn't help. So she reluctantly put aside her plans to tell him more of her faith and left him in his silence. Maybe someday he'd soften some. But until then, she knew that anything she said would cut him off even more.

Turning left off the interstate, she again noted the facts that Sterling's investigation had thus far revealed.

One, Rodney Kent owed six hundred thousand dollars to a less than reputable loan agency. Apparently, Kent's stock trading had become an obsession over the last two years, and he hadn't done too well at it. A rash of bad investments in some speculative Internet stocks had chewed away at his portfolio, and a net worth once close to three million dollars had disappeared. Over the last six weeks, Kent had made more than forty phone calls to Bill Stricker, calls that indicated Kent might be desperate to secure a loan to cover his debts without public scandal.

"You tapped Kent's phones?"

Sterling shrugged. "I keep a couple of investigators pretty busy. Years ago, Kent gambled, apparently. As a young man he ended up in jail a couple of times. Wrote some bad checks to cover his losses. But he stopped all that after he met Chadwick. The day trading apparently scratched the same itch, only it's reputable."

Stopping at a red light, Valerie's thoughts drifted to Sterling's file on the Ayatollah Khatama. The son of a martyred hero to the militant factions in his country, the Ayatollah had an intimate but well-hidden relationship with at least two terrorist groups— the Islamic People's Army and the Committee for International Equality. Both of the groups advocated the destruction of Israel and the militant spread of Islamic fundamentalism. Though a velvet-gloved Muslim in public, Khatama wore brass knuckles under the gloves and funneled money and moral support to his secret allies at every opportunity. His work with Chadwick served his purposes for now, but who knew when his larger goals might surface and what destructive form they might take.

Valerie turned left as the light turned green. Only a couple more miles to the wreckage yard.

Sterling's third file had outlined some sobering facts about Bill Stricker. His company, Applied A&D, had taken more than one hit over the last three years. A&D lost out on an eleven-billion-dollar merger deal with a huge multinational conglomerate and failed to win renewal of a government contract for guidance systems for a fleet of tanks. A research and development project came in over a year late with less than stellar results.

All of this was public information. Stricker's business was shaky. What wasn't as well known was the fact that he had contacted José Zorella as well. José apparently saw his brother, Luis, as the natural successor to Chadwick. But he didn't want to wait for Chadwick to die or retire. In fact, brother José looked at Luis's popularity in his native land and saw him as a future *presidente* of Mexico and perhaps a unifying figure for all of Latin America. With enough money, who knew how far he might ascend.

Placing the Stricker file in her lap, Valerie had faced Sterling. "Did you tap Stricker's phones too?" she asked.

Sterling said. "I tried, tried them all. But Stricker and Khatama have excellent security. Zorella doesn't."

"But if Stricker's so broke, how can he make promises of millions of dollars to Zorella or anyone else?"

"Easy. Maybe he promises, they find a way to stop Chadwick, but Stricker doesn't pay. What could they do? Or he trades the few million he'll give them for the chance to make billions in a better stock price for A&D. It's a good deal for him."

Sterling's last big file had contained information about Cardinal Zolinska. His motives to oppose Chadwick were easy. A true Catholic zealot, he wanted to become pope so he could stop all the nonsense with the Protestants and unbelievers. In his view, contact with Chadwick equaled contact with the devil himself.

Sources said Zolinska was mentally unstable and that a psychiatrist in the Vatican had recently prescribed heavy doses of Prozac for him.

Now, spotting an eight-foot-high metal fence, Valerie braked and looked for the gate. Taking a deep breath, she forced herself to forget the files and concentrate on the present moment. Though Sterling had smaller bits of information in his file on several other people, he had already made his point. Lots of people had motives for wanting Chadwick to fail, and at least a few might actually try to kill him to insure that it happened.

Valerie saw the gate and turned right. The white gravel road inside the gate led to a small but neat white-framed building with green shutters. The building, graced by a thin ribbon of a front porch and three steps leading up to it, sat no more than a hundred or so feet away from the entrance, surrounded by a grove of twisted trees, their leaves the color of the building's shutters. Past the trees, however, the wreckage of scores of cars and trucks and SUVs dotted the landscape. The white building looked like an oasis in the middle of a vast desert of rusted, hump backed junk.

Parking, Valerie hopped out. Hoping the mechanic had arrived, she scanned the area but saw no one. Not waiting, she crunched across the gravel, stomped up the steps, and entered the building, Sterling a step behind. A man in chocolate brown pants, jacket, and baseball cap nodded to them as they entered. A patch over his shirt pocket identified him as "Watson." He sat in a metal chair behind a spotless but cheap-looking wooden desk. A few papers lay in a stack on the desk, but otherwise it was clear.

"Hey," Watson said, standing.

"Hey," Valerie said. "We're looking for a black Suburban that came in on January 26. Owned by Ms. Martha Blevins."

Watson grunted, stuck a pencil behind his right ear. "Yeah, her assistant drove it off the cliff, right down into the ocean."

"That's the one," Sterling said.

Watson stared at him a second, then touched the top of the desk with his right hand. "What you want to see it for?" His eyes followed his fingers as they lightly ran over the top of the wood.

"Just checking it," Valerie said, not wanting to lie.

"For what?"

Sterling took a step forward. "Ms. Blevins asked us to see if her wallet was in the glove compartment," he said, obviously not feeling as constrained by the truth as Valerie.

"Cops already cleaned it out," Watson said, both hands in his pockets. "Didn't say nothin' 'bout no wallet."

Valerie started to speak, but Sterling moved before she could, his hand going to his back pants pocket. Jerking out a wallet, he pulled out several bills.

"I see you run a clean operation here," he said. "And we don't want to mess that up. But we need to see the Suburban and we'll finish within thirty minutes."

Watson took his pencil from behind his ear and studied the writing on its side.

"I'm holding four hundred dollars here," Sterling said. "That's four hundred dollars for thirty minutes, and we won't harm anything, take anything, or mess up anything."

Watson looked up from the pencil. "Thirty minutes?"

Sterling nodded.

Watson pointed the pencil toward the salvage yard. "It's eight rows back from this building," he said. "Fifteenth vehicle on the left side. You got thirty minutes."

Handing him the money, Sterling turned to Valerie and both of them headed out and down the steps. In the yard, she checked for the mechanic again, but he still hadn't arrived.

"Let's take a look," she said, not willing to wait. "We'll hear the guy when he drives up."

Nodding, Sterling followed toward the back of the office. At the eighth row, she turned left and started counting. One wrecked vehicle after another stared back at her, mangled remains of once sleek and shiny machines. For an instant she felt a wave of depression hit again, the wrecked cars somehow symbolic of her own situation, once shiny and sleek and full of life but now battered and bruised and heaped up in a stack of useless bolts and metal and flattened rubber tires.

Her shoulders slumped, she stepped past twelve, thirteen, fourteen. She came to the fifteenth spot. Her mouth fell open and she came to a dead stop on the gravel. She turned to Sterling. He shoved his hands into his pockets.

"It's not here," he said simply.

Valerie stared at the empty spot as if expecting the mangled car to suddenly appear out of thin air. But it still wasn't there.

"Maybe the cops took it for something," Sterling said.

"But wouldn't Watson have known that?"

Sterling nodded. "Probably so."

"Then where is it?"

Sterling shrugged.

"It's gone," Valerie said, trying to grasp what that might mean. "It's gone, and unless I'm mistaken, it wasn't the cops who took it."

THIRTY-NINE

JANUARY 31

Valerie and Casey flew back to Atlanta on Saturday morning, both of them frustrated by a fruitless search for information about the missing Suburban. Though friendly, Martha Blevins offered no new information about the condition of the vehicle, and the people who had serviced it referred them to their lawyers. As expected, the lawyers refused comment. Worse still, the police in Leucadia were tight-lipped. "We're on top of it," they said. "Don't bother yourselves."

With a warm hug and a thank-you for his efforts and friendship, Valerie left Casey at the Atlanta airport. He headed to points unknown and she drove straight to Big Canoe, Georgia, where Chadwick had retreated for the weekend.

Her teeth grinding, Valerie decided she'd move heaven and earth if necessary to keep her uncle from taking one more step down the path he had chosen. She had already called him, of course, the instant she and Sterling left the salvage yard. But he seemed preoccupied and not nearly as concerned about the missing car as she was.

Now, headed north on Highway 400, she wondered how she would stop him. What arguments could she use? She'd lay out everything she knew—the information Casey had given her plus the suspicions she had. Surely, Chadwick would pay attention to the facts, even if they weren't entirely conclusive.

Her body suddenly sagged, and she felt as weary as a soldier who had marched three days without sleep. Her uncle was so trusting of people and their motives he might very well not believe her at all.

The rush of the last several days caught up to her all at once, and she felt completely worn out. What a mess! The energy she'd felt since Kosovo seeped out of her, and she felt depression grab at her throat again.

She stopped along the highway at a hamburger place for a cup of coffee. In the rest room, she washed her face and stared in the mirror. Her pale green sweater and stone-washed jeans hung loosely on her shoulders and hips. Her neck looked bony, like a scarecrow.

She took a deep breath. She'd hardly slept at all since the episode at the junkyard, her fears too active to relax enough to rest. Pushing her hair back, she told herself she couldn't give up. No matter how much he protested, she had to convince Chadwick to bail out of this dangerous game he had decided to play.

Back in the car, she settled down for the rest of the drive and turned on the radio. Flipping through the channels, she found a classical station and eased back in her seat. But even the music failed to calm her. The images of several people flashed through her head—images of everybody who might wish her uncle harm. Bill Stricker, the Ayatollah Khatama, Cardinal Zolinska. All of them had enough motive, money, and power to cause all kinds of damage. But would they kill to achieve their ends? And what about Ted Shuster, who wanted to succeed Chadwick someday? Or Luis Zorella—the most internationally known preacher in the world next to her uncle? Did either of them have the stomach for murder?

Actually, she had no proof that anyone had *killed* anyone. Who knew about Clement's death? Natural or diabolical? And the steel girder that almost hit Chadwick—accidental or deliberate? And Daphne Farmer too. Was it brake failure or murder planned to look like an accident? With the missing Suburban there was no way to tell. She and Casey had tried to impress the importance of finding it upon the police in Leucadia, but they seemed incredibly nonchalant about the whole matter. To them, Farmer's death had come as the result of an accident, and they had too many genuine homicides to go chasing after a missing wreck.

She and Casey had talked about going to the police in Atlanta, but he said he doubted it would do any good if the cops in California weren't willing to cooperate. So they gave up the idea of asking for help from the authorities. Whether she liked it or not, she and she alone had the job of talking Chadwick out of going ahead with his scheme. She turned left off the road, stopped and opened a split-rail gate, climbed back into the Volvo, and drove the rest of the way up the gravel driveway to Chadwick's lodge.

Three minutes later she swerved around the last curve and pulled to a stop in front of the retreat center. Three other cars and a couple of trucks sat off to the right. Climbing out, she decided to go directly to Chadwick. If he'd see her, she wanted to face him now, pour out her heart and see how he'd respond. Grabbing her black briefcase from the passenger seat, she stalked onto the porch.

Valerie found Chadwick alone in his rocking chair in the den, a bedraggled brown robe tied around his waist and a black blanket on his legs. His shoulders were slumped and his hair needed cutting, but his eyes seemed alive and focused on a stack of papers in his lap. To his left a fireplace blazed high, warming the room and casting a soft glow on his face. Though her sweater was wool Valerie still felt cold. She hugged her waist, her briefcase dangling from her right hand.

Hearing her enter, Chadwick glanced up, laid the papers on the floor and indicated a chair to his right. Placing her briefcase on the floor, Valerie walked over, kissed him on the cheek, then sat down.

"Glad you're back," he said. "A good trip?"

She shrugged. "A strange funeral, not exactly in my comfort zone."

Chadwick sighed, the weight of the world obviously on his shoulders. "I pray that all will know the gift of eternal life through our Lord," he said. "But tragically far too many still don't."

Valerie stayed quiet.

"You look tired," Chadwick said. "Thin, too."

"I've lost about five more pounds," Valerie said. "And I'm not sleeping much."

"You need to take better care of yourself."

"I'm trying."

"Good. Look, you've had a tough go of it in the past year, and I've not said much, but I've been thinking maybe you need some time off, some peace and quiet somewhere."

"I thought I'd get that working with you," she grinned.

"Yeah? Well, the best-laid plans . . ."

"I'm making progress," she said. "Just not all the way there yet."

Chadwick put his hands under his blanket. "Just take care," he said. "Give yourself some time."

"I'm okay," she insisted. "What about you?"

"Tip-top shape for an old guy," Chadwick said. "Eating like a horse and nothing keeps me awake, not even this." He pointed to the papers he'd been studying.

"Trouble?" she asked.

"Finances," Chadwick said. "It's a never ending battle in an operation this size. Over three hundred people on the payroll, the Atlanta building, others in Charlotte and Dallas to keep up, the magazine, insurance costs, et cetera, et cetera. Everything takes money, more and more of it. And you know our offerings are way down right now, particularly among our bigger donors. Many of them don't like this peace stuff."

Valerie dropped her eyes. She knew the situation. Not only had Ted filled her in on the details, but the newspapers, especially the religious press, had also reported the discouraging news in blaring headlines. Contributions had faltered badly, down more than thirty percent. The cancellation of the upcoming crusades had confused people, made them unsure about Russell Chadwick's future.

She cleared her throat and picked up her briefcase. She hadn't planned to use finances as one of her arguments against the continuance of her uncle's plans, but if he was worried about them, and that helped her accomplish her purposes, then so much the better.

"If it's that bad, then maybe it's time you gave it all up," she said, snapping open the briefcase. "Shut down the upcoming meeting and go home."

"You know better than that," Chadwick said. "I've already made myself crystal clear."

Valerie pulled out a folder and opened it. "I think you need to see this," she said, handing him the folder. "I just received this information a couple of days ago, but I wanted to give it to you in person. It's unfortunate but . . ."

Chadwick took the materials and leaned back in the rocker. His back stiffened as he read the sheets, peeling them off and tossing them to the floor as he finished each one. Watching him, Valerie wished she could disappear. She didn't like bearing bad tidings to the man she respected more than any but her father. Taking a deep breath, Chadwick flicked the last sheet to the floor and stared up at Valerie.

"Where'd you get this stuff?" he asked through gritted teeth.

Valerie hesitated but knew she couldn't ignore the question or lie about it. "Casey Sterling," she said. "He's been investigating a number of people since you said you were going to Ireland."

"How'd Sterling collect all this?"

Valerie hung her head. "Electronic surveillance, wiretaps, personal contacts, confidants. He's got a broad network, and he's unrelenting once he sinks his teeth into something."

"It's deceitful," Chadwick said. "And I'm sure it's illegal too, at least most of it. It plays to the lowest possibilities of human nature."

"But it's still true," Valerie said. "All of it. You've got enough enemies to populate a small island. I think you're in grave danger. Pope Clement's death might not have been from natural causes. The steel beam that almost killed you—all kinds of suspicion there. And Daphne Farmer? No one can find her vehicle. Not the police, not the salvage yard in California. And Martha Blevins normally makes that drive."

"You have to stretch things some to make all this add up," he said. "You're connecting a bunch of dots that don't necessarily connect."

"I know that," Valerie said. "But it's possible. You have to admit that."

Chadwick rocked a few times. "Yes, it's possible. But don't you think it's a touch paranoid too, always looking for some evil somewhere?"

Valerie stared at the fire. "I know," she agreed. "And before Kosovo I'd have agreed with you that I'd gone off the deep end here. But now . . . I don't know . . . I don't think it is just my paranoia. It's . . . a sense I have, an intuition that something's going on here, something that ties together somehow."

Chadwick grinned, but sadly. He studied his blanket. "In 1967 I traveled to East Germany," he said, his voice soft. "At the height of the Cold War. The CIA told me they had solid information that the Cuban government had hired a Communist hit squad to assassinate me. But you know what?" He faced her again. "I went to East Germany anyway. I trusted God, you see. I knew it wasn't the logical thing to do, but I did it anyway. That's all I know to do. I'm not complicated enough to do anything else. So I'll trust God again, even with this. You should realize that's what I'm going to do. You've known me long enough. I can't do anything else, I just can't."

Listening, Valerie felt more and more desperate. Since she felt she had led Chadwick into this predicament, she had to lead him out, no matter what it took!

"But you've got other goals," she said. "What about the school? Think of all the students who'll miss the opportunity for a Christian education. And the thousands, millions of people who'll never hear the gospel if something happens to you. I know Bill Stricker has threatened you. You can see his connections to Kent and others in those papers." She pointed to the stack on the floor. "Stricker is mean and he's desperate. He—"

"You know I'm not going to let a man like Stricker intimidate me," Chadwick said. "He's a bully with his money, but I don't think he'd stoop to killing someone, no matter how much money that person might cause him to lose."

Valerie started to point out that people had killed for a whole lot less, but she knew she couldn't change her uncle's mind with that kind of argument. She tried another approach. "Then what about the others?" she asked, hating herself for resorting to such a tactic. "Zorella, Blevins, the Dalai Lama, all of them. If someone kills you, he might kill them too. Think of them even if not of yourself."

Chadwick stared into the fireplace again, his jaw working. "I'm not twisting anyone's arm here," he countered. "They all know we're taking a risk."

Valerie felt stumped for a second, trapped by Chadwick's logic and courage. But then, before she could stop herself, another thought slipped out. "Then what about Mildred?" she asked, instinctively tossing out her last card. "You want her to become a widow? And your children, what about them? Grandchildren too!"

Chadwick glared at her and Valerie knew she'd hit a nerve. But then the heat abated in her uncle and he kept his voice even as he spoke.

"Maybe you're right," he said. "Maybe I'm taking it too far this time, being selfish. Perhaps I've gotten so involved I can't see straight anymore."

"Then you'll stop?" she asked hopefully. "Shut it down and send everyone home?"

Chadwick sighed, pulled the blanket off his legs, and pulled himself from the rocker. Rubbing his forehead, he stepped to Valerie and laid a hand on her shoulder. "Mildred has a tumor," he said matter-of-factly. "Doctor says she'll die in less than six months. So if I make her a widow, she won't be one for long."

He walked to the fireplace, leaned on the mantel. "Mildred gave me her blessing in this from the beginning. So did my children. They've known me for so long, they know I'm too stubborn to change once I've made up my mind. So no, I won't shut it down. Whatever happens, happens. It's in God's hands now."

A long minute of silence passed between them. The fireplace crackled as a log broke and sagged into the flames.

"Shouldn't you at least postpone it?" Valerie asked, her last hope fading. "Move it from Stricker's property?"

"We'll have great security," Chadwick said. "Not Stricker's people either. State troopers, local police. And Ted hired some additional professionals. It'll be okay."

Valerie nodded, too numb to argue anymore.

"Lester called me," Chadwick said, shifting subjects. "A couple of hours ago. Asked if he could come back. I said yes. Do you think I should have done that?" He pivoted and faced her again. "Do you think so?"

"I . . . don't . . . don't know," Valerie stammered, disconcerted that he had changed the subject so completely. "He's—"

"He's in Sterling's file," Chadwick completed her sentence for her. "And he's spent some time with Stricker. I know all that."

"But you still trust him?"

Chadwick eased into the rocker again, the blanket in his hands. "Yes, just like I trust Rodney and Ted. Just like I trust you. Lester wants to do the right thing. He just needs some help sometimes in knowing what the right thing is, like almost everybody I know."

Valerie licked her lips. Her uncle's one blind spot, she thought. He believed the best about everybody no matter what, saw the good in them, the potential for Christlikeness. But she knew better. Some people had stepped past the potential for good, had given themselves over to complete and total evil. But Chadwick didn't believe that. No matter how despicable a person had become, he believed they could change. Valerie sighed and hoped that Chadwick's childlike trust in others didn't get him and a whole lot of other people killed.

"I need to go," she said, standing. "I have lots of calls to make, details to handle."

Chadwick nodded. She moved to him, kissed him on the cheek, and headed for the door. Before she stepped out, Chadwick called to her once more. She twisted around.

"I've known about Rodney all along," he said. "He had a gambling problem when he first came to me. His salvation gave him the power to fight it. But the temptation remains strong, and he's battled it for years. This day trading is just another manifestation of the same issue."

"The calls to Stricker?"

"They'll end now. Rodney came to me last night and told me what he'd done. I'll give him the money he needs to pay off his debts. I'll take care of him."

Valerie slumped out of the room. Her uncle took care of everyone—everyone but himself.

———

A telephone in hand, Casey Sterling peered down from his office at CBC and studied a white town car that had pulled up to a curb beneath a maple tree in the parking lot. Though not certain, he thought he had seen the car pull out behind him at the airport, its lean, nondescript presence tailing him like an unwanted shadow. But what sense did that make?

Leaving the window, he stepped back to his desk and took a seat. Punching a number into the phone, he mentally reviewed his security. He never said everything he meant on the phone. He kept files in his computer, but not only were they encrypted, they were protected by the best fire walls computer technicians could provide. He told no one anything that could compromise his sources.

A man answered the phone and Sterling forced himself to focus.

"Casey here, you set?"

"On the move. It's shaping up."

"Did you send me the map?"

"In your email."

"You can't be late."

"I know, time is crucial. Is the green light on?"

He paused and chewed a thumbnail. If he said yes, his whole life would change in the next week. He knew it. Just like that—snap your fingers and alter everything. For some reason, he thought suddenly of Valerie Miller. Would she like the change? Would she support him after it happened?

"There's a sedan in the parking lot here," he said, pushing back his thoughts of Valerie. "You know anything about it?"

"Nope, you want me to check?"

Sterling cleared his throat. "Not yet. Stay focused, can't have you sidetracked. I'll put somebody else on it."

"What about that green light?"

Sterling felt his fingers begin to quiver. He placed his right hand over his left, forcing the shaking to stop before it really started. The thought of Valerie Miller bounced into his head again, and he stood up and checked the parking lot again. The sedan had disappeared.

"I'll call you," he said. "Hold off until you hear from me."

"Can do. I'll wait for your word."

Sterling hung up the phone, grabbed a sport coat, and headed to the door. Maybe he'd talk to Valerie Miller, he decided. Maybe then he'd know whether to move ahead or not.

FORTY

MONDAY, FEBRUARY 2
2 P.M., Rome

His black eyes staring out the window at the falling rain, Pope John Peter spoke into the air, his voice picked up by a speakerphone on a desk no more than five feet away. Though greatly concerned, he easily kept his composure. A lifetime of calm in the midst of political intrigue gave him more than enough focus to handle this latest episode. Thankfully, the man with whom he talked, the Reverend Russell Chadwick, had an equal measure of aplomb.

"I have knowledge that Cardinal Zolinska has more than a little concern over my participation in your alliance," suggested John Peter. "And it seems that he has made himself a conspirator with a number of others who agree with him. But I am not quite sure what, if anything, I should do about him."

"Do you know who he's been talking to?" Chadwick asked.

"Only one of them. It seems he keeps his conspiracies fairly close to the vest."

"Is he aware of what you know?"

"Not all of it, though I have assured him that I'm aware of his displeasure with me."

"I don't think going to the authorities makes much sense."

"Neither do I. We have no proof that he's done anything but plot behind the back of his pontiff to slow down what he sees as unwise Vatican policy. If that was a crime half the members of the Curia would spend the rest of their lives in jail."

Chadwick chuckled and John Peter left the window and took a seat at his desk.

"I will arrive in Denver on Thursday morning with five of my cardinals," John Peter said. "We will take a helicopter to the Stricker complex by that evening and prepare for our joint session on Friday."

"I am grateful for your assistance in this matter," Chadwick said. "You play such a vital role in world affairs."

"I am but a servant of the Lord," John Peter said. "If I can advance the cause of peace, I am glad to make any and all efforts to do so."

"I'll take extra precautions," Chadwick said. "Your Cardinal Zolinska may be in league with some who might want to do more than talk."

"Given what I've heard him say about my predecessor, it may be that he's the leader of such a group."

"A chilling thought."

"But one with some foundation in possibility."

"I'll insist on the tightest security," Chadwick said. "United States authorities and the police here in Denver have assured me they'll cooperate in every way. No one wants any of us harmed. We'll make sure this place is as clean as a whistle."

"I have no doubts you will do exactly that. Until Friday, then."

"Until Friday."

John Peter clicked off the phone and laid his elbows on his desk. For several seconds, he stayed still as a statue. Of all the aspects of his job, he hated this one the most—the constant attention to matters of security. But he knew it had always been this way. Danger lurked in every corner, and plots against the Vicar of Christ seemed as omnipresent as dust in the corners of a country house. In the almost two thousand years since Linus the First had succeeded St. Peter in A.D. 67, forty-five popes had not survived even a year in the papacy. History said that six had definitely died at the hands of assassins, perhaps even more.

John Peter laid his head down on his desk but didn't close his eyes in spite of the weariness that wracked every part of his body. No matter where he turned, someone seemed intent on destroying his efforts, manipulating his words, confusing his motives. Though he'd always suspected it, only the wearing of the papal crown had made it absolutely sure and certain to him. A pontiff slept lightly, no matter the era in which he served.

———

His face dotted with splotches of sweat, Lester Boggett readjusted his seat on the leather sofa and stared across the room at Bill Stricker, who paced furiously out and back in front of the fireplace in his Colorado mountain lodge. Stricker's pipe, having worked overtime over the last two hours as its owner had detailed his latest scheme to stop Russell Chadwick, trailed ashes onto the thick rug that fronted the fireplace. Stricker didn't seem to notice.

Glancing around the room, Lester wiped his forehead and wondered once more if he had done the right thing by leaving Chadwick. To his left waited Ludwig Roth, a big-time business partner with Stricker. Standing by the window another man waited—a bearded man who spoke clipped English and wore one of those turban things like the Ayatollah Khomeini back in the seventies when the United States had so much trouble with Iran. Lester couldn't really pronounce the Muslim's name, but he knew he was connected to Khatama and that he was up to no good, no good at all.

Lester did know a couple of things though. For one, Bill Stricker had pulled this crowd together. Two, they wanted to stop Russell Chadwick at all costs. And three, he had no way to object to anyone here, even if he wanted to.

In a rocking chair by the fireplace, José Zorella ran his fingers through his thick black hair and rested his elbows on the arms of the chair. He liked hanging out with such men as Stricker. Lester could see it plain as day. Money and power—José Zorella craved them like a starving dog craved a bone. His suit coat wedged behind his back, Lester shifted again, pulled the coat out, and laid it across his knees.

Sucking his pipe, Stricker faced the group now. "I don't want any foul-ups," he said, his voice tight as the meeting wound down to a close. "Everything has to run with precision, exact timing. One wrong move and the whole thing will fall apart."

The men nodded as if the same puppet master operated their necks. Stricker looked directly at José Zorella. "Are you all set?"

Zorella smiled hugely. "It will be done."

Stricker sucked his pipe, then faced the man in the turban. "And we have your definite cooperation?"

The man nodded, his bearded chin in his hands.

Stricker turned to Lester. "You sure you can deliver what you promised?"

Lester dropped his eyes. A bead of sweat fell off his brow and plopped onto the thick rug at his feet.

"Lester?"

Stricker's voice demanded his attention.

"I'll do what I need to do," Lester said.

Stricker walked to his desk, a huge mahogany piece with heavy clawed feet and the image of John D. Rockefeller carved on the front. He picked up a manila folder, flipped it open, then pressed a button on the edge of the desk. A second later a beefy man in a plain gray suit entered the room. Lester recognized him as a security officer. Stricker handed the folder to the officer, then asked, "Did you finish the bugging?"

"Every room but yours."

Stricker swept his gaze across his companions. "Remember that," he said. "Every room in this lodge but mine is under surveillance."

They nodded, obviously willing to accept the invasion of their privacy for a broader purpose.

"And the famous Mr. Sterling?" The question came from Zorella, his big teeth shining.

"I'm giving him some of his own medicine," Stricker said with a hint of a smile. "He's had most of you under surveillance. Now it's his turn. I put a tail on him a week ago. Plus a bug and a video guy."

"Did you learn anything?"

"He's canny," Stricker admitted. "Doesn't say much on the phone. But he's up to something. We can't let him interfere."

He turned and picked up a stack of folders from the desk. "I've made copies of our files on Mr. Sterling for all of you." He stepped to each member of the group to hand them a file. The man in the turban refused the file.

"We too have been busy," he said. "We have our own men overseeing Mr. Sterling. Though we thank you for your efforts."

Stricker backed away, his eyebrows arched.

Lester rubbed his thighs with his sweaty hands. These guys played for keeps.

"Everything is in place," Stricker said. "Now, no mistakes. Plain and simple."

He paced to the glass-encased back wall of the room, and Lester's eyes followed. Outside, a thin sunshine barely peeked its face across the mountain, the first light of the day casting narrow shadows on the snow-covered ground.

Past Stricker's shoulders, Lester saw a line of telephone poles running by the house and up the incline of the mountain. Black wire ran from pole to pole as far as the eye could see, crisscrossing through the tall green spruce trees that silhouetted the eastern sky. He rubbed his thighs again, then stood up from the sofa, his sweaty back unsticking from the leather.

By the fireplace, he gazed out the window again. From out of the east, a clutter of blackbirds darted through the trees, their wings moving in concert, almost as if they had a prearranged appointment to keep. Cackling furiously, the birds zipped to a sudden stop on the wires directly out the window past Stricker's profile. Now they lined themselves up, their faces staring into the room at Lester, their beaks curved and pointy. The blackbirds pressed out their wings—once, twice, then settled in as if watching a drive-in movie.

Mesmerized, Lester edged closer to Stricker, his body stiff with tension. For some reason, he found himself counting the birds. One, two, three, four, five. He turned and faced the men in the room. Stricker, the Muslim, Roth, Zorella, himself. Five.

As if waking up from a long sleep, Lester suddenly caught the irony of his presence in the group. He who had fled Chadwick because of his questionable alliances now found himself in a room in a Colorado lodge with a cabal of men with much worse credentials than any of the people now in collusion with Chadwick.

Lester wrinkled his broad forehead, confused as to how all these men had come together. But he did know that in the modern era big business knew no national boundaries, no religious divisions. Odd mixtures of people often joined together for a variety of purposes, and Stricker had pieced this crowd into one unit, all for a common purpose, all lined up now like the blackbirds outside ready to pounce on their unsuspecting prey.

FORTY-ONE

Valerie flew home on Tuesday afternoon, her plans in place. Visit with her mom and dad on Tuesday night and most of Wednesday, then catch a late afternoon plane into Colorado. With the alliance members not scheduled to arrive until Thursday and Bill Stricker's people taking care of local arrangements, she had some business to handle once she arrived, but not so much that she needed to arrive any earlier than that. Besides, Chadwick had ordered her to go home.

"Rest up some," he insisted. "I need you fresh for the weekend."

Too frustrated to argue, she had worked in Atlanta for two days, then dressed in some old jeans, a Duke sweat shirt, and hiking boots and headed to Charlotte. Now, climbing off the plane, she ducked into the car with her mom, exchanged pleasantries, and leaned her ear against the passenger window. The rest of the trip passed in silence and thirty minutes later she walked into her house, her energy lower than she could ever remember. Dropping her luggage on the kitchen floor, she kicked off her boots and sagged into the den, anxious to find a sofa and curl up by the fire.

"Hello, Valerie."

She jerked in surprise as she heard Casey Sterling's voice. She turned to her mom, then back to Sterling. He sat in a leather recliner in the corner, his hair slightly mussed.

"I'm sorry to surprise you," he said. "A maid let me in."

"Mom, this is Casey—"

"I know who he is," interrupted her mother, taking his outstretched hand. "I've seen him on television."

Sterling smiled.

"I'll make some tea," her mom said, subtly giving herself a reason to leave them alone. She disappeared down the hall.

"When did you get here?" Valerie asked, trying to figure out why he had come.

"Ten minutes ago," he said. "Sorry for the shock. I tried to reach you all day."

She eased past him to the fireplace. A hearty flame blazed up, its heat warm against her legs. She faced him again. "Are you set to go to Colorado?" she asked.

He nodded. "Should be exciting. The whole world will be watching."

"Your kind of thing," she said, no rancor intended.

He grinned and she felt drawn to him. "When are you flying out?" she asked, trying to focus on another subject.

"Same as you. Tomorrow afternoon."

"But you came here first?" She meant it as a statement, but it came across as a question.

Sterling stood and moved to the fireplace beside her. She started to move away, but he stepped closer.

"I've done some thinking since I saw you," he said.

"Thinking's good," she said.

He smiled and touched her cheek. "You're confusing me," he said. "And I don't know what's going to happen. But I . . . I wanted you to know why I shake." He dropped his hand to his side. "Don't know exactly why, but it seems important right now that someone knows. Nobody does, nobody in the whole world. Fact is, you're the first person who ever asked me about it. It happens so infrequently no one pays it much attention."

He edged away from her to the window. "The shaking started the day my dad walked out on me and Mama," he said as if talking to himself. "I was eleven and it was November. Cold outside—at least I remember it that way. My mom and dad had fought again. They did that pretty often. He had a drinking problem, and she nagged. He slugged her. She threw a plate."

"I'm sorry," Valerie said.

Sterling ignored her. "I stood on the steps and watched his truck disappear around the corner. At first I wanted him to go, wanted him to carry his cussing and drinking and running around on my mama out of my life forever. But then . . . I don't know . . . I wanted him to stay . . . wanted him to stay and change his life and love me and Mama like he should. I felt awful for wanting him to go, so I started running down the road after him, my legs pumping and pumping for over a mile down that road, pumping until they wouldn't move anymore, till I couldn't breathe anymore.

"I bent over and put my hands on my knees and tried to catch my breath. Then it hit me—the shakes. My whole body, just one huge quivering mass."

He stopped and turned to Valerie again. "It comes and goes now, I never know when. For a while there, I thought it had disappeared. Hadn't hit me for over ten years. Then that night in Belfast it came back. An old demon returned."

"Where's your dad now?" Valerie asked.

"In Swansboro, about to die from liver disease."

Valerie hesitated but then pressed ahead. "Do you ever see him?"

"Nope, not in a long time."

She walked over and touched his arm. He stared into her eyes, his face sad.

"You said something back in Kosovo," she said. "On the bridge with Prikova's son. You said, 'A son belongs with his father.' Do you think that's true?"

Sterling smiled, but ironically. "I say a lot of things. Some are true, some aren't."

"You searched all over Central Europe for that boy," Valerie said. "That was a wonderful thing."

"I'm a prince of a guy. What can I say?"

"You can go see your own father."

"I did't know you had gone into family therapy."

The light from the fireplace bounced off his face, and Valerie saw a veil come over his eyes, as if some interior commander had just ordered him to go into seclusion again.

"I just think that the best way to beat a demon is to face it," she said gently.

Sterling pulled away. "Maybe you should try some of your own medicine."

"I'm trying to do that," she said. "Ever since the Ibar River . . . I'm . . . I don't know . . . different somehow. When this is over I'm going off by myself somewhere and do some serious thinking. I've got my whole life in front of me and I want to find joy again, that happiness we talked about earlier." She touched his arm again.

"I want that for you too. That's why I think you should see your father."

He sighed. "It's a good dream," he said. "But I'm afraid that's all it is, a dream. It's not attainable for most of us."

Valerie started to argue but then decided against it. If Sterling didn't want to make the effort to reconcile with his dad, she couldn't make him.

"So you came here to tell me why you shake?" she said, her brow furrowed.

He nodded, then faced her squarely once more. "I think you should stay away from Colorado," he said. "I don't . . . don't feel good about it."

She laughed and moved to the sofa and sat down. "I'm supposed to be the paranoid one here," she said. "Chadwick has assured me that we'll have security everywhere. He's not going to make the same mistake in Colorado that he made in Ireland."

"I know all about his security," Sterling said. "Everyone does. That's why it's so dangerous. Too many people know too much."

Valerie studied his face for several seconds. He had fear written in his eyes. "You know something, don't you?" she asked.

He hung his head and slipped his hands into his pockets. "I think someone has been following me," he said. "Though I'm not sure who or why."

"Maybe you've upset somebody. One of your investigators stuck his nose too far into someone's business."

He nodded. "It's possible."

"But I don't see how that affects me."

Sterling shrugged. "I don't know. I just think you should keep your distance, that's all."

Valerie rubbed her knees. "Too late," she said. "I'm all set for Colorado."

"Even if it's dangerous?"

On impulse, Valerie stood and took Sterling by the hand. He started to speak, but she put a finger to his lips and led him out of the den, through the living room, and out onto the front porch. Leaving the porch, she turned left and headed to the side yard. Twenty feet around the side, she stopped and pointed at the towering magnolia tree that blocked out the late afternoon sun.

"Here's the tree," she said. She pointed to the scar on her neck. "I fell out of it when I was a kid. But that didn't stop me for a long time. I climbed anything and everything—nothing was too high or too scary—nothing was beyond my reach. Until . . ." She stuck her hands in her pockets.

"Until?"

"Until last year. Now I can't climb anything. This tree? It scares me to death if I get more than two or three feet off the ground."

Sterling stepped to a bottom limb and placed a foot on it. "The wall at your workout club?"

"Same thing. I can't climb it."

He hoisted himself up to a second branch. "So what's all this got to do with your going to Colorado?"

Valerie placed a hand on the magnolia tree. "Well, it's like this. I'm moving toward that happiness thing, I know I am. I can feel it, like a trickle of water growing wider and wider about to drop over a waterfall. But if I let Colorado scare me away, I know I'm stuck. To mix my metaphors, if I back away from Colorado, I'll never climb anything again, and I'm not just talking about trees here. It's bigger than that, a 'defining moment,' as they say. If some vague danger causes me to skip Colorado, I might as well crawl in a corner somewhere and cover my head with a blanket. Colorado is a tree I've got to climb if I'm ever going to make it."

On a higher limb now, Sterling rested his back against the trunk and stared down. She looked up at him, the last rays of the sunlight hitting her face. He stretched out a hand and she took it. Grasping his wrist, she pulled herself up to the bottom limb. He eased down beside her.

"You're a unique woman," he said, still holding her hand, their faces close.

"Not like all the others?"

He grinned. "Totally different. None of them had your . . . your . . ." His eyes clouded over and he glanced down.

"My what?" she asked, her hand pulling his chin back up. "What makes me so different?"

"You know the answer," he said softly. "Your faith. I've never known a woman with your kind of faith. I don't . . . don't know how to handle it. It's so foreign, so beyond me." He shifted, jumped to the ground, and she followed him. They stood by the tree, their eyes still locked.

"I'm not good enough for you," he said. "Not by a long shot." He jammed his hands into his pockets.

Valerie sighed and tried to sort through her emotions. She liked Sterling, she knew that. But the notion of a future with him scared her. And it wasn't just her loyalty to the memory of Michael Del Rio either. Sterling scared her for a host of reasons even more complicated. Though her faith had suffered some in the past year, she did still possess it. But Sterling didn't. His only credo centered in his own success, his own needs and desires. How could she even consider anything but a friendship with a man like that? Not that she felt herself better than him. But she couldn't deny the gulf that existed between them, the incompatibility of their worlds, their views of what was important.

She turned his chin to face her. "It's not a matter of your not being good enough," she started. "But we are different, no way around it."

He nodded, but she continued before he said anything. "I don't know what's going to happen this weekend," she said, "but like I said, when it's over I'm going to come home, try to sort out some things. I'd like to talk to you then, about where I am and where you are."

He nodded. "Maybe you can tell me what you believe."

"I can do that now," she said. "Though I have to tell you my faith is more complicated than it was a year ago."

"Anything worth anything always is," he said.

She studied the ground, wondering what to say. Anything too heavy and she'd lose him, she knew that. But he had opened the door so wide she couldn't let it pass completely.

"Let me try the short version," she said.

"I'm listening."

"A year ago I was naïve, innocent, living what I call a 'Norman Rockwell' life."

"But now?"

"Now the painting has some shadows in it, not all pretty and clean." She licked her lips. "I'm like the man in Mark 9:24 whose son Jesus healed. He said, 'Lord, I believe; help thou mine unbelief.' "

"That man sounds confused," Sterling said.

Valerie smiled. "He's not alone, I can tell you that. I think his problem is pretty true to life. Things happen that make no sense, things we can't explain, things that . . . I don't know . . . cut against the grain of belief in God. But other things—"

"Things like what happened in Kosovo?"

"Yeah, like you showing up at the Ibar River with that boy like you did. I mean, Prikova was within an inch of killing Chadwick. Others would have died too. You saw the situation. But then you show up, a miracle in a moment, Prikova's son in hand."

"Coincidence?" Sterling asked.

"Or miracle. All depends on how you see it."

"And one minute you see it as miracle, the next you see it as pure chance. Faith or doubt."

"Yeah, most people, if they're honest, deal with a touch of both, don't you think?"

Sterling squatted by the tree and stared up at Valerie. "But don't you need to choose one or the other?" he asked. "I mean, can you live with that kind of ambiguity?"

Valerie touched his shoulder. "Oh, I've chosen," she said. "Ninety-nine percent of the time faith wins out. But, now and again, like this past year, I've given in to the doubts. The difference is, I'm learning how to handle it now. I don't let the doubts make me feel I'm not a believer anymore. It's just a phase we go through from time to time. You live through it, pray through it, let others lead you through it."

"People like your uncle?"

"Yeah, I've piggybacked on his faith for the last several months while mine spent some time in the recovery room. But I think I'm mending now."

Sterling stood and stared up through the magnolia. "It is complicated," he said. "You were right about that."

By his side again, Valerie touched his cheek once more. "Let me simplify it for you," she said. "Christianity 101. Jesus loves you. Jesus forgives your sin if you ask. Jesus promises you the gift of an abundant, happy life and eternity to follow if you trust Him. That's where you start. Move up to doubt and faith later."

Sterling smiled. "Back to that happiness thing?"

"Yeah, but not happy as in giddy, laughing all the time. But happy, content, peaceful in spite of some storms."

"Is that what you have?"

She paused, considering the question. "Maybe not completely, but I'm close, I think, real close, and moving closer again all the time. You can too."

"I'll think about it," he said.

For several seconds, they gazed at each other. She thought he might kiss her, and she didn't know what she'd do if he tried. But then, as if a switch had turned off in his head, he backed off and stepped away.

"It's cold," he said. "You better get back inside. And I need to get going. I have a lot to do before Friday night."

Without another word, he led her back to the front door. At the door, he said good-bye, kissed her lightly on the forehead, then turned and walked to his car. Seconds later, he backed out of the driveway, turned down the street, and disappeared around the corner.

For several seconds, Valerie lingered in the driveway, the touch of his lips still warm on her forehead. No matter what happened in the future, she knew she wanted another chance to talk to Casey Sterling. Though she didn't know that she'd ever have any future with him, she wanted to give him every opportunity to know the faith that was daily becoming more and more alive to her again.

Wrapping her arms around her waist, she headed back inside the house. In the kitchen, she picked up her luggage and carried it to her bedroom. Throwing the luggage on the bed, she remembered the worried look in Casey's eyes, the warning he had voiced.

Suddenly concerned, she turned to the desk by her bed, opened a top drawer, and pulled out the pistol her dad had insisted she buy after the fiasco in Costa Rica. Gripping it firmly, she held it out with both hands, her legs shoulder width apart, one eye closed as she aimed at a stuffed cat sitting on her dresser. Pow! She pretended to pull the trigger. Though she had no idea what lay ahead in Colorado, she had learned her lesson well. If Casey Sterling had come to warn her, he knew something. And, though her faith was getting stronger, the image of the falling steel beam and the missing Suburban of Daphne Farmer still gave her enough fright to cause her to prepare herself for whatever lay ahead.

———

Already five miles away from Valerie's house, Casey Sterling adjusted his rearview mirror so he could better see the white sedan that had been following him all afternoon. Though having realized two days ago that he had someone on his tail, he hadn't bothered to duck his pursuers. There was no reason to do so until he knew more about the identity of the man in the car who drove ever so carefully exactly two cars back.

Picking up his cell phone, he punched in a number and settled into his seat. A second later, he heard his mom's voice.

"Hey, Mom," he said, trying to keep his voice light in spite of the loneliness he felt gripping his chest.

"Hey, boy," she said. "Where are you tonight?"

"Charlotte," he answered.

"What's happenin' there?"

"Nothing, Mom, I'm here visiting a friend."

"A lady friend?"

Sterling chuckled. "Yes, a lady friend, but it's not what you're thinking."

His mother sighed and he could hear her disappointment across the miles. She wanted him to get married, settle down, and give her some grandbabies.

"When you comin' home?" she asked. "I been waitin' to see you since you left Ireland. And then that Kosovo thing. Boy you did look good a-standin' on that bridge with that man's boy. Three different women down at the grocery told me they just about cried their eyes out when they saw that. You had us all right in the palm of your hands. Everybody here wants to see you."

Sterling turned right and checked his rearview mirror again. The white sedan remained in place, two cars back. "I'll see after this Colorado meeting," he said. "Maybe Monday."

"You makin' me a promise?" his mother asked, obviously wanting to pin him down.

Sterling gripped the phone tighter. He thought of Prikova and his son, the reunion on the bridge. For some reason he couldn't fathom, he asked about his father.

"Is he any better?" he asked, knowing she'd recognize the reference.

"Nope, worse as a matter of fact. Doc says he might not make it till spring."

"His liver?"

"That and a whole lot of other things. Too much whiskey for too many years."

"Have you see him lately?"

She hesitated and Sterling knew why. More than once he had expressed disapproval that she occasionally visited his dad—that she had gradually forgiven him over the years. For Sterling's money, his dad didn't deserve any such forgiveness. He'd never asked for it and so didn't deserve it. As far as he was concerned, the old man could die alone and unmourned. But his mom felt differently and from time to time tried to tell him so. So far he had refused to listen.

"You're checking on him again, aren't you?" he accused.

"He's dyin'," she said. "I can't kick a man when he's down."

Sterling ground his teeth.

"He wants to see you," she said. "Told me that yesterday. Said he wanted to tell you how proud he was."

Sterling thought of Valerie Miller. She wanted him to visit his dad, give reconciliation a chance. But what did she know about any of it, the whole sordid mess? But then again . . . that moment with Prikova and his son in Kosovo . . . what a great feeling to see son and father together again. But that son and father were separated by war, not by the failings of a man gone bad.

"He had a chance to tell me how proud he was a long time ago," Sterling said, cutting off his train of thought. "I don't know if I can buy it now."

"You're hard, son."

"He made me that way."

"Bitterness will eat you up."

"Bye, Mama."

Hanging up the phone, Sterling checked his rearview mirror again. The sedan was two cars back. He sped up slightly. The sedan matched his speed.

He thought of his dad. The man had so many faults he couldn't name them all. He bailed out on his wife and kid—the worst sin of all. Sterling's face burned with anger. He suddenly noticed his fingers clutched on the steering wheel. The knuckles were white. He heard his teeth grinding in his jaws. His body felt hard as concrete. His mom's words came back to him. "Bitterness will eat you up." He tried to relax but found it impossible.

He checked his rearview mirror again. Maybe his mom was right. He felt eaten up, consumed by resentment toward his dad. But who was he hurting? His dad? Sure. But himself too. How could you feel happy when your heart felt so tight you could hardly breathe?

He exhaled as he slipped around a curve. Maybe he would go see his dad, just for a short visit the next time he dropped into Swansboro. He'd show his dad how well he had done, how much he had achieved—all of it without *his* help.

Sterling's phone rang. Putting aside his decision and keeping his eye on the trailing sedan, he answered quickly.

"Sterling."

"Yeah, Casey man. News from California. I found that black Suburban. The cops had lost it in some paper work, but it turned up earlier today at a police impound area."

"What's the verdict?"

"They're still working it over, but the guy I talked to said it looked clean. No sign of foul play. Brake fluid gone but apparently from natural causes, nothing more sinister than faulty workmanship."

"Sounds like a lawsuit against a manufacturer to me."

"You got that right."

Sterling licked his lips. "Make sure of your information, then check back with me one more time. If nothing else turns up, you're good to come on home."

"I'm on it. Talk to you later."

Sterling signed off and keyed in Valerie's home number but heard a busy signal. He tried to remember her office number to leave a message but couldn't. Hanging up, he decided to wait and tell her the next time he saw her.

He checked his mirror again. The sedan stayed two cars back, keeping pace with his speed. Suddenly tired of the cat-and-mouse game, Sterling pushed his foot into the floorboard and his car jumped ahead, then swerved around a curve. Up to eighty within seconds, Sterling made a hard right turn, then a quick left. Behind him the white sedan made the first turn but lost it on the second. The car skidded and the driver lost control, and the white sedan smacked into a telephone pole and came to a quick halt.

Watching the car disappear in his mirror, Sterling told himself to relax. If everything fell right, he'd become one of the most famous men in the world in just a few short days, and then no one could ever hurt him again. No one. Nowhere. No way.

FORTY-TWO

Valerie plopped into the leather sofa in the room that Stricker's staff had assigned to her, her body exhausted. Her shoes and suit jacket lay on the floor at her feet, and she knew her blouse and skirt looked like used tinfoil. But she really didn't care. The day had worn her out.

Ted Shuster sat at a table beside the sofa, his appearance as frazzled as hers. A stack of papers high enough to dive from lay in front of him, and another stack, the finished pieces, rested on the floor. Busy since 5 A.M. the two of them were now alone, finished for the day with what seemed like a million details. Over a hundred people connected to the Chadwick's peace initiative had checked into Stricker's lodge, and almost three hundred media representatives had taken up residence in nearby hotels. Valerie and Ted and Rodney and Lester had tried to make sure each one was comfortable. In addition, they had also worked on the logistics for the opening meeting at which Chadwick planned to detail his hopes for the next phase of Operation Peace Project.

Valerie studied Ted as he glanced over another paper, then laid it on the floor. The two of them had worked for hours on Chadwick's opening speech, honing each word. But, knowing her uncle, he'd probably toss half of it away.

"I have to follow the Spirit," he'd apologize. "Plan ahead, yes, but don't let that keep you from going where the Spirit leads."

Valerie brushed back her hair and considered the day. All six leaders of the alliance had arrived. Luis Zorella came first, his brother José at his side along with four other Pentecostal preachers—two more Latin Americans and two African Americans. The group talked rapidly with one another, sometimes in Spanish, sometimes in English, and sometimes in an odd mixture of the two.

At noon Martha Sophia Blevins and the Dalai Lama made their appearances—each bringing those they had enlisted, a mishmash of well-known but controversial religious leaders— men and women, young and old, dressed in an array of costumes. Blevins' entourage favored earth tones and straight lines and shells on strings around their necks, while the Dalai Lama's crowd wore orange robes, black sandals, and sported shaved heads and thin wire-rimmed glasses. Watching them, Valerie sensed a strange calm, almost as if the air that surrounded the group had shorn itself of any and all uneasy currents.

The Ayatollah Khatama's people scared her, plain and simple. When they arrived at just past three, they said little and stood rigidly straight as they walked into the hotel. When not stroking their beards, they kept their arms folded and made little or no attempt to greet anyone. Though Valerie knew that the efficient security team that surrounded the premises had screened everyone, she couldn't help but feel that someone in Khatama's group had managed to squeeze a trunk full of explosives into the lodge under one of the shawls they wore draped over their shoulders.

Rabbi ben Moseph made almost no stir as he and his invitees entered. Six men—three in business suits and three in the black Orthodox garb—picked up keys, handed their luggage to hotel attendants, and headed to their rooms. No fuss, no muss, no bother.

Pope John Peter and his cardinals arrived last, a helicopter transporting them to the grounds, a majestic rush of white and red and black landing with a swirl of snow and mountain air.

Standing by her uncle—who had personally greeted each of his allies as they arrived—Valerie bowed to the pope as he entered the building at just past seven. The pontiff humbly returned the gesture, then kissed Chadwick on both cheeks. Finished with Chadwick, the pope faced Valerie, his arms open. Though surprised by the informality, Valerie warmly accepted his embrace.

"Wonderful to see you again," John Peter said, kissing her on both cheeks. "You are often in my prayers." He stepped back and Valerie bowed again.

"We should talk soon," the pope continued.

"At your pleasure," Valerie said. "I would welcome it."

Nodding, John Peter focused on Chadwick again, and the two

men entered the lodge, the pontiff's attendants and cardinals bringing up the rear, their black cassocks, red sashes, and hats in stark contrast to the pope's pure white vestments. A few minutes later, the Catholic contingent had settled themselves in their quarters.

Now, her stomach screaming for food, Valerie picked up a shoe and tossed it at Ted.

"Hey," he said as the shoe bounced at his feet. "Stop playing and get back to work."

"I'm too hungry to work," Valerie said. "Did you eat any supper?"

Ted shook his head. "Did they serve supper?"

"To everybody but us."

"Room service?"

"I'm on it." Valerie pulled herself up and called, keeping the order simple—burgers, salads, soft drinks. Off the phone, she faced Ted again. He looked exhausted but he kept plugging along on the papers, one after the other.

"You should let Lester handle some of that," she said. "Most of it deals with finances."

Ted laid down a piece of paper. "It'll take Lester a while to catch back up," he said. "I'm just doing what I can to make it easier on Russell."

Valerie nodded. She knew the feeling. Though she had her own misgivings about a whole host of things, she knew no way to deny her uncle. The man's integrity and faith multiplied that of people like hers and called out the best in them.

"Do you think Lester is okay?" she asked.

"I'm not sure what you mean."

She stood, walked to Ted's table, and sat down. "I mean, can we trust him?"

Ted shrugged. "I don't know that it matters," he said. "Russ trusts him. That's all that counts." He chewed on the corner of his thumb. "I mean, what can he do to us but walk out again?"

Valerie hesitated. She hadn't told anyone but Chadwick about her suspicions. Would Ted understand? Would he do anything about it if he did? And what could he do that she hadn't already done? Should she try to enlist him to go to Chadwick with her? But wasn't it too late for that?

She sighed. Of course it was. Everyone had already arrived. The fat was in the fire, the Rubicon had been crossed. No matter what she thought, for better or worse, it was truly in God's hands now.

"Nothing," she said to Ted. "There's nothing Lester can do now. There's nothing any of us can do."

————

As the night fell heavier over the mountain, a bank of slow-moving clouds gradually reached out for the moon, and by 2 A.M. the lunar face had disappeared completely. A soft snow started falling, and by three another inch of fresh white powder covered the mountain slopes and furry green of the innumerable and assorted pines that jutted up from the rocky ground. At just past three a pair of heavy black boots crunched quietly through the newly fallen snow, the treads of the boots leaving momentary prints the size of a bear's paw.

Breathing steadily but not heavily, the man in the boots kept his head low and his shoulders hunched as he stalked deliberately into the freshening wind toward his predetermined goal. In addition to the boots, he wore a pair of white Gore-Tex pants, a waist-length coat, a fur-lined hood, and a pair of gloves—all the same color and material as the pants. The only thing not white on him was the black backpack he carried slung between his shoulders and the night-vision goggles that encircled his eyes. To his chagrin, he'd not been able to find a white backpack in the time he had to prepare for this particular work.

The man paused for a few seconds to catch his breath and take his bearings. The plus-three degree temperature and twenty-mile-per-hour wind had numbed his face, but focused on the task at hand, he didn't much notice the chilling conditions. A man in his shoes couldn't afford the luxury of worrying about the weather. Not with what he carried on his back.

Scanning the mountain, he saw a row of floodlights way off to his left and down below, but nothing nearby would illuminate his work in any way. Grateful for the lack of security on this part of the mountain, the man pulled off a glove, wiped the snow off his glasses, regloved his hand, and started moving across the rocky slopes again. The wind and snow seemed to hesitate for a few minutes, making his trek somewhat easier.

It took him less than thirty more minutes to reach the spot he'd chosen two days ago for his package, a spot only twenty yards or so away from a deserted, weather-beaten barn. The barn sat almost nine hundred yards up and away from the area that the locals called "The Stricker Segment"—a pristine section of over a thousand acres owned by the well-known billionaire.

Plopping down on the ground, the man took a moment to make sure he had completely caught his breath. No reason to get careless now. One wrong move and . . .

Grunting, the man told himself to relax. Men like him didn't make those kinds of mistakes.

His breathing even and his heartbeat regular, the man stared out into the wintry night. Nothing moved but the trees bending in the wind. For a second a strange sense of pride overwhelmed him, the pride of a professional appreciating the good work he had almost finished. He took a deep breath, sucking the cold air deep into his lungs. At moments like this, he felt so content, more content than at any other time. Though danger surrounded him, he had managed to avoid detection to deliver his package. In another few minutes, he would finish his task, slip off the mountain, and let matters take their course. He sucked in the air once more and promised himself an expensive cigar and a fine bottle of French wine when he landed on flat ground once again. With what his employer promised to pay, he could afford such extravagances.

Feeling pleased, he focused again on his work. His hands steady, he pulled off his backpack and laid it at his feet. Opening the pack, he slid out the package that lay inside and placed it carefully in his lap. Slipping off his goggles and gloves, he took a thin penlight from the front pocket of his jacket, held it in his teeth, turned his back to Stricker's lodge below, and trained the tiny beam of light at the square black briefcase he had taken from the backpack. Opening the briefcase, he saw the face of an electronic timer staring back. His hands steady, he adjusted the timer for 6:30 P.M., less than sixteen hours away. With the timer set, he closed the briefcase, reset his goggles, and eased himself toward the base of a rock formation that jutted up and out of the ground like a giant chin.

Taking care not to jostle the briefcase, the man wedged it under the back lip of the rock, timer face outward.

For several moments, the man in white sat and stared at the briefcase as if mesmerized. In his head, he saw the clockface click and move. Three-forty-six to three-forty-seven. The imaginary movement startled the man and reminded him to get moving. Tipping his head toward the briefcase as if acknowledging a pretty woman walking by on a sidewalk, he turned his back and scooted away from the darkened rock. Twenty feet away, he slipped his hands back into his gloves, congratulated himself on a job well done, and stalked back toward the protection of the tree line less than a hundred yards ahead. In less than two hours, he should reach level ground again. He licked his lips. He could already taste the wine and smell the cigar.

He never saw what hit him.

The shot came from behind a tree, a single *poof* of sound as a pistol fired, its silencer muffling everything in the quiet night. The man in white slumped to the ground, a spot of crimson the size of a bread plate already spreading out from beneath his left shoulder blade where the bullet had entered the back chambers of his heart.

FORTY-THREE

At just past 11 A.M. a bearded FedEx man drove his delivery truck up to the security checkpoint about a hundred yards below Stricker's lodge and flashed an identification badge at the security officer who met him. The security agent studied the badge for a second, glanced at the truck, then waved him through. Parking the truck at the entrance to the lodge, the man climbed out and headed to the main entry of the Stricker complex. Limping slightly, the man made his way up the steps and over to the front desk. A pair of sunglasses covered his eyes against the bright sun. His shirt seemed a touch too small, almost as if someone had bought it without bothering to check his measurements.

Searching through a brown leather satchel, the man pulled out a thick stack of FedEx envelopes and small packages and handed them to the hotel attendant, a middle-aged woman in a black uniform.

"Where's Phelpsie?" the woman said, obviously surprised that her regular FedEx man hadn't delivered the materials.

The bearded man shrugged. "I'm subbing today."

The attendant took the mail. "Phelpsie back tomorrow?"

"Who knows?"

The bearded man turned and headed back to the door, his left leg slightly out of sync with his right. The woman watched him limp away, then shrugged and pivoted to put up the packages and envelopes. Two envelopes for room 110, one for 114. She worked on through the rooms, slipping the appropriate envelopes, folders, and small packages into the appropriate slots. The stack was unusually heavy today, but that was no surprise, given the unprecedented importance of the guests now residing at the lodge. Room 237, one envelope. She started to stuff the letter into the appropriate slot, then realized it wasn't in a FedEx envelope and it had no return address.

Confused, the hotel attendant stared at the envelope for several seconds. A simple off-white envelope, it was addressed to Valerie Miller, room 237. Hoping to find a return address, she flipped it over but saw none. The woman held the envelope for several seconds, then scratched her head. Should she put the envelope in the slot? Was that breaking the law? She knew a person wasn't supposed to deliver mail with no stamp. But what about a package delivered by a FedEx man that wasn't a FedEx package? Shouldn't the FedEx guy have noticed the inappropriate envelope?

The attendant started to call her manager, but then realized he wouldn't like her bothering him on such a busy day. She waved the envelope in the air as if fanning herself. What to do? What to do? She stared once more at the writing on the envelope. Neat, clear. She rubbed her fingers over the words, and a bit of the ink smeared slightly. Hum. The ink was still fresh. The letter couldn't have been written too long ago. More and more curious, the woman stepped from her desk and walked to the entry of the lodge, her eyes searching for the FedEx man on the off-chance that he had stopped to talk to someone and she could ask him about the letter. But she didn't see him.

Back in the hotel the attendant held the envelope for one more second, then shoved it into the slot for Valerie Miller. Let her deal with it, she thought. No reason to get all bent out of shape over one envelope when she had so many other things to handle today.

————

Almost three hundred yards away behind a snow-laden spruce tree, the bearded FedEx man peered through a set of high-powered binoculars at the huge window that fronted the entry of Stricker's hotel. The FedEx truck sat on the edge of the highway about fifty feet to his right, its engine off. A driver he now knew as "Phelpsie" lay on the floorboard in the back. Though bound at wrists and ankles, gagged and blindfolded, Phelpsie was unhurt. The FedEx man who wasn't a FedEx man had commandeered his truck but had not hurt him in doing so.

Watching the hotel attendant slip the envelope into the slot, the fake FedEx man sagged against the tree, his body wearied by an almost sleepless night. What little sleep he had gotten—less than two hours just before dawn—had scared him more than it refreshed him, scared him worse than anything in a long time. A horrible dream had disturbed his sleep and he didn't have a clue what it meant.

Pulling away from the tree, the fake FedEx man headed off through the woods in the opposite direction from the truck. If anyone could interpret his dream, he suspected Valerie Miller could. Darting carefully through the trees, the man ached for the chance to talk to Valerie. It had been so long since he saw her last, since he had to flee to protect her.

He thought back to that moment in Costa Rica, the moment when he had taken the scroll and disappeared. It had broken his heart to leave her, and it broke his heart to be so close now and not be able to talk to her. But he knew he couldn't, for it was too dangerous for them both. All he could do now was protect her in any way he could. That's why he had kept tabs on her whereabouts in the past year, why he had used so much of the fifty million dollars Willard Madden had given to him to keep current on her. That's why he had sent her the note, why he had taken the chance to come here today. Of course she had to actually receive the envelope and take time to read it for any interpretation to occur.

His heart heavy, Michael Del Rio circled the lodge, came up on the other side, and nestled down in a spot that gave him a clear view of Valerie Miller's room. Once she opened the envelope, he'd have to leave. But until then . . . well . . . if she never opened it, he had an eerie suspicion that everyone in the lodge might die before the next morning came.

———

At just past 3 P.M. Valerie Miller rushed to the desk at the front of the hotel and asked for any and all packages for anyone in the Russell Chadwick party. The attendant, a short Hispanic man with a thin black mustache, checked through several slots, pulling out ten packages and folders and handing them to her. Hugging the stack to her chest, Valerie thanked the man and hustled away. Back in her bedroom, she tossed the materials onto a table she had set up as a desk. The envelope addressed to her wedged itself halfway under her laptop computer.

Leaving the packages, she pivoted and stepped to the bathroom to take a quick shower. With barely an hour left before a last-minute meeting with Chadwick, she desperately wanted to freshen up, change clothes, and lie down for a few minutes. Though everything had gone well so far, her nerves still felt like rubber bands stretched to their limits.

For the next fifteen minutes she reveled in the hot shower as it calmed her jangled nerves, providing a respite from all the memos, last-minute phone calls, and emails she'd handled in the last few hours. With all the media covering this historic meeting, she had talked so much in the last twenty-four hours, she almost hoped she would never have to speak again.

Out of the shower, she slipped into a bathrobe and stretched out on the bed. Though she had less than thirty minutes to rest, that didn't matter. She'd take advantage of every minute.

Closing her eyes, she suddenly realized she hadn't seen Casey Sterling all day. How odd! She sat up, twisted to the table, and pulled a cordless phone from its stand. She noticed the stack of packages by her laptop and realized she hadn't yet checked through them. The phone in one hand, the materials in the other, she flipped through the stack one piece at a time as she dialed.

The answering machine at Sterling's office responded. Searching her memory, she recalled his condominium number and tried it. Waiting, she worked through the rest of the packages and envelopes—three for Ted, one for Rodney, five for Chadwick. Lester had nothing. Another answering machine picked up. Obviously, Sterling hadn't forwarded his calls.

She finished the FedEx stuff and, puzzled by Sterling's absence, laid down the phone. From the corner of her vision, she saw a plain envelope stuck under her computer. She pulled out the envelope and stared blankly at it, her mind still on Sterling.

Try as she might, Valerie couldn't imagine anything important enough to keep Casey Sterling away from the most important meeting of religious leaders in the new millennium. Stumped, she stood and walked over to the window, the envelope still in hand. Staring out, she started to ring Ted and ask him about Sterling. But then she decided against it. Ted wouldn't understand her interest in any specific reporter, and she didn't feel like explaining it.

The sky had grown grayer through the day, and though the sun managed to peek its head through the clouds every now and again, the threat of more snow hung over the place, and a freshening breeze had kicked up as a warning. Valerie shivered and turned back to the room. She tossed the envelope on the bed, slipped on a pair of slippers, and sank onto her mattress. Maybe Sterling had arrived but she just hadn't seen him.

She started to grab the phone to check with the media registration desk but then shook her head. There was really no reason to do that. She didn't have time to talk to him anyway. She would wait until later, after everything calmed down. She stretched out, telling herself to rest for a few minutes. She didn't have long before she had to head downstairs and wade into the crowd again, check out last-minute details, make sure everyone had a place, a credential, an information packet. . . .

She closed her eyes, her hands going behind her head. Her right hand bumped the envelope. Rolling over on her stomach, she picked it up and studied it for several seconds. It was plain and off-white, not a FedEx envelope at all. It had no return address on front or back.

Curious, she opened the envelope and pulled out a white sheet of paper. The paper had no letterhead. She jerked to a sitting position on the bed. She flipped the envelope over again as if a return address might magically appear but it didn't. She read the words on the page.

> *Valerie Miller,*
> *Last night I had a dream—a horrible dream. A mammoth shadow hung over everything. Fingers from the shadow grasped at everyone. I saw danger in the shadow, death. I saw the dream, but I don't know the meaning. But you do, I know that too. I saw you in the dream, your face—you. You read the dream, understood its depths, opened it up for all to see. Know the shadow, Valerie, know it and live. All depends on it. All.*

Valerie read the note again and then a third time, but it still didn't make any sense. Who sent it and why? A shadow? What did that mean? Death in the midst of it? Crazy!

Standing, Valerie studied the envelope again, then the sheet. She read the message over and over but still couldn't decipher it. What kind of danger?

She thought back over the day. A small army of security people had scoured the whole lodge, room to room, door to door, every nook and cranny. A pack of dogs had sniffed and searched for any trace of explosives but had found nothing. Every high-tech gadget in the world had been used to scan every building and everybody. Again, no threat materialized. The security team had checked

Stricker's property from stem to stern and given it a clean bill of health. She had no reason to worry. But now this—this idiotic note.

She glanced at the clock. Almost four. She had to hurry! Putting the letter back on the table, she quickly changed into a tailored black pants suit, white cotton blouse, and flat-heeled shoes. Though the religious leaders would wear their clerical finery, she had a ton of behind-the-scenes work to do. No fancy wear for her tonight. Leaving off all jewelry except her gold earrings, she carefully but hurriedly applied her makeup. Next came her hair—a fast brushup. Lipstick went on last.

Standing in front of the mirror, she thought again of the letter and gritted her teeth. She wanted to leave all her paranoia behind. But now this note. In spite of her resolutions to the contrary, she was unable to shake the feeling that something ominous hung in the air, an evil as real as the clouds that continued to fight with the sun for control of the weather outside.

But the security team had assured everyone. Was she being unreasonable? Still paranoid in spite of her good intentions?

Though chastising herself, Valerie walked to the bedside table, pulled open the drawer, and lifted out her pistol. For several seconds, she stared at it—her mind torn. Should she carry it or not? Then she thought of her uncle and knew she couldn't carry a gun into a meeting where he hoped to consolidate his alliance for peace. Even more, she realized that if she carried a gun it meant she had given in once more to her fears. And she'd promised herself she wouldn't do that again.

Valerie dropped the pistol back into the drawer, grabbed the letter, and bolted from the room, the letter stuffed into the inner pocket of her jacket, her attention to duty momentarily pushing her fears away. Meeting Ted at the bottom of the stairs, she turned left and headed to the cavernous banquet hall where Stricker's people had set up for the opening ceremonies. In that hall in just over two hours, the world's most important religious leaders would map out their design to bring peace to the ends of the earth.

Sucking in her breath, Valerie told herself to stay calm. In spite of everything that caused her to fear—Clement's death, the steel girder that almost killed her and Chadwick, the death of Daphne Farmer and the missing Suburban, now this bizarre note—she still had a job to do. No matter how much she wanted to run, she had come too far to back out now.

FORTY-FOUR

Sweat pouring off his face, Casey Sterling climbed off the commuter airliner at the small Breckenridge Airport and headed straight to the rental car counter. His eyes frantic, he hurried past two other men to the front of the line.

"An emergency!" he apologized. "Life or death!"

The men shook their heads as if disgusted but they let him pass. Five minutes later he rushed from the building, hopped into his car, and screeched out of the parking lot. If he had it figured right, he'd just make it, make it before . . . well, he didn't even want to think about the results if he didn't make it on time.

He checked his watch. 4:20. His support people—camera crew, producer, writer—were already there. He'd talked to them by phone just a few minutes ago.

Turning into the four-lane highway that led from Breckenridge to Stricker's place barely ten miles away, Sterling didn't even bother to tell himself to calm down. He knew such a thought was ludicrous for someone like him, someone so totally driven, someone facing the most pivotal moment of his life. He gripped the steering wheel with his left hand, his right one keying in a number on his cell phone.

The highway began a quick ascent. Rock-faced mountains loomed on both sides in the distance, and dangerous drops of altitude waited just past the steel highway rails to his immediate right.

"Answer me!" he groused ten seconds later when no one picked up the phone. "You've got to be there!" No one responded.

Keeping the phone on, Sterling laid it down and rubbed his

forehead, a vein pulsing in his throat. He needed to reach one more person right now, needed it more than anything he'd ever needed in his life. He briefly considered calling Valerie Miller but then knew he couldn't. She wouldn't understand. Besides, she couldn't do anything about this anyway. It was out of her league, no matter the consequences. He'd managed to get himself into this mess, so he'd have to wriggle his way out.

He tried the phone again. Same number. Same result. He jammed the phone into his thigh and checked the odometer. Only about five miles left. He could make it if he broke every speed law in the state and had no misfortune along the way. He pushed the accelerator to the floorboard.

From an access road on the right a plain white sedan pulled onto the highway, but Sterling hardly noticed. The sedan trailed him for almost a mile, then began to gain quickly. Sterling raised his eyes to the rearview mirror. The sedan had closed to within a few feet of his rear bumper. A man in a Rockies baseball cap sat at the wheel, the hat obscuring most of his face. Sterling lightly tapped his brakes to warn the man to back off. The sedan's front grill tapped the back bumper of his rental car.

"Hey!" Sterling shouted as his car swerved to the right.

The white sedan jerked to the left, then pulled up to his side—the Rockies cap almost even with the front door of Sterling's rental. Sterling glanced over, but the man in the cap refused to look his way. Sterling slowed down a notch. The sedan slowed too.

His face red, Sterling rolled down his window, shook his fist at the man, and shouted at him. The bill of the Rockies cap pointed his way, and he saw that the man had dark skin, a man of Middle Eastern descent, he felt sure. The front of the sedan veered right, and its fender bounced into the side of Sterling's rental.

Sterling grabbed the wheel with both hands, fighting to keep the car under control. The precipice of the mountains rushed toward him, but he jerked the car left and darted back toward the center of the four lanes. The white sedan swerved at him again, and for an instant Sterling wondered about the driver, who he was, why he wanted to kill him. But then the sedan's right fender smashed his car full in the side, and his mind shut down as the rental bounced into the side of the guardrail. A sheet of sparks sizzled though the air as his fender raked along the railing, his tires squealing to straighten out.

Sterling jerked to the left once more, and the car responded and swerved back onto the highway. He caught a glimpse of the white sedan, at least ten feet behind him now, from his side mirror. He heard a pop and thought he'd blown a tire, but then a second pop followed and a third. His back windshield exploded inward, and he realized that the man in the Rockies' cap had fired a weapon.

Sterling lost it. He jammed on his brakes and jerked his car to the left. His front fender smashed into the right door of the white sedan, and the man in the baseball cap stared at him in utter surprise. Sterling's car bounced to the right, but he immediately pulled it back and aimed it at the sedan for a second run. In a blur, he saw a pistol and ducked as a cascade of gunfire passed over his head, the bullets splintering his windshield.

Steering the car to the left again, Sterling roared into the cold mountain air, his anger fueled by the possibility that he might die here on this highway and never have the opportunity to tell Valerie Miller what he'd only recently decided. Plowing his foot into the accelerator, he pounded his car once more into the side of the sedan. The two cars came together just as the snow started to fall again. The two crumpled fenders locked up together, but the white sedan had more weight than the rental and pushed it to the right. The rental and the sedan smashed into the guardrails. The guardrails gave way and the two cars jumped the side of the road and plunged over the edge.

As his car careened down the rocky slope, Sterling banged his head against the steering wheel and a cut the length of a finger opened on his forehead. His car separated itself from the white sedan, rammed into a tree, and the air bag inflated into his bleeding forehead. The car settled to a stop, the loose rocks from the ground clattering under and past his wheels to the bottom of the valley almost a hundred feet farther down. Three seconds later he heard an explosion. Somewhere in his rattled brain he thought his rental had blown up but realized it it must have been the sedan instead.

Momentarily relieved, he tried to pull out from his seat belt but couldn't manage it. He reached for his cell phone to make one final call, but the blood from his forehead blinded his eyes and he couldn't find it. Pushing away the air bag, he tried to unsnap his seat belt, but his fingers wouldn't cooperate. Jerking against the restraint, he wiped blood from his eyes and opened his mouth to call for help. He felt as if he was losing consciousness and grabbed for the seat belt again. This time he unhooked it. But as he reached for the door, consciousness eluded him and he couldn't pull it back.

He saw his mom in an apron in the kitchen in Swansboro, her face lined with age and worry. He saw his dad too, but he wasn't at home. He was on the built-on porch of the trailer where he lived. Casey wanted to love his dad, but it was so hard, so hard to love a man who had never done anything much to deserve it. But he wanted to love him, and he had tried, had tried only a day ago, had driven from Atlanta to Swansboro to see him. A boy needed to be with his father . . . it was true, it was true what he'd said in Kosovo. So he had driven to the rusty trailer where his dad lived less than a mile from the ocean, angel oaks in the yard, adorned with Spanish moss. He had sat on the porch with his dad, the old man's skin the color of bad butter from the disease eating up his liver. . . .

Sterling lost consciousness completely then, his last thought that of his dad in the bed at his trailer, a cloud of cigarette smoke hanging in the air, a look of utter surprise on his face at the unexpected visit of his only child.

FORTY-FIVE

5:05 P.M.

Her mind a jumble, Valerie stood with her back to the wall just to the left of the main platform, Ted Shuster on one side, Lester Boggett on the other. Rodney Kent sat on a chair next to Lester, perched there like a bird on a wire. The four had given up their places in the banquet hall to save room for all the dignitaries about to assemble, but they still had a clear view of the proceedings. A man seated at an electronic keyboard played a soft arrangement, and the aroma of fresh flowers drifted through the air.

For what seemed like the fiftieth time that day, Valerie felt like pinching herself. To the surprise of millions, Chadwick had actually pulled it off. Counting him, seven of the most prominent religious leaders in the world waited in a room at the back of the hall for the ceremony to begin. At least twenty-eight others from a variety of religious traditions had joined them for their march into history.

In spite of her misgivings, Valerie had to admit that the impossible had happened. Whether the alliance could actually usher in an era of peace, she still didn't know. But Chadwick had at least brought the leaders together to give it a try. It was miracle enough to give her hope, she decided, miracle enough.

Ted caught her eye and smiled at her and she felt strangely calm. Maybe her fears were unfounded, maybe . . .

The music grew louder and Valerie's heart quickened. A beam of late-day sun pushed through the window past Ted's profile, and she thought it odd, since it had just started to snow again. She heard a shuffle of feet as the spectators in the banquet hall stood

to wait for the entry of the first wave of religious leaders. She had
an eerie sense of déjà vu and immediately thought of the moments after Chadwick's entry at Prestwick Church in Ireland, the
moments before the explosion, before a slew of people almost
died.

The sunlight on Ted's face brightened even further, and she
gazed outside and saw the huge rock that hung over Stricker's
place like a granite aircraft carrier. On the back side of the rock
she saw snow falling; on the front side the sun blazed in a singular stripe over the lodge. But then the rock's edge caught the
sunlight and blocked it, and a shadow fell over the lodge, a
shadow like a giant hand held over the eyes to snuff out all light,
a hand whose fingers reached out for everyone in the hotel.

The note! The dream!

Valerie almost choked.

Danger in the shadow, said the note! . . . *Know the shadow,
Valerie, know it and live. All depends on it!*

Stunned, Valerie remained still for several moments, wracking her brain, trying to figure it out. But she couldn't. Was she
still so paranoid that a simple shadow could become a reason for
fear? But she'd told herself she wouldn't let that happen anymore. She was past all that now!

She cradled her head in her hands, wondering what to do. She
couldn't run to Chadwick. He wouldn't listen. Ted? Same response. And Casey wasn't here! Like it or not, she had no one
who'd believe her, no one who'd listen. She raised her eyes. The
sun had disappeared completely now and the snow was falling
harder. The music swelled more loudly. The procession had
started but she couldn't focus on it any longer. Though it made
absolutely no sense, she knew deep in her bones that the note
had a message that was beyond rational. But could she respond
to such a message? Should she? Should she trust the unknown
that much?

The first wave of dignitaries paraded past her and took their
seats in the first row, their religious garb a colorful reminder of
the diversity of the group now gathering before her eyes. As if in
a nightmare, she suddenly saw them all under attack, their gar-
ments torn, their faces bloody and panicked by death. She
glanced at Ted as if expecting him to see the same thing, but his
eyes were glued on the processional. Apparently, he saw nothing
else.

She ground her teeth, telling herself to forget the note and the dreams, all her suspicions. Security officers had done their work. No danger hid on the grounds of this lodge, no threat.

Momentarily comforted, she stared out the window once more. The rock loomed over the lodge, and she thought of the words to an old hymn: "Rock of ages, cleft for me, let me hide myself in thee."

But this time the rock didn't comfort her. Its mammoth profile was a lurking presence. The rock created a shadow, but how could a shadow threaten them?

The second row of religious leaders now paraded past, a cardinal in his finest black and red and a Protestant minister from Chicago she recognized. She thought again of the note. *Danger in the shadow ... Know the shadow and live.* But how could you *know* a shadow?

She heard a rustle and knew that Chadwick and the rest of the seven had reached the back of the banquet hall. She glanced at her watch. 5:25. Her heart pounded harder and her neck felt warm.

All at once it occurred to her. You knew a shadow by knowing what cast it! The rock formation above the hotel cast the shadow!

Her mind reeled back to the tragic episode on an island off the coast of Costa Rica. Attackers had come from the least expected place, the direction that had no security, a cliff that jutted up from the ocean behind the mansion where she was staying. People had died and Michael Del Rio—the man she had loved— had disappeared forever. Only hours before he had walked with her on the beach below the cliffs, had picked flowers for her from the wild vegetation by the—

Flowers!

The arrangement sent to her in the hospital after Prestwick! The cryptic message on the card—*That's My Story!* Those were the exact words she had used the last time she talked to Michael! She had tried to explain her faith to him. "It's a matter of the heart," she had told him. "Either way you come down, it's sheer faith. Faith to believe or to disbelieve. ... So in spite of the fact that suffering is real and it hurts and I can't explain it all, that's my story, and I'm sticking to it until someone can show me something that makes more sense than that does."

That's my story!

Michael had sent her those flowers in the hospital! He *was* still alive! Could he have sent her the note? Was he out there, keeping watch over her? Did he have those means, those capabilities? Apparently, so!

She stared out the window, watched the falling snow. And now he was trying to warn her of a terrible danger he saw in a dream. Did God work that way? But why hadn't he contacted her directly? She knew the answer as soon as she asked it. The scroll. Michael had the scroll, and he couldn't take a chance on seeing her, coming into the open like that. So long as he saw the need to protect that document, he'd never reveal his presence to her or anyone else. She wanted to scream as she realized this, to shriek her anger at the injustice of it all. But she knew she had no time for such selfish emotions.

A rock loomed over the lodge and someone—obviously Michael had dreamed a dream, and she was in it, and though she didn't know how the rock could harm her, she knew that it could. Security patrols circled the property and blocked all access from below. But what if someone attacked from above?

Moving briskly but without panic, Valerie brushed past Ted and Lester and hurried toward the nearest balcony. Though not sure exactly what she planned to do, she knew she couldn't stand by and wait to see if she was right or not. If her suspicions were wrong she'd look like a fool. Someone would want to commit her to a mental institution. But what if she was right? What if she wasn't just paranoid? What if what she was doing was really an act of faith, an act of faith in the power of God to use dreams to speak to her and to others? What if she was right but did nothing? That meant almost certain death for everyone now gathering in the banquet hall of Bill Stricker's Rocky Mountain lodge. Given those two choices, she really didn't have any choice at all.

———

Bleeding over his left eye, Casey Sterling jerked to consciousness and instantly became aware of the cold shoving in through the broken windshield of his car. Jamming a hand over the cut, he tried to remember where he was and how he came to be there. The rental car rested on its left side, wedged against a clump of twisted spruce pines. Everything appeared sideways, a swirl of green trees and falling snow and scrabble rock.

Slowly gathering himself, Sterling tried to climb up to the passenger door. But a pain in his right side suddenly cut into him, and he grabbed his ribs and froze in place. For several seconds, he stayed dead still, his head throbbing, his eyes searching through the snow to get his bearings. He pulled his hand from his forehead. At least the bleeding had slowed.

Protecting his ribs as much as he could, he shifted to the left and scanned the part of the car he could see, hoping to find his cell phone. He didn't see the phone. Grunting, he twisted to the back, his eyes busy. But still no sign of the phone. Maybe the force of the crash had thrown it out.

Without warning, his memory returned and he thought of the man in the white sedan and wondered why he had tried to kill him. It made no sense, no sense unless—

He gritted his teeth as he considered the possibility. He had given people at least one reason to kill him, perhaps even more. He checked his watch and knew that he had to move, no matter how much it hurt. He had barely an hour before everything happened and at least four more miles to go.

He checked the passenger side of the car again. No way could he manage that. Even if he somehow climbed up to the door, he couldn't scale the steep incline above the car. Looking out past the broken windshield, he saw that the angle of the incline softened significantly and then leveled out to a reasonably flat surface. If he could work his way out and navigate the incline, then he could reach the level space and move from there.

Sucking in his breath, he reached for a jacket that lay on the floorboard. Grabbing it, he gingerly slipped it on. Then, his right hand against his ribs, he rocked forward toward the broken windshield. If he couldn't go up, he had to go straight through the windshield, over the hood, into the snow. . . .

Sterling pushed his left hand through the remains of the windshield, cleared away as much glass as possible, and grabbed the frame of the car. Using both hands, he hauled himself through the opening, head first, then torso and feet. Grabbing for the nearest tree limb, he swung his feet to the right and slid down through a tangle of pine branches. A spray of wet snow bounced from the trees onto his head as he slid to the ground, and the limb he had grabbed broke off and jabbed him in the ribs.

Losing control, he rolled down the hill, his elbows and knees banging over rocks and scruffy shrubs like a runaway log. Sterling roared as he tumbled, his voice cutting through the snow loud enough to wake a bear from hibernation. He rolled and tumbled and rolled and tumbled until he finally came to rest against a knee-high rock at the bottom of the ravine, his forehead bleeding again, his ribs burning hot, his eyes blank.

For several seconds, he lay as still as death. The earth spun around and around, and he felt like a drunk man run over by an ice wagon. Hugging his coat to his busted side, he closed his eyes against the spinning and wished it would disappear and take him with it. He drifted off. The cold numbed the ripping pain in his ribs. Snow caked into his eyes. The frozen world took over and he knew he needed to pull himself up and move on, but he felt so cold. . . .

But then he thought of Valerie Miller. He had to move. For her sake and his.

Groaning, he pushed himself to a sitting position and glanced at his watch. Fifty-two minutes to go and no way to cross the distance to Stricker's lodge. Glancing up the incline, he saw the rental car balanced precariously against the clump of trees at least fifty feet above. There was no way to climb back up there.

Weighing his options, Sterling stared straight ahead. Only one way to go. Then his hands pressing against his side to ease the pain in his ribs, he stumbled through the snow, his feel staggering past scrub pines and scattered boulders, his eyes working overtime to see, his body numbed to its injuries by the driving wind and icy cold, his mind reeling with panic. Somehow, he kpet moving.

He came to the top of a small ridge and stared down at a snug-looking log cabin, its roof covered with white, a thin light seeping out from one window. The rest of the cabin was dark as a cavern. A metal shed sat nearby, a wooden lean-to attached to its left side.

Almost giddy at his good fortune, Sterling rushed down the slope to the cabin and banged his fists on the front door. No one responded. Shivering but energized by a ray of hope, Sterling stepped to the front window and peered inside but saw no one. He tried the doorknob but found it locked. Pausing for only a second, he considered his options. Seeing no other choice, he lifted a foot and kicked in the door. It took only a minute to inspect the place. No phone. Nothing helpful.

Shrugging, Sterling eased into the yard and headed toward the shed. At the shed he saw a black tarp draped over something under the lean-to.

Sterling moved toward the object, his heart hopeful.

He pulled back the tarp. A snowmobile sat underneath it, its nose pointed out.

Moving quickly, Sterling straddled the snowmobile and spot-

ted a key in the ignition. Turning the key, he almost smiled as
the engine sputtered, then roared into the swirling snow.
Sterling's spirits soared, masking his injuries. But he didn't celebrate long. He had less than forty minutes.

Zooming out of the lean-to and across the yard, he committed
himself to returning the snowmobile as soon as possible. Then, as
best he could, he aimed the machine in the direction of the property owned by Bill Stricker. If nothing else happened he might
just make it in time.

FORTY-SIX

On the front balcony of the lodge, Valerie sucked in her breath against the frigid cold and stared up at the rock through the almost completely dark sky, her eyes busily searching for any sign of danger, any kind of threat. Seeing nothing, she tried to calm her breathing but couldn't manage it. The snow began to fall more heavily, and she knew that if she didn't hurry and do something, the thick snow would block her view of the rock and her moment to do anything would vanish. She heard a door open and pivoted to see Lester Boggett stepping toward her, a scowl on his forehead.

"Shouldn't you be inside?" he asked, his voice gruff.

"Shouldn't you?"

"I saw you come out here a few minutes ago," he said. "Are you okay?"

She nodded toward the rock. "No, I'm not," she said. "But . . . I . . . I can't really say why."

"Put this on if you're gonna stay out here," he said, throwing her a lightweight parka. "Found it on a chair on the way out."

"Thanks." She slipped on the jacket.

"You're still scared."

"Yeah, more than ever. Something's out there . . . something, I don't know . . . something I can't see. . . ." She hesitated, not knowing whether to go on or not. More than once Lester had expressed his disgust with her and his utter contempt for her and Chadwick's dream.

Lester glanced at his watch and she knew he wanted to go back inside. But he continued to hesitate. She got the distinct impression that he wanted to say something else.

She checked her watch too. 6:03. In a matter of minutes all the invited guests would have taken their places. She stared back up at the rock. The lights from the ski slope bounced off it, giving it an eerie glow. But how could the rock harm anyone? Enough security to start a small army patrolled the grounds. She told herself to let it go. She was safe here, as safe as a baby in its mother's arms. She turned to go back inside. But then she twisted back to the rock as a harrowing notion caused shivers to run up and down her spine.

"The rock!" Valerie shouted at Lester, moving down the steps of the balcony toward the ground. "I don't know why . . . but it's the danger here . . . I received a note—"

"What note?" called Lester, his thick body right behind hers going down the steps. "Who sent you a note?"

"I'm not sure," she said honestly. She didn't want to mention her suspicions about Michael. "But whoever sent it had a dream . . ."

Though it made no sense, she felt an insane urge to climb up to the rock, to search it out, find out what lay behind it, underneath it. But she knew she couldn't do that. Even if she had enough time, she didn't have the equipment. A feeling of panic strangled her throat.

"What's a dream got to do with that rock?" Lester asked. "You're makin' no sense."

Valerie grabbed his elbow and used her most persuasive tone. "I know it's crazy," she argued, "but none of this makes any sense, never has. Not Chadwick's dream, not mine either. But I got a letter today, a warning about a shadow, danger and death in the shadow. Think about it. . . . That rock is the shadow, the one thing looming over all of us here."

She saw the possibility as she talked, the notion materializing like a ghost emerging from the snow . . .

"If somebody detonated an explosive under the rock, the whole thing could come crashing down on us. . . ."

As she talked she became more and move convinced that she had figured it out, and her grip on Lester's arm tightened like a vise. "If it crashed, everyone here would die," she continued. "Everyone buried under thousands of pounds of mountain stone! It could happen and no one would ever know what caused it. They'd think it was an avalanche. . . ."

She let go of Lester's arm and stalked toward the rock as if to attack it with her bare hands. "Whatever danger is here is in that rock, and I've got to get up there and find out. I've got to stop this before it's too late!"

Lester grabbed her shoulder, his thick jaw working. "Even if you're right, there's nothin' you can do," he growled. "It's too late!"

Frantic now, Valerie scanned the area around the lodge. She had to scale the mountain somehow. She spotted the pope's helicopter less than fifty yards away.

"John Peter's pilot!" she said, facing Lester. "He'll—"

"No, he won't," he interrupted. "He's inside and we're not breaking into this meeting on some wild goose chase!"

"But I can't just stand here!" Valerie shouted. "I know you think I've lost it, but I'm doing this no matter what you think."

Lester grabbed her right arm and squeezed it tightly. "Okay," he said, his tone suddenly softer. "I'll take you up." He pushed her toward the helicopter. "I flew in Vietnam. Fourteen months in a medi-vac unit."

A blank stare had entered his eyes, and Valerie found herself pulled along by the power of his thick body. Dimly she recalled his history, the years he'd spent in the Marines. But she'd forgotten what he did there.

She knew she should feel grateful for his help, yet she suddenly felt a deep suspicion instead, an intense dread that somehow Lester had come outside with an ulterior motive. But his hand gripped her arm and he pulled her along through the snow, and she knew she couldn't resist. She opened her mouth to scream back toward the lodge, but the wind had almost become a howl. She knew no one would hear her. She closed her mouth and focused on Lester. Within seconds he had pulled her to the helicopter and shoved her inside.

"Stay!" he commanded, slamming the door. Too confused to argue, she obeyed.

He rushed to the other side, crawled in, and searched the instrument panel. A second later a light blinked on and he punched a couple of buttons, flipped a couple of levers, and the engine whirred and sprang to life. A bright light flashed out from the front of the chopper, its illumination casting a piercing beam into the snow.

"Seat belt!" Lester shouted, strapping himself in. "The wind's whippin' up something awful."

Feeling she had no choice, Valerie again obeyed. As the helicopter's engine revved up, its rotor blades flipping round and round, time seemed to slow down. She stared at Lester, afraid of him in one moment, grateful in the next. Had someone sent him outside to make sure she didn't cause a problem? Was he a last line of defense, a protector of those who wanted to destroy Chadwick? Did he plan to carry her up, then push her out of the helicopter, only to claim later that she fell out somehow? Or had he genuinely come out to check on her, concerned for her well-being and repentant over his former actions?

Shivering, she huddled down as best she could and told herself it didn't matter. She had to deal with it one way or the other. Seconds later, the chopper lifted off through the falling snow, its nose pointed toward the looming rock now almost completely obscured. It was 6:15.

———

Inside the lodge, the crowd had assembled and the seven religious leaders had marched down the aisle, their shoulders square, their resolve evident. As previously agreed upon, each of the seven dressed distinctly in the garb of his faith tradition. They had come together out of a desire for peace, each one had confessed. But that didn't mean they agreed on anything else.

"Let the world see our diversity," Blevins had said. "There is no reason to deny the truth of who we are and what we believe."

The seven sat on the rostrum, each of them in plain high-backed wooden chairs. Russell Chadwick was attired in a simple black robe. Blevins wore her usual straight-lined, earth-toned dress, a clear crystal hanging on her neck, her hair frizzier than ever. Beside her sat Rabbi ben Moseph, the only sign of his religion the Star of David that hung around his neck. Appearing bored with the whole procedure, the Ayatollah Khatama stroked his beard, a gray shawl on his slumped shoulders, a black robe licking at the floor over his black sandals. Luis Zorella seemed just the opposite, as rigid as a soldier under inspection, a pinstriped black suit, blue starched shirt, and gold tie and cuff links setting off the white of his teeth and the oiled sheen of his hair and mustache. Beside Zorella, the Dalai Lama waited patiently in his flowing orange robe, his face serene. At the end of the row, Pope John Peter stared straight ahead, his skullcap and cassock matching the cascading snow outside.

Waiting for the music to conclude, Russell Chadwick held his right arm against his side and hoped it wouldn't shake too much when he stood to speak. Searching the crowd, he found Mildred near the back of the room, her sweet smile a reassuring sight in the midst of so much tension. For several seconds, he just looked at her, thinking back over the years to all the times she had blessed him with her encouraging smiles. Though he knew it wasn't possible, it seemed that her smiles actually radiated warmth. No matter how fearful he'd ever been, no matter how anxious, one smile from her warmed up his world and calmed his insides.

He touched his right index finger to the left corner of his lips, their age-old secret signal that passed a kiss from one to the other. She returned the gesture and he smiled. The only sound in the room was the soft music. Chadwick prayed, his eyes open. In less than fifteen minutes, he'd walk to the podium and begin this meeting. But he had deliberately scheduled fifteen minutes of silence before it all began. Though many in the room prayed to a different god than his, he wanted the time anyway, a time for him to cast it all into the care of the Lord Jesus.

From the corner of his eye to the left he saw Luis Zorella stand suddenly, then move to the podium, signaling the musician to stop.

"Forgive me this intrusion," Zorella said. "But I feel that I must speak to this most distinguished group."

He glanced at his brother. Chadwick saw a sly smile on José's face, and he knew immediately that someone had betrayed him.

The snowmobile dipped over the ridge at a dangerously sharp angle, its nose pointed downward toward the back side of the rock that loomed over Stricker's lodge. His hands squeezing the handle grips tightly enough to crush steel, Casey Sterling revved the engine to its highest speed and gritted his teeth.

From somewhere in the distance he heard gunfire and instinctively tucked his neck into his shoulders. Tree bark splintered less than five feet in front of the snowmobile, and something slammed into the back fender of the machine, its force knocking the snowmobile to the left. Fighting to keep control, Sterling hunched low over the snowmobile and kept it pointed toward the rock.

Seconds later, the gunfire erupted again and Sterling's right hand was stung. He gripped the brake and jerked the snowmobile to the left. The force of the movement threw him over the front of the machine and into the snow. Blood seeped from the back of his hand. Rising from the ground, his back wet with snow, he rushed toward the rock and hid behind it before easing his way to the side by the old barn. Scanning the trees in the direction from which he thought the shots had come, he saw nothing out of the ordinary.

Taking a deep breath, he realized he shouldn't feel surprised that someone wanted to take him out. The car that had followed him in Atlanta, the man who had run him off the road, now a sniper—apparently he'd made someone awfully mad. Worse still, whoever it was had obviously discovered his plans for Chadwick's so-called Peace Project.

Sterling rubbed his bloody hand against his pants and crept to the back of the rock. He heard a chomping sound cutting through the falling snow and recognized the sound of an approaching helicopter. But he kept moving anyway. On the back side of the rock nearest to the weathered barn, he found what he had come for—a black briefcase, a briefcase he had paid someone to place about sixteen hours ago.

Though he didn't open the briefcase, Sterling knew what he'd find inside—enough C–4 to blow up the rock and create a mammoth avalanche.

Grabbing the briefcase, he hunched up to hide from the shooter and the helicopter. His hand still dripping blood, he knew he'd reached the end of the line. His ambition had pushed him too far.

He sucked in a breath of air and wondered what had become of the man he'd hired. Had the shooter killed him? Had someone known his plans all along? Was the chopper searching for him, waiting to kill him the instant he showed his head? If the C–4 in the briefcase exploded here and now, Stricker's lodge would be crushed. But who would want everyone in the lodge to die? And why?

Pressing his hand against his side, he lowered his head and closed his eyes. If the chopper didn't leave soon, he'd go up with the mountain, one big whoosh of fire and rock, one incredible end to one incredible scheme.

A wry grin crossed his face. This would be quite a story for somebody! Too bad it wouldn't be him.

———

Hovering in the helicopter above the escarpment that had

spooked her, Valerie examined it as best she could through the
helicopter's lights but saw nothing amiss. With the snow suddenly slowing almost to a stop, the rock appeared serene, a picture made for a postcard, a broad-shouldered back of a mountain,
all decked out in winter white. The cable from the ski lift hung to
her right, its black steel cord stretched out like a clothesline. An
old barn, its sides spindly against the rocky peaks and stout
pines that grew nearby, sat next to the rock. The cars of the ski
lift bounced up and down in the wind, their seats empty but still
busy.

"Everything looks clear!" Lester shouted, his voice loud over
the chopper blades.

Valerie nodded quickly. Even through the snow she could see
that no one threatened Chadwick from this direction, no enemies
lurked in the trees or behind the huge stone. But somehow that
didn't make her feel any safer. The note had stirred up too many
eerie memories, too many shadows from her past.

"We've been up here long enough!" Lester shouted. "You ready
to go back?"

She wanted to say no, wanted to grab him by the arm and
shout that they had to stay and inspect every inch of the mountain to make sure nothing deadly lurked there. But she knew she
had no rational reason to demand any such thing.

"They're going to miss us inside!" Lester shouted, his anxiety
obviously mounting.

The chopping of the helicopter blades must have masked the
sound of the gunfire, and only when something *thump, thump,
thumped* into the tail section of the chopper did Valerie realize
they were under fire. The helicopter dipped suddenly and violently. Lester pulled back on the stick and a look of sheer panic
crossed his face.

"We're hit!" he shouted, his hands busy trying to control the
lurching chopper. "Gotta get it down!"

Valerie saw the mountain rush toward her, the cable from the
ski lift almost directly in front of them. The copter steadied for a
second, and she waited for more shots, but none came. Staring at
the ski cable, an insane notion flipped through her head, and before she could stop herself, she knew what she had to do. The last
time she had faced this kind of danger she had failed, and a man
she'd loved had fallen out of her life like the snow now falling
from the sky. Intuitively she knew that if she didn't do this now,
if she stood idly by and left her uncle in danger, she might as well

jump out of the chopper and let the snow bury her forever. For her life to have any hope, she had to do everything in her power to protect the man who had nursed her wounds and given her another chance.

"Put me out on the ski lift!" she yelled, facing Lester.

Lester's mouth dropped open for an instant, but he quickly recovered. "No way!" he shouted.

She grabbed his bicep and squeezed as hard as she could. "Do it!" she yelled. "Once I'm on the ski lift, I can climb down and check the back side of the rock!"

"You're—"

Another *thump* of gunfire hit the helicopter. Valerie jerked off her seat belt, slid open the door on her side, and moved to the edge of the open doorway. The rock lay a good fifteen feet below. If she could get on the lift chair first and hang down from it, the jump into the snow would be no more than seven or eight feet.

"I've got to do this!" she shouted over the noise. "You either help me or I'll jump!"

The chopper jerked left again as another bullet pounded into its side. Valerie faced Lester and screamed at the top of her voice. "Now!"

"But the cables!"

"Do it!" she shouted.

The copter lurched right and hovered, rocking in the wind directly above the lift chair. Without another word, Valerie took a deep breath and prayed harder than she could ever remember praying. Holding tightly to the side of the passenger exit, she backed out of the chopper, looked down, and placed her feet on the chopper runners. Braced there precariously, the sheer idiocy of the moment suddenly hit her. Everything felt like a dream now, a white nightmare, a freezing scene of surreal proportions.

Lester steered closer to the lift. Valerie glanced down and saw the ground bobbing up and down under her feet, lit up by the lights from the ski slope. Near the old barn she suddenly saw a man with a rifle moving toward them. Her teeth chattering, she started to climb back inside the helicopter but knew she didn't have enough time. Within seconds, the man with the rifle would have the chopper in his sights.

As the chopper bounced up and down in the wind, Valerie reached out with one hand and grabbed the suspension bar above the lift chair and held on. Pushing away from the helicopter, she leaped to the ski lift, grabbed on with both hands, and slid down the suspension bar. Her shoes landed on the side of the lift chair, slipped on the snow, then gripped and held. Sliding down, she bounced into the chair.

The helicopter pulled up and away, and then she saw it plummet suddenly out of sight. She turned away to locate the rifleman, but he had disappeared. In a moment of panic, she wondered if he could see her. She knew she was an easy target where she sat. Then, gritting her teeth, she turned her stomach to the lift chair and her back to the wind. She eased her legs down over the side. Her feet dangling, she took a deep breath and let go.

Inside Bill Stricker's lodge, Russell Chadwick sat in stunned silence. Luis Zorella had been talking for several minutes but now seemed near the end of his speech. Chadwick fought to keep down his anger, to mask the bitterness he felt rising higher and higher with each word that Zorella uttered.

"I and my colleagues"—Zorella waved a hand to indicate his contingent—"have prayed much about this matter. As a result, and in spite of my personal admiration for the Reverend Doctor Chadwick, a man whose faith in Jesus Christ I personally admire greatly, we have decided that we must not go further with this situation. We believe . . ."

Too shocked to respond, Chadwick listened with increasing horror as Zorella poured out his reasons for disengaging. All the reasons sounded understandable. Many of Chadwick's own advisors had counseled him with exactly the same words. But Chadwick sensed something more going on here, something not nearly so innocent as a prayerfully reached decision.

"So that is the best I can do," Zorella said. "I continue to offer my prayers for the alliance but not my personal involvement. I am sorry for the inconvenient timing of my announcement." He looked at Chadwick. "But I finally came to peace with this decision only a couple of hours ago."

From the corner of his eye, Chadwick saw José glance toward Bill Stricker, who nodded his head ever so slightly in José's direction. Chadwick's stomach tightened. Is that what had happened? Had Stricker reached out to José? Were the two of them in league with each other?

Zorella finished and sat down, but before Chadwick could stand, the Ayatollah Khatama held a hand into the air. Chadwick sagged back into his chair and his right arm began to shake.

"I feel that I must also speak now," Khatama said, rising to his feet, "for the sake of my people." He moved to the podium, but Chadwick no longer heard what he said. He saw it all now. Stricker had staged all of this, offered his lodge, brought the leaders of the alliance together, all for the purpose of humiliating and defeating him in front of the whole world.

His heart heavy, Chadwick's eyes searched the room for Mildred. No matter what happened, he knew he could count on her. Finding her, he touched his lip again. She pressed her palms and fingers together, the universal sign for prayer. He nodded slightly. As usual, Mildred brought him back to the important things.

Khatama raised his voice. "For the cause of the great Allah, some are called to do the unthinkable," he started. "Some are called to pour out their very lives on the altar of martyrdom. Some are called . . ."

Not really listening anymore, Chadwick closed his eyes and began to pray. Whatever happened, he wanted to face it with all the humility and grace that God could give him.

The black briefcase clutched to his chest, Casey Sterling heard a series of rifle shots but knew they weren't aimed at him this time. A helicopter dipped and swerved crazily overhead mere feet from the ski lift. A body suddenly emerged from the right side of the helicopter, and for a second he thought the shooter had hit the passenger. But then the passenger leaned out and grabbed the lift chair. The helicopter swooped away as the person on the lift chair fell into the seat and sat there swaying for several seconds.

Watching the person in the lift, Sterling squeezed the briefcase harder against his chest. Valerie Miller!

He saw her auburn hair blowing back from her face, the gusting wind playing with it. But why? Why would Valerie do such an insane thing? Had she found out about his scheme, his crazy notion to make sure that no one in the world ever again forgot his name? The idea that guaranteed that he'd become more famous than anyone, even a television anchor?

His heart thumping against the briefcase, Sterling realized he had less than three minutes. He couldn't wait any longer. If he did, the briefcase would explode and kill everyone, Valerie included.

Tucking the briefcase under his arm, he began to run just as

Valerie Miller let go of the ski lift and tumbled toward the ground.

————

Valerie hit the rock with a thud, her right ankle twisted at an odd angle. A stab of fire burned through her ankle and up her shin, and she grabbed it and lay still for several seconds. Out of the corner of her eye, she saw a man hobbling in the opposite direction no more than twenty yards away. A trail of red dotted the snow behind by his left leg.

The man glanced over his shoulder, and Valerie saw his face in the glow of the ski lift lights. Casey Sterling! But what was he doing here?

Facing forward again, Sterling kept moving, his right arm clutching something to his body.

Valerie heard a gunshot from her left and turned to see an armed man rush forward from a stand of trees some fifty yards away. Forgetting her ankle, she scrambled quickly away from the ski lift, her ankle throbbing in tandem with several scrapes on her knees and hands from the descent. Though trying to stay low, she moved as rapidly as possible, her breath coming in short gasps.

The sound of a snowmobile rushed up from the direction of the lodge below, and she paused for a second to look. Security? Had Lester sent someone up for her? The roar of another engine told her a second machine had joined the first one, and she knew for sure then that someone from the lodge was headed her way. Instantly though, she knew the help wouldn't arrive in time. She had to do this!

A gun fired again and Valerie dropped lower and concentrated on catching Sterling. He had his his head down, obviously focused on the cliffs ahead. But his left leg slowed him and she was gaining fast. Glancing over her shoulder, she saw the man with the rifle drop to his knees and aim. Zigging right, she ducked behind a tree. A shot rang out and she saw Sterling jerk, then stagger, his left hand grabbing his hip. Something fell from his hands and skidded away in the snow.

The sound of the snowmobiles grew louder as she reached Sterling. He lay facedown in the snow, his arms splayed out, blood running from his left hip, a large cut on his forehead, his lips caked with red.

Another shot sounded as she hunched over Sterling. The bullet plunged into the snow only a couple of feet away. On her knees, Valerie rolled Sterling over and lifted his face from the snow.

"The briefcase!" he whispered frantically, opening his eyes. "A bomb . . . less than a minute!"

Valerie jerked her gaze to the briefcase and suddenly realized what Sterling was doing on the mountain!

She saw the sniper running toward her. She pushed away from Sterling and threw herself at the briefcase. The cliffs lay no more than ten yards away and she had less than a minute!

Behind her she heard the snowmobiles rushing her way, and she knew the sniper would surely be closing in for one last shot. She crawled and prayed at the same time, her body working in tandem with her heart.

She grabbed the briefcase and pulled herself to one knee. She heard the sound of a rifle shot and felt a burning in her right shoulder. She staggered but didn't fall. Snow crunched behind her and she knew the sniper was only a few yards away. Without looking back, she steeled herself against another bullet but didn't stop moving. One step, two steps, three more to go to the edge of the cliffs where she could throw the briefcase over and the bomb could fall to the river bottom and explode into the emptiness of the canyon and do no harm.

The rifle fired again. She felt a slice of pain in her right leg, stumbled and fell to her knees. She had only one more step to the edge of the cliffs. If she had to die to do this—

An odd sensation buzzed through her head then, and the snow falling around her face seemed to slow down. The flakes seemed lighter than air, holding themselves before her eyes long enough for her to inspect each one as it passed. A feeling of serenity draped over her, and she wondered for an instant if she had died and now stood somewhere between heaven and earth, a place of momentary transition from one world to the next.

She dimly heard the sound of snowmobiles, but so lovely was her world she paid them no attention. From the corner of her eye she saw her right arm moving, throwing something black and square over the side of the mountain. But the motion seemed separated from her body, as if someone else did it, someone stronger and more determined than she.

The square black thing whizzed out into the air and dropped over the cliffs. She watched it fall until she could barely see it anymore. Then she heard a *WHOOM!* and felt the ground quiver.

For an instant she thought the whole mountain might disintegrate into the canyon. But then the force of the explosion peaked, and everything around her groaned and roared, but the mountain didn't fall. As the sound died away, she heard people shouting and moving and rushing behind her. But she felt distant from all of that, separate and alone, her spirit as peaceful as she'd ever felt it. Perhaps this was the peace of the dead or the dying, she didn't know which.

Someone touched her elbow and she blinked and turned in the direction of the touch, halfway expecting to see the face of Jesus come to usher her home to God. But the face she saw had a cut on the forehead and bleeding lips.

"Case . . . Casey," she mumbled, her eyes dimming.

She felt a hand on her cheek and knew that Casey Sterling lay beside her, his hand on her face. She didn't have the strength to talk anymore, so she just lay there and listened.

"I . . . meant no harm . . . no hurt . . . anyone . . . not the plan . . ." he mumbled. "Sorry . . ." His voice trailed away and he closed his eyes, and Valerie opened her mouth and reached a hand over to his face and touched his lips.

"Okay," she whispered. "Okay."

Everything fell black then, and though she felt the snow falling gently on her face, she could no longer open her eyes to see it.

FORTY-SEVEN

Lacy Drew Sterling held a cup of coffee—black, no sugar—in her long fingers and leaned forward in the rocker where she sat in her simple but neat six-room home. The circles around her eyes were as black as the coffee. Her thin lips covered her teeth.

On an identical rocker across from her sat Valerie Miller, her face equally sad. Beside Valerie on the sofa, Russell Chadwick had taken a spot. A cool but not unpleasant breeze blew in from an open window, and Valerie could hear the ocean rolling in with the breeze. People on the beach for their morning walks were no doubt picking up shells left over from the evening tides.

"I appreciate you both comin'," said Lacy Drew. "I don't cotton much to Atlanta."

"We're glad to do it," Valerie said. "We came as soon as the hospital released her," Chadwick said.

"You all healed now?"

Valerie shrugged. "I'm sore from surgery, but not in any danger anymore. How you doing?"

Lacy Drew sagged into her rocker. A clock on the mantel bonged softly—9 A.M. "Two funerals in one week take it out of a body," she said. "My boy eight days ago, my ex-husband four days ago."

"We've been praying for you," Chadwick said. "I can't imagine the loss you're feeling."

Valerie smiled at her uncle. When she had told him of her plans to come here, he had insisted that he should join her. "Casey deserves at least that much," he'd said. "I'm going too."

Lacy Drew sipped from her coffee, her head down. "Casey was

a good man," she said, staring into her cup, "considerin' all he had to deal with growin' up. His daddy didn't help us much, him or me."

"I'm sorry for that," Valerie said.

"He straightened up some at the end. His daddy, I mean. Moved back here to Swansboro. He and I talked 'bout every day there the last few months."

"That must have meant a lot to you."

"Yeah, it did." The clock ticked on the mantel. Seconds passed.

"I really liked Casey," Valerie said. "He was so smart, so charming."

Lacy Drew smiled, then stood and walked to the window. "I buried him here in Swansboro," she said. "Couldn't stand the thought of havin' to drive to Atlanta to tend his grave site. His daddy's only a plot away from him, mine between 'em. 'Bout a mile down the road. You can hear the ocean from the graveyard, like you can from here."

She waved toward the window as if to show Valerie and Chadwick the spot. "I keep the window open whenever it's warm enough," she continued. "And that's most of the time here in Swansboro."

The weather had turned unseasonably warm, even for this part of South Carolina.

"Casey loved you very much," Valerie said. "Told me so more than once."

Lacy Drew stared at her. "He liked you a lot, you know," she said. "Who knows what . . ." She stopped and changed the subject. "He came by here the day before it all happened," she said. "Wanted to see his daddy."

"Did he?"

Lacy Drew smiled again. "Yeah, less than twenty-four hours 'fore he died. Drove right over there, spent half a day with him. Don't know everything they talked about, but when Casey came back here that night, he seemed calmer than I'd seen him in years, more at ease, happier maybe. I wanted to ask him all about it, but . . . well, you know . . . some things you just don't ask."

Valerie nodded. "I still don't know everything that happened on the mountain," she said. "I guess I never will. But I wanted to come by here and tell you what I did know, what Casey said to me, how he died."

Lacy Drew stared out the window. The drapes, simple floral

swags, danced in the breeze. "Television said Casey saved everybody."

"He did. I don't know how he knew about the bomb, but he found it and took it to the cliffs."

"You helped him," Lacy Drew said.

Valerie dropped her eyes. "I did what I could. But he's the one who found the explosive."

Lacy Drew dropped back into the rocker and studied her coffee again. "I'm sorry your peace plan fell apart," she said to Chadwick.

"Yeah," he nodded, retelling the story the media had dwelt on for days. "Lester Boggett confessed the whole scheme. Bill Stricker had convinced him and Zorella to pull out just as the ceremony began. Create a public relations fiasco for us and destroy everything in one fell swoop. If one of my insiders and my strongest supporter backs out, then everyone backs out."

"Yeah, and Zorella picks up a few hundred million dollars in donations from Stricker," groused Lacy Drew.

"And Lester did it 'cause he thought he was protecting me from non-Christian influences."

"But that wasn't the only problem."

Valerie picked up the story. "No, not even the worst one. The Ayatollah Khatama was a part of Stricker's plan at first. But then he decided to go out in a blaze of glory—die a martyr to the cause of Allah. He knew about the bomb—though he swears he didn't set it. He planned to let it detonate and destroy everybody in the lodge, himself included."

"Some mean people in this world," Lacy Drew said.

"Khatama believed that wiping out such a group would give Islam the best opportunity to advance in the new millennium. With his example as a call to arms for others as militant as he, plus the vacuum of leadership in the other major religions created by his so-called 'heroism,' Islam would emerge triumphant."

"I saw that on the news," Lacy Drew said. "At least a tape of it. The man was givin' his martyrdom speech just before six-thirty. Wanted it to carry right up to the bomb's detonation—a last-minute call to martyrdom to every Muslim in the world."

Valerie nodded. "He told the police he had his people busy for weeks. He knew about Casey's plans to disarm the explosives. Said he had tapped Casey's phones, followed his every move. Retaliation for Casey investigating him. He sent a squad of men after Casey, a man on the highway leading to Breckenridge and the sniper on the mountain who killed Casey's investigator and eventually Casey himself."

"Just about got you too," Lacy said, her eyes moist.

Valerie stared at her hands. "But I survived," she said.

"And so did all the others in the lodge, thanks to you."

"Thanks to her and Casey," offered Chadwick

"What'll happen to Khatama?"

"The U.S authorities have him," said Chadwick. "He'll go to trial for the murder of Casey and his associate."

"He seems proud of himself."

"He's not real repentant, that's for sure. Says his courage will inspire others."

"What about Lester Boggett? And Zorella?"

Valerie shrugged. "It's not a crime to pull out of a religious alliance—even if you do it in front of millions of people watching on television. And Lester left early. He couldn't bear to watch it. He helped me too, by taking me up in the helicopter. Sent security to help. They caught the sniper. He told everyone later he knew he'd gotten mixed up with the wrong bunch."

"You'll forgive him?" Lucy asked Chadwick.

"He's my friend. What else can I do?"

"What'll you do now?"

"I don't know, exactly. Take some time off . . . pray, try to figure out whether I should go on with the peace effort or go back to preaching. I'm not in the best of health, maybe you've heard."

"You're a godly man." Chadwick waved off the statement.

Lacy Drew was quiet for a moment, then spoke to Valerie. "Casey said you told him to make things right with his daddy."

Valerie sighed. "Life's too short for us to let the past eat us up and destroy the joy God wants to give us."

"He said you'd suffered some hard times too."

"Haven't we all?"

Lacy Drew stood and walked to a table by the window. "This came for you 'bout a week ago," she said, handing an envelope to Valerie. "Casey sent it. I've been holding it for you."

Valerie took the envelope. Saw her name and Lacy Drew Sterling's address written in neat blue ink. Her fingers trembling, she glanced at her uncle tore open the envelope and pulled out a three-page letter. Casey had handwritten it, every letter precise and clean.

Valerie,

If you're reading this, then the worst has happened. I want you to know I did all I could to fix things, all the things I'd messed up. I saw my dad just a few hours ago. Like you said, it did make a difference. He and I have hurt each other for years. I kept waiting on him to come to me. He's the dad. He's supposed to be the grown-up. But he wasn't strong enough. You helped me become strong enough to go to him. So I did.

I'm not saying that everything's wonderful now. It's not. I have a long way to go before I can look at him without resentment, without feeling hurt and angry. But we started something. We watched a Braves baseball game for about an hour—nothing dramatic. I rolled his bed out to the porch. We listened to the ocean. His trailer's not but a block or so away, and you can hear the waves lapping. We didn't say much. Then I took him back inside and told him I had to go. He held out his hand to shake. I took it and held it a long time.

I didn't tell him I loved him. I know I should have because I do. But all the absences, all the broken promises, all the suffering made that tough this first time. I wasn't strong enough yet. Next time I see him, I'll tell him, I really will.

He didn't say much when I left. But he opened his arms and I leaned over his bed, then he hugged me and it all seemed okay, somehow. If possible, I'd like for you to go see him and tell him what I said in this letter.

Valerie looked up. Lacy Drew stood by the window, her back to Valerie. Chadwick waited patiently, his hands in his lap. Valerie turned back to the letter.

I want you to know what happened, and what I did. So this is my confession:

A man I hired placed the explosives on the mountain—not to harm anyone but to set up my story. I had it figured this way. I not only wanted to report the story, I wanted the one story no one else had. So why not create the story for myself? I'd plotted it all out. I'd even scouted the area from the moment I heard about the retreat at Stricker's mountain.

Here's how I planned it to work. I would say that I'd received a tip from an informer—I'm a journalist, so I don't have to reveal my sources. Then I would show up at the rock just in the nick of time, cameras rolling. I would toss the briefcase over the cliffs and rescue everyone in the lodge. News programs would plaster my face on television screens for the next month. I would become a celebrity, a hero, larger than anyone. I wouldn't need an anchor desk. I'd be more famous than any of them.

Valerie rocked back in her chair as she saw the implications of Casey's letter. Khatama had told them the truth—his men *didn't* plant the bomb! But they found out about it and they did everything possible to make sure it detonated! But then what? Why had Casey changed his mind? She focused on the letter again.

> *I changed my mind early this morning. After I saw my dad last night, I decided I needed to fix one more thing—if I could. So I called my man in Colorado, but I couldn't reach him. I don't know what happened. Hope he's okay. Someone's been following me and I'm trying to find out who. I'm on my way now to Colorado to disarm the explosive and make things right before it's too late. If you don't think I'm too far gone, pray for me.*
>
> *And one more thing. This faith stuff, I'm working on that too. A long time ago, a church—I should say a preacher—hurt my mom, hurt her bad. I've held that grudge too long. I want to give it up like I'm trying to give up my resentment toward my dad. I've got a lot of questions, but I think that's okay, isn't it? You said some doubts were likely.*
>
> *I'm not sure exactly what I did, but last night, after I talked with my dad, I walked outside on the porch where we'd just been sitting, stared up into the sky, and listened to the ocean. I sensed a presence I'd never felt before. All of a sudden I started to shake. It lasted about a minute. But then it stopped. And when it did, I leaned out over the porch rail and said a prayer to your Jesus. It was strange, but all of a sudden the word "accepted" came to me, and I had a feeling that I'd never shake again. I felt like my dad had hugged me again, only stronger this time. Is that what God feels like? A big hug that says you're home and safe? I hope so. I want to feel that again.*

Valerie's eyes filled and she had trouble reading the last paragraphs.

> *So now I go to make amends. If I don't make it . . . well, just know this. I've decided to move beyond my past, to stop letting it imprison me or keep me from feeling what I want to feel, doing what I want to do, loving who I want to love.*
>
> *So, that's it. I need to hurry. Thanks for everything. And when you're feeling lonely, know this. At least one man will go to his grave loving you.*
>
> *Love, Casey*
>
> *P.S., I wanted to tell you this person to person, but this will*

have to do. One of my sources found the Suburban in Califor-
nia. It looks clean. Check it out for yourself, but maybe this
time you really were just being paranoid.

Valerie laid her head against the chair. Lacy Drew stood beside her now, a hand on her shoulder.

"You okay, honey?" Lacy Drew asked.

For a couple of minutes Valerie rocked back and forth, back
and forth. So much had happened in the last few days—so many
pieces of the puzzle had fallen into place.

The Atlanta police had called to tell her that they had found
the crane operator Ruiz and were convinced from his testimony
that the episode with the steel girder had indeed been nothing
more than a frightening accident. Now Casey had told her the
Suburban wasn't sabotaged. She'd been wrong about so much.
Probably about Clement too. She'd never know for sure.

She laid her head against the rocker once more. But she'd
been right about a lot. The surveillance camera in the front lobby
of Stricker's lodge showed a man she recognized immediately as
Michael Del Rio. Though he had lost weight and had a full beard
and longer hair now, it was definitely him. No doubt about it. He
had dreamed of her, had sent her that note. She had trusted it,
trusted her instincts, and figured out danger. But now it was
over, all of it. The danger was past.

Valerie stood and took Lacy Drew's hands in her own. Chadwick stood too, put a hand on her shoulder. For several seconds,
she wondered what to say, how much to tell. But what good would
it do to tell Lacy Drew or anyone else what Casey had just revealed about his part in the drama at Stricker's? What would it
accomplish if she told her that her son had planned such a thing,
that his own failures led to his death?

Valerie quickly made a decision. She wouldn't ruin the name
of a man who had sought to repair what he'd done, a man who
tried to make amends at the end of his life.

"I'm okay," she said, hugging Lacy Drew. "And Casey loved
you, loved you with all his heart."

The three of them stood there then, the sound of the ocean in
their ears, their tears falling freely. Valerie closed her eyes and
thanked God that Casey, like the prodigal son, had felt God's ac-
ceptance on the night before his death. And, though she hadn't
thought it possible, she thanked God too that Casey had reminded her of a truth she needed to hear again, a truth that

everyone needed to hear—that no one should let the past become a prison that kept them from feeling what they wanted to feel, doing what they wanted to do, loving who they wanted to love.

In those words, Casey had shown her that she needed to move on with her life. Though she should always cherish her memories—good and bad—she should never become a slave to them. Whether she would ever see Michael Del Rio again or not, she didn't know. She wanted to see him, wanted to hold him one more time, even if only to say goodbye. But she couldn't mope around any longer waiting for that to happen. If she wanted to find the happiness she and Casey had discussed, she had to open her arms to receive it, and she couldn't open her arms if she still had them clutched around a past experience she could never recreate.

A verse from Psalms came to her. "Weeping may endure for a night, but joy cometh in the morning." Well, her night had come and gone.

Stepping away from Lacy Drew and her uncle, Valerie wiped her eyes and walked to the window. Listening to the ocean waves, she took a deep breath and brushed back her hair. It was definitely morning for her, she decided, in more ways than one. And for the first time in a long time, she felt truly ready to take on the rest of the day.